ECHOES OF TITANIC

MINDY STARNS CLARK
JOHN CAMPBELL CLARK

HARVEST HOUSE PUBLISHERS

EUGENE, OREGON

Scripture quotations are taken from the King James Version of the Bible.

Cover by Garborg Design Works, Savage, Minnesota

Cover photos © Maxim Ahner / Shutterstock; Bigstock / goinyk; Frank Boston / 123RF

The authors are represented by MacGregor Literary.

This is a work of fiction. Names, characters, places, and incidents are products of the authors' imagination or are used fictitiously. Any resemblance to actual persons, living or dead, or to events or locales, is entirely coincidental.

ECHOES OF TITANIC
Copyright © 2012 by Mindy Starns Clark and John Campbell Clark
Published by Harvest House Publishers
Eugene, Oregon 97402
www.harvesthousepublishers.com

Library of Congress Cataloging-in-Publication Data
Clark, Mindy Starns.
Echoes of Titanic / Mindy Starns Clark and John Campbell Clark.
    p. cm.
ISBN 978-0-7369-2946-2 (pbk.)
ISBN 978-0-7369-4243-0 (eBook)
1. Titanic (Steamship)—Fiction. 2. Corporate culture—Fiction. I. Clark, John Campbell.
II. Title.
PS3603.L366E27 2012
813'.6--dc23

                                                                    2011045882

Printed in the United States of America

12 13 14 15 16 17 18 19 20 / LB-CD / 10 9 8 7 6 5 4 3 2 1

For our daughters,
Emily and Lauren.
Raising them has been
our greatest collaboration.

Our Special Thanks To...

Nick Harrison, who first suggested we base a book on *Titanic*.

Kim Moore, our talented editor and dear friend.

Betty Fletcher, Becky Miller, Katie Lane, LaRae Weikert, and everyone else at Harvest House Publishers who went the extra mile to make this book happen.

Our daughters, Emily and Lauren, who contribute in ways too numerous to count.

We are also deeply indebted to the following people and places:

Harvest House Publishers; Tracie Hall; David Clark; Jennifer Clark; Joey Starns; Gordon Brett; Dr. Denene Lofland; Lee Lofland; *Titanic: The Experience* of Orlando, Florida; the helpful folks at Cramer, LLC (formerly the Cramer Brothers Safe Company) of Kansas City, Missouri; Susan Page Davis; Vanessa Thompson; Stephanie Ciner; Helen Styer Hannigan; the McMullan family; *Titanic: The Artifact Exhibition*; David Trouten; Chip MacGregor of MacGregor Literary; ChiLibris; Sisters in Crime; the Titanic Historical Society; and the Titanic Museum in Indian Orchard, Massachusetts.

Thanks also to BMCC, FVCN, and our connect group: Brian, Tracey, Hannah, and Emiko Akamine; Brad, Tracie, and Payton Hall; and Fanus, Mariette, Jacqueline, Marguerete, and Karla Smith. Truly, we couldn't have done it without your love, prayers, and support!

PROLOGUE

Lower Manhattan, New York
April 15, 1913

The figure stood near the bulkhead, a young woman looking out at the Hudson River. The day had grown windier, not to mention cooler, and her silk hat and spring coat did little to keep out the chill. She made no move to warm herself, however, nor to join the others. Instead, she continued to stare out at the water as the wind whipped at her face and body.

To her, nothing compared to the coldness she'd suffered that fateful night one year before, waiting for the help that wouldn't come till sunrise. As her lifeboat had bobbed in the ocean for hours, the bitter chill had permeated her bones. Even colder, however, had been the frigid waters themselves, which her two beloved family members had been forced to endure. Given the torment they had likely suffered before their bodies finally went still, she had no right to complain of cold—then or now.

More than fifteen hundred people had been left without lifeboats that night and had been plunged into the icy North Atlantic when the ship went down. Would the cacophony of their screams ever fade from her memory? Had her two loved ones joined in with that chorus, their own cries a part of what she'd heard? How long had their misery gone on before they found relief in blessed unconsciousness?

Those were but a few of the many questions that tormented her days and haunted her nights—and had since the great *Titanic* sunk, exactly one year ago today.

By the time the searches had ended, most of those bodies had not been

5

recovered. They had either drifted off with the currents or been pulled down with the ship. Her two family members were among those that had never been found; thus, they had not been given a final resting place in any cemetery. Instead, a small memorial had been erected in Battery Park, in the shade of a gnarled old elm tree. The carved stone was tasteful and elegant, yes, but altogether insufficient as far as she was concerned. No bodies, no headstones, no graves.

No peace in the heart of this survivor.

Foolishly, she had agreed to come here today to this memorial service. She'd thought she could endure a brief ceremony, but just the sight of the two names etched in bronze on a plaque affixed to the memorial stone had been far too much to bear. Let others tend to their ritual.

She needed air. She needed to breathe.

Oh, how she missed them!

The dear man, father to one and uncle to the other, yet father figure to both. He'd been a loving and calming presence to the end.

The young woman, precious cousin, so beautiful inside and out. Raised in the same home, just two months apart in age, they had always been inseparable.

Now she'd be separated from the two of them for the rest of her life.

Standing there, facing the water, she felt the wind whipping at her hat, threatening to whisk it from her head. As she placed a hand atop the stiff fabric surface to hold it in place, her fingers grazed the cold metal of a hat pin.

The hat pin.

She pulled it loose to study it. Never mind that the wind made short work of both head covering and hairdo after that. Soon, the hat was skittering briskly across the grounds of the park, and her long brown locks had fallen loose and were fluttering wildly about her head. She didn't care. She merely grasped the pin in her hand, the tiny gold harp at the end sparkling in the morning sun. She brought it to her lips, pressing the cold roughness of the pin's decorative surface against her skin. Originally, there had been two hat pins, designed to wear separately or as a set. The cousins, as close as sisters, had chosen them together in London the day before they set sail for America. While on the ship, they had taken turns wearing each one, both girls trying to decide which pin they would call their own once their journey was complete. That question had been answered, of course, as soon as she'd climbed into the lifeboat. Simply by default, the one she'd been wearing at that moment had become hers forever—just as the one her cousin had been wearing now lay at the bottom of the ocean, probably still affixed to the hat she'd had on when the unsinkable ship went down.

Again running a finger over the pin's unique design, she closed her eyes. In the past year, the nightmares had grown less frequent, less intense, but her daytime torments had not ceased. She still found herself crying for no reason, still spent far too many of her waking hours trying not to think about all that had happened.

She still ached with guilt and shame for what she'd done.

Only she knew the full reason that she had lived and her cousin had died. She knew because she'd had a part in it herself—a fact that would haunt her for the rest of her days. She rarely spoke of the tragedy, and those close to her had learned not to ask. It was a grief she could only bear alone, a pain that could be understood only by those who had lived through it.

Yet, perhaps even her fellow survivors could not fully comprehend her pain. Certainly, they all felt the grief, the loss, the sorrow. But she also felt *guilt*, a guilt that wrapped around her chest and threatened to choke the air from her lungs and the very life from her heart. Was there any justification for her actions? Any chance of forgiveness? Only time would tell.

She ran her finger along the empty slot in the side of the harp, where the other pin had been designed to fit. Just as this pin set would never be complete without its other half, she would never be complete again, at least not in this lifetime. The best she could do was to live in a way that would honor her cousin's memory and keep her dreams alive. That would start, she decided, by rejoining the others at the memorial stone now, no matter how difficult it was for her.

As she neared the group gathered in remembrance, she spotted him among the mourners, his black overcoat blowing in the wind, and a chill went through to her very bones. The narrow brim of his hat cast a shadow across his eyes, but she realized he must have been watching her because he quickly turned his face away.

Her heart pounded. She knew his secrets from that night, and he knew hers. Would they both remain silent to the end?

Or would one of them end up breaking their uneasy truce, driven by the cries they had both endured, cries that still echoed across the blackest waters of a deep and unforgiving sea?

CHAPTER
ONE

Lower Manhattan, New York
April 3, 2012

Kelsey Tate glanced at the clock and then at the stack of files on her desk. It was three p.m., which meant she had thirty minutes before she'd need to start getting ready for the ceremony. She knew she should use that time to work on risk assessments, but something told her she'd be better off getting some fresh air and clearing her head. The assessments she could do later that evening, once the big event was over. For now, she wanted to run through her speech and somehow find focus. Today had been a busy day at the office, and at the moment all she felt was scattered.

Taking a deep breath and letting it out slowly, she made the decision. Air. Ceremony. Work. In that order.

She locked the files away, straightened her desk, and grabbed her Bluetooth headset for cover. The only way she'd get out of here without being pulled into half a dozen conversations en route to the elevator was to clip the device over her ear and pretend she was on an important call as she went. She loved her front office and the view it afforded her of the busy Manhattan streets below, but sometimes it was a pain having to run the gauntlet of a conference room, an administrative assistant area, and three other executive offices just to get away.

"Is there something proprietary about this?" she asked aloud as she stepped into the hall and pulled the door shut behind her. "Because otherwise, I'm afraid it's just a little too early to buy in. At this point, there's simply not enough data."

Pausing at the desk of Sharon, her executive assistant—or "EA," as she liked to be called—Kelsey told the nonexistent person on the other end of the line to hold on and then said in a low voice, "I'm running out for a few, but I'll be back by three thirty if anybody needs me."

"Got it, Chief," Sharon replied with a brisk nod, her auburn, precision-cut bob swinging loosely around her face.

So far, so good. Continuing on toward the elevator, Kelsey spotted one of her more talkative coworkers coming up the hall, so before he could speak, she gave him a quick smile and continued with her faux telephone conversation.

"Look, we can't justify a buy-in of that size. You know as well as I do that you're estimating the value too high. A million and a half for ten percent is ridiculous."

The coworker smiled in return and continued past her in the hall.

She finally made it to the elevator, pushed the down button, and punctuated her wait with several well-timed brief utterances. "Really?…With that price earnings ratio?…I don't know, I'm not sure about that…How much?"

Finally, the bell dinged and the doors opened to reveal an empty elevator. She stepped inside with relief and removed the device from her ear as soon as the doors whisked shut again. She hated to admit it, but her nerves were more rattled today than she had anticipated, though she wasn't sure why. The announcement she'd be making at the ceremony was an important one, yes, and something she'd been working toward for a long time. But she was no stranger to the podium. She had no fear of public speaking.

It was a more general, vague apprehension she was feeling, almost a foreboding about today's impending event, though she couldn't imagine why. Regardless, Kelsey had these thirty minutes to pull herself together somehow. Then she would return, get ready to go on, do her part, and be done with it.

If only the new public relations consultants hadn't insisted on combining the two separate announcements into one big celebration, she thought as she reached the lobby and walked briskly toward the front door. Though she usually stopped to chat with her friend Ephraim, the building's head of security, she moved on past with just a glance and a wave toward the front desk. Once she was outside, she exhaled slowly, grateful for the warm spring sunshine.

Weather in April in New York City could go either way, but today was warm and dry, thankfully, with just a hint of a breeze.

Turning right, Kelsey merged into the foot traffic moving down the wide sidewalk toward Battery Park. On the way, she thought about the important part of today's ceremony, the announcement of a brand-new scholarship program to be funded by her late great-grandmother's foundation. Adele Tate had survived *Titanic* and gone on to become a successful businesswoman in an era when women in business were practically unheard of. In her later years, she had created the foundation with the express purpose of empowering other women in business. This new program Kelsey would be announcing today was a perfect fit and would provide up to ten scholarships per year to outstanding young females majoring in business-related fields of study.

Kelsey had been pushing for this for a long time, but it wasn't until recently, when her family's firm, Brennan & Tate, had begun taking steps to improve their public relations, that the board was even willing to consider it. The fact that, in the end, the scholarship decision had come down to a PR move rather than any actual altruism didn't bother her. She figured as long as the money was given out to deserving recipients, the end result was the same, regardless of motive.

Kelsey ran through her speech as she continued down the sidewalk and was pleased to get through the entire thing without once having to refer to the notes in her pocket that listed her key points. When she finally reached the corner at Number One Broadway, she looked ahead longingly at Battery Park, a fixture of the city for several hundred years and the perfect greenery-filled end cap to the island of Manhattan. More than anything, she wanted to make her way across the street and into the park to seek out one of her favorite spots in all of New York: the old family memorial stone that honored her two relatives who had perished on *Titanic*. Kelsey loved to visit the memorial, as it always left her feeling connected somehow to her many family members, both living and dead.

But there was no time for that now. Instead, she turned left, and once the light changed she moved with the crowd across Broadway to the triangular-shaped area on the other side known as Bowling Green. At the foot of the triangle was a sprinkling of vendors, and she took a moment to buy a bottle of water from a pretzel cart. Continuing onward, she tried some deep breathing exercises as she angled across the wide base of the triangle to tiny

Bowling Green Park, another of her favorite places to go when she needed a quick breather during the workday. She loved the symmetry of the place and convergence of shapes: a circular fountain inside an oval park on a triangular piece of land. This was a little oasis of greenery in a landscape of cement, its current focal point a ring of vivid red tulips surrounding the fountain.

Kelsey wanted to sit for a while on one of the benches that lined the walkway and take it all in, but she knew she needed to keep moving. At the very least, she slowed her pace and sipped her water and forced herself to get down to what was really bothering her: the other purpose of today's event, the part she wasn't exactly jumping up and down about.

To be sure, she appreciated the honor that was about to be bestowed upon her, and she was proud of having reached this new level of achievement in her career. The problem wasn't the award itself but the big public fuss that was being made over it. Others had earned membership in Brennan & Tate's "Quarter Club" in the past, and the most they had received was a handshake and a little plaque.

She, on the other hand, was about to be trooped out front and center in what the PR firm was practically turning into a circus. Between the handwritten invitations and the catered munchies, they were going all out to promote something that should have happened far more quietly. The best Kelsey could do, she supposed, was to grin and bear it—and try as hard as she could to keep the focus on Adele and the foundation and the new scholarship program. The more publicity for that, the better.

Kelsey let out a deep sigh as she continued through the park. This was the price she paid for being not just an account associate in the company's corporate finance division but an account associate in the corporate finance division who also just happened to be the great-great-granddaughter of the company's founder and the daughter of its reigning president. If there was such a thing as reverse nepotism, she thought, she was living it now. She'd never expected her professional path to be made easier because of family connections, but she also hadn't realized how much harder she'd have to work because of them.

At least she had her mentor and business-savvy friend Gloria to guide her through this current maze of public relations troubleshooting. But she'd be glad when this flurry of promotions was finally over and she could get back to business as usual. She loved what she did—and she was very good at it—but lately she'd spent more time authorizing interviews than she had authorizing investments.

Looking upward, Kelsey watched as a copter lifted off from the heliport at the water's edge, probably taking some important executive to a business meeting. She picked up the pace, exiting the park at the northern end and making her way around a group of chattering tourists who were taking turns posing for photos beside the bronze bull, a statue that had become synonymous with Wall Street and the stock market. Crossing back to her side of the road, she retraced her steps to the office building, allowing herself to take in the sights and sounds and smells of the city that was always so utterly alive and invigorating: car horns blaring the ever-present soundtrack of New York, the doughy smell of pretzels warming in a vendor's cart, businesswomen on their way to appointments in thousand-dollar suits and Uggs, their designer heels tucked inside briefcases for when they reached their destinations.

About twenty feet from her building, Kelsey spied a catering truck idling out in front and stopped short. From what she could see, Ephraim was holding open the door as a trio of uniformed workers dashed in carrying trays of food. Feeling a vague stir of nausea at the spectacle to come, she ducked into an alley on her left and made her way around to the back side of the building.

At the rear entrance, a solid metal door with a keypad above the knob, Kelsey typed in her security code, listened for the click, and stepped inside. Coming in this way, she'd have to take the stairs rather than the elevator, but she didn't care. Right now she just couldn't face the lobby and the excited chaos of the event that was being pulled together in her honor.

Kelsey's office was on the fourth floor, but she continued up the back stairs to the fifth without stopping. Once there, she again had to type in her security code, and then that interior door unlocked with a soft click. The fifth floor back entrance opened into the executive conference room, but it didn't occur to Kelsey until she was swinging the door wide that she might be interrupting some sort of meeting. Fortunately, however, she wasn't. The room was empty.

Stepping inside as the door to the stairwell fell shut behind her, Kelsey paused, relishing in the peace and quiet of the empty space. The fresh air had done her good, but the busyness of the streets had managed to stir up the busyness in her soul. She still felt disquieted, unsettled.

Apprehensive.

Ignoring those feelings, Kelsey glanced around, trying to remember if there was a phone in here as there was in the conference room on the fourth floor. Sure enough, she spotted it on the back wall, mounted between the audio/video cabinet and the broad space where the projection screen hung when it was in use. Lifting the receiver, Kelsey dialed the extension for her EA and told her she was back in the building but would be upstairs with Gloria until it was time for the big event. Sharon read off several messages that had come in while she was gone, none of them urgent, and then said there was one more thing.

"Yes?" Kelsey looked around the room for a clock, hoping her assistant wouldn't take much longer.

"Next time you fake a phone call as you're leaving," Sharon said with a chuckle, "make sure you actually bring your cell phone with you."

Quickly, Kelsey patted her pockets, her face burning with heat when all she came up with was the headset.

"Busted," was the best she could say, and then they both laughed. "So who else knows?"

"Just me. I was putting some files on your desk when I heard a ringtone coming from a drawer. I found your phone in your purse and put it on mute. Hope that was okay."

"Of course. I appreciate it," Kelsey said, grateful for the quick thinking—and discretion—of her faithful assistant. "Would you do me another favor and lock up my office before you head down to the ceremony?"

"No problem, Chief."

They ended the call, and Kelsey decided that before she went to talk to Gloria she would take a few minutes to fix herself up for the ceremony. Hoping to avoid having to go downstairs to her office, she decided to pay a visit to the executive washroom instead, where she knew all sorts of necessities could be found.

Slipping from the conference room into the main hall, Kelsey walked toward the front of the building. Though she had to go past a reception area and several offices along the way, she made it to the primary executive suite without having to pause and chat with anyone. Fortunately, the door to the CEO's office on her left was closed, and the EA that worked for the upper echelon, the exotically lovely Yanni, was busy talking on the phone and simply waved Kelsey on through to the right. With a smile and a nod, she turned and continued down the hallway, past the closed door of Gloria's office, to the executive washroom.

As expected, inside were baskets of toiletries on the wide marble counter. She washed her hands and then helped herself to an individually wrapped toothbrush and a tiny, disposable packet of toothpaste. After brushing her teeth, she unwrapped a fresh comb and ran it through her hair, trying to neaten up the windblown look she'd earned from her walk outside. She followed that with a shot of hairspray, a little dab of face powder, and some lip gloss for the cameras' sake, and then she stepped back, smoothed out her clothes, and studied the full effect in the mirror.

Whenever Kelsey looked at herself, the word that came to mind was "Irish"—not the red-headed, pale-skinned, green-eyed variety that most folks thought were the norm. Instead, she and her family sported a look far more common among the Irish: dark hair, even-toned skin, blue eyes.

Taking a cue from her mentor Gloria—and from her great-grandmother Adele, for that matter—Kelsey always bought the nicest clothes she could afford, knowing they were a business investment of sorts. Today she was sporting a new Hugo Boss suit in a soft gray pinstripe, accented with a red silk blouse and a pair of red Gaetano Perrone shoes. On her lapel was her favorite piece of jewelry, a hat pin she'd inherited from her great-grandmother and often wore as a stickpin instead. Purchased in London the day before Adele and her cousin and uncle set sail for America on *Titanic*, the top of the hat pin was in the shape of a tiny Irish harp, a lovely reminder of their homeland.

The overall look Kelsey always strived for was class, competence, and understated elegance. Examining her image in the mirror now, she felt that today's outfit had really hit the mark. Her layered, shoulder-length brown hair nicely framed her face, and the touch of makeup emphasized her lips and gave a smooth, matte finish to her skin.

Now all she had to do, she decided, was to get through the big event. In the end, though she wasn't looking forward to it at all, at least the new scholarship program made this trouble worthwhile.

Gloria's door was still closed, so Kelsey knocked first and then cracked it open, peeking through to see if her friend was in there by herself or if she had company. Fortunately, she was alone, and though she looked quite startled for a moment, she invited Kelsey in.

"Well, if it isn't the woman of the hour," Gloria said. Papers were spread across her desk, but she quickly shoved them into a single file folder and slipped it in a drawer. "You look gorgeous. Is that a new suit?"

Grinning, Kelsey slowly turned in a full circle. "Gotta look good in the photos. It's all about playing the game, right?"

"I've taught you well, my dear."

Kelsey took her usual seat in one of the two leather chairs facing the desk—a move she'd done countless times before. Yet as she settled in, she detected an odd expression on the older woman's face, as if she were more nervous and apprehensive than Kelsey herself. Worse, in fact. Though Gloria could usually be found looking perfectly polished, at the moment she was anything but, with dark circles under her eyes, rumpled clothing, and not a speck of makeup on.

"Are you okay?" Kelsey asked. She didn't want to be rude, but clearly something was wrong. "You're not sick, are you?"

"Just tired. I worked later than I should have last night. You know how it is."

Gloria obviously didn't want to talk about it, so Kelsey simply nodded and changed the subject, asking about the order of events for the ceremony. Gloria spelled things out, describing what sounded like a two-person show featuring Kelsey and the company's CEO, Walter Hallerman.

Kelsey scrunched up her face in dismay. "What about a board member or two? And don't we want to include somebody from the foundation?"

"Stop trying to deflect, Kels. You know as well as I do that this is all about you. That's the whole point."

Miserably, Kelsey slumped in her chair. "This is getting so old."

Gloria pulled off her glasses and nervously cleaned them with the corner of her blouse. "Hopefully, it won't be for much longer."

Both women knew Kelsey really had no choice—both for her family's sake and for the sake of the corporation. According to management, after Nolan Tate, Kelsey's father and the firm's leader, suffered a stroke last year, the company's value had taken a serious nosedive and now they needed to show that someone else would be carrying on the Tate name, someone who possessed the same sharp gut instincts and business acumen for which the Tates had long been known. As Kelsey was the only other family member who currently worked here, she'd become the logical choice by default.

It was a heavy weight to bear, one that was feeling heavier all the time. She was happy to carry on the family legacy and didn't mind doing her part to bolster the company's image, but she was getting awfully tired of being the center of attention. Last week had been a feature article in the *New York Times* magazine section about the "up-and-comer with the Midas touch." Prior to that, her name and face had been splashed across countless other newspapers and magazines, and she'd even appeared on a few local television and radio interview shows. Now she was about to go through this ridiculous ceremony, all for the sake of reassuring the public that even though Nolan Tate might be sidelined for now, another, just-as-capable Tate was ready to step up and prove that the family gift for investing was alive and well.

"I hope you're right," she said tiredly. "I don't think I can stand much more."

An odd look appeared on Gloria's face, and Kelsey thought she was about to say something important. But then, after a moment, she simply cleared her throat and asked if Kelsey needed any last-minute help polishing her speech.

"No, thanks. It's fine. But what were you thinking, just now? I can tell there's something on your mind today."

The older woman's cheeks flushed. "It's not important. I was...I was going to tell you not to worry, that the end is in sight. Maybe sooner than you think."

"What do you mean?"

Gloria shrugged and looked away, her fingers nervously taking off her glasses, cleaning them again, and putting them back on. Before she replied, the phone on the desk buzzed, startling her so much she practically fell out of her chair.

Face flushing, Gloria resettled herself in her seat and pushed the button for the speaker. Out came the voice of Walter, their CEO.

"I just got downstairs and don't see Kelsey. Have you talked to her?"

"She's here with me now."

"Good. Tell her to hurry up and get down here. We'll be starting in ten minutes."

"No problem."

"Have her take the stairs and use the side door to go backstage. She can wait there until I finish my introduction."

"Will do."

With a click he was gone.

"You heard the man," Gloria said, suddenly using her brightest pep talk voice, though it sounded strained and on edge. She rose, walked to the door, and stood there holding it open. "It's showtime, kid. You'd better get downstairs. Break a leg, or whatever it is they say."

Kelsey stood, feeling oddly dismissed. "Aren't you coming with me?"

"I…uh…I'll slip in the back later."

"But I thought we could go down together."

"I don't think so," Gloria responded without further explanation.

"Listen, are you *sure* you're all right?" Kelsey pressed, moving closer.

The woman wouldn't meet her gaze, though after a moment, much to Kelsey's surprise, her eyes filled with tears. Cooing sympathetically, Kelsey pulled a clean tissue from her pocket and handed it over, asking again what was wrong, if Gloria wanted to talk about it.

"Is it something with work?"

Gloria didn't reply.

"Maybe something personal? A problem with you and Vern, perhaps?"

Even though Gloria's marriage wasn't exactly known to be warm and fuzzy, she seemed surprised at the thought. Shaking her head, she blew her nose and said, "It's…I…" Her voice trailed off as she dabbed at her tears. Then she took a deep breath and slowly let it out.

"I'm so sorry," she said, looking down at the floor and speaking in a soft voice. "Have you ever done something bad out of good intentions?"

Kelsey was surprised. What an odd question for an ethical, no-nonsense woman like Gloria to ask.

"You mean, the 'end justifies the means'?"

Gloria nodded. "Exactly."

"Probably," Kelsey replied, studying her friend's face. "One time when I was a kid, my mother wouldn't buy me the mini marshmallows I wanted from the grocery store, so while she was busy at the checkout, I went back and got a bag off the shelf, tore it open, and started eating them anyway. I figured that once they were open she'd have no choice but to buy them. Of course, I didn't count on her making me pay her back out of my allowance—and then she didn't even let me have the rest of the marshmallows."

Both women smiled, but fresh tears filled Gloria's eyes. "If only this were that simple." She blinked, sending twin tracks of wetness down her cheeks.

Kelsey felt terrible for the poor thing, but she still didn't have a clue as to what any of this was about. Of all the people in this office, Gloria was the very last person she'd ever expect to talk this way, much less to stand in an open doorway and *cry*.

Suddenly, before Kelsey could even think of how to reply, Gloria gripped her by both arms and spoke in an urgent whisper.

"You don't have to go down there, you know," she hissed. "You don't have to do this at all. You could walk right out the back door and go home, and I could tell Walter you weren't feeling well and had to leave."

Kelsey was dumbfounded. What on *earth* was Gloria talking about?

"Why would I do that? It's just a stupid ceremony. I'll get through it, no big deal."

Just as suddenly, Gloria let go of her arms, stepped back, and placed both hands over her eyes. "What am I saying? Don't listen to me. I'm not myself today at all."

Kelsey stood there amidst her friend's meltdown, thinking, *You can say that again*. She wondered if perhaps Gloria had been drinking or something. She didn't smell alcohol on her breath, but she certainly was acting strange— stranger than Kelsey could ever have imagined.

"Enough of this," Gloria said finally, taking her hands from her face and giving Kelsey a broad, forced smile. "Are you ready to go? Because your time's up. Come on, Tater Tot. Forget what I said earlier. I'll walk you down myself."

CHAPTER
TWO

Without another word, Gloria took Kelsey by the elbow and led her down the hall and through the executive conference room to the door for the back stairwell. Kelsey stepped out first and Gloria followed, and then the two women headed side by side down the steps, silent all the way to the first floor. Kelsey wanted to question her friend's odd behavior more thoroughly, but that would have wait until after the ceremony. The company had gone to so much trouble with the event the least Kelsey could do was show up on time.

The bottom of the stairwell had four doors, one on each wall, leading to the outside, to maintenance, to the auditorium, and to the backstage area. Kelsey headed for the latter, but Gloria stopped her by taking her hand.

"Please ignore my ridiculous dramatics," she said softly, giving Kelsey's hand a tight squeeze and then letting it go. "This is your time to shine. I want you to get out there and grab that audience the way you grab investment opportunities."

Kelsey smiled. "That's a good way to put it."

"I'm serious. I know you hate this public relations stuff, but you're doing a great job with it. I promise that a light is at the end of this tunnel. You'll see it soon."

"If you say so."

Taking a deep breath and squaring her shoulders, Kelsey opened the door. She was glad to hear the noise of a chattering crowd, as it meant Walter hadn't yet called things to order. She stepped into the shadows of the backstage space, but much to her surprise, Gloria didn't follow.

"Aren't you coming?" Kelsey asked, turning to look at the woman, who was hovering on the other side of the doorway.

"No. This is as far as I go today."

Kelsey squinted. "I don't understand. You're the reason for much of my success, Gloria. You should be out there by my side."

"No," she repeated. "You need to be seen as the independent, capable businesswoman you are. If I'm up there with you, it weakens the impact. It makes it look like you're still a child learning at my feet."

"But that's exactly what I *am*, metaphorically speaking," Kelsey whispered. "Gloria, there's no way I could do this job without your guidance."

"Sorry, Kels. This is your time to shine. Yours alone."

With that, Gloria gave her one last meaningful look and closed the door. There in the darkness, Kelsey tried to wrap her mind around all that had just happened. She was still trying to make sense of things a few moments later when Walter popped his head through the curtain from out front, just to make sure she was there.

"All set?" he asked brusquely.

"Ready as I'll ever be."

With a nod he disappeared again, and after a moment he began to speak over the noise of the crowd, asking everyone to take their seats because it was time to get started.

As the crowd quieted down out front, Kelsey moved forward to the side of the stage, where she could get ready for her entrance and watch Walter at the podium. Looking out at him now, she saw that he was wearing his usual nondescript yet perfectly tailored Saville Row suit with a white shirt and blue tie. Standing there, he seemed the very image of the powerful Wall Street investment broker. That sense of power came not from any grandiose gestures or broad, sweeping proclamations, but instead the opposite—a reserved, dignified air and no-nonsense style that spoke volumes about his position in the world of finance. Kelsey had always respected Walter, at least until the past few months, when he'd begun scrambling in response to the company's identity crisis. Until then, he'd been an excellent CEO, both before and after Nolan Tate's departure from the firm. Currently, she wasn't so sure.

Soon the audience sounds had ceased and Walter was addressing the crowd, thanking them for coming and welcoming them on behalf of Brennan

& Tate "and the whole Tate family." Talk about laying it on thick. The only member of the family who was even here today was Kelsey herself—and possibly her brother, Matt, if he'd managed to get out of work in time to come. More than anything, she had wanted her parents to be here too, but the consensus was that Nolan was still too incapacitated to be seen in public and that his appearance would undermine the whole event. As Walter had explained it to her, today's primary goal was to make Brennan & Tate appear vibrant and successful and growing. If people saw that the president of the company was now "essentially an old man in a wheelchair who can barely form a coherent sentence," it wouldn't exactly instill consumer confidence.

Thinking back over that awful conversation with Walter, Kelsey finally realized the source of today's apprehension: This was *wrong*. It was disingenuous. Allowing them to exploit her success was one thing, but hiding the full truth from the public about her dad's health was another. Closing her eyes, she thought about how far things had drifted since he'd had the stroke. Nolan Tate would never have pulled the kind of stunts Walter had been green-lighting lately. Kelsey's heart pumped with a sudden surge of anger, and she decided that this was it. She'd play the role today, as requested, but after this she was calling a halt to the entire, absurd publicity campaign. The moment that campaign excluded her precious father—incapacitated or not—from a public event staged in honor of his daughter was the moment it crossed the line.

Her decision made, a surge of peace rushed through Kelsey's veins. For the first time in a month, she felt like herself again: decisive, in charge, ethical. Even as Walter was praising those very qualities from the podium in his introduction, she was scolding herself for having let things get so out of control. Taking a deep breath, she pulled out her notes from her pocket, looked down at them, and read through her key points, telling herself she would make this speech one to remember. She would give it everything she had. She would knock it out of the ballpark. And when it was finished, she would tell Walter Hallerman that it had been her grand finale as far as PR efforts were concerned.

Then she would get back to the business of investing.

Finally, after a few more minutes of Walter's praise, citing Kelsey's summa cum laude degree at Swarthmore and her MBA from Columbia, and telling the audience what a "gifted" and "gutsy" person she was, he turned toward her, smiled, and concluded his intro with the words, "And now I'd like to bring out our guest of honor, Ms. Kelsey Tate."

That was her cue.

Plastering a smile on her face, she walked out onto the stage, shook Walter's outstretched hand, and then took her place next to him, facing the audience as they clapped. As she stood there looking out at the crowd, she was surprised at the number of familiar faces she could see. In fact, from what she could tell, the first few rows of the two-hundred-seat auditorium had been filled with men and women whose businesses *she* had helped get off the ground. Because of her investment work, these people had been able to start or expand their own companies, which had then managed to grow and develop, create jobs, and become profitable for them all. The sight of these people gathered together in one place, in her honor, was both humbling and energizing. *They* were why she did what she did. They were the whole point of it all.

Once the applause died down, Walter proceeded with the award part of the ceremony, again shaking Kelsey's hand as he welcomed her into Brennan & Tate's prestigious "Quarter Club." Turning to the audience, he explained the significance of this honor, that it meant she had brought in twenty-five million dollars' worth of business to the firm. That earned another round of applause, during which Walter's EA, Yanni, came up on stage and handed him a small plaque, which he would then present to Kelsey.

How very Academy Awards of them, she thought wryly. *All this moment needs to make it complete is an evening gown for Yanni and an orchestra to cut off my acceptance speech.*

"On second thought," Walter said, still holding the plaque, "if you folks will indulge me for a moment, I think there's an even better way to do this." With that, he gestured toward the front row and said, "Lou? Would you do the honors?"

"Absolutely," the man replied, rising and quickly bounding up the steps to the stage.

Kelsey grinned as he came, thrilled to see her old colleague and friend Lou Strahan. She hadn't noticed him before, but she couldn't be happier to be sharing the stage with him now.

Once Lou reached them, Walter handed him the plaque and then put an arm around his shoulders and spoke into the microphone.

"Many of you may know Louis Strahan, a former vice president here at Brennan & Tate and now the owner and CEO of the very successful Strahan Realty Trust."

Kelsey saw a number of heads nodding in the audience, and someone called out, "Way to go, Lou!" to a smattering of applause.

"Anyway," Walter continued, clearing his throat, "there's something about Lou you may not know, but it's the reason I've asked him to come up here and present this award to Kelsey on our behalf." Glancing at Lou and then at Kelsey, Walter said, "Five years ago, not long after I came to this firm, Kelsey made her very first investment on behalf of Brennan & Tate. That investment went to Lou to provide start-up money for his new company. As that was the first deal she brokered on her own, and it ended up being such a profitable one for all involved, I thought it appropriate that he be the one to present her with this award today."

With that, Walter took a few steps back and Lou moved to the microphone. Even before he spoke, Kelsey was smiling in anticipation. The man was a real character, intense and driven but also brutally honest and wickedly funny. She'd missed working with him but was pleased he'd done so well out on his own—and that she'd had a hand in helping him get started.

"I won't say much," Lou told the audience with just a tinge of his old Brooklyn accent coming through, "because I know you folks would rather hear from a beautiful young woman than a long-winded old man."

Some of the audience members chuckled, and after a beat Kelsey realized why. Lou wasn't talking about himself. His comment had been intended as a dig toward Walter, who was older than him by a good fifteen years and did tend to get a little long-winded. She stifled a smile and made a point of not looking Walter's way.

"Just let me say," Lou continued, "that I remember well the first day Kelsey started working at Brennan & Tate. I already knew her and liked her, of course, from various functions Nolan had brought her to over the years. But this was different. Now she was going to be a *coworker*. The *boss's daughter*. Can you imagine?"

More smiles, more chuckles.

"Kelsey, I don't mind telling you, the guys in my division took bets that first day on how long it would take before you'd go crying to Daddy over something."

The audience laughed. She smiled, rolling her eyes.

"Of course, this being an investment firm and me being a smart investor, I didn't like the odds." His expression grew serious as he leaned closer to the mic. "I knew the reputation of Kelsey's great-great grandfather, Sean

Brennan, who first founded Brennan & Company more than one hundred years ago. I knew the legend of her great-grandparents, Sean's daughter, Adele, and her husband, Edwin Tate, who together ushered Sean's business through the depression, renamed the company Brennan & Tate, and built it to what it is today. Finally, I knew Kelsey's father, Nolan Tate, one of the finest men I've ever had the pleasure of working with." Again glancing her way, he concluded, "Given all of that, I knew that this young lady wasn't the 'cry to Daddy' type at all. I was right. Instead, she was smart, talented, and hardworking, with the knowledge to back up her instincts. It has truly been my pleasure to work with her, a delight to count her as a friend, and a privilege to present her with this award. Kels, may this be just the first of many honors and accolades to come. Congratulations."

Lou handed her the plaque and they shared a long hug. She was too overcome with emotion to thank him for his kind words lest she start to cry, so she simply gave him a grateful smile as they pulled apart.

"I'm so proud of you, kiddo," he whispered, looking a little emotional himself. With a nod to Walter, he returned to his seat.

Kelsey took a deep breath, assuming it was her turn now, but then Walter surprised her by stepping back up to the mic. Hoping he knew to keep things moving, she stood at his side and took a moment to look down at the plaque and her name engraved there as he talked.

"Before I turn the podium over to our guest of honor," Walter said, "I have one more item of business, a little surprise for her." Glancing her way, he said, "Just this afternoon, I learned that Kelsey Tate has been named by *Forbes* magazine as one of their 'Forty to Watch Under Forty.' Congratulations."

That earned the biggest applause yet, and even Kelsey was momentarily taken aback by such news. PR ploy or not, this was indeed a big honor, one that would no doubt come with a photo and profile in the magazine, garnering her and her firm attention on an international level. Now if she could just wrap up all the promoting and get back to work, she might actually be able to prove whether such an honor was justified.

Finally, Walter concluded his portion of the event and handed the reins over to Kelsey. As he walked off the stage and took his seat down front, she slid her plaque onto the little shelf under the podium, and tried to gather her wits.

"'Forty to Watch Under Forty,'" she mused aloud to the audience as she placed her notes on the shiny wooden surface in front of her and adjusted the microphone. "Wow. I'm deeply honored. Of course, I hope it's not rude of me to say that I'd rather be in something called 'Thirty to Watch Under Thirty,' but I passed that cutoff about two years ago."

Her joke garnered a huge laugh from the crowd, bigger than it deserved. Good. That meant it wouldn't be long until she had them in the palm of her hand. Before she launched into her talk, which would build to a crescendo with the announcement of the new scholarship program, she took a moment to thank various people, including Lou for his kind words, Walter for his support, her investment team, her executive assistant, and her coworkers. She also thanked her mentor, Gloria, but even as she said the words, she looked around and realized the woman wasn't in the audience. Trying not to think about that, she continued.

"Finally, I'd like to thank my father, even though he couldn't be here with us today, and to pass along his regards to all of you. I miss seeing my dad around the office, of course, but I've never missed him more than I do right now."

She shot a pointed look at Walter, who didn't flinch, though Kelsey noticed a few nods of sympathy among those sitting nearby. Her acknowledgments complete, she clasped her hands together, placed them on the podium in front of her, and looked out at the audience, allowing a moment of silence before delivering the most important part of her speech. In that moment, it was almost as if she could feel the room coming together as one, an eager and listening entity ready to hear whatever she'd come to say.

"Just about one hundred years ago today," she began, her eyes slowly scanning the faces in the room as she spoke, "over in Belfast, Ireland, a young woman named Adele Brennan was getting ready for the most important voyage of her life. She was just nineteen at the time, a brave, smart, and resourceful girl who was fascinated with, of all things, *business*, something that was practically unheard of for a woman of her generation."

Kelsey paused to let that thought sink in, and then she continued.

"Making the trip with Adele was her cousin Jocelyn and her uncle, Rowan Brennan. On April tenth, nineteen twelve, the three of them made their way to Southampton, England, and boarded the grandest ship that had ever been built: *Titanic*. They were bound for America, where Adele would be reunited with the father she hadn't seen for sixteen years." Kelsey looked around at the silent, rapt audience. She would have liked to give a more detailed version of Adele's story, but today her time was limited.

"Four days later, as I'm sure you all know, *Titanic* struck an iceberg in the

North Atlantic and sank. Both Jocelyn and Rowan died that night. Of the three travelers, only Adele survived."

Kelsey paused a moment to let that sink in, but as she took a deep breath to continue, she heard a strange sound coming from the back of the auditorium, a low, chanting drone that started out soft but quickly grew louder. Others could hear it as well, and heads began rotating to look. Even Walter turned around in his seat to see what was making such an odd noise.

Kelsey's eyes scanned the auditorium, trying to match the source of the sound with the person making it. Soon, she realized that it was a man, and he was repeating one word over and over. At first she thought it was "ire" or "fire," but after a moment she realized what he was saying: *liar*.

The man stood, shouting the word at the top of his lungs, "Liar! Liar!"

Stunned, Kelsey looked to Walter, but he had already jumped up and was quickly striding up the aisle toward the back of the auditorium. She thought he was going to try and apprehend the man himself somehow, but instead he slipped out the back, probably to alert security.

Everyone else stayed where they were, clearly stunned at this odd turn of events. Suddenly, as quickly as the chanting had begun, the man stepped out into the aisle and pointed at Kelsey. She had never seen him before, and for a moment she was afraid he might pull out a gun and take a shot at her. Instead, he simply cried out, "Lies! It's all lies! The real Adele Tate did not survive *Titanic*!"

That earned a gasp not just from the audience but from Kelsey herself. What was this lunatic talking about?

"The woman who claimed to be Adele was actually an imposter," he continued loudly, his eyes gleaming behind dark-rimmed glasses. "She stole the real Adele's identity, stole this company, and then lived out that lie for the rest of her life!"

CHAPTER
THREE

Kelsey gripped each side of the podium, her mind racing. Someone needed to shut this man up—though a part of her very much wanted to hear what he had to say. He was lying, of course, but he must have some reason for making such a crazy claim.

Suddenly, the back door of the auditorium swung open and two security guards came marching in, followed by Walter. At that moment, as if sensing that the most interesting person at this event was about to be carted away, the media people hopped up from their seats and began moving toward the man, throwing questions at him.

"How do you know this?"

"Why have you come here?"

"What was the imposter's real identity?"

The nature of their questions sent a chill down Kelsey's spine. Were they really going to give this man's words credence? The very notion that the woman who called herself Adele Brennan had been an imposter was absurd!

The room quickly dissolved into pandemonium after that, with the guards grabbing the man's arms and trying to drag him out, the reporters continuing to shout questions, a woman Kelsey didn't know—a tall redhead with short cropped hair—begging the man to "Stop it! Stop it!" and the man himself still shouting even as he slumped down in the guards' grip. A heavy-set man, he used his dead weight to his advantage.

"I came here to tell the world," he yelled as loudly as he could, "that I have proof that the woman who called herself Adele Brennan was actually *Jocelyn* Brennan, Adele's first cousin! Jocelyn assumed Adele's identity after *Titanic* sank and came here to America *pretending* to be Adele so she could steal her inheritance!"

Fortunately, that was all he was able to get out before the guards finally managed to pull him through the door. The reporters followed, the redhead was now screaming at the guards instead of the man, saying, "Don't hurt him! Don't hurt him!" and the people in the audience chattered loudly about what had just happened. From the corner of her eye, Kelsey saw Lou jump up from his seat and join the fray, no doubt to help with damage control.

Someone needed to speak up quickly in Adele's defense. Kelsey thought about doing it herself, but she knew such words coming from the woman's great-granddaughter would be seen as biased and wouldn't carry much weight.

Mortified and desperate, Kelsey looked down to see that today's honored guests seemed decidedly uncomfortable. In the front row sat Pamela Greeley, the well-respected head of Queen's Fleet Management Group and one of the older people present here today. Pamela's career in the world of finance had overlapped with Adele's, maybe even as far back as the late sixties. Though they never actually worked together in the same place, they had numerous business dealings over the years, and Pamela had looked up to the legendary Adele Brennan Tate as her own personal hero and the kind of businesswoman she aspired to be. Kelsey knew this because Pamela had been one of the speakers at Adele's funeral and had said as much to the congregation gathered there. Kelsey had only been nine years old at the time, but she clearly remembered Pamela's heartfelt words because they had echoed her own thoughts. Grandma Adele had been Kelsey's personal hero too, the kind of woman *she* wanted to grow up to be.

Looking to Pamela now, Kelsey implored her with her eyes, wishing she would come up and publically refute the claims of the man who had just disrupted the entire ceremony. Anyone who had known Adele knew that she was a woman of honesty and integrity. To call her an imposter was like saying Mother Teresa was selfish or Babe Ruth wasn't much of a hitter. Adele had been the very *embodiment* of ethics, and everyone who knew her knew that. Pamela didn't take the cue, however, so Kelsey gave up, knowing it would be rude and presumptuous to call the woman out by name and specifically ask her to come up and defend Adele's honor.

If only Gloria were here! She, too, had known Adele, had known the kind of person she'd been. Why wasn't she around to help?

Walter had only been with the firm for about five years, so Kelsey wasn't sure if he'd ever known Adele personally or not. Regardless, he was missing at the moment too, having stayed with the security guards and the raving lunatic who had ruined her ceremony. Ditto with Lou, who was also MIA.

Feeling like a deer caught in headlights, Kelsey looked out at the whole auditorium, which was now half empty. The roar of the voices of those who left could still be heard coming from the lobby, and those who remained were perched in their seats and looking up at Kelsey, unsure, as if they were too polite to leave but hoping she was about to dismiss them.

Finally, she took a deep breath and said the only thing that came to mind. "I'm so sorry about all of this. I suppose we'll have to speak with the caterers about what they put in the punch."

Her joke landed a few chuckles, but mostly the crowd looked antsy and ready to bolt. Growing more serious, Kelsey continued.

"Obviously, there is no truth to that man's allegations. I'm not sure what he was hoping to achieve here, but rest assured we'll get to the bottom of it. In the meantime, maybe we should go ahead and try to wrap things up. I apologize that our ceremony has been cut short."

Glancing down at her notes, Kelsey tried to decide what parts—if any— of her talk she could salvage. "Before I was interrupted," she said, lifting her eyes and looking out at the audience, "I was telling the story of my great-grandmother, Adele Brennan. Why don't we just jump ahead to the part of that story that, to me, most clearly demonstrates her tremendous gifts and talents as a businessperson."

She went on to tell that part of her tale, how Adele's husband, Edwin, was happy to be the behind-the-scenes administrator and facilitator while Adele was the star rainmaker. "They made quite a pair, and between the two of them managed to keep this company afloat through the crash of nineteen twenty-nine and the Great Depression."

Scanning the faces in the room, Kelsey was pleased to see that she seemed to have regained their full attention. She continued.

"When this company was at its lowest point, it was Adele's idea to invest in businesses run by women, immigrants, and minorities. That's part of what helped save Brennan & Tate at a time when other investment firms were going belly up all around them. No other company would take a risk on these types of businesses, but my great-grandmother knew her roots and knew who to believe in. With that vision, not only did she and Edwin bring this place through some difficult years, but they also gave a chance to so many who came to them for financial help. For the second time in her life, Adele had been brought down to nothing and found the will and strength to survive and ultimately thrive. Her legacy is still with us today."

At that, the audience surprised Kelsey by bursting into enthusiastic applause. Smiling, she waited for the applause to wind down, and then she added, "It's in the spirit of that legacy that I'd like to make the following announcement on behalf of the Adele Brennan Tate Foundation. My great-grandmother created the foundation when I was just a little girl, but I well remember her enthusiasm for its goal of empowering women in business. On tables out in the lobby, you probably saw some reports about many of the good works the foundation has been able to do. Now I'm thrilled to announce their newest effort: The Adele Brennan Tate Scholarship Fund, which will provide up to ten substantial scholarships per year to young women who demonstrate academic excellence in business-related courses and clear evidence of an entrepreneurial or investment-related spirit."

More applause, and though Kelsey was still devastated by the bizarre turn of events, she was glad at least that she'd managed to get to the main part of the ceremony anyway.

"I know this has been one of the more, uh, *unique* events you've probably been to this week," she quipped, "but I hope what you remember most from this afternoon isn't the outburst of a stranger but the legacy and generosity of a truly upstanding, ethical, and memorable woman, Adele Brennan Tate, who was brilliant in business, charitable in life, and absolutely, positively who she said she was. I'd stake my life on that."

With those words Kelsey thanked everyone for coming. The members of the audience leaped to their feet and gave her a standing ovation. Yet, as convincing as she felt she'd been, she knew it wouldn't count for much because none of the media people had even been in the room to hear her wrap things up.

Now that the ceremony was finished and she was coming back down from the adrenaline rush of her closing words, she found herself feeling momentarily disoriented. What should she do next? Mingle with those who had stayed? Go out to the lobby and help handle the press? She was trying to decide when she heard her name being called, and she turned to see Lou standing off to the side of the stage, right where she had stood during Walter's introduction.

"Come on, kiddo," Lou said, and that was all she needed to hear.

With a final smile and a wave at her audience, Kelsey walked out the way she'd come in, giving Lou a quick embrace and then letting him lead her through the backstage shadows to the stairwell door. She thought they would be going upstairs or maybe outside, but instead he led her to the one door of the four she never, ever used, the one for the maintenance area.

The door didn't even have a keypad for entry, but instead just a regular knob and deadbolt that were always locked. At the moment, however, the door was propped slightly open by what looked like an Italian leather shoe. To her surprise, Lou pulled the door the rest of the way open and then slipped his foot into the shoe.

"Lou! Are those Testonis?"

"Berlutis," he replied. "Not the cheapest doorstop around, but it was all I could think of to do."

He gestured inside, and she moved forward up the narrow, grungy hallway that ran past the building's HVAC system and maintenance supply area.

"Where are we going?"

"They need you in security, but this was the only way to get you there without going through the lobby."

They continued forward, finally coming to a stop in front of the door at the end of the hall. Lou reached across Kelsey to give it a sharp knock, and it immediately swung open to reveal the imposing figure of Ephraim Jones, head of security.

"Hey, Kelsey," he said in his low rumble of a voice. "You okay?"

"I've been better," she replied with a wan smile.

"I hear that."

Moving back, he swung the door open all the way and gestured for them to come inside. Kelsey stepped forward but then glanced back to see Lou hesitating in the hallway. For the second time today, someone she needed and trusted was about to stay behind at the worst possible moment.

"Oh, no you don't. You're coming with me," Kelsey said to him, grabbing his wrist and pulling him inside.

"I don't work here anymore, remember?"

"That doesn't matter right now, Lou. I need you."

He hesitated and then did as she asked. "I'm here for you, kiddo. You know that."

Together they followed Ephraim around the corner to the security office.

Standing nearby was Walter, a security guard, and a woman named Carole from the public relations firm. At the far end of the room was the man who had disrupted the meeting, deep in conversation with the spiky-haired redhead who had also been part of the ruckus. The two of them were arguing in hushed whispers, and at the moment they were so focused on each other that they didn't even seem to notice Kelsey had come into the room.

Walter, however, greeted her with a hug and an apology, much to her surprise. "I'm sorry I abandoned you in there," he said in a low voice. "Carole told me you did an excellent job of calming everyone down and wrapping things up. I knew you would."

Kelsey glanced at the PR woman and then back at Walter. "Thanks, but I don't know what good it did. All the media people had already left by then."

"They didn't go far," Ephraim said, gesturing toward a bank of security screens. The image on the left was coming from one of the lobby cameras, and Kelsey could see that the space was packed wall-to-wall with people. No big surprise there. They had gotten a whiff of a big story and weren't going to go away until they knew who this man was and what it was he'd been trying to say.

The next screen over showed the lobby at a different angle, near the doors to the auditorium. Moving closer, Kelsey could see several members of her investment research team, along with her EA, Sharon. They were huddled together talking, and when Sharon glanced up toward the camera, the worry on her face was clear.

"So what's the plan here?" Kelsey whispered, looking apprehensively toward the pair at the other end of the room. Now that she was getting a closer look at them, she could see that the man was in his mid-sixties with messy gray hair, thick glasses, and cheap, ill-fitting clothes. The woman looked to be a few years younger than he was, though that might have been because of her more youthful orange hair color—obviously from a bottle—and the spiky style she wore it in. How had these two possibly slipped past security and into the ceremony?

"The plan," Walter said, "is to get this man out of this building and then out of New York City before any reporters can get their hooks into him."

"Where does he live?"

"Florida, but that's not where we want him to go just yet. Too easy for the reporters to track him there. Instead, I offered him a limo to Vermont, a week at my sister's bed-and-breakfast near Burlington, and five hundred dollars spending money for while he's there if he'll keep his mouth shut. He's not having any of it, but the woman with him is trying to talk him into it."

Kelsey's eyes widened. Walter was trying to pay off this lunatic? That was absurd! The man had come here, made libelous accusations about her great-grandmother in public, and disrupted a big corporate event in the process. Now he was getting *rewarded* for it? Before Kelsey could voice her objections, Lou muttered, "Excuse us, Walter," took her by the arm, and pulled her out of the room and around the corner.

"Don't blow your stack here, kiddo," he whispered. "I don't always see eye to eye with Walter Hallerman, as you know, but I think in this case it's the right move. This kook's done enough damage already. Let him get shuttled out of here and tucked away till the dust settles. You can follow up more privately later."

Kelsey wanted to scream, but she knew Lou was right. She fully intended to question the man now, before he left, but otherwise the only real move they had was to get him as far away as possible from that crowd of reporters in the lobby.

"Fine." Though she agreed to the plan, she still wasn't happy as they returned to the other room.

"I suppose I'd better get back out there," Ephraim said in his deep voice, still eyeing the milling crowd on the screen. Looking at Walter, he added, "Are you sure you don't want us to call the police?"

"Nope. We'll handle things in here ourselves. But thanks anyway."

Nodding, Ephraim headed to the main security door that led to reception. As soon as he swung it open, the noise of the crowd came rushing in.

"Sounds like the vultures are circling," Lou said as the door fell closed behind him. "I don't get it. Why is this turning into such a big deal? Adele's been dead for more than twenty years. Whether this guy's telling the truth or not, it's practically ancient history by now."

The PR lady turned and addressed Lou and Kelsey as well. "I'll tell you why it's a big deal," she hissed softly. "For starters, we're not just talking about Adele Brennan Tate, well-known Wall Street icon. We're talking about a woman who also happened to be a survivor of *Titanic*. This man just served up the juiciest *Titanic*-related scandal anyone's heard about in years. To make matters worse, the world's already in a *Titanic* frenzy right now because of the anniversary."

"Anniversary?" Lou asked.

"Yes," Kelsey told him. "We're coming up on one hundred years since the ship sank."

"In about a week and a half," Carole said, "April fifteenth. I have you booked solid for that whole weekend, the fourteenth and fifteenth."

Kelsey nodded, resisting the urge to groan, as Carole continued.

"Anyway, with this big hundred-year anniversary coming up, there's not a media outlet in existence that wouldn't kill for some huge story they could tie in with it—and the more outrageous that story, the better."

Lou sucked in a breath through clenched teeth. "Got it. Wow. Talk about bad timing."

Walter, who had been studying the screen, interrupted their conversation. "Carole, why don't you go out there and spread the word to all B & T employees that they should get their things and go on home? I don't want anyone hanging around tonight. Have them leave the building as quickly as possible. I know they are curious about what's happening, but we need to clear out the lobby as much as we can—plus I don't want any of them getting questioned by reporters."

"Agreed."

"Then see if your people need help schmoozing our special guests out the door. I know the reporters and photographers aren't going anywhere, but if we can at least get everybody else out, it'll help."

"Will do."

As she headed for the same door Ephraim had used, Walter added, "After you've done that, Carole, you and your people are free to go too. We'll deal with all of this tomorrow."

"Good idea," she replied, "though I'll wait to take off until after the caterers have all their stuff out."

With that she was gone, and Kelsey was glad. More than anything, she wanted to talk with the man who had ruined her speech with his insane accusations about her great-grandmother, but there was no reason for the PR woman to hear all the gritty details, whatever they might be.

"Where's Gloria in all of this?" Lou asked Kelsey softly. "I didn't even see her at the ceremony."

Kelsey was trying to decide how to reply when Walter answered for her.

"She's up in her office. I just talked to her. I told her what happened and that we needed her down here ASAP to help with damage control, but she said she wasn't coming. She's not feeling well."

Kelsey could feel heat rising in her cheeks. Though she was as put out with Gloria as it sounded like Walter was, she felt the urge to defend the woman. She was obviously dealing with something difficult. If she wasn't up to attending the ceremony, it stood to reason that she wouldn't be coming down to help out in its aftermath, either.

"You know she would be here if she could," Kelsey replied, but as soon as she said it, she remembered the woman's odd behavior before the ceremony and wondered if that were really true. Something weird had been going on with Gloria today.

"All I know is that she's been extremely unhelpful in all of this," Walter snapped. "If she's so sick that she can't get herself down here, then she needs to go home."

"I'll talk to her once we're done," Kelsey assured him.

"Well, well, well," the man said suddenly from the other end of the room.

Kelsey looked up with a start, her heart pounding. Apparently, he had just realized she was here.

Putting a halt to his discussion with the redhead, he stepped forward and put out an arm as if he intended to shake Kelsey's hand. In response, she simply stood where she was and clasped her hands behind her back. She had no intention of doing any such thing.

"Miss Tate," he said with a nod, getting the point and letting his hand drop. He didn't seem embarrassed—nor hostile, for that matter. Mostly, he just looked pleased to see her. "How do you do? I'm Rupert Brennan."

She'd been all ready to go on the attack, but then she faltered at the mention of her great-grandmother Adele's maiden name. "Did you say Brennan?"

"Yep. Rupert Brennan. I'm your second cousin, once removed."

CHAPTER
FOUR

Kelsey was dumbfounded, staring at the stout little man in front of her. Her *cousin*? This lunatic was a *relative* of hers? Trying not to look as astounded as she felt, she cleared her throat and asked the man in an even tone if he would care to sit down so they could talk.

"Certainly," he replied, as jovial as if they had just met at a family reunion picnic.

"I don't think this is a good idea—" Walter began, but Kelsey cut him off with a sharp glance. It was *her* great-grandmother the man had impugned out there. She had a right to know what he'd come here to say.

As Walter backed off and Lou moved up and to the right in a more protective stance, Kelsey pulled out two rolling chairs from in front of the security screens and placed them facing each other a few feet apart in the middle of the room. They both sat.

"Why did you do this?" she asked, taking the lead. "Why did you come here and disrupt our ceremony like that?"

The man looked at her for a long moment, all traces of warmth disappearing from his gaze. "Because it was time for me to be heard. It was time for the world to know the truth about the woman who came to America claiming to be Adele Brennan."

Kelsey could feel anger boiling up inside of her, and she knew it was coming not just from this man's words but his odd attitude. Still, letting him see that anger would get them nowhere, just as she would never wear her heart on her sleeve in a negotiation with a potential client.

36

"Let's back up a little, Rupert," she said, keeping her voice even and trying not to choke on the man's name. "Will you tell me exactly how you think you and I are related?"

He nodded, almost eagerly, saying that he was the grandson of Quincy Brennan, who was Jocelyn's brother and Adele's first cousin.

"The same Jocelyn who was traveling to America with Adele when *Titanic* went down?" she asked.

"Yes! When Jocelyn made that trip, her father came along but her mother and baby brother, Quincy, stayed home in Ireland. Eventually, Quincy grew up and fathered a son, Ian, who grew up and fathered me." Smiling, he added, "Lucky for my dad, when he immigrated to America as a young man, *his* ship made it all the way here without hitting any icebergs."

Kelsey cringed at this guy's lighthearted attitude about one of the saddest, most senseless tragedies of all time.

"Anyway," he continued, oblivious to the effect he was having on her, "because my grandfather Quincy and your father's grandmother Jocelyn were siblings, that makes your father and me second cousins, which makes you and me second cousins once removed. Simple. See?"

Lou huffed, looking at Kelsey. "Why are you wasting your time with this guy?" With his expensive suit, black slicked-back hair, and short, muscular build, Lou cut an imposing figure. But she knew he was all bark and no bite. Beneath his dark glower, he was probably every bit as confused as she was.

She ignored his comment and asked, "What makes you think Adele was an imposter?"

"I have proof," Rupert replied. "The real Adele died the night *Titanic* sank, as did her uncle, Rowan Brennan. Of the three, only Jocelyn survived, but when she was rescued from the lifeboat and realized the other two were dead, she made a decision. On the rescue ship they asked her name, she said she was Adele Brennan, they wrote it down, and that was that. Once she got to America, her father didn't know she was actually Jocelyn 'cause he hadn't seen Adele since she was three years old. He bought Jocelyn's story, hook, line, and sinker, and welcomed her as his daughter."

Kelsey sat back, astounded at this man's claim.

"So, basically, you're saying your grandfather's sister stole her cousin Adele's identity and lived out the rest of her life as a lie?"

"Yep. And I have proof."

"And what kind of proof would that be?"

A smug, self-righteous expression began to spread across his face. "I'm saving that for the courts to see."

"The courts?" Kelsey asked, glancing at Walter. "Let's not get ahead of ourselves here. It's up to management, of course, but I doubt we'll be pressing charges."

"Pressing charges? What are you talking about? *I'm* suing *you*—and your company too."

"You're *what*?" Kelsey cried, standing. She'd reached her limit for pretending to be calm. "Why? What for?"

"For half of Adele's inheritance."

She stared at him, incredulous. He continued.

"It's complicated, but it has to do with an old family will. Because of the fraud perpetrated by Jocelyn Brennan, Adele's father's estate was paid out incorrectly when he passed away. Fully half his fortune should have gone to his nephew, Quincy and, obviously, down the line to Quincy's heirs. Instead, it went to Adele—who wasn't really Adele at all. Get it?"

Kelsey did *not* "get it," but at the moment she wasn't going to waste time trying to sort out the details. Closing her eyes, she took a deep breath, held it in, and then slowly let it out. Whether there was any merit to this guy's claims or not—and surely there was not—it didn't matter. The truth was that any "inheritance" that might have been passed down to Adele from her father had evaporated in the stock market crash of 1929. He had retired by then, and it was up to Adele and Edwin to keep the company afloat. If not for their efforts in getting them through the tough economic years following the crash, not only would the business have ended in bankruptcy, but when Sean died about ten years later, he wouldn't have had any fortune to leave behind to her anyway. Opening her eyes, she looked intently at Rupert and tried to explain just that.

"Do you understand what I'm saying?" she concluded. "There was no fortune to be had. The only reason Adele's father had any money at all when he died was because Adele had earned it *for* him."

"Ah, but there's still the matter of the bonds," Rupert replied triumphantly. "Don't forget he had those."

At the word "bonds," both Walter and Lou sprang to life.

"*That's* what all this has been about?" Walter cried, throwing his hands in the air.

"You gotta be kidding!" Lou said with a laugh.

"What bonds?" Kelsey asked, looking from one to the other.

Walter was the first to answer, saying that part of the "legend of Adele" was that she'd come to America with a handful of bonds purchased in England with her father's money, and that those bonds had grown quite valuable over time. Word had it that over the years whenever things got tight at Brennan & Tate, all Adele had to do was cash in one of those bonds and then she would use the proceeds to get them through the difficult spot.

"I've never heard that story."

"It's an old chestnut," Lou said. "Like Sasquatch or the Jersey Devil."

"Unicorns or leprechauns," Walter added.

Both men laughed, but Kelsey wasn't finding anything funny about this situation. Turning to Rupert, she again took her seat and spoke to him earnestly and calmly.

"Look, bonds or not, if you feel that there's a problem with how one of our ancestors' estates was paid out, this isn't the way to address it. You can't go around accusing my great-grandmother of being an imposter in a public forum when she's not even here to defend herself."

"I told you, I have proof—"

"Proof or not, Rupert, you're going about this all wrong. Before anybody sues anyone, what we need to do is get someone experienced in trusts and estates to sit down and review the facts and see if we can't figure out if your claims have any merit. This matter can be worked out privately and fairly. There's no need for any more public outcries, okay?"

She was trying to sound as calm and reasonable as she could, so she was surprised when Rupert's cheeks flushed a bright red, his shoulders slumped, and he cast his eyes downward. Behind him, the redhead cleared her throat and took a small step forward.

"The problem is," she said in a tentative voice, "he's already tried that. Nobody will take the case."

The room fell silent. And though Kelsey was still upset about what this man had done, she also found herself feeling sorry for him. Clearly, he was unstable. He didn't need justice. He probably just needed medication.

The redhead came and knelt beside the man's chair.

"Come on, Rupert," she said softly, "you had to know this is how it would end."

He closed his eyes tightly shut, refusing to respond.

"These nice people coulda sent you to jail, and instead they're willing to forgive and forget. More than that, they're gonna give you some money and a vacation and even a limo to take us there. Have you ever been in a limo before?"

Eyes still closed, he shook his head from side to side.

"Me neither. See? This'll be fun. We'll do like Miss Tate said and go on a nice little trip and handle things in a more private fashion later. She seems very fair. They all seem fair. So what d'ya say, huh? Shall we go for our ride in that big, fancy car?"

They all seemed to hold their collective breaths until finally Rupert Brennan gave one nearly imperceptible nod.

Exhaling with relief, Kelsey stood and stepped away as Walter told them he already had the limo waiting on standby just around the corner. Then he looked to the remaining security guard and said to have the limo pull up front.

"Up front?" the guard replied, reaching for a walkie-talkie at his belt. "Wouldn't it be smarter to take them out the back?"

Walter shook his head. "The reporters in that lobby need to see him leaving or they will never go away."

Nodding, the security guard conveyed the message as Kelsey pulled Walter aside.

"What makes you think he'll make it all the way to the limo without having another outburst?" she whispered.

Walter glanced at the man, who was still in his chair, slumped in a heap. "Not to worry. I'll escort him out personally."

Seeing on the screen how rabid those reporters were getting, Kelsey wasn't sure that would be enough. She glanced at the security guard and said, "Please don't use pepper spray or do anything violent if the situation gets out of hand. That could only make things a thousand times worse."

He chuckled. "There's no pepper spray around here, Miss Tate. This being an office building, we generally don't carry any weapons. I know that Ephraim keeps a Taser in his desk, but he's the only one certified to use it."

"Okay, good," she said. While she hated the thought of Rupert going out there and becoming verbal again, she could only imagine the PR nightmare that would ensue if some kind of force were used against him—especially if it ended up getting caught on film and replayed on the six o'clock news.

"Don't worry, ma'am. This will go fine," the guard assured her. "I used to work stage door security on Broadway. If I can get Hugh Jackman into a limo without him getting his clothes torn off, I can get this guy out of here and on his way without any disruptions."

She smiled and thanked him, somewhat relieved.

A crackle from the walkie-talkie was followed by the voice of Ephraim, who told them that the limo was out front. The guard took charge then, and in a calm, steady tone he explained exactly how this was going to go, that Walter would stand to Rupert's right, the redhead to his left, and the guard would lead the way. They were to ignore everyone and everything between here and the limo and not answer any questions or stop to pose for any photographs.

"The driver has your money," Walter added, looking from Rupert to the redhead. "If you can make it out of here without any further problems, you'll be given that money once you reach your destination."

"Thank you, sir," the woman replied, helping Rupert out of his chair.

"Once they've driven off," Walter said to the security guard, "I need you and Ephraim to make sure that if anyone tries to hail a cab with the intention of following, there's enough of a delay that the limo's out of sight before they go. The limo will be doing a few evasive maneuvers, but if somebody's persistent, that won't be enough by itself."

"No problem, sir."

Turning to Kelsey, Walter said, "After they've left, I'll stay out there and take questions from the reporters. I'll try to spin things as best I can."

"Do you want me with you?" she asked wearily.

To her relief he shook his head. "No, I want you leaving here right away— out the back door. How do you usually go home?"

"You mean what streets do I take?"

"No. Subway? Bus? Walk?"

"Oh. Walk. I always walk. I'm just over in Battery Park City."

"Okay. Well tonight I want you to take a cab. Lou? You on it?"

"Absolutely."

Kelsey started to object but then thought better of it. Let Walter do what he had to do, and she would do what she had to do.

Things happened quickly after that. Without a word of thanks or good-bye or apology from Rupert or the redhead, they left with Walter and the guard. Only Lou and Kelsey remained in the security office, watching them file out the door and form ranks. Once it shut behind them, Kelsey turned her attention to the screen showing that part of the lobby.

She held her breath as she watched them go, the guard parting the crowd ahead of them. He really did seem to know what he was doing, and with Walter and the woman shielding Rupert from each side, their little group made it all the way out to the curb and into the vehicle without incident. Thank goodness.

"All right," Lou said, standing next to her, also watching the screen. "Let's get you out of here."

"Not so fast," she replied. "I need to go up and talk to Gloria first."

Lou frowned. "Sorry, kiddo. I told Walter I'd get you into a cab and that's what I'm going to do."

They argued for a moment, and then Kelsey settled the matter by saying they would let Gloria decide. She grabbed the nearest phone and dialed her extension. When the woman answered on the first ring, Kelsey asked if she could come up so they could talk.

"Absolutely not," Gloria replied vehemently. "You need to get away from here as fast as you can. Don't speak to anyone, and don't stop anywhere along the way. Just go straight home."

"And do what once I get there? Paint my nails? Surf the web? Gloria, today was a disaster! I have to do something about it or I'll explode." Much to Kelsey's chagrin, at that moment her voice broke. Pausing, she swallowed back a sob and tried to get control of herself. It was one thing to be strong in front of Walter and the others, but now that the only ones to hear her were Lou and Gloria, dear friends both, she was finding it a bit harder to maintain her composure. "I…I was hoping you could help me figure things out… both why this happened and what we're going to do about it."

Gloria was quiet for a long moment. When she finally spoke, the sharpness was gone from her voice. Clearly, she could tell Kelsey was at her limit.

"Go home, Tater Tot," she said gently. "I know this is all very confusing and upsetting, but I promise you, it'll all make sense soon. Do you hear what I'm telling you? Trust me on this."

Kelsey closed her eyes, willing herself not to cry. She had always been able to trust Gloria before. It seemed she had no choice but to trust her now.

"Fine," she whispered. They said their goodbyes and she hung up the phone.

Lou and Kelsey left the office the same way they had come in, only this time he didn't wedge a thousand-dollar shoe in the door. Instead, he made her wait inside the stairwell while he went out to see if the coast was clear and to hail a cab. A minute later she heard a knock, so she opened the door and looked out.

"All right, kiddo, time to roll," Lou said, gesturing toward a cab idling at the curb. As she climbed into the backseat, Lou handed a twenty to the driver. "Take her to the Hudson Arms building in Battery Park City. If you stick around until she's safely all the way inside, you can keep the change."

Quickly, Kelsey rolled down her window. "Lou, don't be silly. I can pay for—"

He brushed off her objections. "I have a meeting in midtown in half an hour, but I'll call you later tonight after I get home. Okay?"

"Okay." She gave him a smile and a soft thank-you. As the cab pulled away, she turned to see him watching her go, fatherly concern evident in his furrowed brow. Then he gave a final wave and headed for the main street to hail a cab of his own.

CHAPTER
FIVE

Settling back against the seat of the taxi, Kelsey closed her eyes, realizing that a big part of her really did want to go home. She was exhausted. Gloria had been right to send her away.

"Your father, he is the overprotective type, eh?" the cabbie asked in a heavy accent. "Trust me, this is good thing. Too many young women in this city have no one watching out for them."

She didn't correct his misconception. Lou may not have been her father, but he'd always been a father figure to her. Now, with her dad so incapacitated, it felt good to have someone step in and fill that role, even if it was just for today.

A few minutes later, as they turned onto her street and the cab pulled to a stop in front of her building, Kelsey realized she'd left her purse back at the office. Worse, inside that purse were her phone and keys. She hesitated, trying to decide whether she should have this man drive her back to where he'd picked her up or if she could get into her apartment some other way. Weariness won out. Suddenly, the last place on earth she wanted to be was at Brennan & Tate. Now doubly grateful that Lou had paid her cab fare, she thanked the driver, climbed out, and was pleased to note that he remained at the curb, just as Lou had requested, until she got her next door neighbor to buzz her in and she was safely inside the building.

Thanks to the fact that the same neighbor kept a spare of her door key, soon Kelsey was in her kitchen in jeans and a loose sweater, making herself a hot cup of tea and counting the minutes until she could plop on the couch.

What a day.

What a nightmare.

The telephone had not stopped ringing since she'd walked in the door, but she had no intention of talking to anyone right now. As the electric kettle came to a boil, the phone started to ring yet again. Leaning over to glance at the caller ID screen, she saw the name of a local newspaper. She listened for the pause after the third ring that told her the call was being routed to voice mail, and then she picked up the phone, turned it over, and flipped the button to shut off the ringer.

Finally, once her mug of tea was ready, she squeezed past the exercise equipment filling the space intended for a kitchen table and made her way over to the living room area of her small, one-bedroom apartment. With a heavy sigh, she sat down on the love seat and sipped her tea, eyes closed, trying to recover from all that had happened.

Outside, she could hear cars honking, tires rumbling, distant sirens wailing—even the long, low horn of a ship out on the river. She loved living in Manhattan, especially this part of Manhattan, she thought as she set her mug down on a coaster on the end table and rested her head on the overstuffed arm of the little sofa. But at the moment she wished she were somewhere far away, maybe at her grandfather's house down at the Jersey shore, where life was simpler and slower and she always felt safe and loved.

Kelsey must have dozed off briefly, because when she opened her eyes with a start, she realized it was nearly dusk. Standing and stretching, she clicked on the lamp, crossed to the window to lower the blinds, and then reached for the TV's remote control. Might as well see if the story of Adele had made the six o'clock news after all.

Half an hour later, she'd caugh the story on all of the major networks and on a CNN offshoot. Fortunately, no one seemed to have any footage of the actual ruckus in the auditorium, but they had all managed to get cameras rolling by the time Rupert and the redhead were escorted from the building and put into the limo. Walter had done a pretty good job of speaking to the press after that, and the clip most of the stations had chosen to run had him attributing the incident to "*Titanic* fever run amok."

All of the channels showed professional head shots of Adele and of Kelsey, but somehow CNN had managed to get hold of a full-length picture of Rupert as well. He wasn't exactly attractive in person, but the photo they had chosen made him look positively ugly—not to mention a tad deranged.

A candid snapshot that looked as though it had been taken during a hunting trip, he was dressed in camouflage clothing, leg waders, and a grimy old sailor's hat. Worse, in his hands he was cradling a shotgun. Either Brennan & Tate was lucky, or their PR firm was even smarter and faster than Kelsey had given them credit for. The juxtaposition of images spoke volumes about the truth behind the incident. Obviously, this was a case of some crazy, backwoods yokel coming to the big city and trying to cash in on the hard work of some very upstanding, highly respected business people, past and present, one of whom had even been a *Titanic* survivor in her youth.

Thinking about the way the media had portrayed things, Kelsey was relieved, but in a way she almost felt sorry for the guy yet again. If he'd acted out of maliciousness or ill-intent, then of course he deserved what he was getting. But as neither seemed to be the case—that he was, instead, simply a man in possession of some *Titanic*-sized delusions—he shouldn't have been made to look so foolish.

Refusing to feel guilty for something completely out of her control, Kelsey flipped off the TV and popped a frozen dinner into the microwave. She wanted to draw the family tree and then add in the information from Rupert's claims, just to get a better picture of what he'd been trying to spell out. It would have been easier to do so using an app or an ancestry-related website, but seeing as how she'd left both her phone and her laptop at the office, she'd have to do this the old-fashioned way, with pen and paper.

Sitting down on the floor at the coffee table, she ate her dinner as she worked. She decided to start with herself and her brother, Matt, at the bottom and work her way up, creating a chart. She only got as far as their parents, however, when she realized she hadn't even contacted them yet about what had happened today. Mortified, she immediately got up and retrieved the phone. Though her father may or may not understand what she was saying depending on how lucid of a day he was having, her mother definitely needed to hear this from Kelsey herself and not by accidentally running across it some other way, such as online or in the newspaper.

Unfortunately, there was no answer at her parents' house, so she left them a message saying there had been a big problem at the office today and that she needed to talk to them about it as soon as possible. It was odd not to find them at home, she thought, glancing at the clock on the microwave as she disconnected the call. These days, taking her father anywhere was so much trouble that her parents rarely went out at all anymore, except for doctor visits and the like. Where could they possibly be at a quarter to seven on a Tuesday night?

Frustrated, she dialed Matt instead, thinking he might know where their parents could be. She thought his call was about to go to voice mail too when he surprised her by answering.

"Hey, Kels," he said loudly, "sorry about the noise. I'm on my way home from work. I was just about to head down into the subway. Listen, I'm so, so sorry I couldn't make it to your thing today. I thought I'd be able to pull it off, but then one of my students had a big meltdown when I caught her cheating on an exam, and after that things kind of fell apart. There was this whole big drama with her and me and the dean, and it dragged on all afternoon. I feel terrible about it, but there was nothing I could do."

Clearly, he was oblivious to what had happened at Brennan & Tate, so rather than competing with the street noises to bring him up to speed, she simply told him the same thing she had said in the message she'd left for her parents, that there had been a big problem at the office and that he should go straight home and turn on the TV to see what he had missed. "Try the Headline News channel. The story's on their loop. Oh, and don't talk to any reporters, okay? They'll probably start calling you soon, once they track down who you are and how they can reach you."

As soon as she said it, she realized that maybe her parents were home after all, but that they, too, had simply turned off the phone's ringer, as she had, because they were being badgered by the news media.

"Did you say reporters?" he yelled, his voice nearly drowned out by what sounded like a passing train. "What are you talking about?"

"Just turn on the TV as soon as you get home and then call me!" she yelled back before hanging up the phone.

How frustrating. Glancing over toward the fridge, she thought about hopping on the stair stepper to work out some of her tension but decided she was getting too far off track. First things first. She would check her messages to see if maybe her parents had called earlier, and then she would get back to work on her family tree.

Dialing into voice mail, Kelsey was shocked when the automated system announced she had twenty-seven messages. *Twenty-seven? Lou wasn't kidding. The vultures are circling.* With a heavy sigh, she carried the phone over to the love seat, sat down, and began working her way through from the beginning, finishing her now-cold dinner as she did.

Just as she'd suspected, the messages were primarily a mix of media requests and well-meaning and/or curious friends calling to find out first-hand what had happened. Most of the calls could be deleted after the first sentence or so, and she quickly worked her way through, barely pausing until she reached message number seventeen and heard the voice of Gloria.

Snapping to attention, Kelsey pressed the button to make the message start over again and then listened more closely this time.

> *Kelsey, it's Gloria. I don't know why you're not answering your cell, but I thought I'd try your home phone. Please contact me as soon as you get this. I know I told you to leave and go home, but I've changed my mind. I'm ready to talk now. I need to tell you some things, Kelsey. Please. It's urgent. Before I lose my nerve.*

Sitting up straight, Kelsey listened to the message once more, just to make sure she was hearing correctly. What was Gloria talking about? Pulse surging, Kelsey quickly zipped through the rest of the messages, just to see if she had left any others. Sure enough, there was one more, message number twenty, and that time her voice sounded even more frantic than it had before.

> *Kelsey, call me! Please! If you can't reach me by phone, come back to the office. I'll be here. I'm not leaving tonight until I tell you what I have to say. Please. Where are you? Call me!*

The message ended with a sob and then a few clicks before it went dead, as if Gloria had been so overcome with emotion that she could barely even hang up the phone. Poor thing!

Face burning with guilt for having turned off the ringer and missed Gloria's calls, Kelsey dialed the office and then punched in the woman's extension as fast as her fingers would go. It rang five times and went to voice mail, so Kelsey left a brief message and then tried Gloria's cell. It, too, went to voice mail, so she left another message, hung up, and then began pacing while she waited for her to call back.

Nothing.

When the phone still hadn't rung after five minutes, Kelsey tried both of Gloria's numbers yet again and then, on the off chance that she'd changed her mind and gone home, called there too. No answer anywhere. Eventually, Kelsey knew she had no choice but to head back over to the office. In Gloria's message, she'd said she wasn't leaving until they talked, and if Kelsey couldn't reach her by phone to just come back. That's what she would have to do. Glancing at the clock, she saw that it was now almost seven fifteen. She hoped that meant enough time had passed since the incident that everyone, including the press, had gone home by now.

Kelsey went to the bedroom closet and rooted through a few spare purses until she came up with one that had some money in it, just in case. Slipping the bills into her pocket, she grabbed a jacket and her spare apartment key and headed out.

Down at street level, she was almost at the front door when she spotted a small cluster of people gathered on the walkway outside. With a gasp, she darted behind a pillar, her heart pounding. Reporters. Of course. She should have expected this.

Careful to keep out of the sightline of the front windows, she inched along the wall until she was able to turn the corner and head for the back exit instead. Unfortunately, that meant walking out between two extremely smelly dumpsters, but it was worth the trouble. Five minutes later, she was at the elevated walkway over West Street, and no one even knew she'd left her building.

Kelsey's commute from home to work was just under half a mile, an easy walk at any time of day but especially now, when there was less foot traffic to contend with. As she quickly covered the distance and neared the office building, she thought about going in through the back but decided to take a peek around front first, to see if the coast was clear.

Fortunately, it was. From a discreet vantage point on the opposite side of the street, she could see through the tall front windows of the lobby that the only person in there at the moment was Ephraim, sitting at reception. Moving quickly, she crossed at the corner and then sprinted to the front door. It was locked, but as soon as he spotted her, he buzzed her in.

"Thanks, Ephraim," she replied, stepping inside and pulling the door firmly shut behind her. "What are you doing here this late? Don't you guys usually knock off around six?"

"Yeah. Not tonight, though. After all the mess this afternoon, I thought I'd stick around a little longer, just to be safe."

"Well, I'm glad you're here—and happy to see that the crowds are gone."

"Been this way for 'bout an hour now," Ephraim replied. "Some of those people were pretty persistent, but Mr. Hallerman got 'em all out of here eventually, thank goodness."

"Is he still around?" Kelsey asked and was relieved when Ephraim said no, that Walter had gone back upstairs for a few minutes once everyone else was gone, and then he'd come back down and left for the night.

"Looked bone tired to me," he added.

"I know the feeling. How about Gloria Poole? Have you seen her tonight at all?"

Ephraim said no, that he hadn't seen Mrs. Poole coming or going this afternoon or this evening. "'Course, there was an awful lot of confusion here, as you know. There's a chance she came through and I just didn't notice. That's what I told her husband, anyway."

"Vern? Was he here?"

"Yeah, 'bout an hour ago. He said she called and asked him to come to her office, so he did, right from work. But then once he got here and I let him up, he couldn't find her. By the time he left, he seemed pretty mad."

"I can see why. Actually, she called me too. I'll see if *I* can find her." Kelsey couldn't imagine where on earth Gloria could have gone. "You haven't seen her on the security cameras anywhere? Not even on the ones for the fifth floor?"

Ephraim shook his head. "The only security camera on fifth shows the elevator landing and the reception area, that's it, and I definitely haven't seen her come walking through there."

"Well, if by some chance she calls or comes down here, tell her I'm looking for her, would you?"

"Will do. Holler if you need me."

Kelsey thanked him and went around the corner to the elevators. Thinking she might as well start by checking Gloria's office first, she pressed the button for the fifth floor. Once there, she stepped out into the vestibule and turned left, toward reception, feeling strangely watched. At the door she punched in her security code, waited for the click, and then went inside.

The Brennan & Tate fifth floor reception area was small but strikingly elegant, with a sleek mahogany reception station at the center and several groupings of chairs and low tables along the perimeter. The color scheme was pleasant, a muted mix of browns and yellows and greens with splashes of more vivid colors in the abstract artwork adorning the walls. The focal point of the room, however, was the mahogany-and-glass display case in the far corner, placed there as a memorial to Adele Brennan Tate a year or two after she passed away. Inside the case, restored to museum quality, was the clothing she'd been wearing the night *Titanic* sank.

Artfully displayed on a dressmaker's dummy, the outfit consisted of a pale blue floor-length dress covered by a darker blue overcoat with white fur trim, white gloves, a white fur hand muff, and a blue velvet hat with a pale blue hatband. Other memorabilia had been acquired later by Kelsey's father and added around the clothing, including a cup and saucer from the White Star Line, a menu from *Titanic*'s second-class dining room, and a White Star pen and stationery. Front and center were two books: a copy of Adele's memoir of *Titanic*, that she'd had printed in a limited quantity, and the white leather-bound Bible given to her by her husband on their wedding day.

Kelsey had been just ten or eleven years old the first time she had seen this display, and she hadn't liked it at all. Something about the dressmaker's dummy—bearing the same height and dimensions as Adele herself when she'd been alive—looked all too real, like the headless ghost of a woman who had died while dressed for a cold night in 1912. Over the years, however, it had grown on her, and these days she actually looked upon the display fondly, as if it embodied the very spirit and nature of Adele herself. Gazing at it now, Kelsey couldn't help but remember the accusation that Rupert had made this afternoon, that the woman who called herself Adele had actually been a cousin merely *posing* as Adele. No matter what "proof" he thought he had of that claim, Kelsey knew it wouldn't bear out. She was one hundred percent sure Adele had been exactly who she'd said she was. This temporary besmirching of her name would pass, and all Rupert Brennan would end up proving was that he was in need of serious help.

Moving on through the reception area, Kelsey entered the same hallway she'd walked down earlier today and followed it to the executive suite. She saw that everything looked closed down except for Gloria's office, which was fully lit up. She went there now, hoping to see the woman sitting at her desk, but the room was empty. Kelsey stepped inside anyway, looking for a note or something that might indicate where Gloria had gone. She saw nothing of relevance on the desktop, so she took a peek in the lower desk drawers just to see if Gloria's purse was there. It was, in the left bottom drawer. Good. That meant she was still somewhere in the building—unless she'd accidentally gone home without it, just as Kelsey had.

Coming back to the doorway, Kelsey called out Gloria's name, but there was no reply. Fearing she really was ill, as she'd told Walter earlier, Kelsey went from there to the executive washroom to see if Gloria was inside.

She was not.

From there Kelsey made a quick tour of the rest of the fifth floor, peeking in the copy room, the meeting rooms, and several offices, but most everything was dark. As she neared the far end of the hall, Kelsey wondered if maybe Gloria could be in *her* office on the fourth floor, though she couldn't imagine why. At the very least, perhaps she'd left a note there for Kelsey or sent a text or voice mail that had more information about where she was now.

Kelsey ended her search of the fifth floor near the executive conference room, so she decided to take the stairs down to the fourth floor rather than going all the way back to the elevator bay. She'd already checked the conference room earlier on her hunt for Gloria, but one peek had showed her it was dark and not in use. This time, however, she flipped on the light as she went inside so she wouldn't bump a hip or a shin as she cut through to the back stairwell.

She'd taken several steps across the well-lit room before she froze, realizing that someone was in there.

In a moment that turned seconds into hours, she simply stood and stared, trying to make sense of what she was seeing at the other end of the room.

On the wide expanse of wall, the metal covering for the projection screen hung crooked, its cord dropped down from the lower side. At the other end of that cord hung the body of a person. A woman.

Gloria.

At least she thought it was Gloria. The body was wearing Gloria's clothes. It had Gloria's hair. But the face was purple, such a dark purple that it was hard to tell. Strangest of all was the neck, around which the cord for the projector screen was wrapped. The skin there was purple and red and even bloody. The colors of death.

Gloria was dead.

Kelsey fell to her knees and began to scream.

She was still screaming five minutes later, when Ephraim found her and called for the police.

CHAPTER SIX

April 10, 1912

ADELE

Adele Brennan stood at the hotel room window and looked out at the busy streets of Southampton below. It was early, but already men were funneling in from every side and pouring down the main avenue toward the White Star docks.

"They look like rats scurrying out from their hidey-holes," she said, watching the continuous stream of young men with their packs slung over their backs walking along the streets, their breath forming puffs of smoke in the early morning chill.

The sight reminded her of her home in Ireland in more ways than one. Not only had she watched the shipyard workers similarly head down to the docks of Belfast, but for the past three years the ship they had been heading toward each morning was *Titanic*. Now that ship had been relocated to Southampton, England, and was ready to set sail on her maiden voyage across the sea. Just as the shipyard workers had done back home, these men were also streaming toward *Titanic*.

"How excited they must be to staff the finest ship ever built," her cousin Jocelyn said from the other side of the room. "Da says these workers are the best of the best."

"For the price of passage, they ought to be."

"I wonder what kind of accent your father speaks with these days," Jocelyn said from her perch in front of the mirror, changing the subject. Do you

53

ever think about whether he has begun to speak in the American style now that he has lived there for so long?"

Adele turned away from the exciting scenery of the window to look at her cousin, who had been pinning up her hair for what seemed like the last half hour.

"I would imagine he still sounds somewhat the same. Many of his friends and business associates are a part of New York's Irish community. As long as he's been surrounded by enough regular speech all these years, he should have retained his ear for it."

Adele crossed to sit on the end of the bed, still amazed that they would be leaving for America in just a few hours. One week ago she had been home, getting ready for this next big step in her life. Today they would board the ship that would take them across the sea to a new world and a new life. As exciting as that was, it was also quite melancholy. She might never stand on this side of the ocean again in her lifetime.

"Perhaps Mr. Myers can teach us a few American phrases before we get there," Jocelyn said. "We don't want to sound like complete foreigners, you know."

Adele eyed her cousin suspiciously. "Mm-hmm. I know what phrases *you* want to hear."

Jocelyn paused, hands in the air, to give her cousin an inquisitive look. "What?"

Adele grinned. "Oh, like, 'Miss Oona Jocelyn Brennan, will you marry me? Will you warm my hearth and love me unconditionally forever and forever?'"

"That's better than what you want to hear," Jocelyn retorted. 'Miss Beatrice Adele Brennan, will you accept our offer? Will you invest for us and labor here unconditionally forever and ever?'"

Adele frowned. Just because she had an interest in business didn't mean she had no other interests at all.

"Are you going to sit there and fool with your hair all day?" she snapped, rising from the bed and moving toward the window. "We need to get downstairs."

Jocelyn dropped her arms and turned around in her chair. "Why are you acting this way this morning?"

"What way?"

"Pacing, snapping at me, making fun. This isn't like you at all." Jocelyn's voice softened as she added, "Are you frightened of the voyage? Or of what comes after?"

Adele studied her cousin. Jocelyn was a born nurturer, a quality that was usually quite endearing. But sometimes her nurturing felt more like mothering, and today that mothering bordered on smothering.

"Thank you for your concern," Adele replied, trying to sound sincere, "but I suppose it's more excitement than anything else. I'm eager to get downstairs and meet up with Uncle Rowan before Mr. Myers gets here. Why is it taking you so long to dress?"

Rebuffed in her attempt at compassion, Jocelyn returned her attentions to the mirror, her lips pursed, avoiding the question.

"Wait a minute," Adele said slowly, her eyes narrowing. "I know what's taking you so long. You're nervous about meeting Mr. Myers."

"What are you talking about?"

"It was fine when we thought he was just some older gentleman my father sent here as his representative," Adele said, a hint of a smile on her lips, "but from the moment last night when we were told he's practically our same age—and quite dashing besides—everything changed."

Jocelyn was silent for a moment as she finished her hairstyle and moved on to placing her hat just so. "Perhaps," she replied. "But I don't think I'm the only one. I noticed you're wearing one of your new dresses already. I thought you were going to save that one for when we disembark in America."

Adele could feel her cheeks flush. "Headmistress says that first impressions are important. As Mr. Myers is a representative of my father's company, I realized that it was important his first impression of me be a favorable one."

Jocelyn slid her new hat pin into place and rose from her chair at last. Watching her, Adele could see the teasing glint of her eyes change to a look of sincerity.

"Dear Adele, do you honestly doubt what Mr. Myers' reaction to you will be?"

Adele shrugged. "I don't know what my father told him or what he is expecting."

Jocelyn's features flooded again with compassion as she stepped toward Adele and took her hands. "I guarantee you, cousin, that this Mr. Myers will find you charming, polite, and refined—everything your father desired when he paid for your finishing school education."

"You really think so?"

"Of course I do," Jocelyn said earnestly, dropping her cousin's hands and taking a step back. "Just look at you! You're beautiful, well dressed, articulate, intelligent…You even have a mind for business, which is a rarity among women."

Adele didn't object, even though she usually did when her cousin made such comments. It had long been Adele's opinion that many women had a mind for business. They just didn't recognize it for what it was.

"I, however, am the one who will probably come off as some uneducated culchie," Jocelyn continued as she packed the last of her things in her suitcase.

"*Culchie*? But you're a *townie*. We both are. Besides, you are every bit as 'finished' as I am. Don't forget the hours we spent after each class, where I showed you everything Headmistress taught that day."

Jocelyn shrugged modestly. "And it all felt fine in Belfast. Yet you know how we were made to feel in London in the past few days. Nothing about us has been right or fashionable—not our clothes or our accents or even our luggage, for that matter. You saw the way the porter in the hotel sneered when he spotted our shabby old bags."

Adele shook her head, and this time it was her turn to be compassionate.

"Jocelyn Brennan, I feel sure there is a big difference between London and New York City. From what Father says in his letters, people in New York aren't so bound by class and wealth. They honor ideas, industriousness, and vision. If Mr. Myers is a true American, he won't judge either of us by our hair or our clothes. He'll engage with our minds and judge us by our intellect, our conversation, and our ideals."

Jocelyn grinned. "I'm sorry, cousin, but in that dress, intellect is not the first thought that will come to his mind—nor any man's mind, for that matter."

She chuckled as Adele felt herself blush again.

"You know you are the prettier one," Adele said.

"You know you are the smarter one," Jocelyn replied.

And then they grinned. It was their old balance, the way they measured their differences in the labels they had given themselves years ago. Lately, though, as Jocelyn had begun to expand her world by reading and the discussion of ideas, and Adele had begun to blossom and to pay more attention to her appearance, those differences had begun to even out. According to Aunt Oona and Uncle Rowan, both girls were smart *and* pretty. Adele knew that was true of Jocelyn. Sometimes she almost believed it of herself as well.

The question was whether this Mr. Tad Myers would see things the same way, or if he would take one look at them and sneer, just as the porter had sneered in their fancy London hotel.

CHAPTER
SEVEN

Kelsey sat in the reception area just down the hall from where the police were viewing the corpse and processing the scene. Next to her sat Ephraim, who had been glued to her side for the last hour. Though he had already been excused by the police and told he could leave, he had chosen to stay. Somehow, he seemed to know she wasn't up to being alone right now, that she needed a friend. At the moment he was the best kind of friend, because he seemed content to remain silent, a solid physical presence who neither pestered her about how she was feeling nor offered up empty platitudes to try and make things better.

Near the door stood a policeman in uniform. He hadn't said much, but Kelsey knew she was expected to stay where she was for the time being—and that it was his job to make sure she did.

No worries there. She'd do anything she could to help them figure out exactly what had happened and why one of the most important people in her world was now dead.

Dabbing at her eyes with a crumpled tissue, Kelsey kept listening for the elevator, hoping her brother would get here soon. In the wake of this horrific nightmare, he was the only one she'd been able to think of to call. Matt had promised to come from his apartment on the Upper West Side as quickly as he could, but twice now she'd heard the elevator ding and had been disappointed to see someone other than him coming around the corner. The first time, it had been a couple of people with the police department. The second time, it was Walter, the first person Ephraim had called after he'd contacted the police.

Though the CEO had been kind and solicitous the moment he saw Kelsey and learned she was the one who had discovered the body, she hadn't said much to him in return. She'd already spent more than enough time with Walter Hallerman today. At this point, the sight of him just made her feel weary.

At least he hadn't stayed there in reception with her and Ephraim. Instead, he'd received permission from the cops to go to his office, where Kelsey imagined he was on the phone with the company lawyers or whomever else one spoke to when a dead body had been found hanging from a projection screen in one's conference room.

Eventually, a man of about fifty wearing a suit with a badge clipped at his belt came into the reception area from the hallway and introduced himself as Detective Hargrove. Kelsey thought he might bring her into some back room where they would talk, but instead he pulled up a chair right there in reception, whipped out a narrow notebook from his inside suit pocket, and asked her to tell him in her own words what had happened.

In a voice that sounded monotone and flat even to herself, Kelsey recounted her story for the third time this evening. She gave him the basic facts, starting with her visit to Gloria's office prior to the ceremony and ending with her walk across the executive conference room when she spotted the body. Tears spilled from her eyes as she spoke, but she made no attempts to wipe them away. "I just can't make sense of this." Her voice broke as she concluded her tale.

"Let's back up a little bit," he said, flipping through his notes. "You said you spoke with Mrs. Poole around four this afternoon, just before you went from the stairwell to the backstage area. Correct?"

"Yes."

"And that's the last time you saw her alive?"

Kelsey nodded. "I mean, we talked on the phone later, but that's the last time I saw her in person."

"How did she seem then? What was her demeanor?"

Kelsey wasn't even sure how to answer that question. All over the map? Totally out of character? Crying one minute and giving a pep talk the next?

The problem was, if this man hadn't known Gloria while she was alive, he sure wasn't going to be able to get to know her now that she was dead. Yet, as the detective assigned to this case, it was up to him to figure out exactly how she had died, and why. Kelsey wasn't sure he could accomplish that. She had known Gloria for years, and even she couldn't say what had been going on with the woman and why she'd been acting so strange.

As honestly as she could, Kelsey tried to explain her final encounter with Gloria. She stressed several times how unusual such behavior was for this woman who had otherwise always been the consummate professional. To his credit, Detective Hargrove seemed to take her at her word, listening intently, taking copious notes, and asking questions that were phrased as respectfully as possible. His face was expressionless throughout, but the tone of his voice had a kindness to it that she appreciated.

It wasn't until he asked her to again describe the two messages that Gloria had left on her home phone that Kelsey thought of her cell, still sitting in her purse in the bottom drawer of her desk where it had been all afternoon and evening. In the messages Gloria had left on her home machine, she had said she'd been calling Kelsey's cell phone. She told that to the detective, saying that if they were lucky, there might be more information on there about what had been going on.

Ephraim offered to go down to the fourth floor and retrieve the phone, so Kelsey gave him the code that would unlock her office door and then asked him to bring her whole purse, explaining where he could find it.

While he was gone, the detective began pursuing a new line of questioning, one that shed insight into what he was thinking about Gloria's last minutes of life.

"You think she killed herself?" she asked, though it came out sounding more like a statement than a question.

"We haven't ruled it out."

Kelsey thought about that. "She wasn't exactly the suicide type."

"What's the suicide type?"

"Hopeless? Depressed? Self-destructive?"

He jotted something in his notebook. "How about the opposite? Did you see any euphoria here at the end?"

She shook her head, saying that except for Gloria's weird behavior prior to the ceremony today, she had been pretty even-tempered lately, as always.

"Have you noticed her settling her affairs in any way?"

"You mean, like writing a will?"

"Or making changes to her insurance, telling people goodbye. Anything like that at all?" He waited patiently while Kelsey searched her memory.

"Not that I noticed," she said finally. "She always finished her projects. She wasn't a procrastinator. But tying up loose ends so she could kill herself? No." She became more certain as she spoke.

At that moment, they were interrupted by yet another ding of the elevator. Still no Matt. Instead, Ephraim came walking around the corner holding Kelsey's purse far out in front of him, as though it were full of snakes.

"What's wrong?" she asked, hesitant to take it.

"Nothing," the burly man replied. "I just didn't want anybody to think it was mine."

Stifling a smile, Kelsey took the purse from him, opened it, and pulled out her cell phone. She pushed the button and the screen sprung to life, indicating twelve missed calls, four voice mails, and seven text messages.

She had the feeling that the detective would have preferred she review those voice mails on speakerphone so he could listen in too, but she did nothing of the kind. She specialized in investments, and some of her calls could be financially related and contain confidential information.

In the end, she told him Gloria had called five times and left a message twice. Those she did replay on speakerphone for him, but neither message shed any new light on the matter.

Then she went through the text messages. Of the seven, three were from Gloria. Her first two were more of the same—Call me, I have to talk to you—but the final one came as a complete shock. Sent at precisely 5:52 p.m., it looked like a suicide note. It said:

> Goodbye, Tater Tot. I'm so sorry for what I've done. Please forgive me for taking what wasn't mine and for ending my own life. With love and regret, Gloria

"Tater Tot?" the detective asked.

Tears sprung into Kelsey's eyes. "It was her pet name for me."

He was quiet, waiting for her to go on, so she explained. "My last name is Tate. When I first started working at the office, she would refer to me as Little Tate and my father as Big Tate. I guess it just evolved over time. Somehow Little Tate became Tater Tot."

The detective nodded, a flash of pity reflected in his eyes. "Any idea what she's talking about where she says 'Forgive me for taking what wasn't mine'? What did she take?"

Kelsey shook her head slowly. "I don't have a clue."

Truly, she was stunned. Unable to stop reading and rereading Gloria's message, she kept zeroing in on those four words: *ending my own life.* There was nothing ambiguous about that at all. Either someone had murdered her and faked this note, or Gloria really had killed herself.

"How did she...What method..." Kelsey cleared her throat and tried again. "I mean, I know I saw the body and all, but I don't understand how it worked. Technically speaking, I mean. How did she do it? For that matter, how do you know it wasn't an accident?"

Another ding of the elevator, and this time the person who came around the corner was the one Kelsey had been waiting for all along: her brother Matt. Tall and lean with a runner's build and a friendly face, he was the most beautiful sight she'd seen in a long time. The moment he spotted her, he rushed to her side and pulled her into a hug.

Kindly, the detective excused himself for a few minutes and left the room. While he was gone, Kelsey brought her brother up to speed on all that had happened—both this afternoon and this evening.

When she was finished, Ephraim said, "Looks like you're in good hands now, so I guess I'll head out."

They both thanked him for staying until Matt got there, and then he was on his way.

Once they were alone, Matt caught Kelsey up on his side of things, saying that when he saw the news clip and then couldn't reach her on the phone, he had headed straight over to their parents' house. Sure enough, as Kelsey had suspected, they were home. They had just stopped answering their calls after the fourth or fifth intrusion by a reporter.

Still unable to reach Kelsey, they had ended up calling Walter to get the whole story, and he had filled them in as best he could.

"Miss Tate?" the detective said from the doorway, interrupting their conversation and gesturing for them both to come with him. They stood and did as he asked, though halfway down the hall, Kelsey realized where he was bringing them. Hesitating, she gripped Matt's arm, her eyes glued to the conference room up ahead.

Noticing that she had come to a stop, Detective Hargrove came back and assured her that the body had already been removed from the scene. Reluctantly, she allowed herself to be led all the way to the door of the conference room, though she was relieved when the detective said they weren't to step inside.

Gesturing toward the projection screen, the detective showed how Gloria could have used the cord to kill herself.

"That screen is designed to be opened and closed electronically by pushing the button on the wall there, but it also comes with a cord so it can be done manually. The best we can figure, Mrs. Poole climbed up on that chair there, wrapped the cord around her neck and tied it off, reached over and pushed the button to lower the screen—which would in turn raise the cord—and then she jumped. That simultaneous motion of coming down from the chair and being pulled upward by the cord did the job. Frankly, I'm surprised that thing could hold her weight long enough to kill her, especially if she thrashed around."

Standing in the doorway, Kelsey couldn't help but picture what he was describing. Between that and her memory of the sight of Gloria's dead body once she'd come upon it, she could feel the bile rising in her throat.

"And how do you know it wasn't an accident?" Matt asked. "She could have tangled up in the cord somehow without realizing it and then unknowingly bumped into the button."

"Highly doubtful," the detective replied. "The button that raises the screen is too far from the cord to have been hit by accident. Even with an arm stretched all the way out, she probably could just barely reach it as it was."

Kelsey's stomach churned at the thought. With a quick, "Excuse me," she dashed up the hall to the restroom, where she promptly vomited.

A while later, once the nausea had passed and she'd cleaned herself up, Kelsey came out of the bathroom and returned to reception, where she spotted not just Matt and the detective but Gloria's husband as well.

The moment their eyes met, they moved together into an embrace, one that brought a fresh onslaught of tears to Kelsey's eyes. Vern was also crying, sniffles that soon became deep, wracking sobs. Eventually, Kelsey pulled away and led him over to a chair.

Just as Ephraim had stayed there with her, Kelsey felt she should stay with Vern, at least until a family member had arrived to take her place. Fortunately, even though the detective had told Matt he was finished with Kelsey for now and she was free to go, he allowed them to stick around.

As Vern told his side of things, the story sounded somewhat similar to hers. According to him, he'd been finishing up at work when Gloria called around five thirty and said she needed him to come down to the office right away.

"She said she was going to do something very difficult and she wanted me by her side when she did it. I had no idea what she was talking about, but she sounded so worked up I figured I better do as she asked and get down here."

"So you came right away?"

"Yes, sir. Took the train from Twenty-Third to Rector."

"And what happened when you arrived here?"

Vern shrugged. "Ephraim let me in. I came upstairs and went right to her office, but she wasn't there. I called out her name a few times and wandered around looking for her, but after a while I gave up. By the time I left, I was pretty aggravated."

"I'm sorry to ask this, Mr. Poole, but when you were looking around for her, didn't you think to check the conference room?"

Vern shook his head. "I might have opened the door and looked inside, but the light was off. I mean, I knew she wouldn't be sitting in the dark, so I just continued on and kept looking elsewhere." With that, a fresh sob gurgled from his throat, and the poor man collapsed into a sobbing mess. Kelsey patted his back, knowing she had done the same thing when she'd been looking for Gloria herself.

As Matt went on a hunt for a box of tissues and Kelsey tried to comfort Vern, the detective sat quietly, reviewing his notes and waiting for the man to get a hold of himself. Once Vern had regained his composure, he apologized for having fallen apart like that.

"It's certainly understandable," Hargrove replied evenly.

Vern reached for another tissue. "Can I ask you a question, Detective?"

"Yes?"

Kelsey was afraid that he was going to ask the same thing she had, about the mechanics of the suicide. Instead, he looked up at the man, clearly in agony, and said, "If she really did kill herself, do you think the reason she called me down here was so I would be the one to find her body?"

CHAPTER
EIGHT

Simply asking the detective that question had brought Vern to a fresh onslaught of tears. As he cried, Kelsey considered his words.

"Do you think the reason she called me down here was so I would be the one to find her body?"

The very idea nearly broke Kelsey's heart. Vern was a strikingly handsome man even now in his sixties, but over the years he'd proven to be, as Gloria liked to put it, "all flash and no substance." While Gloria had worked her way up the corporate ladder at B & T and amassed enough personal wealth through wise investments to keep the two of them in a tony condominium overlooking Gramercy Park, he'd flitted from job to job and served primarily as arm candy for Gloria's corporate functions.

Truly, their relationship had been an odd one. But the thought that she might have staged her own death so that he would be the one to run across her body first was sickening. Could Gloria really have done something like that? Surely, even at the lowest point in their marriage, she hadn't been capable of that kind of cruelty.

The detective seemed to sense that Vern's question was rhetorical because he didn't answer. Instead, he just looked back at the man sympathetically and asked if the two of them had been having marital problems.

Vern took another tissue and blew his nose. "If that was what she was trying to do, I probably deserved it."

At that point, the detective looked over at Kelsey and tilted his head as if to say it was time for her and Matt to leave. She nodded, grateful to be dismissed. Kelsey and her brother headed for the elevator, leaving the two men to continue their conversation in private.

When they reached the first floor and stepped off, Kelsey was surprised to see the flashing lights of a police car right outside, a uniformed officer standing near the door, and a cluster of curious onlookers peering through the front windows. Except they weren't just curious onlookers, she realized as she got a better look. They were reporters.

"Oh, man," she moaned. "I should have anticipated this."

The fact that the vice president of management recruitment and training for Brennan & Tate had been found dead in the company's executive conference room was newsworthy by itself, but coming on the heels of the incident here earlier today, it was positively titillating. Of course the media was coming out in droves—and it was probably only going to get worse as the night wore on.

They asked the security guard at the front desk to call them a cab. When it arrived, the cop manning the door escorted them out to the vehicle. After running the gauntlet of several dozen shouting voices out on the street, once they were inside the cab and speeding away toward her apartment, she was exhausted.

"You Wall Street types sure do live the exciting life," Matt teased.

"Hah. Thank goodness Wall Street isn't actually involved here. Can you imagine if Brennan & Tate were a public company instead of a private one? Then, along with all of those reporters, we'd also be dealing with an angry mob of stockholders demanding to know what's going on and what it'll mean to their bottom line."

They were quiet for a moment, watching as the cab reached the end of the street and turned right onto Battery Place.

"Well," Matt replied, "speaking as a stockholder in this privately held corporation, do you have any idea what today's events are going to mean to the bottom line?"

Kelsey rolled her eyes. "Leave it to the econ prof to have one eye on the numbers."

"I'm just sayin'. Unlike you, who receives an increase in shares every year that you work there, I'm pretty much capped out at my family dole of one percent."

"Hey, nobody made you become a teacher instead of a businessman," she replied, smiling. "You were perfectly welcome to join the rank and file at the family firm if you wanted to. Still are. You certainly have the brain for numbers."

"Maybe, but with neither the patience nor the interest, that brain wasn't going to do me much good there. Guess I far prefer theorizing about money than I do actually trying to earn it."

"As long as Tiffany likes ramen noodles," she teased with a shrug.

"Hey, Tiffany's on the tenure track at NYU. Once we're married, she'll be the one bringing home the bacon."

"And you don't mind being a kept man?" Kelsey asked. She was only kidding, but the moment the words came out of her mouth, she thought of Vern, who in a sense had been Gloria's "kept man" for the past thirty years.

"Yeah, if I had no assets, maybe," he replied. "But as long as I have my B & T stock, I'm not a 'kept man.' I'm an heir with a temporary cash flow problem."

Kelsey laughed. She'd forgotten how much fun Matt could be, especially when he was trying to lighten a dark mood.

"Well, then, to answer your original question," she said, "I wouldn't exactly bank on that one percent to remain at its current value for long." The topic was complicated, so rather than go into it there in the cab, she suggested he come up for coffee at her place and she could tell him more about it.

Despite a small throng of reporters at Kelsey's building when they arrived, she told the cabbie to drop them at the front door. As they mounted the steps and questions were being shouted out to them from left and right, a part of Kelsey was tempted to stop and reply. But she knew better than to field questions with words that could get twisted around or misinterpreted for the next day's news. Instead, once she got to the top of the steps and unlocked the door, she turned and gave them a smile, an apology, and a simple statement.

"Gloria Poole was my business mentor and a dear friend. Along with everyone else at Brennan & Tate, I will deeply mourn her passing."

With that she thanked them all and went inside, Matt following along behind and closing the door in their faces. She collected her mail from the row of boxes, and then they took the elevator to the tenth floor. Once they were inside her apartment, Matt went to the TV to look for a news channel while Kelsey headed for the kitchen and read out the flavor names for all the coffee pods in the cabinet.

"That one," he said, interrupting her about halfway through. "Hazelnut raspberry cream decaf."

While he made himself comfortable on the love seat and continued to flip channels, she brewed first one steaming mug of coffee and then the next, carried them both into the living room, and sat down on the tiny sofa next to her baby brother. Together, they watched several different reports about Gloria, and in every case the conclusion was drawn by the reporters that her death tonight and the scene with Rupert earlier today had been somehow connected. And while Kelsey could see why that was the natural conclusion to draw, she couldn't imagine what the one might possibly have to do with the other. She said as much to Matt, and they tossed around ideas for a while but couldn't come up with any theories that connected the two events.

Ultimately, their conversation came back around to the discussion they had been having in the cab, about the value of Brennan & Tate stock and the impact today's incidents would have on it. To help Matt fully understand, she had to go back a bit and describe for him the bigger picture of what had been going on at the compnay lately.

She started with what he already knew, that the company had originally been founded by their great-great-grandfather, Sean Brennan, back in 1904. Even though it had grown since then into a multimillion dollar corporation with nearly fifty employees, it was still thought of in the finance world as a "family business," one synonymous with the Brennan and Tate names. Their father, the highly respected Nolan Tate, had served solidly at the helm for decades, but after his stroke last year the company's value had begun to plummet from a high of seventy million before Nolan's stroke to a low of thirty-six last December.

"Ouch. Merry Christmas."

"I know, right?"

In January Walter had called in consultants, who identified the problem as "a lack of public confidence in the wake of Nolan Tate's sudden departure from the firm." Something drastic needed to be done to restore that confidence, so they ended up hiring a big public relations firm to come in and fix things. The goal was to show the world that even though Nolan was no longer around, the Tate name was still alive and well in his daughter Kelsey. The impression they were trying to give was that she possessed the same sharp instincts and business acumen for which her family and her firm had long been known. It was a heavy weight to bear, one that had been feeling heavier all the time. But the general consensus was that their campaign was succeeding even better than predicted. These days, B & T's value was back up in the high fifties, she was a rising star in the financial realm, and the impression people were getting was that not only did she possess the same talents and instincts as her father, but that in time she may just prove to be as adept at successful investing as her great-grandmother, the legendary Adele Brennan Tate herself.

"So basically," Matt said, nodding in comprehension, "these people built a whole campaign around Adele and how her gifts have been passed down through the generations to you."

"Correct."

They were both silent for a long moment.

"Guess I can see where you're going with this," he said finally. "Besmirching the name of Adele the way that guy did today could wipe out the significance of your entire campaign and put the value of B & T stock at an even lower point now than it was when you started."

"Exactly."

Matt let out a long, slow sigh. "Well, then," he said philosophically, "that leaves just one last question, only now it applies to you instead of Tiffany."

"What's that?" Kelsey asked, leaning her head back against the couch and looking over at her brother.

"How do *you* feel about ramen noodles?"

CHAPTER
NINE

Kelsey awoke the next morning with swollen eyes and a bad headache. The night before, after Matt left, she'd gone to bed and cried herself to sleep. Today, however, she had no time for grief. She took several ibuprofen and thought about what lay ahead. There was much to do if she wanted to learn more about Rupert's claims and Gloria's death. Surely, if she worked diligently enough, she could get down to the truth behind both events, much as she and her team regularly dug up the facts on the people and businesses involved with each potential investment.

After a hot shower followed by a cold compress on her swollen eyes, Kelsey took a long time with her makeup and hair. She also dressed with care, not wanting to give the reporters she encountered today anything to criticize about her appearance. A navy-blue Ann Klein skirt and jacket felt right, and she paired it with a cream-colored blouse.

Out of sheer habit, she reached for Adele's hat pin, the one with an Irish harp at one end that she frequently wore on her lapel. When she realized what she was doing, she set it back in the jewelry box and looked for something else. Deep inside, a part of her felt guilty, as though the rejection of the pin was somehow a rejection of Adele herself. But that wasn't it. Her action of intentionally *not* wearing the pin had to do with focus and resolve and the need to face this situation head-on without any preconceived notions about what the true, bottom-line facts might actually be.

Adele had been, after all, a flesh and blood person, one who had flaws and made mistakes and, yes, even kept a few secrets. In theory, it was conceivable that she could have been someone other than who she said she was. On the other hand, Kelsey knew to her core that she wasn't. Adele had *not* been an imposter.

So much for remaining objective.

Still feeling that nagging twinge of guilt, Kelsey picked the harp pin back up and held it in her hand. According to Adele, it had come as part of a set of two, bought for her and Jocelyn by Jocelyn's father. This half of the set had been hand tooled out of gold and was in the shape of an Irish harp. The other half, she'd said, was equally beautiful but had been made of silver and formed the shape of a string of musical notes. Each of the pins could be worn separately, but what made the set so unique was that the two pins could also be clipped together as one and used that way, with the silver musical notes seeming to rise up from the harp like a song.

Looking at the pin up close, it was easy to see the small slit in the side of the harp where the companion pin had been designed to attach. She'd asked her great-grandmother about that slit several times when she was a little girl, but whenever she did, Adele had become upset and changed the subject. It wasn't until Kelsey went to her father with the same question that she finally learned the truth: The slit was to hold the pin's mate, but that mate had been pinned to the hat of Adele's cousin Jocelyn the night *Titanic* went down. When Jocelyn's body disappeared, her pin had gone with it.

After Great-Grandmother Adele passed away, Kelsey learned that the harp hat pin had been left to her in the will. Even as a child, she recognized the significance of that and took on the full weight of the responsibility. She had allowed her mother to store the pin in the family safe until she was older and ready to take care of it. She'd meant to retrieve it at nineteen or twenty but ended up not asking for it until after she graduated from college. Once the pin was in her possession, Kelsey found herself thinking more and more about the other half of the set, the one with the silver notes on top. Surely, a pin set that lovely and unique hadn't been manufactured only once. There must be others out there somewhere.

As time went on, whenever she would pass an antique store or a collectible shop, she would find herself stepping inside and searching the glass cases for the mate to her pin. She knew how much Adele had pined for her late cousin her entire adult life, and even though both women were now gone, it seemed to Kelsey that if she could just find a duplicate of the missing pin, she would somehow bring closure to Adele's heartache as well.

Kelsey knew full well how silly that sounded, which is why she had never shared with another soul the thinking behind her hobby of collecting antique hat pins. Correction, she thought now. She had told one person: Cole Thornton. But that was a good five years ago, back when she thought they would be together forever. As it turned out, she'd been mistaken on that.

Only once had Kelsey requested a professional opinion about the likelihood of her ever finding the pin she so earnestly sought. After a thorough examination, the expert had told her that the set had likely been one of a kind, handmade by an artisan in England, and that no match would ever be found. But he hadn't been able to say that with one hundred percent certainty, so still she searched—in shops, on eBay, at flea markets and antique shows. Perhaps, she realized now, that obsession had been a way of staying connected to Adele even after she was gone.

Kelsey's thoughts were interrupted by the sound of a buzzer. Carefully placing the pin back inside her jewelry box, she closed the lid and headed for the intercom mounted beside the front door. Before she asked who was there, she leaned around the corner to check the time on the microwave. It wasn't even eight o'clock in the morning! Who could be here at this hour?

Afraid this might be a new tactic by a persistent reporter, she pushed the button and asked in her sternest tone who was there.

"It's Lou," a familiar voice said in reply.

With a grin she pressed the button that would let him in downstairs and then quickly straightened up her kitchen and living room until she heard his knock at her door. When she swung it open, she expected to see the warm, smiling face of her old friend. It was Lou all right, but he definitely wasn't smiling. In fact, he looked mad.

"What am I, chopped liver?" he demanded.

"What's wrong?"

"What's wrong is that you won't answer your phone and you haven't returned any of my calls. Worse, I had to find out what happened last night by hearing it on the news this morning!"

The man seemed genuinely upset, so Kelsey invited him in. She offered him breakfast, but he said he'd already eaten.

"I'll take some coffee, though, if you have it," he replied, sitting down on a stool at her tiny kitchen bar. "And since it's eight o'clock in the morning, bring on the high-octane stuff and keep it coming till I tell you to stop."

Kelsey did as he asked, and once he was settled with a hot beverage in front of him, she toasted herself a bagel and covered it with cream cheese. As she did, she apologized earnestly to Lou for having upset him. She explained about the numerous calls from reporters and the need to turn off the ringer, but she admitted there was no excuse for not contacting him once she got home last night to tell him about Gloria.

"Did you really find her body? That's what they said on the news anyway."

Kelsey nodded. "It was horrible, Lou. I was cutting through the executive conference room on the fifth floor when I flipped on the light and spotted her hanging from a cord by her neck."

He shook his head slowly from side to side and mused aloud about what would lead a person to do something like that. "That is," he added, "if it really was a suicide. Any chance it might have been foul play, like they were saying on TV?"

"The detective who interviewed me seemed to be leaning more toward suicide," she told him, "but they were definitely pursuing both possibilities."

Lou was silent for a long moment. When he finally spoke, there was a deep sadness to his voice. "You know, back when I was at B & T, Gloria was a very good friend to me."

"Oh, I know. When you left, she was the one who guided me in brokering the start-up money for your company."

Lou shook his head, and Kelsey could tell that there was something he wanted to say.

"What is it?"

He shrugged. "I was just thinking how much happier she would have been in the long run if she'd done what I did and left the company five years ago, once she found out that she'd been passed over for promotion."

Kelsey thought back, remembering some of the details of that difficult time. Five years ago, her father had been forced to take an early retirement, doctor's orders. Nolan had been having prolonged and significant blood pressure problems, and his doctor said if he didn't at least take a leave of absence from his very demanding job, he was going to end up having either a heart attack or a stroke.

Knowing he had no real choice in the matter, Nolan had devised what he thought was a sound exit strategy. He changed his own title from CEO to president, a position he could fill in a part-time, limited capacity with the goal of serving as a consultant who could be brought in from time to time to weigh in on important matters.

At the time everyone assumed he would be promoting Lou to fill the CEO position left vacant by the restructuring, and once Lou was in the top spot, the expectation was that Gloria would step into the position he'd vacated as COO. Instead, Nolan surprised everyone by leaving both Lou and Gloria exactly where they were in the hierarchy and bringing in a man from the outside, Walter Hallerman. Kelsey had been fairly new at the firm then, but even she had been able to see what a poor job her father had done of engineering the transition.

Lou and Gloria had both been devastated by the decision—not to mention deeply offended. It had been a stressful time at Brennan & Tate, with lots of closed-door discussions and whispered asides and tense interactions. In the end, Lou had made the decision to leave his job and strike out on his own. With Nolan's eventual blessing, B & T ended up investing in Lou's new business. In the first deal Kelsey had ever brokered on her own, she had managed to obtain a significant amount of money for him, enough for Strahan Realty Trust to get rolling and eventually establish itself as a significant part of the New York financial scene. Business had continued to go well, and that first investment was still providing significant returns.

Gloria, on the other hand, had chosen to stay at Brennan & Tate despite the significant snub. Swallowing her hurt and anger, she poured all of her energies into her job and continued to serve the company well. It was a choice that many at B & T had questioned, but as the boss's daughter, Kelsey had never been privy to the thinking behind Gloria's decision.

Now Lou was sitting in her kitchen, sharing with Kelsey the depth of Gloria's rage and pain back then. "I think if she'd gotten out, like I did, and made a new life for herself elsewhere, she might still be alive. If it really was suicide, I gotta wonder if at least part of it was about all that unresolved hurt from being passed over by your father five years ago. Otherwise, why do the deed at the office, you know? It's almost like she was trying to send a message."

Kelsey swallowed a bite of her bagel. "I disagree, Lou. Gloria and I have worked together closely ever since, and I've never had the feeling she was repressing anything. When my dad ended up having his stroke last year anyway, in spite of the early semi-retirement and the things he'd done to lower his blood pressure, Gloria just kept saying how sad it was that he had gone through all the grief of restructuring the upper echelon and in the end it hadn't really gained him a thing. She was talking about *Dad's* grief, not her own. Does that sound like someone who was harboring resentment? When someone's been terribly wronged, do they turn around and show pity for the one who wronged them?"

Even as she asked the question, Kelsey remembered the scene from the day before, in the security office with Rupert Brennan, when she'd been surprised to find that in the midst of her anger at the man she also found herself feeling kind of sorry for him. Rolling that around in her mind for a bit, she wondered if maybe Lou had a point. Certainly, Gloria had been devastated when she was passed over for that promotion. Consummate professional that she was, perhaps she'd only been wearing her game face these past five years, swallowing down her true feelings under the guise of "getting on with the business of business" as she liked to say.

Unable to come to any definite conclusions, they decided to change the subject. Their conversation lightened somewhat after that, with Lou having a second cup of coffee and Kelsey finishing up her bagel and placing her plate in the tiny dishwasher. Then he rose and said he needed to get going.

"I have a busy day ahead of me," he said, "but I knew I had to touch base with you first and make sure you were okay." Looking into her eyes, he added, "*Are* you okay, Kels? You seem really good, considering everything that happened yesterday, but it never hurts to ask."

Kelsey smiled, reaching out to give his arm a pat. "It's sweet of you to worry about me, but I promise you I'll be fine. Today, more than anything, I just want to start gathering some facts. For starters, if I'm going to counter the claims of Rupert Brennan, I need to make certain I really know what I'm talking about."

"That a girl."

Squeezing back around the end of the bar, Kelsey walked Lou to the front door and thanked him again for coming.

"I know you and I don't see each other all that much these days," he told her, "but I hope you know I always have your back, just like you had mine five years ago when you invested in me."

They shared a hug, and as they pulled apart Lou told her he'd had one other reason for coming here this morning. With that, he reached into his inside jacket pocket and pulled out a small box wrapped in gold paper and topped with a silver bow.

"I'd planned to give it to you at the reception after the meeting yesterday, but then things got out of hand, and...well, here."

She took the box from him and began unwrapping the paper.

"This probably still isn't the right time, but sometimes there *is* no right time. It's just a little congratulatory gift I got for you."

"You didn't have to do this," she said, tearing off the last of the paper and removing the lid from the box.

Inside was an even smaller box made of black velvet, and she took it out and popped open the spring-hinged lid to reveal the treasure inside. It was a pin, a very tasteful and elegant lapel pin. Made of gold, it formed the shape of a capital Q, and at the letter's center was a diamond. "Oh, my," she whispered.

"Like it?" he asked, grinning shyly. "I had it made special for you. For the Quarter Club."

Taking it carefully from the box, she separated the backing from the front and pinned it to her lapel. "I love it!" After checking her image in the hallway mirror, she gave him another hug. "Thank you, Lou. Thank you so much." Pulling back, she added, "Actually, don't you have one kind of like this?"

He nodded. "Yeah, it's pretty close. I got mine years ago, from your father, when I was inducted into the Quarter Club. I know he's as proud of you as I am, Kelsey, and if he was in good enough health, he'd be the one giving you this."

Kelsey's eyes threatened to fill with tears, and she fought hard to keep them at bay.

"You know, kiddo," Lou said kindly, "this too shall pass. Even if right now it doesn't feel like it."

"I know," she whispered, nodding.

"You wear that pin proudly, okay? Especially now, in the middle of all this mess. You've achieved great things for your family's company, and there's a lot more in store for you ahead. Let this pin remind you of that."

"I will," she promised. "I absolutely will."

By the time Kelsey finished getting ready for the day and started downstairs, it was nearly nine a.m. Though she'd hoped to get an earlier start than that, she was still glad she and Lou had taken the time to visit. These days they didn't see each other very often, but when they did she was always reminded of how much she missed working with him.

To avoid the reporters, Kelsey had called for a cab to pick her up on the back side of the building. She hoped this would all be over soon and she could go back to her preferred modes of transportation, walking and the subway, both of which were a lot cheaper and usually faster as well.

The back door of Kelsey's building had no window, so she held her breath as she swung it open and stepped outside, hoping the coast was clear. It was.

The cab was idling at the curb when she came out, so she walked quickly between the two dumpsters and then dashed the rest of the way just in case, practically leaping into the back seat of the bright yellow vehicle. She was relieved to have made it this far unscathed.

But then she glanced to her right and realized someone else was already there in the backseat. "Oh, I'm so sorry." Kelsey reached for the door handle to get out. "I thought this was the cab I had called for."

"It is, Kelsey."

Startled, she turned to look at the woman. In her early fifties, she was dressed in cheap, ill-fitting clothes, her spiky, close-cropped hair dyed vivid orange. Kelsey stared at her, trying to make sense of what she was seeing.

"Sorry if I frightened you," the woman told her with a smile. "I'm not sure if we ever officially met yesterday, but my name's Rhonda. I'm Rupert Brennan's sister."

CHAPTER TEN

April 10, 1912

JOCELYN

Despite the time Jocelyn had taken to fix herself up, the two girls arrived in the hotel lobby just a few minutes late. Jocelyn's father was not waiting for them near the café, as agreed, but rather at the base of the curving staircase. He was dressed more formally than his daughter had anticipated, and when he spotted them, she noticed he pulled out his pocket watch and gave it a look.

"Sorry we're late, Da," she said, giving him a kiss on the cheek when they reached the bottom stair. "It was my fault, not Adele's. My hair would simply *not* behave."

She expected his usual indulgent smile, but instead he seemed distracted. "Is something wrong?" she asked.

Focusing on her and her cousin, he replied, "No, not at all. We're just pressed for time. I'm afraid there's been a slight change in plans."

Jocelyn and Adele looked at each other.

"I have some final business to attend to this morning, so I need the two of you to remain here and meet up with Mr. Myers on your own. I shouldn't be long, and then we can all proceed to the ship together."

"May I go with you, Uncle Rowan?" Adele asked eagerly.

Jocelyn looked askance at her cousin, not surprised to see that she cared more about business than she did about meeting a handsome young man.

"I'm sorry, Adele, but this one is just for me. Maybe next time. Besides,

77

it wouldn't be proper for Jocelyn to host Mr. Myers alone, even in a place as public as the hotel's café."

Jocelyn could clearly see the disappointment in Adele's face. This was the second time she had been left out of the business meetings that had taken place during the journey to Southampton. The day before, while still in London, Rowan had met up with Mr. Myers at the site of some new business venture and had stayed there so long that the girls hadn't even had the chance to make the younger man's acquaintance before it was time to depart. Mr. Myers had parted company with Rowan in town, spent the night at his hotel in London, and was coming in on this morning's train.

"Don't look so sad, Adele," Rowan cajoled. "At least you and Jocelyn had a lovely time at that department store in London yesterday, didn't you? You found some beautiful baubles." He gestured to the new pins both girls wore on their hats, each one half of a matching gold-and-silver set they had chosen together and would share.

"Yes, we did, Da," Jocelyn responded when Adele did not. "We really appreciate your buying them for us. We will be fine here with Mr. Meyers. How will we know him when he arrives?"

Rowan returned his attention to his daughter. "I have arranged for that. You two can go on into the café, and he will be directed to you when he gets here. I am sorry to leave before you are even settled at your table, but I must be at my meeting in a few minutes. I'll return before the three of you are finished with breakfast, I promise."

"That will be perfect," Jocelyn replied cheerily, wishing Adele would get that frown off of her face. The girl could be so maddeningly single-minded sometimes.

Once her father was gone and they were alone and seated in the restaurant, Jocelyn urged her cousin to relax, saying she couldn't always expect to take part in the world of business, which, after all, was man's domain. As soon as she said it, Adele's eyes flared, and it looked as if she was about to embark on one of her lectures. Fortunately, before she could get out a word, the waiter was leading a young man to their table and she had to hold her tongue.

Mr. Tad Myers was dashing indeed, with light blond hair, sparkling brown eyes, and elegant attire. He greeted each of them with a smile and a bow, and then he took his seat. It looked as though Adele was about to make the introductions, so Jocelyn squeezed her hand and jumped in to speak instead.

"It's so nice to meet you, Mr. Myers. I am Adele Brennan, and this is my cousin, Jocelyn." Jocelyn smiled at Adele and winked. Switching identities was a game they used to play whenever they were in the company of someone new and feeling mischievous.

"Pleased to meet both of you," Mr. Myers said. "Please call me Tad." Looking to Adele and assuming she was Jocelyn, he added, "Isn't your father joining us?"

"No, I'm sorry," Adele replied, giving her cousin a kick under the table. "My…father…sends his apologies, but he had some additional business to attend to and will be joining us afterward."

To Jocelyn's dismay, Tad looked extremely disturbed by this news. He excused himself from the table, saying he would be right back, and they both watched as he went to speak with the maître d'.

"Well, that was quite rude," Jocelyn whispered. "I wonder why it matters."

"Never mind him," Adele hissed. "What are you doing?"

"Just trying to help lighten the mood. You need to relax, cousin. It's only a lark. We'll tell him the truth eventually."

Tad returned to the table before Adele could object any further. Though he was clearly upset, he put on a friendly face and proceeded to order their beverages.

"Miss Adele will have black tea, I believe," he told the waiter as he gestured toward Jocelyn, "and Miss Jocelyn would like Earl Grey. Just coffee for me, please."

Once the waiter was gone, Jocelyn asked how he had known which teas were their favorites. As she said it, she realized that if they maintained their switched identities much longer, they would both be forced to drink a tea they disliked. Still, she wasn't ready to call a halt to their game just yet. Adele continued to sit there quite humorless and stiff, and Jocelyn was determined to keep the ruse up until her cousin rediscovered her missing sense of play.

"Your uncle mentioned it last night. I make a point of remembering things about people."

Jocelyn returned his gaze, knowing that his handsome brown eyes were something she would not easily forget.

Making conversation, Jocelyn asked Tad about his train trip, but somehow Adele soon managed to steer the conversation in the direction of business by asking him what title he held at Brennan & Company.

He explained that he had been hired right out of college to apprentice with one of their investment research teams and then advanced from there to his current position of associate. From the way he talked, it sounded as if he were intent on working his way up in the company—to the position of president, if possible—and that he wasn't ashamed to admit it.

Adele peppered the poor man with questions about the company, its investments, and more, though Jocelyn wasn't sure whether she did so because she was actually curious about such boring things or if she was just hoping to keep the topic away from them and their identity switch. Either way, the man seemed happy to satisfy her curiosity—until she came to the topic of the business matter that had brought him to London and to yesterday's meeting, from which she had been excluded.

In response, he waved a hand dismissively and said, "Oh, the details would bore a woman. Trust me. It was nothing all that interesting. Just investment talk and such."

Bad move, Mr. Myers, Jocelyn thought, suppressing a smile. She expected smoke to come pouring from her cousin's ears at any moment.

To keep any explosions at bay, she quickly jumped in and changed the subject, relieved when her father finally appeared at their table, looking far more relaxed and happy than he had when he'd left. He greeted Tad with a handshake and an apology. Tad asked where he'd been, a question so direct it could only have come from an American. When Rowan was as dismissive with his answer to Tad as Tad had been to Adele, the young executive's expression seemed to darken a bit.

Rowan sat at the table, helped himself to a scone, and unwittingly began a conversation that addressed each girl directly, making it perfectly clear which was which. Once Tad caught on to the prank they had been playing on him, his scowl turned to an out-and-out glower.

Jocelyn was mortified. She'd only meant to lighten the mood, and instead her silly little game had backfired. When the waiter appeared and diverted Rowan's attention, she leaned forward and spoke in a whisper.

"I apologize for our earlier introductions, Tad. It's just a game we play sometimes, but I realize now it was utterly inappropriate in this setting."

"I don't appreciate being made a fool," he whispered in return.

"I'm glad you know how that feels, then," Adele countered. When the waiter walked away, she turned to her uncle, asking, "Were the interest rates sufficient enough for an investment, or does the lower potential for return from the purchase of bonds have you leaning toward stocks instead?"

From Tad's startled expression, it was clear Adele had made her point. To make matters worse, for some reason Rowan seemed quite reluctant to answer her question and quickly changed the subject. An air of discomfort hovered over the rest of their meal, so Jocelyn was thankful when they were done and her father urged them to return to their room to finish packing.

"It's time to check out of the hotel and get on over to *Titanic*," he said jubilantly as he paid the bill.

While Tad headed to the hotel's lobby to wait for them, Rowan walked to his room on the first floor and the girls started up the staircase to theirs on the third, Jocelyn apologizing to Adele as they went.

"I am so sorry, cousin. It seems I've made a mess of everything."

"Don't worry about it," Adele said, surprising Jocelyn with her reply. "I'm glad you did it. Our Mr. Myers deserved exactly what he got in there."

Then she marched on ahead, her anger showing in the heavy stomp of each step.

CHAPTER
ELEVEN

K elsey was dumbfounded. There in the cab next to her sat the woman who was supposed to be far away in Vermont by now. Instead, here she was, acting as if sitting in the back seat of someone else's taxi was the most natural thing in the world.

"What are you doing here?" was all Kelsey could manage to utter.

"If you want to know the truth, I took a gamble and I'm happy to say it paid off."

Kelsey sputtered, trying to respond. She knew she must have looked and sounded like an idiot at the moment, but she could barely form a coherent thought, much less get that thought into words. She was about to tell the woman to get out when Rhonda spoke to the driver and informed him that he could go. The cab pulled into the traffic and began the long drive uptown.

"See," Rhonda continued, "I wanted to talk to you, but I was afraid if I called first you would hang up on me, and if I went up and knocked on your door or something, you might even call the police."

"You better believe it."

She nodded. "So finally I decided I was just going to wait out in front of your apartment building this morning till you came out and ask you if you wanted to grab some breakfast or something. But then when I got here, I realized a bunch of reporters were already waiting for you. I was afraid they would recognize me—by my hair, you know—and start asking me a bunch of questions, so I knew I couldn't wait there with them. That's when I took a gamble. I figured you would use the back exit out of your apartment building today. I've been waiting for almost an hour and a half. I was about to give up and go away when I saw a cab pull in at the curb and just sit there. I got in but told him to wait, that we were a party of two. I had a feeling you'd be down any minute. And I was right! You were, and now here we are."

Her little speech finished, Rhonda let out a contented sigh and settled back against the seat, clasping her hands together over the giant purse she was cradling in her lap. Then she turned and looked over at Kelsey expectantly.

So many emotions were roiling around inside that she didn't even know which one to latch onto. Fear? Anger? Defensiveness? At least this woman didn't come across as unstable—not in comparison to her brother Rupert, anyway.

First things first, she told herself, trying to calm down and think more clearly. "Why aren't you in Vermont like you're supposed to be?"

Rhonda smiled, looking chagrined. "Well, not to put too fine a line on it, but technically *I* wasn't the one sent away yesterday. Rupert was. I had no intention of leaving."

"But the limo—"

"Aw, that limo zigzagged around town for a long time first, I guess to make sure nobody was following us. Before they started heading north out of the city, I asked the driver to drop me off at my hotel."

"So what you're saying," Kelsey said slowly, "is that you're still here in Manhattan but Rupert is up in Vermont as promised?"

"Exactly. I'm gonna go up there and join him tomorrow. I already got a rental car reserved and everything. But I just couldn't go yesterday. I just couldn't."

"Because you needed to speak with me first?"

"No, because I saw a Broadway show last night and it was so good that I'm going back to see it again tonight. Plus, our room at the Wilton Plaza is nonrefundable."

Kelsey didn't know whether to laugh or groan. Taking a deep breath, she looked out the window to gauge their progress.

"Did you say the Wilton Plaza?" Kelsey asked, an idea coming to her. "We'll be going right past there in a little while. We'll drop you off as we do."

She should have posed it as a question rather than a statement, but she'd meant her comment to sound just rude enough for the woman to get the point.

To her surprise, however, Rhonda's face lit up. "Why, thank you! That would be real nice. Save me some walking."

Leaning forward, Kelsey told the driver he needed to make a stop at the Wilton Plaza on their way.

"Okay, lady," he said, putting on his blinker. "but that's going to take us up Eighth. Heavy traffic this time of day."

"No, stay on Tenth till you get to Forty-Fourth and then cut over."

"Fine."

Settling back in her seat, Kelsey looked over at Rhonda and asked what it was she wanted to talk about.

"Mostly, I just wanted to apologize for my brother's behavior yesterday. That was a real nice ceremony y'all were having and a good speech you were giving. If I had known he was going to disrupt everything like that, I never would have let him go in the auditorium in the first place."

"Let's start there. Why *was* he at the ceremony? You're both from Florida, right? What are you doing in New York? And how did you even know about the award?"

"The letter," Rhonda replied. "Rupert got a letter a couple of weeks ago inviting him to come."

Kelsey stared at her. How was that possible? Who would have knowingly invited these people?

"A letter?" she managed. "From whom?"

Rhonda blinked her long, thick lashes—probably extensions. "We don't know. They didn't sign their name."

Kelsey swallowed hard. "Do you still have that letter? I'd like to see it."

"Actually, I might just have it in here." Rhonda opened her purse, which was almost a tote bag, it was so large—a black, faux-leather sack that seemed to be filled with a jumble of cosmetics, pieces of loose paper, and miscellany.

"See, Rupert's the one who brought it, but I got so tired of seeing him read and reread the thing over and over during the flight that I took it away from him. I believe I shoved it in here…"

As she talked, Rhonda rifled through the bag, reaching into its depths and hauling out handfuls of flotsam and jetsam that she piled onto the seat next to her.

"Wait!" Rhonda pulled out a crumpled envelope, held it up, and squinted at it. "Yep, here it is." She extracted the letter, smoothed it on her knee, and handed it to Kelsey. "Now let's see if I can fit all this stuff back in here."

While Rhonda reloaded her cargo, Kelsey studied the letter. Printed on plain white paper, it read:

> *Dear Rupert,*
>
> *You should know that on April 3 at 4:00 p.m. there will be a ceremony at the offices of Brennan & Tate in New York City, during which the Tate family will continue to perpetuate the lie that Adele Brennan Tate survived the sinking of Titanic. You and I both know that Jocelyn was the one who survived, not Adele. I hope you will consider taking the opportunity to appear at this ceremony and put an end to the Tate family's lies.*
>
> *So you do not bear this burden alone, I am enclosing $500 in cash for you to use toward any traveling expenses you might have getting to New York City. I am also enclosing a recent article from the New York Times about Kelsey Tate, so you can see how she praises her great-grandmother Adele and tells the heroic story of her surviving Titanic. (What a lie!) Finally, I'm enclosing an invitation to the upcoming meeting, which you will need to show at the door in order to get in.*
>
> *Bear in mind, your time is running out! If Brennan & Tate is sold, you may lose your right to inherit any part of Sean's fortune. Don't let this happen! Seize the opportunity to set the record straight now. Those of us who know the truth about that fateful night on the ship will be forever in your debt.*
>
> *Sincerely,*
> *A Friend*
>
> *P.S.—If you decide not to go to NYC, you can keep the money anyway. I don't have the nerve to sign my name to this letter and would prefer that you not try to figure out who it's from. Thank you.*

As Rhonda had said, there was no signature at the bottom. But whoever wrote it clearly believed that Adele Brennan Tate, a legendary icon of investing, also was a lying impostor.

"May I see that, please?" Kelsey asked, reaching for the rumpled envelope.

"Sure." Rhonda handed it over and finished loading the last of her things back into her bag.

There was no return address printed on the envelope, but Kelsey studied the postmark, which had been stamped *New York, NY,* on the top, *Mar 17 2012* in the middle, and *10006* at the bottom. It looked like any other letter mailed from Manhattan. The only significant bit of information that the postmark offered was the zip code, which was the same zip code as Brennan & Tate. In any other city in the country, that might not be so significant, but given that there were eight or nine different zip codes in Manhattan's financial district alone, that really narrowed things down. If this letter hadn't been mailed from their office, at the very least it had been sent from somewhere within a five- or ten-block radius of it.

"May I keep this?"

Rhonda frowned. "I'm sorry. I would say yes, but it's not mine to give."

Kelsey reluctantly tucked the letter inside the envelope and handed it over, though what she really wanted to do was drive to the nearest police station and have them dust both the letter and envelope for finger prints.

"Just do me a favor and don't throw that out," she said earnestly.

Rhonda assured her that she wouldn't, but the sight of her shoving it back into that disaster of a handbag wasn't exactly comforting.

"So has anyone from Brennan & Tate contacted you or Rupert in any way other than via this letter?"

"Recently? No." Rhonda was shaking her head when she paused, eyebrows raised. "Wait. There was a message from somebody on my machine at home yesterday."

"At home?"

"In Florida. They called my house yesterday morning, but we were already on our way here and didn't get it in time. In fact, I didn't even check my messages until just before I went to bed last night. By then, it was too late to do any good anyway."

"Who was it?" Kelsey asked.

"She didn't leave her name, but it sounded to me like the one who handled things with us the last time."

Kelsey blinked. "The *last* time?"

"Yeah, when Rupert got himself all worked up and tried to say he wasn't bound by Daddy's agreement. I thought he was wrong, but I let him go ahead and give it a shot. You never know. I mean, if his theory's right and Adele really was lying, then he and I got a lot of money coming to us. No offense."

Kelsey was too startled and confused to speak. So many questions pounded in her brain that she couldn't even figure out which one to ask first.

"Anyway," Rhonda continued, pulling a cell phone from her coat pocket, "I don't think I deleted it. You want me to play it for you?"

"The message from yesterday? Yes, please."

Rhonda dialed into her voice mail and handed Kelsey the phone. "Just press one and then it'll start."

Kelsey did as instructed, put the phone to her ear, and listened:

> *Hello. I'm trying to reach Rhonda Brennan. It's urgent and has to do with her brother, Rupert, and a meeting he may be attending in New York City later today. Please contact me as soon as you get this message. Please.*

The call ended with the caller leaving her cell phone number, but Kelsey already knew the number the voice was going to say before she said it.

Overcome with a wave of nausea, she handed Rhonda back her phone.

Gloria.

The message had come from Gloria.

Kelsey looked at Rhonda. Her mouth was moving and she was saying something, but Gloria's words were the ones pounding in Kelsey's brain:

"You don't have to go down there, you know. You don't have to do this at all. You could walk right out the back door and go home, and I could tell Walter you weren't feeling well and had to leave."

Kelsey sucked in a deep breath, a chill going through her. Gloria had known that Rupert and Rhonda were planning to come to the ceremony yesterday. She'd known but she hadn't stopped them—and she'd never said a word about it to Kelsey at all.

CHAPTER
TWELVE

When the cab crossed 40th Street, Kelsey knew they were getting close to Rhonda's hotel. And though she would rather have avoided the encounter altogether, she had to admit that it had given her some good information. It had also raised a number of new questions as well.

"Listen, can we back up a little bit?" Kelsey asked with some urgency as they rumbled across 41st. "Just a little while ago, you were talking about the message on your phone and you said it sounded like the woman from the last time. What last time? What are you talking about? I hate to sound stupid, but as you can see, I've never heard about any of this stuff before."

Rhonda nodded. "Well, Rupert's a lot more familiar with all that than I am, but I'll tell you what I can. Our side of the family has tried to straighten this whole thing out a couple of times before."

"Straighten out in what sense?"

"My daddy came and talked to your daddy and tried to make him understand that we had some money coming to us. Your daddy didn't think so, and in the end they had to bring in some lawyers and work it all out that way."

Kelsey stared at Rhonda in disbelief. Her father had dealt with these accusations in the past? Why had he never told her anything about it?

"When was this?" she asked, wondering if maybe it had happened when she was away at college.

"The first time I was in my early thirties and busy with two little babies at home. Guess you could say I was kinda preoccupied with taking care of them, but I do remember hearing my father ranting and raving about it. Adele Tate had just died a couple of months before, and he couldn't stand knowing that all her money was getting passed down the other side of the family. It wasn't fair, not when he knew for a fact that half of it should have been coming to us."

Keeping her expression blank, Kelsey did the math. Adele had died when Kelsey was just nine years old, so if the first time this has come up was pretty soon after that, it made sense why she'd never heard about it. She'd been a child at the time. There would have been no reason to involve her in matters of money and wills and ancestry disputes.

The cab lurched as the driver turned right onto 44th Street. Just a few blocks to go.

"So after they brought in the lawyers, the matter was settled?"

"For the time being, anyway. Again, I don't know all the details, but in the end I know our daddies came to some sort of settlement over the whole matter. Your daddy paid out a bunch of money, and my daddy signed a paper that said he promised to keep quiet about everything and never bring it up again."

"And did your father honor that agreement?" Kelsey asked, still trying to wrap her mind around what Rhonda was telling her.

"He sure did. I know he wasn't completely happy about it, but I guess he figured a little money was better than none at all, and at least it was a lot easier than having to go to court and prove our case and all of that."

"So where does Rupert fit in with this?"

"Well, that first time around, he was younger than he is now and more hotheaded too. He was furious at our daddy for taking that deal. I don't even think for him it was about the money. It was more important to him that the world know the truth, that this woman who called herself Adele was not who she said she was."

Kelsey was actually glad when they hit heavy traffic on the other side of 9th Avenue and came to a dead stop. Though this conversation had turned out to be more fruitful than she'd expected, there was still more that she wanted to know before they parted ways.

"Anyhoo," Rhonda continued, gazing with excitement at the billboards and posters lining the front of one Broadway theater after another, "Rupert kind of stewed in silence for a number of years, but when our father passed away, he refused to keep quiet anymore."

"And when was that?"

"Oh, 'bout 10 years ago now. Rupert figured that once daddy was dead, that agreement to keep quiet died with him. The internet was catching on then, you know, so Rupert used it to do some poking around and tried to dig up even more proof than our daddy had. He finally found something, and so back in '02 or thereabouts, he came up here to confront your daddy and convince him that our side of the family was still owed a bunch of money."

Kelsey sat up straight, listening intently. In 2002 she was graduating from college and going on to graduate school. Once again, there would have been no reason for her father to tell her about any of this. It had probably never crossed his mind to do so, and she hadn't been around to hear anything about it.

"So what happened that time?" Kelsey asked, frustrated when the traffic cleared up ahead and they quickly made the next block.

"That time your daddy didn't deal with it much at all. Instead, it was a woman…I can't quite remember her name. Lake? Pool? Pond? Some kind of water."

"Poole? Gloria Poole?"

"That's her. Anyway, she handled things that time around. At first she was nice about it and all. She even offered us a whole new settlement with more money, but a part of that settlement was just the same as before: If Rupert took the money, he had to promise he would never say anything about any of this ever again. No way was he going to agree to that. Like I said, for him it was more about the principle of the thing. He wanted the world to know what really happened back then, but the people at your company were ready to do anything they could to stop that from happening."

"So were they finally able to come to some sort of agreement?" Kelsey asked.

"No. In the end it all got kind of nasty. Once Rupert turned down the new settlement, that Gloria lady got pretty tough. She brought in a whole team of lawyers, and they went through the original agreement our father had signed. Seemed like they proved it was still enforceable even after all these years and even though the man who signed it was no longer living. It was something about how our father had signed on behalf of the entire family, present and future. Rupert talked with a couple of lawyers of his own, and in the end he finally had to give up. He hasn't been happy about it, but there wasn't much he could do."

Kelsey thought about that. It wasn't hard to picture Gloria taking matters into her own hands and wrapping up the matter of the delusional cousin swiftly and legally.

"And has anything happened with all of this since then?"

Rhonda shook her head. "No, Rupert just kind of put it out of his mind, but then when that letter showed up a few weeks ago, well, that was like pouring gasoline on a campfire. Especially that part about if the company got sold we'd lose any chance of ever getting the money we were owed. Rupert didn't know how that could be true, so he did some research and sure enough found something called an 'innocent buyer law.' What the letter said was right. Because of that law, if the company got sold our chance at any sort of settlement would be gone."

"Maybe so," Kelsey replied, "but isn't that kind of beside the point? Brennan & Tate isn't for sale. It never has been and never will be. It's our family's firm. It'll be owned by Tates for generations to come."

Rhonda shrugged. Looking out the window, she seemed to be growing antsy. Soon, the Wilton Plaza was in sight up ahead, and as they drew nearer, Kelsey tried to think of what other questions she wanted to ask.

"What can you tell me about this proof Rupert has? I know he said he was saving it for the courts, but if he ends up suing us, he'll have to hand it over during discovery anyway."

"I've never seen it myself, so I'm not exactly sure what it is, but I do know it's some sort of document that's been passed down through our side of the family. Our father seemed to think it was significant. Rupert does too."

Kelsey couldn't imagine what that document might be, but she felt certain it wasn't all that rock solid. Otherwise, Rupert or his father would have won this battle years ago.

"Anyway, I'm glad we've had this time to talk," Rhonda said, "and I really appreciate this ride back to my hotel. Mostly I just wanted to apologize for my brother. He's actually a nice guy once you get to know him, but he's just so obsessed with *Titanic*—and with what happened to Jocelyn and Adele—that he tends to go a little crazy. He's been consumed by this issue for years."

Kelsey, too, was glad they had had this opportunity to talk, though as they came to a stop in the front of Rhonda's hotel in the heart of the theater district, she couldn't help but feel a bit cynical. What had been this woman's intention exactly in coming here to New York? Watch her brother impugn someone who wasn't alive to defend herself, destroy that woman's legacy and the value of the company she'd left behind, and then take in the sights and catch a couple of Broadway shows? Unbelievable.

"Look, while I appreciate your apology, Rhonda, I have to ask what you thought was going to happen once you came up here. Didn't you realize what your brother was going to do at the ceremony?"

Reaching for the door handle, Rhonda paused and turned back to look at Kelsey.

"Not really, no. I had a feeling this was a bad idea—the whole trip up here, I mean—and I tried to talk him out of coming, but he wouldn't listen to me. He never does. So I knew I had to come along too. I figured if anything happened, at least I'd be here to help smooth things over afterward."

Kelsey wasn't convinced. "But you had to know he was going to pull *something*."

"Well, yeah, but I never expected him to go off like that in public. I thought he'd get through the ceremony and then try and talk with you in private. I'm really sorry. You gotta believe me."

With a final goodbye, Rhonda stepped out of the cab, closed the car door, and headed on into her hotel. The cab quickly pulled back out into traffic to bring Kelsey to the destination she'd first given him, her parents' house. Settling into her seat, Kelsey reviewed the surprising things she had just learned. Out of all the new information she'd gleaned from Rhonda, the fact most prevalent in her mind at the moment was that Gloria had known Rupert would be coming to that ceremony and hadn't done anything about it.

Why not? Why hadn't she stopped it? At the very least, why hadn't she warned anyone? She had known, but she'd never said a word! The thought made Kelsey feel so hurt and so angry that she didn't even know what to do with those emotions.

She took in a deep breath and blew it out between pursed lips, telling herself to calm down. She needed to strip the emotion from all of this and look at things objectively. Closing her eyes, she tried to picture that last encounter with Gloria, up in her office just before the ceremony. The woman had been acting incredibly odd, at turns sad and happy and anxious and weepy and evasive...and most of all stressed.

Of course she'd been stressed, because she had known what was about to happen. She had known but she hadn't said anything even to her protégé, the young woman she'd mentored all these years and who was now about to go out on that stage and get publicly humiliated.

Opening her eyes, Kelsey realized something else. This had to be the reason, the real reason, why Gloria hadn't been willing to participate in the event herself. She'd said her absence was all about helping Kelsey to give an impression of independence. But the truth was, she'd bowed out of that ceremony because she knew exactly what was going to happen there and she didn't want to be around to see it.

If so, could that really have had something to do with this Adele-as-imposter situation? Gloria had tried numerous times last night to reach Kelsey before she died. In her messages and texts she had apologized, but without saying what she was apologizing for.

"Have you ever done something bad out of good intentions?"

Maybe that's what had happened with Gloria. She had done something bad, something that had to do with Rupert and Rhonda and what took place at that ceremony. Afterward she'd been so wracked with guilt about whatever it was she had done that she couldn't bear to live any longer. Gloria did something bad out of good intentions and lived to regret it.

Correction, Kelsey thought as they finally turned onto the street where her parents lived. *Gloria may have regretted it, but she hadn't lived. She died—and she took her secrets with her to the grave.*

CHAPTER
THIRTEEN

Doreen Tate opened the door of the three-story brownstone and welcomed her daughter inside. As she did, just the sight of her mom's sweet, nurturing face brought tears to Kelsey's eyes. She may have been thirty-two years old with a prestigious job and a riverfront apartment and a whole world separate from that of her parents, but once in a while it felt good to be somebody's little girl.

Kelsey's mother hugged her fiercely, stroking her hair and cooing soft words and promising it was all going to be okay. Of course, such kindness only served to make Kelsey cry. Somehow, it had been easier to face the day in full-on business mode, ready to ask questions and gather facts and get to the bottom of things. But now that she was being shown compassion, she feared she might lose it completely.

Her mother was full of questions about all that had been going on, so after Kelsey fixed her face in the bathroom, she went back up the hallway to the bright, sunny kitchen and sat at the table, answering as best she could. Kelsey had plenty of questions for her mother in return, as she was hoping to confirm the things she'd just learned from Rhonda in the cab. Unfortunately, her mother didn't remember a whole lot about the whole Adele-false-identity thing and couldn't confirm or deny much of what had happened back then.

As they talked, Doreen brewed a pot of Jamaican Blue Mountain coffee, Kelsey's favorite. Soon she was serving it to her daughter at the table along with a delicate plate of the most heavenly smelling banana bread Kelsey had ever encountered.

The presentation was lovely, and the sight of such artfully served food made Kelsey smile. She'd always been closer to her father than to her mother, not necessarily because she liked him any better but simply because they had more in common—including interests and talents and even personalities. She and her father were so much alike, both of them focused and business minded and visionary, with a tendency to work too much and a brain that jumped to conclusions that could sometimes make them seem callous. Her mother, on the other hand, had always been a far more nurturing and creative soul. The poor woman had had so little interest in stocks and bonds and investments and money that she'd spent much of their family time with her eyes glazed over, enduring the shoptalk while she tried to pretend she cared.

Still, Doreen Tate had always made the perfect corporate wife for her husband, Nolan. After a lifetime of devoting herself to his needs and his dreams, facilitating his career and providing him with a near-idyllic home life, it just didn't seem fair that once he'd retired and had the time to shine some of that attention back on her, he'd ended up having the stroke. A server by nature, Doreen had never complained. But Kelsey knew it had to break her mother's heart sometimes to realize that her handsome, vibrant, brilliant husband had been reduced to a weakened, trembling man in a wheelchair who could barely string more than a few words together at a time.

"How's Dad today?"

"Do you mean in relation to all that's going on or just in general?" Doreen carried a second plate of banana bread to the table for herself and took a seat across from Kelsey.

"Both." She slid a bite of the warm concoction into her mouth and had to close her eyes as she chewed, it was that good.

"Well, generally speaking, he seems pretty much on the ball this morning," she said, neatly placing a cloth napkin on her lap. "But I can tell this whole thing has affected him deeply. He even cried himself to sleep last night."

"Poor Dad," Kelsey said, trying not to picture it. "Which do you think bothers him more? The attack-on-Adele thing or the death of Gloria?"

Doreen put down her fork and gaped at Kelsey in surprise.

"Oh, honey, Gloria, of course. He knew the woman her entire professional life. He respected her and depended on her and considered her a dear friend for many years. You know that."

Kelsey nodded, chagrined. "Has he given an opinion on the cause of her death? I mean, whether he thinks it was suicide or…uh…something else?"

"Yes. He feels that the Gloria he knew would never have killed herself. He's sure it has to have been a murder. I didn't know her nearly as well as the two of you did, of course, but I agree. Gloria Poole was a born problem-solver, the kind of person who never accepted defeat and rarely took no for an answer. She wasn't the type to give up and commit suicide. Don't you agree?"

Kelsey did agree, and she had said pretty much the same thing herself to the detective last night. But the more she'd been thinking about it, the more she wasn't so sure. "Up until yesterday, Mom, I would have agreed with you completely. But if you'd seen the way she was acting before the ceremony, if you'd heard the things she was saying..." Her voice trailed off. "I don't know. She was acting so strange yesterday that I'm at least willing to consider the possibility."

Her mother sighed softly in reply.

"I don't know," Kelsey continued, "maybe in a sense it's just easier for me to think it was suicide than to consider the possibility of a m-murder. Listen to me. I can hardly get the word out of my mouth. I mean, come on. *Murder?* In the executive conference room at Brennan & Tate? If that's really what it turns out to be, we're talking about a whole different ballgame here. Mom, you can't imagine how many people were in that building yesterday or the kind of chaos that was going on after everything was disrupted. Almost anyone could have sneaked upstairs and done that to her and then simply slipped back out undetected. The list of suspects would be ridiculously long. If you ask me, that detective had better hope the coroner ends up calling it a suicide. Otherwise, he has his work cut out for him."

"I see what you mean."

"And as far as the company's concerned, I can't even think about the possibility of murder without getting a headache. For starters, there'd be a whole host of liability issues. If she was murdered, we'd be forced to address safety concerns, security procedures—and we'd have insurance increases, not to mention the added expense and effort of trying to get around the stigma of someone having been killed right in our own office. A lot of people work in that building, Mom. From a business perspective, murder would be a nightmare. Whether it seems in character for Gloria or not, we all better *hope* it was a suicide."

Kelsey took another bite and looked up at her mom as she chewed, surprised to see that she was looking back at Kelsey with disdain.

"Do you hear yourself?" Doreen whispered. "Can you stop for a minute and listen to what you're saying?"

It took a moment for Kelsey to understand what her mother was getting at, but when she did she had to resist the urge to roll her eyes. What was the big deal? She'd spoken like an executive, her mind jumping first not to the human element but to corporate concerns. So what? She knew her words must have sounded harsh, but this was her reality.

Okay, in a sense, her mother was right. Maybe she had sounded a little cold and unfeeling. On the other hand, her mother lived in a whole different kind of world than Kelsey did. Doreen Tate could not begin to understand what it would be like to be in her daughter's shoes.

Kelsey took in a breath and was about to speak out in her own defense when Doreen cut her off to continue her lecture.

"When did your heart check out of the equation entirely and turn you into this, this automaton? This shell? I didn't raise you to be this way. I taught you to have compassion. I taught you to put others first, to care about their needs. Your whole life, I tried as hard as I could to help you understand the value of living a balanced life, to avoid the tunnel vision that a big-time business career can bring. I've seen it dozens of times in colleagues of your father's, and now I'm sitting here seeing it in you, and I can't believe I didn't recognize it before. I don't even know who you are right now. I love you, honey, but I do not know you. What could possibly have happened in your life to bring you to this?"

Doreen stood and turned away, busying herself at the sink as she angrily wiped away a few tears of her own. Stunned, Kelsey remained at the table, her heart pounding with guilt and grief and shame. Her mother was right. Somehow, in the past few years, she'd turned into exactly the kind of person she had never wanted to be.

Why? What *had* happened to bring her to this? Even as she asked herself that question, she already knew the answer.

Cole. Her breakup with Cole Thornton. Five years ago, she'd had at least some compassion, some selflessness, some sense of that balance that her mother had tried to instill in her. Kelsey had been so happy back then, loving her new career, dating a fantastic man, making big plans for the future. That future had been all about Cole, who was everything she'd ever wanted in a husband. Smart and sweet and funny and handsome and successful and attentive and considerate and loving, he was everything she'd ever dreamed of in a mate.

By the time things started to go wrong, they had already exchanged the "I love yous." They had already had the joking, flirting what-if conversations about how many kids they could see themselves having and where they would most like to live in the future and when might be the best time of year for a wedding.

Then, in the space of a few weeks, everything had fallen apart.

She didn't think about that period much anymore, but back then it had consumed her every waking thought. It was her investment in Lou's company that started it all, just one single stupid business deal that messed everything up. She knew she'd been the one to start the ball rolling by undercutting Cole's investment proposal with a better one. In her defense, the proposal he'd put together for Lou had been poorly done and extremely insubstantial, considering the data. At the time she'd known she could do far better, and so she did. Afterward, she told herself that Cole was too timid to be good at this job, that he wasn't visionary enough to spread his wings and really fly with it. Even Gloria had assured her that in offering Lou a better deal than Cole had she was just doing business as usual. After all, she couldn't go easy on a coworker just because she happened to be dating him.

But he hadn't seen it that way.

When her deal with Lou was announced and Cole realized what she'd done, he'd been devastated. To him, it was bad enough that she'd slipped in behind his back and stolen an investment opportunity he'd been actively pursuing. But the fact that she'd done it with neither warning nor apology had made it unacceptable. Adding fuel to the fire was the fact that she'd tossed out a few careless comments about the situation to the woman who had been her administrative assistant at the time. That woman had a big mouth, and before Kelsey knew it, things she'd said to her privately about Cole had been spread from one end of the company to the other. Of course she'd fired the woman soon after, but that had been small comfort. By then the damage had already been done.

When it was all over, Cole had ended not just his relationship with her but with the company as well. He broke up with her, quit his job, and walked out of her life completely. From what she heard, he'd even stopped going to the little church they had been attending together, though she could have told him not to bother. Once he was gone, she never went back there anyway.

Kelsey wished she could explain all of that to her mother, that she could help her understand how the loss of Cole from her life and the pain that came with it was the thing that had started her down the wrong road she'd been on ever since.

In the wake of her breakup with Cole, she had buried herself so deeply in her work that over time she had become this person she was now, one who could witness the gruesome death of a beloved friend—a tragedy of monumental proportions—and process it in terms of damage control.

This was not who she wanted to be.

Before Kelsey could articulate any of these thoughts, her mother surprised her by turning around and apologizing for her outburst.

"I'm sorry, Kelsey," she said, leaning her hip back against the counter and drying her hands on a towel. "We all have different coping mechanisms. You've been through a horrific trauma, and if you need to focus on the business side of the situation to get you through this, you have every right to do so. It's certainly understandable. I shouldn't have said anything."

Her eyes filling with fresh tears, Kelsey stood and went to her mother and wrapped her arms around her and told her that no, she was right. Everything she'd said was true. "I don't want to be this way, Mom. I really don't."

"Oh, honey," her mother cooed, once again stroking her hair. "Maybe this can be a wake-up call for you then, you know? One that helps you get back on track."

"Maybe."

The two women shared a long embrace, and when they pulled apart Kelsey excused herself to go repair her makeup. Once she'd fixed the damage and had a solid hold on her emotions, she emerged from the restroom and went in search of her father. She found him right where she'd expected, in what used to be the living room but now served as pretty much the extent of his limited world.

This space that used to be the very heart of the home was no longer a plush, inviting gathering place. Gone were the custom couches and the big wooden coffee tables and the Hubbardton lamps. Instead, now the decor centered on a hospital bed, a portable toilet, and an old man who could usually be found slumped in a corner in his wheelchair.

Refusing to think about all of that right now, Kelsey put on a brave smile, pushed the door open further, and leaned inside.

"Hi, Dad," she said, trying to keep her voice light.

He looked up to see her, his reaction subtle but definite, a shifting of the shoulders and a brightening in the face.

"Somebody's glad to see you," the aide said, giving her a warm smile.

"I'm glad to see him too," she replied, crossing the room and giving her father a big hug.

By the time she pulled away, the aide had discreetly left them alone, for which she was grateful. These days, it was hard enough to talk to her father about regular, day-to-day kinds of things, but harder still to do so when someone else was there. She couldn't imagine trying to have this particular conversation with an audience present.

She pulled up a chair to sit facing her father and asked how he was doing.

"Gloria," he mumbled in reply, tears filling his eyes.

Blinking back her own tears, Kelsey placed a comforting hand on his arm. "I know, Dad. It's just awful, isn't it?"

They sat together in silence for a long moment, both of them acknowledging the passing of their dear friend. Across the room the grandfather clock ticked loudly, the pendulum swinging back and forth, counting away the minutes of her day. Kelsey had never liked that clock, but at the moment something about its steady rhythm felt calming to her soul.

"Dad, I need to talk to you about something else," she said. "It's about the other bad thing that happened yesterday."

He grunted. "Liar liar man?" he replied, causing her to smile.

"Yes, the disruption by the man who yelled out 'Liar! Liar!' Listen, I've kind of looked into things and had some conversations, so I have a general picture of what that was all about. I know this matter has come up twice before. Is that correct?"

He managed a nod. "Cor-rect."

"And I believe it ended with a settlement the first time and some legal threats the next?"

He nodded again. So far, so good.

"Okay, then. I just wanted to ask if there's anything about this situation that I ought to know, anything I need to say or not say, you know? Do you remember much about the specifics? Can you give me any guidance here at all?"

Since her father's stroke, his speech was slow and often disjointed. Sometimes he seemed confused, but Kelsey wasn't sure if he was really lost temporarily or just couldn't string words together to express himself. Often she sensed frustration as he tried to get his thoughts across.

It also took a long time for him to respond, as if all input had to work its way through a faulty computer before it could kick back out on the other side. Breathing deeply, she practiced patience and waited for what he might say.

"Always thought..." he said slowly, and then he shrugged. "Dunno."

"Don't know what?"

He shrugged again. "Might be true."

She blinked, studying him.

"Might."

Kelsey narrowed her eyes.

"Wait a minute. What? What might be true?"

Her father shrugged. "Adele."

She thought for a moment.

"Are you saying Rupert's claims might be true, that Adele was actually her cousin Jocelyn just posing as Adele? Are you kidding me?"

"Can't prove. Settled."

"Adele's identity couldn't be proven or disproven, and that's why they were willing to sign a settlement? Is that what you're saying?"

He nodded.

"What about DNA testing? Did you try that?"

Her father blinked, trying to form an answer with his lips. Finally he blurted something that sounded like "mothers down to fathers." She took it to mean that there was some DNA complication because of the way the lineage played out. Then again, the science of DNA was growing more sophisticated all the time. Perhaps what couldn't be done five or ten years ago was perfectly doable now.

He let out a loud sigh and ran a hand over his face.

"I'm sorry, Dad. You're tired. I shouldn't wear you out."

"Sean's will," he said.

"Sean Brennan's will? He left everything to Adele, didn't he?"

Her father nodded, but tentatively, as though there was more to the story—which there certainly was. He went on, but his words were a bit garbled now. Kelsey leaned close.

"Settlement within."

She puzzled over that, repeating it back to him. "A settlement within? Within what? The firm, maybe?"

"Settlement," he said again. "With eee-un." He pulled his lips back and bared his teeth. "Eeeee-un."

She thought for a moment then said, "Ian? You reached a settlement with Ian."

Looking deeply relieved, he nodded.

Oh, great. Now they were caught in a loop. They had already covered this. "Right. Yes. I knew that, remember? I mentioned it a minute ago?"

He just stared at her, his jaw slack. Feeling bad for having snapped at him, she went with the repetition, hoping it might bring up other memories for him of that time. "So neither you nor Ian could prove anything conclusively about Adele's true identity, but there was enough of a question there that you offered the family some money to go away and keep quiet. A settlement. A payoff in exchange for a gag order—at least until Ian died and Rupert tried to stir things up again. Right?"

Nodding, Nolan seemed to be trying to say something—either "right" or "Rupert"—but finally gave up and mumbled instead, "Liar liar man."

Kelsey realized he was smiling, and she grinned at him in return. "That's right. Rupert's the liar liar man."

She had so much she wanted to learn, but she could tell she was quickly wearing her father out. "I know this isn't easy for you, Dad. I appreciate your trying."

He nodded, running a hand over his face again.

"Just one last question. It's about bonds, the bonds that were part of the legend of Adele. Do you know what I'm talking about?"

"Bonds," he repeated.

"Right. The bonds. Did Great-Grandma Adele ever actually have any bonds, or was that just a myth?"

He pursed his lips for a long moment, almost like he was trying to whistle. Finally, she realized he was attempting to make the sound of a "t." After a moment, he got it out. "True."

"It's true?" she asked, her pulse surging. "There actually were bonds, really valuable bonds, that Adele used to get the company through tough times?"

He nodded. "T-true."

"Did she use them all up or were there some left?"

He tried to answer but mostly sputtered in frustration.

"Sorry, Dad, let me try that again. Did Adele use the bonds all up?"

After a beat, "No."

"Are there any left?"

A longer pause. "Yes."

Sucking in a deep breath, Kelsey took a moment to let that word roll around in her mind. There had been bonds, yes. There still were bonds.

Yes.

CHAPTER
FOURTEEN

April 10, 1912

ADELE

W ithin an hour, all irritations and frustrations faded away in the excitement of boarding the ship. Adele couldn't believe she was actually stepping aboard the finished *Titanic* at last. For three years she and her fellow
citizens of Belfast had watched the vessel go from a steel skeleton on dry land
and then a shiny, floating shell on the water to a fully appointed ship here
at the White Star docks in England. And though their little group would be
staying in the ship's second-class cabins down on the F deck, she was excited
to learn upon boarding that for a short while they were welcome to tour the
upper portions of the ship if they desired, as apparently the first-class passengers would not be arriving for at least another hour.

They started by heading down to their staterooms to take a look. Adele
and Jocelyn eagerly took in every detail of the gorgeous ship as they went,
though the two men adopted an air of sophisticated indifference. Adele
found their attitude both amusing and irritating, knowing full well they had
to be as excited and impressed as she and Jocelyn were.

Truly, the ship was the most elegant thing Adele had ever seen. From the
oak-lined passageways to the well-stocked second-class library to the elegant second-class smoking room, Adele and Jocelyn were dumbfounded
and impressed by it all.

They especially loved their stateroom, once they found it, a small but
graciously appointed space with two beds bunked along the left wall, a

convertible sofa on the right, and in between a fold-up washbasin cabinet that the steward said would supply fresh water from a holding tank. The room also featured two mahogany wardrobes, each fitted with drawers and a mirror, and under the sidelight was a small but comfortable-looking upholstered chair. All in all, the room was quite impressive, far better than one might normally expect from second class. As the two girls stood in the doorway gazing in at it, Adele commented that they were the first passengers to ever use this berth.

"You're right," Jocelyn whispered reverentially. "What a historic moment for us both!"

They shared a smile. Many others would use this room over the coming years, but they could always say they had been the first.

"Ready for our tour?" Uncle Rowan asked, appearing behind them in the white-walled hallway. His room was on the same deck, not far from theirs. Apparently Tad was also on F deck, though his room was down a completely different corridor.

The four travelers made their way back upstairs and began their tour on the promenade deck, a first-class-only area that ran the entire length of the ship. As they were standing there admiring its length and appointments, they were joined by another gentleman, one Uncle Rowan seemed to have been expecting.

When he introduced the fellow as Mr. Neville Williams of Transatlantic Wireless, Adele realized instantly who he was. This was the man Rowan and Tad had met with in London the day before. Adele's father was extremely interested in investing in Mr. William's company, which was the reason he had sent a representative over to London in the first place. Tad Myers had crossed the ocean charged with the task of escorting Adele and Jocelyn and Rowan back to America, yes, but prior to that he was to meet with Mr. Williams, learn more about Transatlantic Wireless, and evaluate it as a potential investment on behalf of Brennan & Company. Uncle Rowan had attended that meeting along with Tad yesterday, and though the young American had dismissed the company as an unwise investment choice, Rowan hadn't seen things quite that way. He hadn't bought in as of last night, but as soon as Adele could get her uncle alone, she would ask for more details of this morning's "change in plans." She had a feeling that he'd slept on the matter and awakened this morning with a different intention, despite Tad's negative evaluation. She could only assume from Rowan's jubilant attitude and easy manner with Mr. Williams that a transaction had taken place that morning and he was now in possession of investment bonds from Transatlantic Wireless.

"Mr. Williams is a first-class passenger," Uncle Rowan explained to the girls now as he made the introductions, "but he has come aboard early just to give us our very own customized tour."

Soon their group of five set off, and Adele realized that she liked the man right away. Mr. Williams seemed a true British gentleman, yet not one mired in convention. He was also quite knowledgeable about the ship and made for a fascinating tour guide indeed.

As they moved through first class past the darkly paneled male-only smoking room and then the more feminine reading-and-writing room, conversation between the three men turned to the business model of the White Star line, which involved catering to passengers' growing demand for beauty and luxury.

"And this room is the perfect example of that," Mr. Williams said when they reached the first-class lounge. "It is considered by many to be the finest room afloat."

Looking around, Adele could believe it. The magnificent space, with its gold and green decor, intricately carved oak paneling, and large marble fireplace, reminded her of pictures she had seen of the palace of Versailles. There was even a cupola in the ceiling, fitted with intricately cut glass panels that allowed a gentle illumination of the entire space.

As they continued down to a lower deck, Adele decided to insert herself into the topic and give her own opinion on the matter. Like many in Belfast, she had read extensively on the various issues besetting the White Star Line and their multimillion dollar investments in *Titanic* and her sister ship, *Olympic*. And though the company repeatedly touted its emphasis on luxury, she felt that behind closed doors their real emphasis had been to tap into the ever-growing third-class-passenger market.

She said as much to their little group now, adding that while she knew that White Star's public emphasis was indeed on luxury, their bottom line was probably far more dependent on plain old steerage.

When Adele finished, she realized that everyone in their group had grown silent, all eyes on her. After pausing to give her a piteous smirk, Tad continued on his way down the staircase. Jocelyn smiled politely and kept going as well.

"You are completely correct on that, young lady," Mr. Williams said to Adele with a broad smile. "From what I understand, steerage class offers the best return per passenger per mile traveled. Jolly good of you to pick up on that. Your uncle told me you had a head for business."

At that moment Mr. Williams became Adele's favorite passenger aboard the entire ship.

Their group continued the tour with a visit to a Turkish bath, a swimming pool, and a squash court, and then they rode the lift back up to B deck so they could climb the famous grand staircase while it was still open to them. Once they were up on the boat deck, they looked at the large gymnasium there. The equipment inside was varied and interesting, and included machines for horse riding, rowing, bicycle racing, weight lifting, massaging—even camel riding. Jocelyn seemed fascinated by them all, but Adele just kept wondering why such machines were necessary when a person could far more easily just go outside and take a walk.

The final stop on their tour was the most important, Mr. Williams explained, and in fact was the main reason he had chosen to sail on this ship. He led them forward along the first-class promenade, and when they reached a low barrier that separated the passengers from the ship's crew area, they were met by a young officer. He brought them through the gate and into the nearby deckhouse. There, they walked down the corridor until they came to the Marconi operating room, which housed the ship's wireless equipment.

"As you know," Mr. Williams said proudly, "our company developed a major component of what you are about to see here. I predict that someday we will all be communicating via the wireless."

The area was bigger than Adele had expected and was comprised of three separate rooms, including one that was soundproof to house the noisy equipment.

"This technology is simply amazing, and *Titanic* is one of the first ships to be fitted with a rotary spark gap. This greatly reduces the transmission jamming problems on older units. It's our technology that makes that improvement possible—and someday soon we hope to eliminate all jamming issues entirely."

Mr. Williams pointed out the workers in the room: Mr. Phillips, the senior operator, and Mr. Bride, the junior operator. Though they each gave a polite wave, the men were fast at work and far too busy to stop and chat.

"As you can see," Mr. Williams pointed out, "these two are sending and receiving messages, status updates, weather reports, and much more."

Mr. Williams thanked the men for their time and they all turned to go. As they were leaving, Adele saw the posted price chart for sending telegrams—twelve shillings and sixpence for the first ten words, and nine pence per word thereafter—and then took note of the paid passenger messages that had already started piling up prior to departure. With a wink to Mr. Williams, she said, "That's a nice revenue stream if I've ever seen one."

Grinning conspiratorially, he nodded. "White Star knows exactly what they're doing. Better yet, half of these two men's salaries is being paid for by the Marconi company, so personnel costs are particularly reasonable."

Mr. Williams concluded the tour by bringing them back to the passenger area of the ship. They parted ways with him there, and though Adele was sorry they weren't all traveling in the same class together, her disappointment lifted a bit when she learned they might be able to spend some time with him during the voyage anyway.

Adele's step was light as the four of them headed back down to their own section of the ship. They settled into their staterooms, and then shortly before noon they heard the great steam whistles blow. Quickly, they joined in with their fellow passengers and moved up to the second-class Promenade. There they stood among the suspended lifeboats, leaning out from the deck to watch as five tugboats chugged into place, preparing to move the ship from the dock sideways and out toward the river. There was excitement on board the ship, of course, but out on the quay, which seemed to be packed with thousands of well-wishers, people seemed equally thrilled. As the massive vessel finally began to move away from the dock, everyone waved and cheered.

And though Adele and Jocelyn didn't know a soul ashore, soon they found themselves joining in, enthusiastically waving and cheering as well. The ship's next stop would be Cherbourg, France, and so with that in mind they bid a fond goodbye to England's shores, hearts filled with both joy and loss, comforted by thoughts of the wonderful adventure they knew lay ahead.

CHAPTER
FIFTEEN

Kelsey scooted closer, looking intently into her father's face. "Do you have these bonds, Dad? Do you know where they are?"

He stared at her for a long time, and then slowly his eyes filled with tears. "Gloria," he whispered.

"Gloria?" she asked. "Gloria had the bonds?"

He couldn't seem to answer her question, so she tried again.

"Did Gloria *spend* the bonds? Did she cash them in?"

More silence. He was looking very tired.

"How about this, Dad. Was Gloria the one in *charge* of the bonds? Like, in charge of their safekeeping?"

At that Nolan's face lit up, and he gave a definite nod. "The wonder!" he cried.

"The what?"

"The wonder."

"Wonder? Are you saying 'the wonder'?"

He nodded. "Wonder," he whispered. "The wonder."

Sitting back, she tried to figure out what he was telling her. "I don't know what that means, Dad. Does it have something to do with Gloria?"

He just stared at her, again whispering, "The wonder."

After that he closed his eyes. Trying to make sense of it all, Kelsey sat quietly as she rolled his words and phrases around in her head. What she really needed to do was talk to someone who could fill in the many blanks in the story. All of this stuff had happened long before Walter even worked at the company, but she realized he might know enough about it that he could be of some help anyway.

Kelsey was about to wrap things up with her father when his head slowly tilted forward and a soft snore escaped from his lips. Smiling tenderly, she smoothed out the cuff of his sleeve and tucked an errant lock of hair away from his forehead.

Then she kissed him gently on the cheek and left him there to rest.

She found her mother out in the courtyard, snipping away at a bare, spindly hydrangea bush that had been allowed to get out of control. As she worked, Kelsey told her about the conversation she'd just had. Unfortunately, Doreen could add no additional insights and had no idea what he might have meant by "the wonder."

"I'm finished here for now," Doreen said, stepping back from the bush and dropping the last of her clippings into a bag. "I think I'll go check on your father myself. Will you be staying for lunch? I could heat up last night's leftover soup. Yvette made a saffron mussel bisque."

Kelsey was tempted. The woman who cooked for her parents was a wonder in the kitchen, and her specialty was rich, aromatic soups. But with no time to linger today, she would have to take a rain check. "Thanks, no, I should get rolling soon. I just need to make a call first."

"Okay, well, I'll be in the living room if you need me." With that, Doreen headed into the house as Kelsey pulled out her phone and dialed the office. Once the automated system answered, she typed in Walter's extension, and as she waited for him, she moved over to a sunny spot and settled herself down on the wide, flat brick rim of a raised flower bed.

The sun felt good on her arms and face, and she closed her eyes and tilted her head back to take it in. By the time she heard Walter's voice on the other end of the line, it took a moment for her to snap back to attention.

"Hey, Walter, it's Kelsey. How are things there today? Has everyone heard the news?"

He cleared his throat. "About Gloria? Yes, I decided to tackle that head-on with a full staff meeting first thing. Most of them had already heard but didn't have many details. There were lots of questions and concerns. As you can imagine, some people in the office aren't taking it well."

"I'm sure."

He went on to explain that the police had closed off the back half of the fifth floor, and that the people with offices in that section had been relocated to meeting rooms on the fourth. He said that Detective Hargrove had set up shop in the Human Resources department and was bringing people in individually to question them.

Kelsey was a bit taken aback. They were still actively investigating? Swallowing hard, she said, "I'm guessing that's not standard procedure with a suicide. Does this mean they've decided Gloria was…" her voice trailed off. Somehow, she just couldn't bring herself to say the word.

"The police still haven't said one way or the other," Walter answered quickly. "They're playing this all very close to the vest."

"I wonder why."

"I don't know. Hargrove is a reasonable enough fellow, but maybe that's just the way he operates. On the one hand, it's frustrating, because I'd like to be kept apprised of the situation. On the other hand, if he's not even telling me, that means it's not likely he'll go blabbing things to the media either."

"That's good, at least."

Kelsey heard a soft buzzing and looked up to see a pair of bumblebees hovering around a still-dormant azalea bush.

"As for the employees," Walter continued, "I gave everyone the option of taking the rest of the day off, and a few took me up on it. We also have a counselor coming in around noon for anyone who might feel the need to talk."

"Good move. What are you doing about Gloria's clients?"

"Well, the police confiscated her computer, but she was tied in directly with the server, so that hasn't posed any serious problems as of yet. Right now Yanni is going through her active case files and divvying those up among the staff. Ordinarily, I would have funneled most of them straight to you, but considering the situation I knew that wouldn't be an option."

Kelsey thanked him, grateful that he realized she wasn't up to it—and might not be for a while. First thing this morning, she'd left a message on Sharon's phone telling her to reschedule all of her appointments for the next few days. At some point during that time, she would have to sit down with her own account list and start making calls, just to touch base and reassure all of her clients that things were fine and it was business as usual at Brennan & Tate. But she couldn't even attempt to do that until she felt sure she could pull it off. She had to sound as though she actually meant it.

"Have you talked to your father yet?" Walter asked. "I know I should go over there and tell him about all of this personally, but I'm still tied up doing damage control."

"Not to worry," she replied, brushing a fallen leaf from her skirt. "I'm at my parents' house right now, and my dad and I just had a nice long talk. He's devastated, of course, but mentally speaking he's having a very lucid day." She went on to explain about their discussion of the whole Rupert Brennan situation. "Believe it or not, Walter, this conflict goes way back, to the early nineties. Only that time, the person making the claims about Adele being an imposter was Rupert's father, *Ian* Brennan."

"I can stop you right there," he replied. "I had a long conversation with our lawyers last night. They had a big file on the matter, which they photo-copied and sent over first thing this morning. I've been reading through it for the past hour."

Kelsey breathed a deep sigh of relief, feeling stupid that it hadn't occurred to her to get this info via the lawyer route.

"So what have you learned?" she asked, shifting to a more comfortable position. "Do you know what kind of 'proof' Rupert Brennan thinks he has?"

"Yep. It's all in here."

"Oh, thank goodness. Do you have time right now to tell me about it?"

"I can take a few minutes." He rustled some papers and then said, "Just to be clear, you know the basic Brennan family history, right? That around the turn of the century Sean Brennan left Ireland and came to America. His wife Beatrice and three-year-old daughter Adele stayed behind, though he planned to bring them over once he was established here."

"Of course. Sean was my great-great-grandfather. He came over in 1896, I believe."

"That's what it says here. Anyway, it took a few years, but once they were finally making plans for his wife and daughter to come over, Beatrice con-tracted diphtheria and died. That left six-year-old Adele alone in Ireland with no mother and an absentee father. Rather than bring her over here by her-self, where Sean would have to hire a caretaker for her, the decision was made that she would be taken in by Sean's brother, Rowan, and his sister-in-law, Oona, who lived in Belfast. They would raise her along with their own two children, a daughter named Jocelyn, also six, and a toddler named Quincy."

Walter wasn't telling Kelsey anything she didn't already know, but it was still helpful to hear things laid out so systematically. He went on to describe Sean's progress as a businessman in the States, how with help from a few afflu-ent members of the Irish community he had landed a low-level job at a Man-hattan bank. He had an affinity for numbers and money and quickly worked his way up to management. In 1904, he left the bank to open his own investment firm, Brennan & Company. With the strategy of primarily investing in forward-thinking businessmen such as Edison and Marconi, he made good fairly quickly. Once Marconi won the Nobel Prize in 1909, Sean wisely began channeling more and more funds toward wireless technologies, and most of his investments began paying off nicely.

Of particular interest was a new start-up in England called Transatlantic Wireless, Ltd., which manufactured an integral component of the Marconi system. Transatlantic Wireless was looking to drum up substantial funds for the expansion of their factory, and Sean learned that one of the founders of the company, a man named Neville Williams, was planning a trip to the United States in April 1912 to meet with potential investors. He had chosen to cross over on the maiden voyage of a brand-new ship, *Titanic*, because it would actually be using the newest Marconi wireless system on board.

The more Sean learned about Transatlantic Wireless, the more he wanted to get in on the ground floor. Eager to beat out other investors, he made the decision to preempt Neville's trip to the States by sending a representative to London to meet with the man there first, before he even left London.

Around that same time, Sean had been communicating with Oona and Rowan about Adele. She was nineteen by then, smart and pretty but with few satisfactory prospects in Ireland either for marriage or work. It seemed the right time to get her out, especially because of the rumblings of trouble throughout the British Isles and the flaring up of issues and conflicts throughout Europe that would eventually lead to the first world war. Sean urged all of them to come, but Oona had no interest in leaving her homeland. She did, however, agree that Jocelyn might do well to make the move along with her cousin. In the end, the plan was for Rowan, Adele, and Jocelyn to come to America. Adele would stay, Rowan would visit for a few weeks, and then he would head back home, and Jocelyn would make the decision as to whether to stay in America with her cousin and uncle or go back to Ireland with her father.

Neville Williams encouraged Sean to book passage for his family on the maiden voyage of *Titanic* too. He said he would get together with them on the voyage to show them the new wireless technology in action. Thus, Sean timed his representative's trip to England just prior to the dates for that voyage. The man was to meet with Rowan and Neville at the Transatlantic Wireless office on April 9, 1912, in London regarding investing in the company, and then he and Rowan and the girls would sail back to America together on *Titanic*, which was to sail the next day.

Eventually, the plans were all set. As Rowan, Adele, and Jocelyn prepared for their trip first to London and then on to Southampton, Sean made the decision of who among his employees would make the voyage to England to serve as his representative. He finally decided on a young upstart named Tad Myers. Though Tad was relatively new with Brennan & Company, he was ambitious and eager to take the assignment on.

All seemed to go as planned—up to the moment *Titanic* hit an iceberg and sank in less than three hours. Though Tad and Adele each made it onto a lifeboat, Rowan and Jocelyn did not. They perished in the sinking, and their bodies were never found.

Once the ship that rescued the survivors, *Carpathia*, reached New York, Sean welcomed the daughter he hadn't seen for sixteen years and grieved with her as well. Though she'd been devastated by the tragedy, his hope was that in time she would recover and make a new life for herself here.

What he didn't expect was the news given to him by Tad Myers one year after the sinking. According to Tad, the woman calling herself Adele Brennan was lying. She wasn't Adele at all, Tad insisted, but was instead Adele's *cousin*, Jocelyn Brennan, just pretending to be Adele. Tad claimed that Adele had died the night *Titanic* sank and that for some unknown reason, once Jocelyn realized her cousin was dead, she'd taken the opportunity to assume her place.

Kelsey interrupted Walter to clarify. "Wait a minute. You're telling me these claims of Jocelyn posing as Adele trace all the way back to nineteen thirteen?"

"That's right. Sean had trouble believing it, but this guy Tad put up such a stink that he finally ended up sending Adele away to school at Swarthmore while he tried to sort things out."

"Why did it take a whole year for him to say something?"

"Apparently, he claims he kept waiting for her to admit the truth herself. She had told him she would but never did, so finally he spoke up."

"So what happened then?" Kelsey asked breathlessly.

"That's where things get a little muddy," Walter replied. "It seems that Sean decided the best way to answer the question was to write to Oona over in Ireland and ask her. In his letter, he laid out the situation and enclosed a photo of the young woman who was claiming to be Adele. He asked Oona to tell him whether the person in that photo really was Adele or if it was, instead, Jocelyn."

"Clever thinking," Kelsey said, heading back into the house. The wind had picked up and she was feeling chilly, plus she wanted to find pen and paper and once again attempt to jot down a family tree.

"In the letter Sean wrote to Oona," Walter continued, "he said that if it turned out that it *was* a photo of Jocelyn, he would of course confront her about the situation but would do so with sensitivity, considering the trauma she'd been through. He pledged continued financial and familial support for the young woman regardless, whether she ended up being his daughter or his niece. He also promised to continue sending money over to Ireland in support of Oona and Quincy, especially now that Rowan had passed away."

"Does the file have a copy of that letter?" Kelsey asked, stepping into the kitchen and pulling the door shut behind her.

"Yes. It also has a copy of the photo. It's an old black-and-white of a somber-looking young Adele, posed on the front steps of what I think is the old Brennan house on Liberty Street."

Rooting through the kitchen drawers, Kelsey finally came up with pen and paper. She sat at the table, and as they continued to talk, she began again an attempt to sketch out the Brennan family tree.

"So all we need is Oona's response to settle this whole matter. What did she write back and say?"

She could hear more rustling of papers on Walter's end as he told her, "Well, see, therein lies the problem. Oona saved this letter and photo that Sean sent to her, and it ended up getting passed down to Quincy with her papers. When Quincy died, it came to the attention of his son, Ian, and that was when he first realized that Adele's identity had been questioned. Call it exhibit A."

"Exhibit A? Are you saying this is the proof Rupert was talking about, the proof that Adele was an imposter?"

"This is the proof Rupert's father had, yes. But by the time Rupert came back and tried again himself after his father died, he had also managed to unearth a sworn affidavit from Tad Myers in which he officially made those claims against Adele."

"But all this letter does is raise the question. It doesn't give any answers. It doesn't prove anything."

"I know."

"So what did Oona write in response? *That's* the letter that matters."

"Yes, it is. Unfortunately, that letter no longer exists."

Kelsey groaned.

"It's not that they didn't try to find it. This report details the extensive search the attorneys made through the company's archives and through Sean's personal papers, but Oona's response letter was never found. They concluded that Sean must have gotten it, read it, and at some point thrown it out without thinking—or maybe destroyed it intentionally, depending on what it said."

"Wow. That's not good. So where does the report go from there? Were they able to find any sort of proof of her true identity?"

"In a sense. Hold on a sec." He rustled around some more, and as Kelsey waited she jotted in the various names she could think of for her tree, adding lines to show how everyone was related.

"Here it is," Walter said. "I'll read it to you. 'It is the conclusion of this researcher that the woman claiming to be Adele Brennan was most likely telling the truth. This conclusion is based primarily on two points of evidence. One, company records show that a Mr. Tad Myers left Brennan & Company approximately six weeks after the date on Sean Brennan's letter to his sister Oona asking her to identify the woman in the photo. The assumption is that Oona wrote back confirming Adele's identity, which thus showed that Tad Myers had been the one who was lying. After he left, Myers disappeared for a while but then it was reported that he moved to California. Three years later, he contracted pneumonia and died at the age of twenty-seven.'"

"Could he have been paid off to keep quiet too?" Kelsey asked, worrying about how far back this conspiracy went.

"It doesn't say." He resumed his reading of the report as she worked on her diagram. "'Two, the issue of Adele's identity seems never to have come under question again. See attached documents for numerous references over the next twenty-six years, until Sean Brennan's death, where he repeatedly referred to Adele as his daughter. He died in nineteen thirty-eight, and she inherited his entire estate.'"

"That seems pretty clear to me. It was Adele's word against Tad's, and she was the one vindicated in the end."

"You could interpret it that way."

"So why the settlement, Walter? Their 'proof' doesn't seem all that conclusive to me. Why did my father give them money?"

"Because it was cheaper than going to court, for one thing. But primarily he did it to keep them quiet. You know as well as I do that much of this company's cachet hinges on the 'legend' of Adele, starting with her being a *Titanic* survivor. Mess with all that, and you might end up messing with the bottom line of Brennan & Tate."

"But if Rupert's father couldn't prove his claims…"

"Don't be naive, Kelsey. Do you think that matters? Just having the question raised in the first place is enough. In the eyes of the world, Adele would be convicted without a trial. Besides, if it came to a trial, your father didn't really have any more solid proof than they did, and it is too risky to put a case like that before a jury."

Kelsey knew he was right. The decision to pay them off, as infuriating as that must have been, had probably been the right one.

"Any idea what Tad's motivation was for lying about it in the first place?"

"No, but one could speculate. Perhaps he did seek some sort of payoff. Or maybe he was threatened by Adele's ambition or her business acumen. He was a rising star at Brennan & Tate before she came along. Maybe he just didn't like all the attention she stole away from him, especially the attention of her father."

"Could be."

"That would be my guess, but who can say, really?"

Kelsey hated that they didn't know why Tad had done it. It's not as though they could go back in time and ask the man himself. If only Adele had addressed this situation in her memoir! But Kelsey had read that book cover to cover a dozen times, and from what she could recall, the man who came to England as her father's representative had shown up in all of about one sentence, maybe two at the most.

For some reason, Adele had chosen to omit this part of her story. Consequently, the facts of what really happened between the two of them back then were anybody's guess.

CHAPTER
SIXTEEN

M oving on, Kelsey asked Walter if he could explain to her the basis for Rupert's claims. "I mean, why does he think they are owed some money? He said something yesterday about this having to do with a will?"

"Yes, with Sean's will, actually. Hold on."

As she waited, Kelsey finished her sketch as best she could then picked it up and studied it. It read:

```
                    Father ——— Mother
                       |            |
         Oona ——— Rowan       Sean ——— Beatrice
            |                         |
  Wife ——— Quincy    Jocelyn    Adele ——— Edwin
     |                                 |
Wife ——— Ian                    Jonah ——— Mary
   |                                     |
Rupert   Rhonda —— Husband        Nolan ——— Doreen
             |                             |
        Kid      Kid              Kelsey      Matt
```

"All right, got it," Walter said through the phone. "In his will, Sean left everything, quote, 'to my living descendants, and if I have no living descendants, to my brother, Rowan, or, if he is no longer living, to Rowan's descendants.'"

Kelsey had him read it again, only this time she traced her finger along the family tree as he spoke. She still didn't understand how Adele's true identity could have made any difference, but then she traced it out again, this time pretending that Adele had died on *Titanic* and Jocelyn was the one who lived. In that case, Sean would not have had any living descendants, so everything would have gone to Rowan's descendants instead. "Walter, was Oona still alive by the time Sean died?"

"Uh…let me see…no. Oona died in nineteen twenty-three."

"Okay. So if we know Oona was no longer living and we pretend that Adele was no longer living, then according to Sean's will, everything would have gone to Rowan and Oona's descendants. That would mean half to Jocelyn and half to Quincy, right?"

"Correct."

Kelsey closed her eyes. "So if Adele was not really Adele but was instead Jocelyn, she would have received only half of Sean's estate, not the whole thing. When she died and her fortune passed down from her to Grandpa Jonah, he should have received only her half, not the whole thing. Right?"

"Yes," Walter replied, "Half was definitely hers to give. But if she was Jocelyn pretending to be Adele, then the other half should not have gone to her. It should have gone to Quincy, and from Quincy down to Ian, and from Ian down to Rupert and Rhonda. That's the money they want, the money they say is owed them. If Adele died on that ship on April fifteenth, nineteen twelve, then they are correct. They should have received half of Sean's estate when he died. If Adele—the real Adele—lived to the ripe old age of ninety-six and died in her sleep of natural causes, which is what you and I believe happened, then they are incorrect and are not owed a penny. Does it make sense now?"

"It does." She took a deep breath and blew it out slowly. "I appreciate your taking the time to explain all this to me. It's complicated, but I think I get it."

"Good."

"Just one more question, and then I have something to tell you about."

"All right, but we need to wrap this up. I have a meeting in a few minutes."

"Sure. I'm just wondering where DNA fits in with all of this. Aren't there

ways now to test different descendants from the same family line and figure out if and how they are related? Seems to me we should be able to test
Rupert and test me and then from that information know if his claims are
true or not."

"I asked one of the lawyers about DNA testing last night. According to
him, it wouldn't help in this case because of the way DNA is passed down
through the sexes from one generation to the next. In this situation, he said
the most DNA would be able to prove is whether or not you and Rupert
share a common ancestor—which we already know you do. The specifics
of who that common ancestor is can't be determined. That would take an
unbroken female line or an unbroken male line, such as mother to daughter
to daughter or father to son to son, but you don't have that. Jocelyn had no
sisters to trace through."

Kelsey exhaled slowly, her shoulders sagging. Walter asked her to hold on
for a moment, and when he came back on the line he apologized but said that
the people had arrived for his meeting and he needed to go.

"I understand, but I just have one more thing, real quick, about the bonds."

"The bonds Rupert referred to yesterday?"

"Yes. You and Lou told me that the bonds were just a myth, but I asked
my dad point-blank if they ever actually existed and he said yes, they did.
Better than that, I asked him if there are still any left, and again he said yes."

She expected Walter to express shock or elation at that news, but instead
he merely gave a soft grunt so she continued, explaining that according to
her father, Gloria had been the caretaker of the bonds. "I asked him where
they were stored, and he kept saying something that sounded like 'the wonder.' Do have any idea what he meant?"

"'The wonder'? Never heard of it."

"He repeated it several times. I'm almost certain that's what he was saying. The wonder."

Walter was silent for a long moment. "Listen, Kelsey, I don't mean to be
hurtful, but I know it hasn't been easy for you to accept the, uh, reality of
your father's condition. He says a lot of odd things, most of them nonsense.
From what I understand, that's part and parcel with a stroke."

Kelsey clenched her teeth. She knew what Walter was saying, but she also
knew her father well enough to know when he was spouting nonsense and
when he was fully lucid. Just a little while ago, in the living room, he had
been utterly, completely lucid.

"Anyway," Walter said, "thanks for calling in, and I'm glad to know you're doing okay. The PR team is here now, so I really do need to go."

Just the mention of public relations made her want to shudder. "I hate to ask this, but do you need me in that meeting?"

"No, though I appreciate the offer. As you can imagine, our PR strategy now has to do a complete one eighty. Just yesterday we were beating the drums far and wide to proclaim the name of 'Tate' from the rooftops. Now, the *last* thing we need is to reinforce the connection between you and your great-grandmother and this company. I'm sorry, but you're going to have to stay away completely. I don't see what choice we have right now."

Though Kelsey didn't exactly appreciate the way he'd phrased it, she knew what he was saying. It was the same issue she'd had to explain to her brother last night, that the fallout from Rupert's public outcry was going to have a huge impact on the company's bottom line. A besmirching of the good name of Adele Brennan Tate, even if unfounded, was the same thing as a besmirching of the company that carried her name. And the more the name of Kelsey Tate was promoted, the more people were reminded of that connection.

They ended their call, and then Kelsey went in search of her mother. She found her in the living room, seated beside Nolan's wheelchair, almost as if they were sitting together on the couch the way they used to. When Kelsey entered the room, her mother was reading to her dad from a book, an old favorite of his that Kelsey quickly recognized.

She told her parents that she needed to go but for her mom not to get up, she would see herself out. Crossing the room, she gave them each a peck on the cheek, but then, as she was standing there chatting with her mother for just a moment longer, her father suddenly spoke.

"Proud."

Both women turned to look at him.

"What did you say, dear?" Doreen asked.

He didn't reply right away, but then Kelsey realized that his eyes were riveted to the new pin on her lapel, the golden "Q" with the diamond center that had been given to her by Lou.

"Proud," he said again, the corners of his mouth turning up into a crooked smile.

Fresh tears immediately filled her eyes.

"Thanks, Dad," she whispered, trying to blink them away. "Lou gave it to me this morning. He said that you gave one to him years ago, so now he was giving one to me." She was about to add that she wished her father could have been there at Brennan & Tate for the ceremony, but considering how the whole event had unraveled so disastrously, she realized now it was a good thing he hadn't come after all.

Once the pin had been called to her attention, Doreen complimented it as well, but Kelsey could tell that her mother didn't really get it. She seemed to think that the significant thing here was the pin itself. Only her father understood that what really mattered was what that pin represented.

In the past, Kelsey and her dad had shared many a work-related victory, something they usually met with a high five and a hearty "Way to go!" Missing those moments so badly she could feel an ache deep in her chest, Kelsey knelt down beside his chair and held up her open palm just a few inches away.

"Can you believe it, Dad? I finally made it into the Quarter Club."

It was a struggle, but finally he managed to raise a trembling hand and press it against hers. "Waaaay," he said, which was all he could manage to get out. It was enough.

"Yeah, way to go, huh?" she whispered.

Then, with a last goodbye, she stood and walked out of the room as quickly as she could, somehow managing to hold in her sobs until she had gathered her things and made it all the way outside.

CHAPTER
SEVENTEEN

Kelsey went to a bench on the corner of the next block, sat down, and allowed herself to cry. Though her sadness was bubbling up from deep inside, hers were silent tears, and not a single person who passed by even noticed. Or perhaps they did but pretended not to.

Once she'd gotten control of herself, Kelsey headed to a deli on Lexington and went into the restroom to put herself back together again as best she could. After that she bought an egg salad sandwich and a bottle of water then made her way to the subway entrance and took it straight down the island, all the way to Wall Street. The subway ride took almost half an hour, but from there it was a quick, two-minute walk to the office.

As she drew closer, she looked up ahead for the sight of any reporters or photographers hovering outside the building, but the coast looked clear. Once inside, she saw that Ephraim was manning the front desk, but at the moment he was busy with someone, so Kelsey just gave him a wave and continued on to the elevator.

Up on the fourth floor, Sharon looked surprised to see her but also somewhat relieved. Kelsey invited her into her office, shut the door, and asked how things were going. Though Kelsey was never one to congregate around the water cooler, she managed to stay up on all the office scuttlebutt via the shrewd eyes and ears of her ever-alert executive assistant.

Sharon shared all that had been happening—the announcement, the dramatics, the shuffling around of office space—but she didn't tell Kelsey anything she hadn't already learned from Walter. When she was finished, they spent a few minutes going over the calls that had come in during the morning and the various appointments Sharon had managed to shuffle around for the next few days. After that, Kelsey said that she'd be working in her office for a while and that she didn't want to be disturbed.

"You got it, Chief," Sharon replied, rising to go. "Anybody who tries to get in here will have to go through me."

Once she was alone, Kelsey turned on her computer, but rather than logging in as herself, she wanted to try going in as Gloria. According to Walter, though the actual hardware of Gloria's computer had been removed by the police, virtually anything of importance would still be on the server. And though she wasn't even sure what she was hoping to find, she just wanted to poke around a little bit to see if anything unusual jumped out at her.

Last month Gloria had been out with a bad cold for almost a week but had called Kelsey repeatedly for help with various matters that required her to sign in under Gloria's name. She still remembered the password, 5tgbNHY6, because of how easily it typed out in a line straight down the keyboard and back up again. Her hope was that it hadn't changed since then. The IT department made everyone on the system go to a new password each month, but perhaps Gloria's reset cycle was different from hers.

No such luck. Kelsey tried it once but her entry was rejected with the dreaded response, *Invalid Password.* She considered trying a few guesses but didn't dare because she knew the system would lock her out completely after two more tries. Instead, she called the extension for Yanni, the EA Gloria shared with Walter, hoping to get the password from her. Yanni didn't answer, however, so rather than leaving a message, Kelsey just hung up and headed upstairs to Gloria's office herself on the off chance she might find it there, scribbled on a piece of paper or something. The woman wasn't big on technology and tended to cling to old habits.

The door to Gloria's office was closed. When Kelsey swung it open, she was startled to see Yanni there, leaning over the desk, her long, black hair hanging in a straight, glossy sheet. She straightened, quickly dropping her hands to her sides.

"Yes?"

Kelsey explained what she needed, but Yanni apologized, saying she wasn't privy to Gloria's password.

"Any idea where I could get it?" Kelsey asked, her eyes taking in the space where Gloria's computer used to be. The polished desktop was bare now except for the phone, an empty inbox, and a small potted plant.

To her core, Kelsey could feel the void of what was missing from this room—not just the computer, but Gloria herself. Standing there, Kelsey tried to picture her mentor sitting at the desk, inviting her in or offering some advice. But slowly that image began to morph into something else entirely.

Gloria's purple face. Gloria's limp body hanging from a cord.

Dead.

Suddenly dizzy, afraid she might faint, Kelsey gripped the door frame. Yanni must have seen that something was wrong, because she jumped forward to help Kelsey over to Gloria's desk chair, where she sat.

"Are you okay?"

"I think I just need to sit here a minute," Kelsey said, pressing a hand to her forehead and closing her eyes. After a long moment, the dizziness seemed to pass. Once it did, she was left feeling a little embarrassed.

"I'm sorry. I guess it just hit me that she's really gone. Something about seeing her empty desk, you know?"

Yanni nodded, assuring her that it was perfectly understandable. She looked as if she were about to say something else when the sound of Walter's voice came ringing from down the hall, calling Yanni's name. She excused herself and then dashed from the room gracefully despite her three-inch heels, the magenta scarf artfully draped around her neck flowing behind her as she went.

It wasn't until she was gone that Kelsey realized the woman's dark eyes had been red and swollen. Though the relationship she had shared with Gloria hadn't been nearly as chummy as the one Kelsey and Sharon had, the two women certainly had a mutual respect for each other. It wasn't surprising that Yanni would mourn Gloria's passing.

They all would, each in their own way.

Kelsey was feeling better, so she began to snoop around a little, opening drawers and gently rifling through their contents, looking for some notepad or scrap of paper that might contain Gloria's current password. She couldn't help but notice that Gloria's sticky notes and paper clips and other supplies were much more neatly organized than the jumble in her own drawers downstairs. But the only pads of paper she found were completely blank, stacked in the bottom drawer beside a small tray of neatly-labeled keys. *Washroom. Display case. Supply closet.*

Pulse surging, Kelsey checked the tags on every key, hoping against hope that one might read *The Wonder*. No such luck, but as she was going through them it struck her that Gloria was the caretaker of many things around here. It made sense that she would have been the one in charge of storing the bonds as well.

I'm sorry for taking what wasn't mine, her suicide text had said.

Was it possible that she had taken something that had been in her charge? Was it possible she had taken the bonds?

Refusing even to consider it, Kelsey put the thought out of her mind and continued her search. The only other place she could think of to look for paper was underneath the telephone, where Gloria always kept her "scribble pad." To Kelsey's surprise, when she lifted up the large, multi-lined office phone, the pad was right there where it always was. The police must have missed it when they took away Gloria's things as part of their investigation.

It probably didn't matter anyway. It wasn't as though Gloria used it for writing down important information. She just liked to doodle and jot down notes to herself whenever she talked on the phone. Kelsey doubted she would have written her password there, but she skimmed the pages just in case.

She didn't see any likely candidates but pocketed the pad anyway, partly for sentimental reasons and partly so she could take a closer look at it later for any clues to Gloria's odd behavior.

Back downstairs, Kelsey stopped at Sharon's desk on the way to her own office and asked if she would call the IT department to get Gloria's password. A few minutes later, she was scanning through the scribble pad more slowly this time when Sharon buzzed her and said that IT wouldn't give it to her without permission from Walter.

Kelsey grunted in frustration. "Fine. Can you take care of that for me, please? I know he's in a big meeting right now, but tell Yanni to interrupt him. It's important and it'll only take a second."

"Sure. I'll get back to you."

Kelsey clicked off the phone, wishing such a simple request didn't have to be so complicated. The thing was, most people in the company used passwords that were sequential in some way, just to help them remember month to month what their passwords were. But what was sequential to 5tgbNHY6?

Suddenly, on a hunch, she turned to the computer screen and decided to take a guess, knowing that would still leave one try before the system locked her out. Instead of typing 5tgbNHY6, Kelsey tried shifting her finger over one row. She typed 6yhnMJU7 and pressed enter. After a beat, the screen came to life.

Welcome, Gloria.

"Yes!" she whispered.

Grinning, she buzzed Sharon to tell her never mind on the password, and then she began to poke around. Mostly, she just wanted to get a picture of Gloria's recent activity and see the kinds of things she'd been working on and dealing with before she died. Maybe one of them would offer a clue to why she had ended up dead.

She began by doing file searches by keyword, starting with her own name, "Kelsey." That brought up numerous documents, but they were all ones she and Gloria had worked on together. There was nothing there she didn't recognize.

Trying a different approach, she wondered if perhaps Gloria had been dealing with any serious personal issues Kelsey hadn't known about, ones that could have possibly led to suicide. She tried "marriage," "marriage counseling," "marital problems," and "depression." Those brought up nothing, so she put in "Vern," but even Gloria's husband's name linked to surprisingly few entries, all quite innocent looking.

Next, she focused on the stolen identity issue, trying "Adele," "Jocelyn," and then "settlement." The first two resulted in nothing, but the third came back with way more results than she felt like slogging through. She tried narrowing those down by adding the name "Rupert," and that time it came back with just half a dozen files. Skimming the list, she decided to take a moment and click through each one.

It looked as though most of them were from ten years ago, the last time Rupert showed up and started making trouble. Gloria had apparently written to the man five different times, and though her letters had started out nicely enough in the beginning, they had steadily progressed toward more "cease and desist" language. The final one contained a strong message and numerous legal warnings and ended with the words:

> *Make no mistake, if you persist in pursuing these ridiculous, unfounded delusions, you will feel the full weight of our legal team crashing down upon your shoulders. Please understand that this is not a threat—it is a promise.*
>
> *Sincerely,*
> *Gloria Poole*

Kelsey read that last paragraph twice, understanding how such a missive could have shut him down for a while. She couldn't imagine how Rupert must have felt when he got this letter. Was it possible that he'd been stewing in rage ever since? If so, could that rage have led him or his sister to act out in some way that had ended up resulting in Gloria's death?

Kelsey was thinking about that as she double-clicked the last file on the list. It opened and she began to read:

Dear Rupert,

You should know that on April 3 at 4:00 pm there will be a cere-mony at the offices of Brennan & Tate in New York City, during which the Tate family will continue to perpetuate the lie that Adele Brennan Tate survived the sinking of Titanic…

Kelsey gasped. This was the letter, the one that Rhonda had shown her in the cab, the one that had been sent to Rupert anonymously, encouraging him to come to the meeting and "seize the opportunity to set the record straight."

Heart pounding, Kelsey sat back in her seat, her head spinning. She couldn't believe it. The letter that got Rupert all stirred up again and convinced him to come here and disrupt the ceremony had been written by none other than Gloria herself!

Kelsey was still trying to process that thought when Sharon buzzed her. She wanted to ignore it, but she knew if she did that a knock at her door would be next. Gathering her wits about her, Kelsey pushed the button to answer.

"Yes?"

"Sorry to bother you," Sharon said, "but Walter wants to see you in his office."

"Did you tell him never mind on the password?"

"Yes. I don't think it has anything to do with that."

"Okay then. I'll head up as soon as I'm finished here."

"Um…" Sharon's voice had an odd tone, and Kelsey frowned at the speak-erphone. "He said right now."

"Fine. Thanks."

He'd probably finished his meeting with the PR folks and wanted to give her a rundown. And while Kelsey wanted to hear what they had to say, she was still so shaken by what she'd just found among Gloria's documents that she did not feel like having this conversation at the moment.

Still, he was the boss. And he needed to know what she'd just found among Gloria's documents. After taking a moment to print it out and save the letter to her local drive, she signed out of the computer, grabbed the page from the printer, and headed upstairs to Walter's office.

When she got there, she was surprised to see him waiting for her at his door. His face was rigid, his hands clenched at his sides, and he greeted her with a curt, "Kelsey, *what* are you doing here?"

Startled by both his words and his tone, at first she didn't even know how to respond.

"Sharon said you wanted to see me."

"I don't mean what are you doing here in my office," he said, stepping back so she could come inside and he could close the door, "I mean in the building. I told you not to come in."

She sat, blinking at him. "You what? Why? When?"

"When you called me from your parents' house," he replied, practically yelling. "I said we needed to distance ourselves from the whole emphasis on the Tate name, and I told you *not* to come in."

Kelsey's face flushed with heat, though she wasn't sure if it was from anger or embarrassment. "No, you didn't, Walter. You said don't come to the PR meeting. You never said don't come to the *office*."

He sat back and harrumphed, his cool, Wall Street demeanor cracking around the edges. Finally, he spoke. "You can't be here, Kelsey."

She simply stared at him.

"You need to leave the building and not come back until things have calmed down. I'll tell you when it's okay to return, but I don't want you on the premises until then. Do you understand?" His mouth remained tight, and his eyes seemed hard and impersonal.

"No, I don't. Walter, I have business to conduct. I have open cases I'm working—"

"I understand that. I'll go through your schedule with Sharon personally and see which things must be taken care of while you're out. If I need you, I'll let you know, but otherwise you have to distance yourself from this company completely and immediately."

A lump was growing in Kelsey's throat. She wasn't sure she could speak, so she looked down until she felt she had regained control of her faculties.

"You can't do this to me," she said, looking back up, her voice breaking at the end.

"Listen," he replied, softening just a bit, "this isn't forever. It's just for right now. I'm sorry, but I would prefer that you stay away."

Kelsey eyed him narrowly. "You'd *prefer* that I stay away? From my own office, from my family's own company?"

"Yes. I'm sorry, but for right now this is how it has to be."

Stunned, she stood, folded the letter she'd printed out, and slipped it into her pocket. She turned and walked to the door. As she reached it, she realized Walter was at her side. He swung it open to reveal the massive, uniformed figure of Ephraim just outside. The kindly man had been a loyal employee of this company and a friend of hers for years, but at the moment he couldn't even look her in the eye.

"I hate to have to do this, Kelsey," Walter said, "but I've asked Ephraim to escort you from the building."

CHAPTER
EIGHTEEN

April 11, 1912

JOCELYN

When Jocelyn awoke, it took her a moment to remember where she was. Then it came to her as she looked around: *Titanic!* They were aboard the ship *Titanic.*

Last night she had been disappointed when Adele chose the top berth, but now that it was morning she was glad. Jocelyn liked to be first up, and her position on the bottom bed allowed her to slip out from the covers without disturbing her cousin. Back at home, those calm, early morning moments alone while the rest of the household slept always helped Jocelyn to organize her thoughts and communicate with her Maker before the busyness of the day set in.

Of course, it was a bit harder to be quiet in this small room, where things were unfamiliar and the washbasin was mere inches from where Adele slept. Somehow Jocelyn managed to get dressed and make herself generally presentable regardless. Then, with a final glance toward her cousin, she slipped from the room into the corridor, eager to take a walk on deck and clear her mind. She would have preferred to leave Adele a note, but she had nothing with which to do so. She decided that acquiring pen and paper from the library was goal number one for the day.

The hallways were quiet except for the passing of a steward and the occasional fellow early morning riser. Jocelyn was tempted to make her way up to the boat deck, where the second-class passengers were allowed access to the outdoors, but she headed for the enclosed promenade on C deck instead, reasoning that though the day's temperatures would likely again be moderate, at this hour the air would still be quite chilly.

Fortunately, there wasn't a soul in sight. She was tempted to take a seat on a bench but decided to do some walking first, just to get her blood going. She would have liked to pay a visit to the gymnasium and try out the camel-riding machine, but that part of the ship was restricted to first-class passengers except while they were in port.

Breathing deeply, Jocelyn began to stroll along the outer edge of the enclosed promenade, looking through the windows at the first glints of light along the horizon and considering the significance of the day. In a few hours the ship would stop to take on passengers in Queenstown, Ireland, and then in the afternoon it would finally head out to sea for good. Though Jocelyn would likely return to these shores within a month or two, today might be Adele's final glimpse of her homeland forever.

Last night the ship made a similar stop in France, though there wasn't much to see from their vantage point far from shore. As their steward explained, the harbor was too shallow for a ship of this depth, and thus transfers had been made via smaller tender boats. She assumed the same would hold true for Queenstown as well.

Despite their disappointment at not having been able to see a new country, the girls had enjoyed getting to know their way around the ship—or at least those portions that had been allotted to the second class. Truly, their accommodations had to be as fine as any other ship's first class. The dining saloon had been especially elegant, and their evening meal had far surpassed everyone's expectations.

All in all, their first day aboard had been an extremely pleasant one with a single exception, that of Tad's dismissiveness of Adele's ambitions. The more time they spent in his company, the more blatant his scorn had become. Late yesterday afternoon, he had crossed the line. When Adele mentioned her intentions upon reaching America of attending college in New York followed by a career in finance with her father's company, Tad had actually laughed out loud in response. Adele was used to others' attitudes regarding her ambitions, but such a rude and blatant reaction had left her looking startled and hurt. Jocelyn knew she had to do something to make things right again. Slipping away, she had quickly secured pen and paper from the second class library and written her cousin a note of encouragement, which she gave to her soon after.

The more she thought about it now, Jocelyn decided she might have a word with Tad today as well. He was obviously taken with Adele, but he had no comprehension of the damage his attitude was doing to her spirit, not to mention its impact on any chance of a relationship between them.

Jocelyn put the matter to prayer, soon moving on from that topic to the questions in her heart about her own intentions upon reaching America. She was as uncertain about her future plans as Adele was certain of hers. The focus of this trip was primarily to get Adele settled in her new homeland. Jocelyn's father was eager to spend a month or so visiting with his brother, Sean, Adele's father, but then he would be returning to Ireland. At issue was whether Jocelyn would return with him or stay in America with Adele and Uncle Sean. Both options were open to her, but thus far she had not been able to make a decision on the subject. Adele was especially eager for Jocelyn to remain there with her, of course, so much so that eventually Jocelyn had had to ask that she keep her thoughts about it to herself. "As I consider this decision," Jocelyn had told her just a week ago, "the last thing I need is to be nagged and cajoled and pestered by you." Since then, Adele had done fairly well at adhering to Jocelyn's request.

The rest of the family was divided on the matter. Her little brother Quincy hoped she would return, while her mother was conflicted about it, wanting her daughter to come back to Ireland but knowing that America offered far more opportunities and prospects for her than Belfast ever would.

Sean and Rowan both felt strongly that she should stay in America, especially in light of the political troubles brewing at home. But it was one thing to visit a new country, and quite another to set up residence there and commit to staying forever.

As always, the matter is in Your hands, Lord, Jocelyn prayed now. *Please guide me according to Your will.*

As the sun rose fully above the horizon, other passengers began drifting into the enclosed promenade. Her walk complete, Jocelyn settled herself into a deck chair and watched all of the activity from there for a while. Eventually, she noticed a father with two young boys, one of about four and the other perhaps one or two. As they were speaking French, she assumed they had boarded last night in Cherbourg. The father looked as if he was having a difficult time, so Jocelyn went over and asked if he needed any help. He replied in fairly good English, and though he seemed reluctant to accept her offer, it was clear he hadn't much choice in the matter.

Both boys were crying fitfully, so Jocelyn picked up the younger one and began bouncing him on her hip and cooing to him softly. The father introduced himself as Mr. Hoffman and said that the boy she was holding was named Lola and the older one was Louis. Though the father's English was passable, it was clear that the children understood only French.

At least children of all languages knew loving tones and silly faces, and soon both boys had calmed down and were clinging to her contentedly. Finally, Mr. Hoffman said that they needed to get ready for breakfast. Handing back little Lola, a darling child with sparkling eyes and soft, curly hair, Jocelyn said she hoped to run into them again and also to make the acquaintance of Mrs. Hoffman. In response, the man simply shrugged and ushered the boys away.

Watching them go, Jocelyn decided it was time for her to leave as well. Adele would be up soon and wanting breakfast. Jocelyn's stomach had begun to growl, so she was more than happy to accompany her cousin to the dining saloon. As she headed down toward the F deck, she was further tormented by the alluring smells of food preparation—coffee and waffles and other delights—wafting through the halls. Still, she felt sure she had enough time to make a quick detour along the way to the second-class library, where she gathered up several pens and a small stack of paper to have as needed in their stateroom.

Adele had just finished getting ready for the day when Jocelyn arrived. She took the opportunity to make herself a bit more presentable now that she didn't have to move around so quietly, and then as soon as the bugle call sounded, the two of them set off for the dining saloon. Breakfast was a magnificent affair, with a variety of meats and breads and fruits fit for a king. Afterward, the cousins headed to the open area on the boat deck to enjoy the sunshine and the view.

As they bundled up and stepped outside, Jocelyn was glad to see that though the morning air was still quite cool, the sun felt warming to the face. They stood looking out toward the rear of the ship, gazing down at the open area below, including the third-class promenade and, beyond that, what a fellow passenger called the "poop deck." Adele seemed to enjoy learning the many nautical terms they were continuously encountering on board, but Jocelyn was more fascinated by watching all of the people scurrying around below.

As they kept an eye on the time and waited for the ship to reach Ireland, they couldn't help eavesdropping on the many conversations happening on every side. One woman kept exclaiming about all the famous people she'd learned were aboard—including the film actress Dorothy Gibson.

They were eventually joined by Tad, and Jocelyn shared these tidbits with him. While he didn't seem to care much about the actress, he was eager to learn more of the rich and famous businessmen aboard, especially John Jacob Astor, the richest man in New York City, and other New Yorkers such as Isidor Straus and Benjamin Guggenheim.

Tad's eyes gleamed as he exclaimed, "Oh, how I wish we were traveling first class! I'd have Colonel Astor begging me to work for him in no time!"

Jocelyn found his comment rather rude, considering that their passage had been paid for by Adele's father, but she held her tongue. Tad seemed to have a tendency of blurting things out before thinking, and she tried to give him some grace, assuming it was caused by a cultural difference between their two countries.

Soon, Tad and Adele were discussing the various accomplishments in the financial realm of their wealthy fellow passengers, and Jocelyn began to feel bored. She had no desire to meet streetcar magnates or railroad executives. She just wanted a glimpse of Miss Gibson.

After a while, Adele excused herself, saying she needed to warm up inside, perhaps even have some hot tea, but she would be back in time for the ship's landing in Queenstown at eleven thirty. Jocelyn knew she ought to go with her cousin but instead chose to stay, thinking this might be the perfect opportunity to speak with Tad privately about his behavior toward Adele.

Drawing him over to an emptier area of the railing, Jocelyn lowered her voice and spoke gently but truthfully, explaining that she wasn't sure if he understood how much it hurt Adele's feelings every time he made fun of her ambitions. The conversation went surprisingly well, as he was quite gracious and receptive in return. As they talked, Jocelyn couldn't help thinking what a fine man he was and what a handsome couple he and Adele would make. Jocelyn rather fancied him herself, but she resolved to keep those feelings in check. Tad Myers was an employee of Adele's father, not to mention a citizen of Adele's new country. It made more sense for him and Adele to become a couple. After all, Jocelyn didn't even know which country she would be calling home a few months from now. More importantly, if she did end up going back to Ireland, how much better would it be to leave her cousin in the care of a handsome young executive who just happened to be her father's employee *and* a potential fiancé.

Jocelyn and Tad ventured inside and then walked down the finely carved oak staircase. Tad excused himself when they reached B deck and entered the men's smoking room. Jocelyn proceeded down one more deck and passed through mahogany doors that led to the library. The spacious room was to her liking, and she took a seat in an upholstered chair at one of the writing tables. She turned on the small electric lamp at the center of the table and removed pen and paper from the drawer. Looking across the room and out of the large windows draped in silk curtains, she thought of the luxury she now found herself in. What a contrast to the land they just sailed away from, where life was much harsher. She caught a glimpse of that land outside the window and wondered what life would bring to her and her cousin now that they had left all they had ever known behind them.

If only Adele could stop focusing so much on business and see what was right in front of her! With that thought in mind, Jocelyn started a new letter, one that urged her cousin to remember the importance of balancing work with family. Adele always loved getting her little notes of insight and encouragement. Jocelyn would try her best to provide that encouragement now when she knew Adele needed it most.

CHAPTER
NINETEEN

As soon as the elevator doors closed them in, Ephraim looked at Kelsey, his expression dark.

"I'm so sorry, Kelsey. This goes against my grain, having to walk you out of here like this."

They reached the fourth floor, and much to Kelsey's chagrin, Ephraim got off the elevator with her and followed along behind as she made her way down the hall to her office. When they neared Sharon's desk, the EA looked up, her eyes flying open wide.

"What's going on?" Sharon whispered, jumping up and following Kelsey into her office despite Ephraim's looming presence.

"It seems that Walter and the PR firm have decided that I'm a liability to the company at the moment. With all of this scandal surrounding the Tate name, he wants me out of here until further notice, simply because I *am* a Tate. He thinks my presence reinforces that connection at a time when they need to achieve the opposite of that."

Sharon's green eyes widened even further. "But this is *your* company, Kelsey! Don't you own like half the stock?"

"Personally, I only own three percent, which isn't enough to stop this from happening," Kelsey replied. "My family owns thirty percent total, but even that doesn't give us controlling interest."

"So go to the board of directors," Sharon urged, "and tell them what happened. I bet they'll put a stop to this nonsense right away."

Ephraim cleared his throat. "We need to get going, Kelsey."

She nodded at him and then turned back to Sharon. "Let's see how things go over the next few days and then I'll decide. For right now I'm going to trust Walter in this. My father has always believed in him, and you know what a good judge of character he is."

Sharon looked as if she might burst into tears at any moment, so Kelsey paused to move around the desk and give her a long hug. As she did, she whispered in her EA's ear.

"Eyes and ears, Sharon. Be my eyes and ears."

When they pulled apart, the girl wiped a tear from her cheek and gave a slight nod. After that, Kelsey slung the strap for her computer case over her shoulder and grabbed her tote bag and purse.

"Guess that's everything for now," she said, glancing around the room. As an afterthought, she walked over to the windowsill, grabbed one of the framed photos there, and shoved it down into her tote bag.

With that, she was off.

As hard as it was to do so, she would hold her head high and walk out of here with pride. But as she walked past nosy coworkers, stepped into the elevator with Ephraim, and watched the doors slide shut, she couldn't help but think, *This would never have happened to Adele. She wouldn't have let it happen.*

They traveled the rest of the way down in silence. When the doors slid open, Ephraim walked with her across the lobby and held the door for her.

"Want me to get you a cab?"

"No thanks." Her jaw set, she was stepping out of the door when Ephraim said her name. She turned and looked up into his sweet, dark face, his soft brown eyes.

"Yes?"

"If there's anything I can do for you, you just tell me. Okay?"

This time, the tears filled her eyes before she could stop them. "Thank you, Ephraim. I appreciate that." She took a deep breath and blew it out slowly, regaining her composure. "I'll be okay. I just wish I knew what had been going on with Gloria here at the end and why she ended up dead. Unless you can explain that to me, I'm afraid there's not much else you can do."

An odd expression coming over his face, Ephraim stepped outside with her and let the door fall shut behind them.

"I can tell you this much," he said in a low voice. "I do know that Mrs. Poole and Mr. Hallerman had a screaming fight on Monday."

"What?"

He glanced around and lowered his voice even further. "Monday afternoon, around three o'clock, Mrs. Poole came down and asked me to unlock the auditorium so she could get things set up for the big ceremony the next day. She was working for a while by herself, but maybe half an hour later I overheard voices, so I figured someone was helping her. But then the voices started sounding kind of mad, so I checked it out. Mr. Hallerman was in there with her, and they were hollering and fighting up a storm." He hesitated. "I'm no gossip, Kelsey, and I wouldn't mention this at all except that I had to tell that detective about it when he interviewed me, and after that he just kept coming back to it and asking me a whole bunch of questions. What did I hear? What did they say? What did they do? In retrospect, it made me wonder if I should have said something to someone sooner."

Kelsey's eyebrows lifted. She'd left the office on Monday around two and had been tied up in meetings the rest of the afternoon, so she'd missed this event entirely. Then again, if something disruptive had happened in her absence, Sharon would have told her about it. Why hadn't she said anything? A big fight between the two highest-level executives in the company—especially one that happened just a day before one of them ended up dead—was definitely big news.

At Kelsey's request, Ephraim gave her the same information he'd given the detective, which wasn't much. He hadn't paid any attention to the specifics of the argument, so all he could remember of their conversation was how it ended. Ephraim had made his presence known and asked if everything was okay. The two had simply glared at each other, and then Walter had said something like, "I'm calling an emergency meeting of the board," and left.

"And that was it?"

"That was it. I asked Mrs. Poole if I could help her or if she needed anything, but she just snapped at me and told me to go away. There were tears in her eyes, so I just figured she was embarrassed for me to see her cry. She left the building pretty soon after that."

Once again, Kelsey felt as though her head were spinning. She'd been so forthcoming with Walter about all she'd learned, yet he'd held back this very pertinent fact from her? Something definitely wasn't right here.

Thanking Ephraim one more time, Kelsey turned to her right and began walking briskly down the block toward Battery Park. She couldn't bring herself to go home just yet. Her mind was spinning, her heart was aching, and she felt utterly and completely lost.

When she reached the park, she made her way toward the family memorial stone, which was practically hidden among some trees near the southeast end of the park. Strolling down an offshoot path that led her among those trees, she reached her destination.

Simple yet elegant, the memorial was made of a solid block of Irish blue limestone that was about five feet high by a foot across. On the front was an inlaid plaque that read:

> In loving memory of
> ROWAN AND JOCELYN BRENNAN,
> Father and daughter,
> who perished together on *Titanic*
> in the early morning hours of April 15, 1912

A few lines down from that was a second plaque with the words: *Ar dheis Dé go raibh a anam dílis,* which she knew was an Irish expression along the lines of "May your faithful soul be at God's right hand." Though the memorial had been erected by Sean Brennan just a year after *Titanic* sank, the Irish plaque had been added by Adele herself several decades later in honor of her father's passing. Following the tradition, Adele's son, Jonah, had put in a stone bench nearby, in honor of his mother after she died. As Jonah was still alive and well and living at the Jersey shore, nothing had yet been added in his honor to carry on the tradition. Even at eighty-nine, he was in excellent health. With a start Kelsey realized that there was a good chance he would outlive his own son. How heartbreaking would that be for the poor old guy? They would have to come up with something together to place here in honor of Nolan, a task she'd always thought she and Matt wouldn't have to face for many years.

Sucking in a deep breath, Kelsey moved over to the stone bench and sat facing the sculpture. Being here always made her feel more connected to her ancestors, but especially to her great-grandmother. She just wished the woman were here now to tell her what to do. Gloria was gone as well. Even her dad was practically as good as gone. That left Walter, who apparently wanted nothing to do with her.

Aching with loss and loneliness, Kelsey reached into her tote bag and pulled out the framed photo she'd grabbed from her office. She held it in her hands and studied it now, a group shot taken in 2007 at her father's sixtieth birthday celebration. In the picture was the grinning birthday boy himself,

Nolan, front and center, and he was surrounded by Gloria, Lou, and several others, including Kelsey and the handsome man next to her, Cole Thornton. Looking at the photo now, she realized that this was the group's last real golden moment. Not long after that dinner, the dominoes had begun to tumble.

Now here she sat, just about as alone and lost as she'd ever been.

At that moment, Kelsey's phone began to ring from her purse, and though she intended to send the call straight to voice mail, when she looked at the screen and realized it was Lou, she went ahead and answered.

He said he'd just been calling to see if she was doing okay, but soon he got far more than he'd bargained for, listening as she spilled out the lower points of her day, sharing her grief and dismay over one bad thing after the other. When she was finished, he asked if there was any way he could help.

"Not unless you can convince Walter to let me back in the building. Either that, or turn back the clock a few days so we can keep Gloria alive and make everything work out differently this time."

Lou gave a sad chuckle. "To be honest, Kels, I'd probably have better luck at turning back time than I would at convincing Walter Hallerman to do anything."

She sighed, knowing no love was lost between Lou and Walter, the man who had essentially stolen the CEO position at Brennan & Tate out from under him.

"Actually," he added, "I bet there's one way I can help. I think I can take a pretty good guess at what Gloria and Walter were fighting about."

She sat up straight, eager to hear what he had to say. "I'm listening."

"Okay, well, you know I've tried not to burn any bridges with B & T in the hopes that someday my own firm might be large enough to merge back in. In fact, I've had a standing offer with your company for the past year, but so far Walter hasn't been interested in taking me up on it."

"Yes, I know all about that," she said, wondering where he was going with this.

"Lately, rumor has it that a much bigger corporation than mine now also has its eye on B & T. On Monday they made an offer too, but theirs is going to be a little harder to refuse than mine was."

"Why?"

"Because from what I hear, it's somebody big, which means that if Walter and the board don't play their cards right, this could turn into a hostile takeover situation. I have a feeling that the reason he and Gloria were fighting was because reportedly she was in favor of the deal. In fact, I heard she was pushing him pretty hard to accept their offer."

Kelsey thought about that for a moment. She tried to keep her eyes and ears open too, but she'd not picked up one whiff about any of this from anyone. Why had Gloria not confided in her? For that matter, why hadn't Walter brought her into the loop?

At the thought of a hostile takeover, Kelsey's chest tightened. If that went through, her family company could end up being dissolved into some big conglomerate. Even if she somehow managed to hang on to her position, Brennan & Tate as she knew it would cease to exist.

"Who is it, Lou?" she asked, almost afraid to hear his answer. "Who's the big company trying to buy out B & T?"

"I wish I could tell you, kiddo. All I know at this point is that it's somebody big. That doesn't exactly narrow things down. Your guess is as good as mine."

Kelsey thanked him for the information and ended the call. Then she sat there for a long time, looking over toward the memorial. She thought about her great-grandmother and how much this spot had meant to her, how much this whole city, in fact, had been a part of her, had been in her blood.

When Kelsey was about seven or eight years old, Adele had begun taking her for what she called her "Accomplishment Walks" through the city. The woman had been quite old by then but was still very spry. Their walks always started somewhere different, but every few blocks she would stop and point out some nearby building or window and tell her, "I helped fund that company's start-up," and then she'd go on to elaborate. She'd say things like, "Twenty-five years ago, I gave them thirty thou for sixteen percent, now they're at three mil, which means my original thirty is up to almost five hundred. That's a net profit of about four hundred and seventy thousand dollars. Not bad for an old lady, eh?"

At those times, even when Kelsey didn't understand what her great-grandmother was actually saying, she still hung on her every word. She'd found the lingo fascinating.

Great-Grandma Adele didn't just talk money. She also loved to tell Kelsey about the various people who owned the businesses she'd invested in. Often, they were women or immigrants or minorities—folks who couldn't seem to get much cash the conventional way. But Adele knew a good thing when she saw it, and she liked to say that she often banked as much on the person as on their product or service. Kelsey had always admired Adele, but those walks had helped to reinforce her desire to grow up to invest in people and their businesses as well.

Now she rose and walked over to the memorial, reaching out to run her fingers over the Irish words on the plaque that had been added by her great-grandmother. At that moment, for the first time ever, Kelsey did not feel close to Adele at all.

Was it possible that Rupert was right?

Had she actually been Jocelyn, pretending to be Adele?

Kelsey could think of only one person who might be able to give her some answers: her grandfather, Jonah Tate. As Adele's son, he just might be able to fill in some blanks. And as Kelsey's grandpa, he also might be able to soothe some of the hurt.

With new purpose Kelsey turned away from the memorial and headed through the park toward Battery Place, the street that ran along in front. She could run home, throw together a few things, and be on a train by one thirty, heading south on the North Jersey Coast line. If anyone still alive knew Adele Tate's deepest secrets, it would be Grandpa Jonah.

CHAPTER
TWENTY

Kelsey ended up catching the two thirty train from Penn Station, and as soon as they made it through the tunnel, she fell asleep and ended up dozing almost the rest of the way.

Her grandfather was waiting on the platform at Bay Head when she arrived, and he greeted her with a warm hug and a kiss.

"You look wonderful, Grandpa!"

"So do you, young lady."

She knew he was lying, that she was tired and disheveled and had never looked worse, but she didn't say so. He was just being kind.

He put her bag in the trunk of his old Buick and drove south on Highway 35 about twelve miles until they reached the coastal town of Seaside Park, a narrow strip of land nestled between the Atlantic Ocean and Barnegat Bay. His snug little home sat directly across the street from the ocean, with the bay just three blocks behind him. Grandma Tate had died twenty-five years ago, and Jonah had lived here alone ever since. Nowadays he was checked on regularly by a professional caretaker, who also did some light cleaning and laundry, and an agency brought his lunch five days a week. But otherwise he had thus far managed to maintain his independence. As a retired ship captain and member of the merchant marine, if he couldn't be out on the water, he at least wanted to live as close to it as he could.

Despite the fact that Grandpa Jonah was well off, he lived in a modest way, his needs few and his home small but comfortable. Situated on oceanfront property worth well over a million dollars, the house itself was essentially worthless, comparatively speaking, and he couldn't have cared less. These days he spent most of his time advocating for causes related to his fellow merchant marine veterans from World War II. When he wasn't doing that, he could usually be found across the street, sitting on the beach in his favorite grimy old canvas chair, surf fishing for bluefish and striped bass. As the sign that hung in his kitchen proclaimed:

The secret to a happy life
is in the hanging on and in the letting go.

Years ago Kelsey had asked him what that meant, and with uncharacteristic seriousness he had replied, "Let go of your hurts, your grudges, and any possessions that aren't a necessity. Hang on to your memories, your loved ones, and most of all your faith. Do that, Little Bit, and your life will be more rewarding than you could ever imagine."

Those in the family whose entire worlds revolved around money—the investing of money, the accruing of money—had trouble understanding his perspective, but his was a life of such peace and simplicity that they had to respect him for it nonetheless. Grandpa Jonah lived quietly down here in the sunny, loamy, salty world of the Jersey Shore, and he really was the happiest, most contented person she had ever known. That said a lot for his lifestyle—and often left her questioning her own after almost every visit.

His spare bedroom had a window facing the ocean, but because of the raised boardwalk across the street and the tall sand dunes beyond, the water wasn't actually visible. Kelsey settled into that room now and changed into more comfortable clothes. The walls there bore a collection of nautical mementos, not the kind to be had in a gift shop but the real deal. A mounted brass cleat held a robe, and between a faded old maritime flag and a framed photograph of Jonah's last ship sat a sturdy shelf sporting a compass, several fancy jade boxes he'd picked up in foreign ports, and an old copper ship lantern. On the opposite wall hung a framed map of the Atlantic Ocean and some old navigational charts.

Once Kelsey was settled into the guest room, she went out to the kitchen, where her grandfather was pulling food from the refrigerator and setting it out onto the counter.

"Bacon and eggs all right for supper?" he asked.

It was only five o'clock and she wasn't hungry yet, but she grinned just the same.

"I love it when you make me breakfast for supper. What should I do—set the table?"

"That'd be fine." The old sailor whistled as he went about fixing their dinner. Once the bacon began to sizzle on the stove, Kelsey laid the table for two and took out bread for toast. As she worked she couldn't help but think about how ironic it was that the son of a woman who had nearly perished on *Titanic* had devoted his life to the sea. Then again, Adele had always been one to confront things head-on. After all, by naming her son Jonah, hadn't she been stubbornly refusing to let that sea get the best of her in the first place?

"What else can I do?" Kelsey asked, setting out the butter dish.

"Sit down and take it easy," he replied.

She pulled out a chair at the maple drop leaf table and sat, only then realizing how tired she was despite her nap on the train.

"Tell me about all this brouhaha on the news," he said as he cracked some eggs in a bowl. "I know you didn't come all the way down here just for the free omelet. What's going on, Little Bit?"

Kelsey sighed. "It's a mess, Grandpa. What have you heard so far?"

"Just what I've seen on the news, and then your brother called me this morning and filled me in some more. Sounds like one of our Brennan cousins came to a big event at your office yesterday and stood up and yelled at you, making all kinds of crazy accusations."

"That's about right."

"Too bad he ruined your party. Matt said you were being given some big award or something."

She glanced down, about to show him her Quarter Club pin but then realized it was in the bedroom, still clipped to her jacket.

"Yeah, well, it wasn't that big of a deal. All I care about at this point is figuring out the truth about my great-grandmother." She didn't add that she also wanted to know how Gloria had really died and why. The thought of that was so overwhelming that she was going to stick with the Adele stuff for now. "Please tell me there's no truth to that story about Jocelyn stealing Adele's identity when the ship sank. Can you?"

He turned and set a plate of bacon on the table. "I can try. Nolan told me all about this fella the last time he made a fuss. I don't believe a word of it."

"You don't?" Hope and relief filled Kelsey's heart. "Is that just a feeling, or do you *know*?"

"Just a feeling." He must have seen how her face fell because he quickly added, "She was my mother, Kelsey. Everything I ever knew about her tells me she was a truthful person. I honestly don't believe she could have assumed someone else's identity. Adele Brennan Tate could not have been the person she was and lived the life she lived if that life had been based on a lie." He turned back to the stove for the eggs.

"It does me good to hear you say that. Dad seemed to have some doubts. I don't know what to think anymore or how we can possibly prove it either way. According to my boss, DNA testing isn't an option."

"You don't need any fancy tests to know the truth," Jonah replied.

"Then why are there still doubts about this stuff? How could my own father think it's true?"

Jonah sat down and shook out his napkin, his shoulders looking surprisingly narrow and small as he placed it in his lap. The dear man was showing his age, and his weathered face bespoke the years he'd spent out in the sun and wind. Thank goodness his wits were as sharp and clear as they had ever been.

"Let's pray," he said gently. "Then you can tell me about your friend Gloria."

He reached out and clasped Kelsey's hand and bowed his head. She bowed hers as well with mixed feelings of frustration and nostalgia. Once upon a time, she'd thought she had a faith in God every bit as strong as her grandfather's. And though she'd never had a big moment where she'd renounced that faith or intentionally turned her back on God, somehow she had slowly moved Him into the background of her life—until He had disappeared from it entirely.

Why had she let that happen? Had it been yet another facet of her breakup with Cole, part of that slow descent into unfeelingness that her mother had accused her of this morning? Doreen had called Kelsey an automaton, a shell. Automatons and shells didn't have souls. But she did, and suddenly, in this tiny kitchen filled with the smell of bacon and the distant cry of seagulls and the sight of the most faith-filled person she'd ever known, that soul felt unprotected and alone, like a little girl standing barefoot in the snow and peering in through a window at a cozy, warm room with a fire in the hearth. For the first time in a long, long time, a part of Kelsey wanted to go into that room. How odd that until this moment she hadn't even realized how cold the snow was around her feet.

"Our mighty God," Grandpa said with soft reverence, and Kelsey's heart twisted. She missed this.

"We come before You in humility," Jonah went on. "You are the One who knows all. You are in control of this fallen world. Lord, help our Kelsey to see some sense in what's going on around her. Give her an extra measure of Your wisdom. Help her in the many decisions she has to make. We thank You for this food, and for Your grace, and for all Your many good gifts to us. Amen."

"Amen," Kelsey whispered, tears blurring her vision. She blinked them away and picked up her fork.

"So," Grandpa said when she'd had a few bites of crispy bacon and perfectly cooked eggs. "Tell me about Gloria."

"I miss her so much. Did you know her? I can't remember."

He shrugged. "I met her once or twice at company parties Mother or Nolan dragged me to, but I don't recall that we interacted much."

"She was a genius when it came to business, Grandpa. Well, maybe not as good as Great-Grandma Adele, but she was very good. So professional and intelligent. I looked up to her. She trained me. She taught me so much."

"Was she well liked?"

"Um, I guess. I mean, she was always very professional, not what anyone might call chummy, but she was nice and decent and helpful. People liked her well enough."

"Seems Nolan told me she wasn't happy when he brought that Walter guy in."

"No, she wasn't," Kelsey said. "She stayed on, though, so I assumed she got over it. I *thought* she had remained loyal to the company to the end."

Grandpa eyed her keenly. "Thought?"

Kelsey sighed. "Today I did some digging and learned a few things that surprised me. As it turns out, Gloria knew Rupert Brennan was going to come to the ceremony yesterday but didn't do anything to stop it. I thought that was bad enough, but then I learned that *she* was the one who encouraged him to come there in the first place! I was shocked. Now I don't know what to think."

"Maybe that's why she killed herself. Remorse for hurting the company and people she cared about, like you?"

Kelsey pressed her lips together for a moment. "Maybe. *If* she killed herself. Though she may have been murdered, you know."

He grunted, his fork poised in midair. "They said that on the news, but I just thought they were being sensationalistic."

She exhaled deeply. "No, that's a possibility. The police won't say, and I don't know what to think. For now I'm just biding my time, hoping we'll have more answers soon. Until then I'm going with suicide. I can't bear to think about the alternative."

He nodded, seeming to understand. "Either way, Kelsey, I'm really sorry all this has happened. It's a big load for you to carry. Too bad your father can't help you with it."

"I know. And it gets worse. This afternoon Walter banned me from the office and even had me escorted from the building by security!" She explained what had happened, and though she'd expected her grandfather to become angry on her behalf, maybe even offer to storm down there to the office and give Walter Hallerman a piece of his mind, instead he just ate eggs and nibbled on bacon and let her tell her story. Somehow, his calm response lent calmness back to her.

"I'd give anything for the letter Oona sent back to Sean," she said, "the one that answered the question of Adele's identity. But that's long gone, apparently. Now we're almost back to where poor Adele was a hundred years ago, faced with the task of proving something almost impossible to prove but that we already know to be true."

"Well put, my dear."

Her eggs were growing cold, so she took one last bite and pushed her plate away.

"Grandpa," she began, settling back in her seat, "if I'm so sure and you're so sure, why isn't my father sure?"

Jonah shrugged. "I wouldn't say he thinks Adele was a fraud. More likely, he's just open to the possibility. Your father was always a pragmatic man. I have a feeling that as long as the company wouldn't be hurt by it, he doesn't really care either way."

"But she was his grandmother. He loved her dearly."

Jonah was silent for a long moment as he finished clearing his plate and drank down all his coffee.

"Well," he said slowly, "let's think about this for a bit. In the aftermath of such a tragedy, what would a father rather believe— that he lost a daughter or that he lost a niece?"

"I don't follow."

"I'm talking about Sean Brennan. Think about it. Two young women were coming to America, his daughter and his niece. He learns one of them didn't make it. If you were him, which would you rather believe? That you'd lost your daughter or that you'd lost your niece? I know it sounds cold, but speaking as a father, I can tell you for a fact that he'd rather have lost the niece."

"But Sean barely knew Adele, and even then only from letters. He hadn't been with her in person since she was three years old. Why would it matter?"

Jonah studied her for a moment. "Ask any parent and they'll tell you why. Take my word on that. There's a bond there regardless, one deeper and more pervasive than you could ever imagine."

She nodded, suddenly feeling young and inexperienced and foolish. At thirty-two *she* could be a parent by now. The fact that she wasn't made it harder for her to grasp his logic.

"Put it this way," he said kindly. "Your father loves you so much, as you know."

"I know."

"Well, being such a pragmatic man, and having such a deep love for his own daughter, Nolan probably looks at this through the eyes of a loving father and assumes that whether the survivor was really Adele or not, Sean would have been willing to pretend his daughter survived, just to save himself the heartache of having lost his child—the child he'd never had a chance to get to know before then."

She considered his words. "Even if he knew it was a lie?"

"Maybe—as long as that meant he still got a daughter out of the bargain. What I'm saying is that I imagine this has probably been your father's thinking all along, that whether the young woman who stepped off *Carpathia* was Jocelyn or Adele, all Sean wanted was to love her and care for her and give her a decent life. If she said she was Adele, then to him she would be Adele, case closed."

"Case closed for him maybe," she replied. "But what about now? What about all these generations later, when her identity is coming under question yet again?"

Jonah stood and carried his plate to the sink, and then he poured himself a fresh cup of coffee. Rejoining her at the table, he sat back with a creak of the chair, took a sip, and met her eyes with a look of challenge.

"Maybe the question now is, what's really important here? The truth or the money?"

She shook her head, not understanding.

"If Rupert Brennan is right," he explained, "then from what I understand, he's owed some money, correct? So my question to you is, are you more concerned with learning the truth, regardless of the consequences? Or are you more concerned with protecting your money, regardless of the truth?"

Kelsey's face flushed with heat, and for the first time in memory she felt anger toward her grandfather. How dare he ask her that? How dare he question her integrity?

"No disrespect, Grandpa, but I'm offended by your question. *Really* offended. Those people—Rupert and Rhonda and whoever else is on that side of the tree—they're family. They descended from the same ancestors we did. As nutty as they may be, if the woman who actually survived *Titanic* was Jocelyn, then they have every right to what's theirs. I would never begrudge them that. The money isn't the problem."

"No?"

"No! The problem isn't the damage that their claims could do to the company. The problem is the damage their claims could do to the memory of Adele Brennan Tate, a woman I happened to love and respect very much! *That's* what matters."

By the time Kelsey finished, she was practically shouting, her hands clenched tightly at her sides. To her surprise, however, the old man simply smiled.

"Good," he said, nodding. "That's all I wanted to hear."

Unclenching her hands and placing them flat on the table, she groaned in frustration. "Why do you always ask these kinds of questions, Grandpa?" she demanded. "Are you trying to make me crazy?"

"Nope. I'm just trying to keep the focus on what's really important."

"Well, what's really important for me right now is to figure out the truth. That's why I wanted to come here today, because I was hoping that was something you could help me with."

Nodding more somberly, he rose from the table, went to the sink, and turned on the faucet. Realizing he was about to do the dishes, she got up and took his place, insisting that he sit down and let her do it. "One cooks, the other cleans. That's the rule," she told him sternly.

"Yes, ma'am," he replied, moving around to the side of the table and taking a different seat so he wouldn't be in her way in the tiny kitchen.

"What do you know about any of this, Grandpa? About when your mother first came to this country and found that her identity had been challenged? Did she ever mention any of that at all? Because I never heard a single word about it before yesterday. For that matter, I've never heard much about Jocelyn either."

Kelsey found a plastic tub and a bottle of dish detergent in the lower cabinet. Soon the tub was in the sink, slowly filling with hot, steamy water.

"Well, as you know, my mother never talked much about her past to anyone—especially not about her time on the ship or what it was like the night it sank. But she did write about it extensively in her diary. I have to say, it would have been pretty hard for anyone to fake that stuff, especially the parts about Jocelyn."

"I don't know," Kelsey said, turning off the faucet and plunging the dishes into the soapy water. "I've read that story a dozen times, and I don't recall that it had much to say about Jocelyn at all."

"Well, the printed version doesn't. But she wrote an extremely detailed account of each day at sea, and the sinking and everything, in her handwritten one."

Kelsey gasped, spinning around from the sink.

"Her *what*?"

"Her diary."

Heart pounding, Kelsey wiped her hands on the front of her shirt. "I've never heard of any handwritten diary. The thing I was talking about…"

Her voice trailed off as she quickly walked into the living room and over to the bookcase where she knew he kept a copy. She rooted among the nautical tables and books about sailing ships and steamers and finally returned to the kitchen with a small, printed booklet in her hand. She held it out to him, showing the cover that read *Titanic: One Survivor's Story* by Adele Brennan Tate.

Kelsey opened the booklet and flipped through the pages. "See? I don't think this was traditionally published, but it was obviously typeset and printed and bound. There's nothing handwritten here."

The old man nodded. "That's the printed version she dictated to a secretary for publication. I'm talking about her personal diary, the one she started keeping just before she set sail on *Titanic* with Jocelyn and Rowan."

Kelsey couldn't believe it. How many more family secrets was she unaware of?

"Where is that diary now?" she asked, her voice practically a whisper.

Jonah shook his head. "I'm sorry, but I have no idea, hon. Haven't even thought about it for years. But I saw it many times when I was younger."

Her legs growing shaky and weak, Kelsey sat, dumbfounded. "Are you telling me it's just been misplaced? Or do you think at some point it was destroyed?"

"Oh, I'm sure it's just been misplaced," he said, his brow growing furrowed as he thought about it.

Kelsey placed her elbows on the table and leaned forward.

"We have to find that diary, Grandpa. It could be the key to everything."

CHAPTER
TWENTY-ONE

Kelsey awoke the next morning to a quiet house. Sunlight was streaming into her room, and when she slid the window open an inch, she could hear the waves pounding the shore on the other side of the dunes. It was chilly outside, though, much chillier than in the city. Cold air rushed in through the opening, so reluctantly she pushed the window closed again. Then she pulled on her robe and followed the smell of fresh coffee to the kitchen.

Propped against a mug on the counter next to the coffeemaker was a note Grandpa must have written last night when he set the timer for the coffee. She picked up the little piece of paper and read his spidery script.

Sorry, hon. I've gone through everything else I have here, but I can't find the old diary. Ask your parents. Maybe one of them will know what happened to it.

Deeply disappointed, Kelsey poured herself a mug of coffee and added cream and sugar. Last night the two of them had spent hours rooting through old boxes and bins and trunks trying to find that diary—to no avail. In the end Jonah had finally insisted that she go on to bed, though he promised to get through the last of his papers before he turned in himself.

Still no diary. She couldn't imagine the family losing something so important!

Kelsey glanced at her watch. Her parents wouldn't be up for another hour.

She would call them then, but in the meantime she decided to go for a run. More than anything, she needed to clear her head.

Fifteen minutes later she was dressed in an odd assortment of layers and walking across Ocean Avenue toward the boardwalk. As she began jogging, she could feel her body slowly growing looser and warmer, and soon she removed her outermost layer and tied it by the sleeves around her waist. As she'd expected, she passed only a few other early morning joggers and a single bicyclist as she went.

Kelsey always forgot how much she loved it here until she came back and was reminded again. Though she could do without the more touristy towns along the Jersey Shore, this sleepy little place always felt like a haven to her. The people were friendly and the pace was slow, and when she wanted to get away from the city and clear her head, it was the perfect destination.

When Kelsey was halfway to her turnaround point, she found her mind wandering back to last night's prayer at the dinner table. Looking up at the beautiful sky now and listening to the rhythmic waves on the other side of the dunes, it wasn't hard in this moment to have faith in an almighty God. The hard part was taking that faith back to her busy life in the city, where the evidence of God's hand was often supplanted by that of man's. Somehow, looking at a beautiful ocean sunrise always made her feel closer to her Creator, yet looking at a tall and beautiful skyscraper did not bring God to mind at all. Thinking about that now, she realized how faulty her logic was. If God made man, then skyscrapers, just like mountains, would not exist if God Himself did not exist.

Reaching the next block, Kelsey picked up her pace a bit, thinking back to when she was a teenager. Her parents' faith had always been a more occasional thing—worship service on Christmas and Easter, saying grace on Thanksgiving, trying to be "good" year-round—and she'd always thought that was all there was to it. But then a friend had invited Kelsey to the youth group at her church.

To the people there, faith was a daily walk. Joy and peace were abundant. Life came with a guidebook called the Bible, and at its core were all of the bottom-line truths she needed to know. Looking back on all of that now, she couldn't decide if her experience had been genuine or just run-of-the-mill teenage dramatics. Kelsey had felt things so *deeply* back then, her highs so high and her lows so low. On the night she went forward at a Christian concert, she had felt as transformed, as euphoric, as *bound* to Christ as a bride to a groom. She'd thought those feelings would last forever, but of course they hadn't. Once the "high" faded, she'd been disappointed, but she'd remained faithful, at least until she went away to college.

After that, God got shifted from the center of her life to the sidelines. And while she never actively, consciously rejected God, she had definitely wandered far from Him.

There had been a time, back when she and Cole were dating and starting to grow more serious, when the two of them had begun to go to church together. Another couple had invited them to join a new Bible study class geared to their age group, one that was just starting up. On a whim they had tried it and ended up liking it far more than they had expected to. They continued to attend regularly, almost every week—until their breakup. After that she'd been too heartbroken to go to any of the places they had frequented together, including church. As that fell by the wayside, so did her focus on God.

She hadn't even thought about this stuff in a long time. It was as if being with her grandfather—a man whose faith was an integral part of his life, woven into his soul—had woken something up inside of her. Again, her mind went back to that feeling of being on the outside looking in and desperately wanting what she could see. She didn't know if this sudden hunger for God was just a reaction to the trauma of the past two days or something genuine, but it was worth thinking about. For the time being, though, she would table this mental discussion. A whispered prayer or two couldn't hurt anything, she supposed, but there was already enough on her plate to think about without throwing God into the mix as well.

When Kelsey reached 1st Avenue, she was more than ready to shift from the boardwalk to the beach. Finally finding her footing on the damp, packed sand close to the water, she once again began to jog, feeling the pull of the softer footing in the back of her calves and thighs. It felt good.

Thus far she'd had a rotten week, one of the most rotten weeks of her life. But in this moment, with the sun warm on her face and the ocean gently lapping at the sand and the sight of seagulls up ahead gliding languorously on currents of air, she allowed herself to let go of all the pain and grief and fear and simply enjoy the moment. All too soon she would be back where she started and life would come crashing in again.

The rest of her run was wonderful, and once it was over, she used the walk back across the sand and through the dunes as her cooldown. By the time she reached her grandfather's house, he was up and dressed and in the kitchen, whistling as he made a pot of what smelled like oatmeal. She greeted him with a smile and a hello but continued on toward her room, eager to get in the shower and wash away the sand and sweat before she had breakfast. She turned on her phone as she was gathering her clothes and toiletries, but even though she heard several telltale dings of incoming messages, she ignored them for the time being and continued on to the shower.

Twenty minutes later, dressed in a sweatshirt and jeans with her wet hair combed out straight, she returned to her room, picked up the phone, and took a look at the screen to see who had called. To her surprise, she had four texts and eight voice mails waiting for her. She pressed the button to see who had called, wondering what new development had led to so many messages.

It didn't take long to find out. Though some of the calls had been from concerned friends and colleagues who had just heard the news about Gloria's death, there were three messages from Sharon. The first two simply urged her to call into the office as soon as possible, but the third went into more detail. *Kelsey, it's me again. Walter just called together the staff and announced that the company is being targeted for a hostile takeover by Queen's Fleet Management Group. Please call me!*

Queen's Fleet? That was Pamela Greeley's company. Kelsey lowered herself to the bed.

Not now. Not them.

Queen's Fleet was known throughout the industry as "Clean Sweep," as in an acquisition by them meant all top-level executives gone, whether they were good at their jobs or not. Queen's Fleet always cleaned house of upper management when they did a takeover to make way for their own people.

How could Pamela, the CEO of Queen's Fleet, attempt a takeover of B & T? She had known and respected Adele. They had considered each other friends. Now Pamela was going to take over Adele's company, her very legacy? Kelsey pictured the woman sitting at the ceremony two days ago and realized why she'd been silent while Adele's name was being besmirched, offering no help in her defense. It was because she already had plans in the works to destroy what Adele had built.

Kelsey had to speak with her. She had to talk to Pamela in person, face-to-face. She wanted to march in there and demand to know how she could dare do this. But she couldn't just fly off the handle at her; she needed a plan. She would have to tread carefully, or she might end up making a bad situation worse.

She took a deep breath. Better to wait until she had more information before she did anything.

After a quick text to Sharon—*Got your message, will call later*—she went into the kitchen and told her grandfather that she was sorry but she needed to go. She had to get back to the city as soon as possible.

He frowned. "What's up?"

"B & T is being targeted for a hostile takeover."

He glanced at the clock. "Well, do you want to look up the train schedule, or should we just head on up there now and take our chances?"

"Let's go," she said. "I can be ready to leave in ten minutes."

"Well, then, so can I."

She ran to her room and changed into the only nice outfit she'd brought, a maroon shirt and a pair of black slacks. Though the outfit wasn't quite dressy enough for the office, it was better than the jeans and sweatshirt she'd been wearing.

Kelsey threw the rest of her things into her overnight bag, made the bed, and turned off the light. Her grandfather was waiting at the door, a mug in one hand and keys in the other. He gave the mug to her, and she smiled when she looked inside to see a steaming serving of oatmeal with raisins, a little brown sugar sprinkled on top and a spoon resting against the rim.

"Aww, Grandpa," she cooed.

"Gotta eat," he replied gruffly, stepping outside and locking the door behind them.

On the way to the station, he asked her to explain what a hostile take-over was exactly. "I mean, I've heard the term, but I don't really know what it means."

Kelsey wiped her mouth with a tissue. "Well, a takeover is simply when one company acquires another company by buying up their stock, or some-times by exchanging stock. It's called a 'hostile' takeover when the manage-ment and the board of directors of the company being taken over don't want that to happen."

"And that's what's going on at B & T?"

The traffic light ahead turned yellow, and though Kelsey wanted him to run it, he slowed to a stop instead.

"Yes."

"That's bad?" he asked.

"Very."

"What can you do about it?"

Kelsey took a bite of oatmeal, thinking about that. "I'm not sure. At least this isn't something that happens all at once, so a lot can change before it's all over."

The light turned green and he accelerated as she continued.

"First, the acquiring company, in this case Queen's Fleet, makes an offer to management at the target company, in this case B & T. If the offer is turned down, then the acquiring company has the option of taking its offer directly to the stockholders. If they send out a letter to the stockholders notifying them of their offer, that means a hostile takeover is underway. Then there's a meeting held where a vote is taken, and if the stockholders vote to accept that offer, it's pretty much a done deal."

"Has that gone out yet? The letter to the stockholders?"

"I assume so. I'll call my assistant once I'm on the train to find out more of the details. I haven't received such a letter yet, but it could have come in this morning's mail."

"Well, I'm a stockholder too. If you want, I could call my broker and ask him."

She smiled. "That's okay. Sharon can fill me in."

They rode along in silence, and Kelsey took in the passing scenery as she finished her breakfast. They were driving north on 35, but with every cross street, she could look to their right and see sand dunes at the end of the block. Even in the midst of this turmoil, they were a calming sight.

"I know that the family doesn't own a majority stake anymore," Jonah said, "but isn't it possible that this thing won't go through anyway? I mean, what if enough other stockholders vote no? Then it ends there, right?"

Kelsey nodded. "Yeah, but I doubt that's how it'll play out. Pamela Greeley doesn't do anything by chance, Grandpa. I have a feeling she already has enough votes lined up to win this thing or she wouldn't be moving forward."

"What do we do? What will *you* do?"

She took a deep breath and let it out slowly.

"I don't know yet," she said. "But if you feel like praying for me over the next few days, please do. Trust me. I'll need all the help I can get."

Once they reached the station, Kelsey gave her grandfather a quick hug and kiss goodbye before grabbing her things and running inside. Unfortunately, she'd missed the 10:10 train by just five minutes. The next one wasn't until 11:10, so she bought a bottle of water from a vending machine and found a quiet corner of the station to wait.

She needed to call Sharon, but before she did that, she pulled out pen and paper and dialed into the messages on her home phone. There were a ton, most of them media, but some from concerned friends and coworkers. She had almost gone through them when another one started and a familiar voice came to life.

> *Kelsey? It's...um, it's Cole. Listen, I know it's been a while since we talked, but I heard about what's going on at Brennan & Tate, and I wanted to call. I'm so sorry about all of this. It sounds like you've been through the ringer. Anyway, I just...I wanted to check on you. Make sure you're okay, and all that. Don't feel like you have to call me back if you don't want to. I just wanted to touch base and see how you were doing and let you know that if you need any help, don't hesitate to call me. As you probably know, I have my own firm now, with a top-notch team in place, so if you need us to do anything for you, really, please call. No charge, of course. I mean, I'm offering as a friend, not like trying to get your business or something. Anyway, I'm babbling now, I guess, so I'll hang up. Hope you're all right. Okay, well, bye. Oh, wait, you probably need my numbers, duh.*

He went on to leave three different ones, cell and home and office, and then he said goodbye one more time and hung up. Kelsey was so stunned to hear from him that she played the message through three more times before she remembered to write those numbers down.

Cole Thornton.

Coming out of the woodwork and back into her life.

She disconnected the call without listening to the rest of her messages. When the train came half an hour later, she was still sitting there, staring into space, trying not to think about how good it had been to hear the sound of his voice.

CHAPTER
TWENTY-TWO

April 11, 1912

ADELE

After a delicious lunch, Adele and Jocelyn went up to the B deck prome-nade, both glad to see that the day had grown much warmer. Adele had forgotten her hand muff and fur hat in the stateroom, so she was relieved when she realized she wouldn't need them after all.

As it had since late that morning, Ireland sat in the distance and contin-ued to taunt them both, surprisingly visible from where *Titanic* was anchored several miles off shore. The ship had been stationary for nearly two hours but would be departing soon.

The third-class promenade deck below had grown far more congested while they had been inside eating, and it was clear to see that the ship had taken on a number of new steerage-class passengers during their stop. Adele hadn't seen anyone new in second class, but she felt sure there would be at least a few additional people because she'd seen stewards preparing more of the rooms for occupancy.

The ship was scheduled to set sail again at one thirty, and Adele was deter-mined to stay and keep watching the horizon until her homeland disap-peared in the distance completely. She was saying as much to Jocelyn when a nearby passenger, a priest, interrupted to explain that the rest of the day would be spent moving in a direction that would have them running along-side the coast, and thus they might well be able to see Ireland for the entire afternoon.

Both girls found that thought comforting, that they would be given more time for a final farewell than just the next twenty minutes or so. They decided to stay exactly where they were just long enough for the initial departure, and then they would go to the library for reading material and relocate to the enclosed promenade, where they could alternately watch and read much more comfortably.

As the clock ticked closer to their departure time, Adele suddenly sensed an odd disturbance among her fellow passengers. Turning to look upward, she took in the shocking sight of a man's head, black with soot, peeking out from the top of the ladder inside the aft funnel. She decided that he must be a stoker just trying to take in the final view of his homeland, as she was; perhaps breathe in that last breath of sweet Irish air before setting sail. But those around them took a much dimmer—and more ridiculous—view, saying it was a bad omen of which they should all take heed.

Either way, the excitement of the sight was soon forgotten when the ship's horn gave three deep blasts, so loud from their vantage point that they could *feel* the sound as well as hear it as the engines sprang fully to life.

Then they were off.

The sight of land receding in the distance tore at Adele's heart even more than she had expected it to. To her delight—but also her dismay—down on the third-class promenade directly below, a passenger took out a set of Irish pipes and began to play a dirge. They sailed from Ireland to the tune of "Erin's Lament," a sad and mournful goodbye to a land more beautiful than any other on earth.

Listening, Jocelyn took hold of Adele's hand and gripped it tightly, and when the song was over they clung to each other in a long embrace.

"Please stay with me in America," Adele whispered, even though she had promised herself she wouldn't pressure her cousin on this matter. "I cannot bear to leave my homeland and lose you too!"

Pulling away, Jocelyn gave her an encouraging smile, always the motherer.

"Do not worry, cousin," she said. "Whether I stay with you there or come back with my father here, you and I will always be bound together in our hearts."

Adele nodded, knowing it was true. God had blessed her with a cousin, a sister, and her dearest friend all in one. Moving again to the rail, they remained side by side for a long time, unable to tear themselves from the sight of the rolling green hills slowly receding in the distance.

"I don't know how my father did it," Adele said softly, trying to imagine how Sean Brennan must have felt when departing from this same shore sixteen years before. Not only had he been saying goodbye to his homeland, he was also leaving his wife and young daughter behind.

"He went to America to make a better life for all three of you," Jocelyn replied. "I know it must have been difficult, but at the time he thought he would be bringing you both over to join him within a few years. He didn't know that his wife would die shortly after. He was just trying to do the right thing."

Adele nodded, grateful for Jocelyn's wisdom. "You're right, cousin. None of us knows what the future holds."

"That's why we do the best we can and trust in our heavenly Father," Jocelyn replied, linking elbows with her cousin. "No matter what happens, we find strength in our relationships and comfort in the arms of the God who loves us all."

CHAPTER
TWENTY-THREE

Kelsey had a lot of calls to make, so as the train rattled toward Manhattan, she started by dialing Sharon, hoping to get all of the details of this latest development. Without taking time for chitchat, the EA jumped right in, telling her that Walter had gathered the staff together first thing this morning and told them what was going on. He said that he'd recently turned down an offer from Queen's Fleet Management Group for the purchase of Brennan & Tate, but they hadn't taken no for an answer. Now Queen's Fleet was going straight to the stockholders to try and overthrow management and pursue the purchase in a hostile takeover. Since that meeting, according to Sharon, not much else had happened around the office. Mostly there was just a lot of whispering and closed-door conversations. Kelsey imagined that probably half of her coworkers had already gone online and started looking for a new job.

After hanging up with Sharon, she called her mother to ask for the whereabouts of Adele's old handwritten diary. Doreen didn't even know such a thing had ever existed, but she promised to ask Kelsey's dad.

"Don't expect much, though," she added. "He's not having a good day."

Kelsey's heart sank, both for her sake and his. "No?"

"I think the events of the last two days have finally caught up with him. He hasn't said a word all morning. He just keeps dozing off to sleep. But I'll ask him your question just the same. You never know. He might feel better this afternoon."

Once that call was over, Kelsey found her fingers dialing the cell number

Cole had left for her in his message earlier. This wasn't exactly the best time to be reconnecting with an old boyfriend, but he was still enough of an insider in the New York financial scene that talking to him might be helpful.

That's all this was, her calling Cole to get some input on her situation.

A strange feeling swept over her as she listened for the ring, and she realized she was bracing herself. She anticipated a surge of emotion, and she didn't want that. She liked to stay in control, especially in business conversations. And that's what this would be. That's all this would be, a business conversation between old colleagues.

"Kelsey?"

Her heart lurched. "Hey."

"Wow. Hi. Thanks for calling back. Are you okay?"

She put a hand up to the ear she wasn't using to block out the rumbling of wheels on the track. "Yes, thanks. Sorry for the noise. I'm on a train, heading into the city. I spent last night down in Jersey, at my grandfather's. I...I just wanted to tell you I appreciated your call."

"No problem. I wasn't sure if I should contact you or not, but after this last development, I couldn't help myself. Sounds to me like you've been hit with a triple whammy. First was that bizarre scene at your Quarter Club ceremony, then Gloria's death, and now a hostile takeover attempt? Good grief, you must feel as though the sky is falling."

"Just call me Chicken Little."

He chuckled. "Well, Miss Little, I meant what I said in my message. If there's anything I can do for you..."

"Thanks, Cole. I'm just trying to get a handle on the situation and go from there. I'm not really sure what we're up against yet. I was hoping you might be able to give me some insight as to the word on the street."

"Ah," he said, and she could almost picture him at his desk, leaning back, stretching out, propping one leg over the other. "To be honest, now that I'm working out of Chelsea I'm not all that in sync with you Wall Streeters anymore."

Kelsey was disappointed. It would have been nice to get a little perspective from someone outside the company.

"In fact," he continued, "the only reason I knew about all this was because my sister saw it on the news Tuesday night and called me. When I looked into it the next day, I found out about the hostile takeover too. Man, when it rains, it pours, huh?"

Kelsey smiled to herself, glad to know that Cole's sister still thought information about her was worth sharing with her brother.

"Seems I'm not exactly in sync these days either," Kelsey admitted. "And I'm definitely not in the inner circle of B & T. Frankly, I'm kind of working from the outside in."

"What do you mean not in the inner circle? You *are* the inner circle. And not just because you're a Tate. You're the rising star there, Kels. Don't let all this recent stuff make you feel otherwise."

She sighed. "Oh, Cole, that was just media hype, designed to compensate for my father's absence from the firm."

"Don't sell yourself short." Cole's vehemence surprised her. "Look, when your father had his stroke, Brennan & Tate would have sunk if it weren't for you. From what I understand, your presence and performance and demeanor in the past year have given everyone hope. It's not just about your name. You have Adele's gift—and everyone in town knows it. Once all of this mess is behind you, you're going to take the company to new heights, I have no doubt."

Kelsey closed her eyes. If someone like Cole could have such high expectations of her, what were the employees and stockholders feeling now that she'd been ousted from her family's firm?

"Thanks for the vote of confidence, Cole, but at the moment I'm feeling pretty low and insignificant."

"Well, quit that." His half-teasing tone made her smile. "Listen to me. A lot of people thought that once Nolan stepped down, the company would falter. But instead you rose up as the new star. You may be young, Kels, but you're already the lifeblood of that place."

"Thank you. That means a lot, especially coming from you." Unexpected tears filled Kelsey's eyes, and she wiped them away. "But with this hostile takeover on the horizon, I surely haven't managed to save the day this time. I don't even know much about what's going on, and it feels crummy."

"Well, if you think we can help with that, give me a call. Like I said, I have a top-notch team at your disposal. We can dig up anything on anybody."

She smiled. "Oh, yeah? What color blouse am I wearing right now?"

Without missing a beat, he replied, "Chermouse silk with dark pants."

Kelsey laughed. "Chermouse? What's that?"

"A really good fake name for a color. Thought I might just slip that one by you." They shared a chuckle.

"Good try. You got the dark pants right but my top is maroon."

"Oh, yeah? I bet it looks great on you too."

There was a long silence, and Kelsey wondered if he was flirting with her or if that had just slipped out by accident.

"Anyway," he said, clearing his throat, "you hang in there. In the long run, this current mess will end up being a little blip on your otherwise upward arc."

"Your mouth to God's ear."

She smiled, but she realized there was a measure of truth to what he was saying. She had been on an upward arc—at least until Rupert's scene at the ceremony had broken it in half and sent her tumbling to the ground. Given that Gloria had engineered the man's appearance there, had that been her intention, to break the upward arc Kelsey was on? But why?

Who would mentor someone for all these years and then turn around one day and cut them off at the knees?

"Cole, can I ask you something?"

"Sure. Anything."

Kelsey shifted in her seat to get more comfortable. "I was talking to Lou Strahan yesterday, and he said that when my father passed Gloria over for promotion five years ago, she was absolutely devastated and has probably been smoldering with bitterness ever since. Do you think he could be right about that? I always thought she took it in stride. At least, that's how it looked from where I was sitting. But now I'm wondering if all that mess back then really did hit her harder than I realized."

He was silent for a long moment.

"Gloria *was* really shocked back then," he said. "And deeply hurt. I guess it's possible that she may have held on to her bitterness about it. Lou was passed over too—and just as devastated—so he probably knows what he's talking about."

Kelsey watched out the window as the train slowed down for a brief stop at the Spring Lake station. "Yeah, but he says the problem was that she stayed on at the company, which kind of forced her to stew in her own juices. The only way he was able to get over it was by leaving completely and starting fresh somewhere else."

"Yeah, I remember," Cole said softly. "You had a big part in helping him get that fresh start."

Kelsey was mortified she had brought that up. For a moment she couldn't think of what to say. She didn't know how to break the long silence.

At last Cole spoke, addressing the matter head-on. "Hey, that's water under the bridge, Kelsey. And you know things worked out great in the end—for him and for me. I might never have made the jump to start my own business if things had gone the way I thought they should. And I *really* love what I'm doing now."

"I'm happy for you, Cole. I truly am."

The train started up again as their call was winding down.

"Well, like I said, I just wanted to make sure you were okay. You hang in there, and if you think you can use my team's services, we're here for you. Don't hesitate to call."

Kelsey smiled. Cole would surround himself with the smartest and the best, she was sure of that, but she already had a great team of her own.

She thanked him one last time and then they hung up. For a while she allowed herself to sit back and stare out the window and bask in the memories of the man. Rattling along toward the next stop, her mind went back to the day she and Cole had met, at that first church youth retreat back in high school.

The two of them had ended up on the same team during recreation time and had instantly hit it off, their game-playing strategies merging perfectly and resulting in the winning capture of the other team's flag. After that they had become "youth group buddies," but never anything more. Cole had been really cute, but he was shorter than her by half a head and his voice tended to squeak at all the wrong moments.

They went away to different colleges, but through letters and emails and the occasional call stayed in touch over the years, just as friends. Cole had always been super smart, a real numbers guy, and when he graduated with a Wharton MBA in 2004, it wasn't hard for Kelsey to get him an interview at the family firm.

What a shock that had been, the day he came walking into Brennan & Tate for his meeting. Gone was the little boy with the pretty eyes and the squeaky voice. In his place was a *man*, six foot plus, nice build, incredibly handsome. Truly, the sight of him had knocked her breathless.

He'd seemed equally taken by her, and once they were reunited and working together, their friendship deepened and eventually turned to romance. That romance had come to an end a year later, thanks to her thoughtless actions and stupid ambition.

Kelsey sat up straight, suddenly remembering that Gloria had been a big part of things back then as well. *Gloria* had been the one who had first come to Kelsey with Lou's business plan and suggested she work something up despite the fact that Cole was already on it. *Gloria* had been the one who had told Kelsey the details of the miniscule offer Cole had made to Lou and laughed with her at how ridiculous it was. *Gloria* had been the one who had assured Kelsey that business was business and personal was personal and that one had nothing to do with the other.

Try telling that to Kelsey's heart after Cole was gone.

Was it possible that Gloria had intentionally sabotaged their relationship back then? Had she *wanted* the two of them to break up?

Suddenly, she found herself looking at all of Gloria's actions in a new light. If the woman was capable of bringing in Rupert Brennan and unleashing him at the ceremony, what else had she been capable of? What else had she done to wreak havoc in Kelsey's world?

More importantly, why had she done it? What had been her motivation?

Kelsey's first, knee-jerk reaction was the thought that this was personal, that underneath that caring exterior, Gloria hadn't liked her at all and had wanted to hurt her out of spite. But was that true? Or had her motivations lain elsewhere and Kelsey was just collateral damage?

She thought about that. If it was personal, maybe she'd done it because she'd been jealous of Kelsey's early success. Maybe she'd even been afraid Kelsey would be promoted ahead of her. That could very well have happened in a few years, as everyone knew that Nolan had always hoped for his daughter to head up the company eventually. Cole's words were some comfort, and yet there was a flip side to his assurance that she was of prime importance to B & T. *Had* this been personal, aimed at Kelsey herself? Was Gloria determined to keep her from ever taking the helm, regardless of what that required?

Shifting in her seat, Kelsey considered the other alternative, that this hadn't been personal at all but rather part of something much bigger, something aimed at the company at large. Could Gloria have been working behind the scenes to sabotage the entire corporation? If Kelsey was as pivotal to B & T as Cole seemed to think, maybe Gloria's actions constituted an act against B & T itself. After all, an attack on Kelsey *was* an attack on B & T.

She took out the battered letter Gloria had sent to Rupert Brennan and read it again, trying to stay calm and objective. When she came to the last paragraph before the postscript, she paused and reread it.

*Please note that if Brennan & Tate is sold, you may forever lose
your right to inherit any part of Sean's fortune, thanks to what is
known as "innocent buyer" laws. Don't let this happen!*

Right there in the letter, she'd said "if Brennan & Tate is sold." Had that
just been a general hint at a future possibility, or did it imply foreknowledge
of the impending hostile takeover? Maybe this whole Rupert mess had been
all *about* the takeover.

Needing to organize her thoughts, Kelsey took out pen and paper. At the
top of the page, she began writing a list of every person and entity that had
been involved thus far. She wrote out *Kelsey, Gloria, B & T, Rupert, Rhonda,
Walter, Pamela, QFMG*—and then she stopped. Something with those last
letters had caught her eye. She'd seen the same notation recently, QFMG.
But where? Pulse surging, she opened her purse and dug around in the depths,
feeling not unlike her cousin Rhonda. Finally, her hand closed around Gloria's scribble pad and she pulled it out. She scanned the scrawled notes until
she found it, there on the third page and jotted in Gloria's handwriting:
Sched. mtg. with P @ QFMG.

Kelsey closed her eyes for a moment. This whole thing seemed incredible.
Had Gloria been working with Pamela in secret toward a hostile takeover of
B & T? If so, how could she have done that? How could Gloria, one of the
company's most loyal employees, have been such a traitor?

Most importantly, if she *had* done it, then why?

Doing the math, Kelsey quickly tried to figure out how much B & T
stock Gloria owned. Between the shares granted to her as a member of
management and additional incentive stock plan grants over the years, the
woman had probably amassed enough stock by now that she owned a good
five percent of the company. A percentage that high would have made her
an appealing inside partner to Pamela in her attempt at a takeover. Had the
two of them been working together?

Had Gloria been a traitor in their midst?

Kelsey mentally reviewed the consequences of Gloria's latest actions:

She had disparaged Adele's legacy.

She had gotten Kelsey banned from her own office.

She had caused the value of B & T to plummet.

The thought hit Kelsey like a punch in the stomach. That had to be
why Gloria had done all this: She'd wanted to devalue the stock! She'd used
the Rupert mess to sully the company name and drive down the price

of shares, which in turn would make the hostile takeover possible and affordable.

That had to be it. Just look at how things were falling into place, she thought. The stockholders were probably frightened enough by the plummeting stock value by now to accept an outside offer. The employees were already eyeing the door. Soon, Pamela's bid for takeover would be a success, and B & T as they knew it would cease to exist.

Gloria and Pamela must have been working together all along. Despite Pamela's reputation for cleaning house, she had probably agreed to make an exception in this case, offering Gloria a tony position within the new, merged version of B & T—perhaps even the top spot. Gloria was all about power, and looking at the big picture made Kelsey realize that, sneaky as it was, this was the type of thing Gloria would have been capable of doing without another soul ever catching on.

But if things were going Gloria's way so perfectly, then why had she committed suicide?

And if she hadn't committed suicide, then why had someone killed her?

There were just so many questions and not nearly enough answers. And as desperately as Kelsey wanted to get to the bottom of things, she had to admit she would never be able to solve this alone—especially now that she wasn't even allowed in the building.

Quickly, she grabbed her phone and called Sharon again. This time she told her she wanted to assemble her research team, that she needed them to meet with her somewhere off-site to lay out a plan for how they could fix this situation. Sounding a little uncomfortable at the thought, Sharon nevertheless promised to talk to each of them and get back to her as soon as possible.

While she waited, Kelsey jotted down a list of the many questions that needed answers and the various ways the team could go about finding them. By the time she reached the city, she wanted to have mapped out a complete plan of attack. Half an hour later, just as the train was about to go into the tunnel, a text came through from Sharon.

> Whole team on board with plan, excited to help. Meet at
> 6 at the High Yield Café on Stone St.

Thank goodness, Kelsey thought, tucking her phone into her purse and gathering up her stuff. She hated to have to wait that long, but six o'clock was better than not at all. And now that her team was behind her, at least she had a fighting chance

Closing her eyes, she whispered aloud as she waited for the train to come to a stop underneath the massive Penn Station. "Lord, please let me save my family's company as well as my great-grandmother's legacy."

CHAPTER
TWENTY-FOUR

Kelsey made her way through busy Penn Station, switching over from New Jersey Transit to the subway system without ever having to go above ground. Soon she was crammed in tightly with her bags, rumbling south toward Rector Street Station. Half an hour later she emerged into the sunlight, jolted by the difference between the calm, salty sea air of the shore and the noisy, bustling city that surrounded her now. Hoisting her bags on her shoulders, she walked to her home a few blocks away.

As she neared her apartment building, she was relieved to see that it looked as if the reporters had all given up and gone away. She entered through the front door without being approached by anyone, and she was upstairs and in her apartment by two p.m. That gave her four hours until her meeting, which was plenty of time for both tasks she wanted to accomplish.

After making herself a late lunch, she took out her laptop and settled down at the kitchen bar. She pulled up her contact list and got ready to start making the calls she'd been trying to get around to for a day and a half. She had a feeling Walter would not be happy with her for doing so, but on this matter she would stand her ground. Distancing herself from the company for the world at large was one thing, but disappearing without a word to her clients was something else entirely.

She went through her entire list of active clients, dialing them up one at a time and giving them the same basic spiel. She said she was calling to touch base and to reassure them that while Brennan & Tate was currently facing some challenges, the company was actively working to solve those challenges as quickly as possible. In the meantime, she added, though she might have to hand over some of her accounts to her coworkers temporarily, she wasn't going anywhere and, most importantly, the clients' interests were *not* going to be forgotten in the shuffle.

Fortunately, the calls went better than she had expected. There were a few clients with big deals pending who were understandably nervous, but otherwise almost everyone seemed appreciative that she had contacted them. In general, people seemed to be taking the situation in stride, sounding neither hostile nor skittish but primarily curious. Though she had no answers for most of their questions, she did what she could to be reassuring. By the time she was finished, she felt much better, and she hoped they did too. They certainly seemed to.

Then she changed into one of her favorite tailored jackets, a pale beige blouse, and black jeans. She completed the outfit by fastening to her lapel the pin Lou had given her. She would wear it with pride, hoping it would continue to remind her of her hard work at B & T and all that she'd done there. No one was going to take that away from her without a fight.

Before going to the meeting, she would be making a detour on the way to pay a visit to Vern Poole. Kelsey hated to drop in unannounced, but she wouldn't stay long. She just wanted to ask him some quick questions, make sure he was okay, and find out if any funeral plans had been firmed up yet. As angry as Kelsey was at Gloria, and as confused as she was about her recent behavior, she still felt bad for the woman's husband. The poor guy had been such a mess the other night, and her heart had really gone out to him.

On the way from the apartment to the subway station, she slipped into her favorite neighborhood bakery and bought a delicious-looking lemon cream Bundt cake. Then, with the box in one hand and her purse in the other, she got on the train at Rector Street and rode until she reached Union Square station. From there it was a quick five blocks straight up, from Fifteenth to Twentieth, before she reached Gramercy Park and the gorgeous old red brick building that Vern and Gloria had called home for the last twenty or so years.

Kelsey was standing directly across the street, waiting for the light to change, when she saw a familiar figure emerge from the building's front door. Despite her four-inch heels, the woman glided gracefully down the steps and across the wide pavement, coming to a stop on the other side of the street at the same light Kelsey was waiting for. It was Yanni, looking strikingly beautiful as usual in a light gray dress-length all-weather coat, cinched at her tiny waist by a wide silver belt. When the light turned, rather than crossing, Kelsey stepped back out of the way of the other pedestrians and waited there as Yanni came toward her. She'd probably gone by Gloria's place to drop off some of her personal things from the office. If so, perhaps she would be able to give Kelsey an idea of how Vern was doing before she headed up there herself.

Yanni didn't notice Kelsey waiting, so she called out her name before she was all the way past. In response, Yanni jumped, clearly startled.

"I'm sorry. I didn't mean to frighten you," Kelsey said with a smile, stepping closer. "I saw you crossing the street and thought I'd wait on this side for you. I wanted to ask you a question."

Yanni forced a smile in return, though she did not look at all pleased to have run into Kelsey. In fact, she looked downright upset, as if she were ready to bolt at any moment. With a sinking feeling in the pit of her stomach, Kelsey wondered if Walter had been turning the employees against her, starting with his own assistant.

"Kelsey, hello," Yanni said, recovering from her surprise. She gestured off behind her and to the right, speaking more quickly than usual. "I was just over at the salon, getting a blowout. Big date tonight. You know how it is." She smiled even wider, but that smile did not reach her eyes.

Kelsey hesitated, the situation shifting in her mind. There was no salon in Gloria's building, not that she could recall. More significantly, Yanni's hair did not look freshly styled at all. If anything, it looked disheveled, as did her makeup, for that matter. If this was Yanni's idea of dressing up for a hot date, she needed a better mirror.

Clearing her throat, Kelsey tried to sound nonchalant as she said, "Oh? Who do you use? I've been looking for somewhere new ever since my last haircut. My girl butchered me."

"No way," Yanni said, her cheeks coloring a bright pink. "Your hair looks beautiful. It always does. If I were you, I wouldn't change a thing."

"Still, it never hurts to get a good lead on a new place. What's the salon called?"

Yanni faltered for a moment and then said, "My stylist is Maurice, but I can never remember the name of the place. 'Hair' something. It's a couple of blocks that way." She pointed up the street before turning to Kelsey again. "But from what I understand they might be going out of business soon. No point in starting up somewhere new if they're only going to close down anyway."

Kelsey nodded, her face neutral but her mind spinning. What was Yanni trying to hide?

"Anyway, I need to get going. Mr. Hallerman thinks I left early today to run to the bank, so I would appreciate it if you don't say anything to anyone about seeing me here."

"Sure. No problem. Since I'm banned from the office right now anyway, I don't know who I would tell." She was about to meet up at a restaurant with her EA and her whole team, but she didn't think it necessary to mention that fact. She had no intention of telling anyone about her encounter with Yanni—at least, not unless the need arose for some reason.

As the woman turned to go, Kelsey decided to push things a little bit further. "I was just about to check on Vern and drop off a little something. I never know what to bring when someone has passed away, but I figure you can't go wrong with dessert, right?"

"Guess not."

"That's their building across the street there. They have a condo on the sixth floor."

Yanni hesitated, clearly flustered, and then she pointedly looked at her watch and took another step away. "I'm sure he'll appreciate that," she said evenly. "This can't be easy for him. Gotta go. See you around."

"Yeah, see you."

Kelsey stood there at the corner and watched Yanni walk away, wondering what that had been about. As Gloria's executive assistant, she could have had plenty of legitimate reasons for being in the building, especially now in the wake of the woman's death, such as dropping something off or getting something signed.

So why had she lied?

The light changed and Kelsey stepped in with the crowd to move across the street. She had to give her name to the doorman in the lobby, and after he called upstairs to announce her arrival, she continued on to the elevator. Her mind was still rolling around various possibilities when she reached Vern's door. She was about to knock when it swung open and he stood there waiting for her. Unlike Yanni, he didn't seem flustered at all. For a moment, she wondered if he even knew the woman had been in the building.

Putting that from her mind, Kelsey gave him a hug and told him she was sorry for dropping by without calling first but that she wasn't going to stay. "I just wanted to check on you and see how you were holding up," she continued. "Oh, and here." She handed the boxed cake to him. "This is a little something to have in the house in case any guests come in from out of town."

He seemed genuinely touched as he took the box from her and placed it on a hall table.

"I'd love to invite you inside, but I was just heading out," he said as he grabbed his keys from a hook by the door and walked into the hall. "I'll go down with you."

"How are you holding up, Vern?" Kelsey asked as they walked toward the elevator. "Is there anything I can do for you?"

He shook his head. "No. I've been getting by and I have a lot of support from family, friends, and people from the office."

Kelsey considered the possibility that Vern and Yanni were having an affair. The two of them had certainly had numerous interactions over the years at various work-related functions. Many of those had ended up being a combination of social time and after-hours business, with Gloria being pulled away to handle some important matter or another, leaving Vern to fend for himself. It wouldn't have been unusual for his wife's secretary to step in and entertain the man in her absence. Perhaps something had developed between them. Of course, he was a good twenty years older than the strikingly beautiful Yanni, but some girls went for older guys, and he was a handsome man, his silver hair and lined face only serving to make him look more distinguished.

Then again, if he'd been having an affair with another woman, would he have been quite so distraught the night Gloria died? Kelsey had been by his side and had seen how genuinely heartbroken he was. Had that been the behavior of a man who was cheating on his wife?

Suddenly, a comment he had made that night popped into Kelsey's mind. He had asked the detective whether or not he thought Gloria had meant for him to be the one to find her body. Between sobs, Vern had said something like, *If that's what she was trying to do, I deserved it.* At the time, Kelsey had taken the comment generally, as in he hadn't been the best husband in the world. Now, she realized, he could have been speaking more specifically, and those were the words of a man who was guilty of some tangible act.

"So I ran into Yanni just now, outside," she said nonchalantly as they stepped into the elevator and she pressed the button for the ground floor.

Looking completely unruffled, Vern nodded and said, "I asked her to come over and help pick out Gloria's burial clothes. I figured that since she worked with her every single day, she'd probably know best what Gloria would have wanted. I'm hopeless at that sort of thing."

She studied him for a long moment, knowing with everything in her that not only was he lying right now, he'd probably been lying to his wife for so long that he'd become a master at it. He stood silently next to her, watching the numbers change on the elevator display.

Finally, deciding that it was none of her business anyway, Kelsey let the Vern–Yanni connection go and asked about the funeral arrangements instead. He gave her the name and address of the funeral home and said that visitation would be tomorrow night from six to nine.

"The burial will be Saturday morning," he added, "but that's for immediate family only."

"Got it. Thanks." Kelsey had to wonder exactly what constituted "immediate family" for the Pooles. Gloria and Vern had no children, and she knew Gloria's parents were gone. Outside the office, the woman's life must have been a sad, empty affair. No wonder her job was all she had lived for.

Kelsey had one more line of questioning for Vern. She tried to think how to phrase what it was she wanted to know. Finally, she just came out with it. Nothing ventured, nothing gained.

"Can I ask you a strange question, Vern? It's going to sound odd, but I really, really would appreciate an honest answer—a one hundred percent honest answer, okay?"

"Okay…" he said, suddenly looking nervous. Poor guy, he was probably expecting her to ask about Yanni. Instead, she launched into an issue of far more importance to her right now.

"Five years ago, when my father went into semiretirement, everybody at the company expected him to the fill his absence by promoting from within. Instead, he brought in Walter Hallerman from the outside and made him CEO."

Vern nodded, and as he did she couldn't help but detect in his expression something like relief. She continued.

"I know Gloria was very hurt and angry about all of that back then. What I want to know is…well, it's kind of hard to say this…"

"It's okay, Kelsey. What do you want to ask me?"

She let out a breath and looked off to the side, a sudden sadness overwhelming her. "What I want to know is if she ever really got over that, or if she remained bitter for the rest of her life."

"*That's* your question? I don't understand. Of course she got over it. It's been five years, for goodness' sake. She was none too happy at the time, you're right about that, but eventually she moved on. Why would you think she hadn't?"

Kelsey shrugged. "Because since she died certain things have come to light, things she did recently that seem, um, pretty malicious. What I'm trying to figure out is if she'd been acting out of anger—either at the company or at me—or if there was some other reason for her actions."

Vern's eyebrows raised. "Malicious?"

Kelsey could feel her cheeks growing hot. As mad as she was at Gloria, it still felt terrible maligning the dead this way. "Malicious toward me, Vern. I don't want to go into detail, but what I'm trying to figure out is whether she was acting to hurt me personally or if she was trying to inflict damage on Brennan & Tate."

Vern didn't answer but instead just looked at her incredulously.

The elevator reached the ground floor and the doors opened.

"I know it sounds crazy, but I have…evidence that she hasn't exactly been acting in the best interests of the company. I have a feeling I know why, but before I pursue that I just wanted to double-check with you." Stepping out of the elevator, Kelsey turned toward Vern, locking eyes with him. "Was Gloria mad at me? Was she holding some sort of grudge against me? Did she hate me? Or was this all about what happened in the past and I just got hurt in the process?"

Vern slowly shook his head, and either he was a very good actor or he was genuinely stunned by her questions. "I honestly don't know what to tell you, Kelsey. You have to know as well as I do that Gloria loved you dearly. You were like the daughter she never had."

Tears threatened at the back of Kelsey's eyes, but she willed herself not to cry.

"She loved the company too," he continued. "She lived and breathed Brennan & Tate. I don't know what kind of evidence you have, but I'd have to see it to believe it. I mean, sure, she had her occasional irritations with management or frustration with a client or a coworker, but who doesn't? Gloria was as dedicated as they come."

Kelsey nodded skeptically.

"I'm sure it's no secret that her career and her company ranked far above her marriage. Far above *me*. I learned to live with that a long time ago. But if you're going to sit here and tell me she didn't love you or love that place with all her heart, I have to say you're wrong. Dead wrong."

They grew silent as his words hung in the air between them. Kelsey wasn't all that surprised at what he was saying, nor at the conviction with which he was saying it. Before she found that letter on Gloria's computer, she would have said the same things to anyone else who asked.

But now she knew differently.

She walked silently through the lobby toward the door to the street, Vern following along behind her.

"Is there any chance your evidence could be wrong?"

"I found an incriminating document on her computer."

"Someone else could have put it there, Kelsey. Someone else could have been trying to make her look bad, though I can't imagine why."

"That thought crossed my mind at first, but so many things have come to light. Gloria was up to something before she died. I guess I just wanted your opinion as to whether her actions were against me personally or against the company."

They reached the door and Vern pulled it open. "Well, as her husband, I'm telling you the answer to that question is *neither*. She loved you and she loved B & T. All the evidence in the world couldn't convince me otherwise."

Kelsey nodded, moving out onto the sidewalk. When she turned back toward him for a thanks and a goodbye, she realized that an odd look had come over his face.

"What is it?"

He shrugged. "I was just thinking…well, she *had* been acting kind of strange the past few weeks. Very stressed, very anxious. It got so bad that the other day I told her she needed to go see her doctor and get something for her nerves."

Kelsey thought about that. Though she and Gloria interacted frequently at work, they had both been busy lately on different projects and had barely done more than speak as they passed in the hallways—and even that happened only once in a while. The last time they had spent more than ten minutes together had been almost four weeks ago, when they had met up on a Saturday morning and gone to the Union Square farmers market together. Now Kelsey realized that if something had been bothering Gloria, she wouldn't have been around her enough to know it.

"Any idea what was stressing her out? Was it something to do with work, or maybe something personal?"

He shrugged, eyes darting away. "I assume it was work. She spent almost all of Monday night down at the office."

Kelsey squinted. "This past Monday night? The night before she died?"

He nodded. "Yeah. I mean, she came home at a decent hour—earlier than usual, actually—but then she got a call around ten or ten thirty, one that got her all worked up. Said she had to get back to the office to handle a crisis. By the time she got home again, it was almost morning. She probably slept all of an hour, and then she had to go back to work."

Unfortunately, he couldn't remember anything of the phone conversation that had sent Gloria to the office that night and didn't even know who she'd been talking to. Kelsey asked if they could check the caller ID, but he said it had come on her cell, and that was being held by the police for now.

Kelsey thought of what Ephraim had told her the day before, that Walter and Gloria had had a big argument in the auditorium on Monday afternoon. She had a feeling that the call later that night had been a continuation of their argument—though what had brought the woman back to the office and kept her there until dawn, she had no idea. At least that explained why Gloria had looked such a mess on Tuesday prior to the ceremony. She'd pulled an all-nighter, something she was too old to do.

With a final hug, Kelsey thanked Vern for his help, and he thanked her for the cake and the visit. Then she made her way back to the subway and down to the financial district as quickly as she could, thinking over their conversation all the way there.

CHAPTER
TWENTY-FIVE

The High Yield Café was located on Stone Street, a lovely little cobblestone lane about six blocks from the office. Lined with restaurants on both sides, the street was closed to traffic and was one of Kelsey's favorite dining spots, especially in the summer, when the restaurants moved some of their tables outside for dining alfresco.

In April, however, it was still chilly enough that she would have to be content with sitting indoors. Fortunately, their usual café was more of a lunch spot than a dinner draw, and at five fifty on a Thursday night it was half empty. The hostess was happy to set her up at a table for six, and soon she was settled in, facing the door and waiting for her group to arrive.

Despite the rush hour subway ride, she'd managed to make it to the restaurant a little early, and she was glad. Not only would she be here to greet her guests when they arrived, but she'd also have a few minutes to clear her head and focus. The waitress brought her a cup of decaf coffee, and she sat and sipped it as she thought about her research team.

Things moved fast in the world of investing, and lots of information had to be assembled quickly. Her group of highly skilled individuals, each with a different area of expertise, could research the various elements of a potential investment and help guide her to make wise decisions. Along with Sharon and herself, the team was comprised of a financial analyst, a background researcher, a technical expert, and an advisor, each one among the best in the company and handpicked by her.

With every prospect who came their way looking for financing, Kelsey and her team would go into action, whether that prospect was pushing an invention, creating a plan for a new business, or helping with the expansion of an established company. It was up to her and her team to evaluate the background of the prospect and their business or idea. Once that had been done, it was much easier to determine whether the proposal in question would be a good investment for Brennan & Tate or not.

Three or four years ago, the procedure had been for Kelsey to take her team's findings to Gloria, who would then make the final decisions about the investment, based on the team's information and her own experience, instincts, and other factors. But for the past year Kelsey had been making final recommendations herself. She had done quite well thus far, bringing in good money for the firm. The *Q* on her lapel attested to that.

Her hope tonight was that she could use her team's investigative skills to solve the issues that had risen up this week and were threatening to destroy both a company and a legacy. She would present them with the information she had managed to collect thus far—about Gloria, Rupert, and Queen's Fleet Management Group—and then they could run with it, using their knowledge and resources to come up with some answers or at least a solid theory or two.

Kelsey glanced at her phone to see that it was 6:02 p.m. They should be arriving any minute, so as she continued to wait, she pulled from her purse the questions she'd written up on the train. She skimmed through the whole list, starting with, *Why was Gloria trying to reach Rhonda the day she died?*, and then she jotted down a few more, ending with, *What were the terms of the takeover offer and how did the board respond?*

It was a start. Some of the questions were closely connected, and she was sure the answers would overlap. There was just so much she needed to know. Thank goodness they had agreed to help her!

After a while, Kelsey checked her phone again and was startled to see that it was nearly six fifteen. Where was everyone? They were usually a prompt bunch. Time was money in their business, after all. Frowning, she was about to call Sharon and ask what was holding them up when the restaurant door opened and in stepped Walter Hallerman. Kelsey's breath caught in her throat, and for some strange reason she almost felt guilty, as if she'd been trying to get away with something bad and had been caught red-handed.

Walter spotted her and began winding his way between the tables to her place in the corner. She sat there watching him come, her pulse surging. His face was grim, and she knew she was about to be reprimanded. She could just feel it.

When he reached the table, he stood there stiffly, glaring down at her.

"Your team isn't coming, Kelsey."

She took a deep breath and told herself to remain calm.

"And why not?"

He shook his head. "I already told you that your access to the company has to be limited. That includes not using B & T resources to run your own maverick agenda."

With that he turned and walked away.

Furious, Kelsey sat there steaming for a long moment. But then as the door swung shut behind him, she grabbed her things, tossed a ten on the table, and got up. She ran after him.

"Walter!" she called, once she was outside on the sidewalk. He turned to face her. "What are you keeping me away from? What are you trying to hide?"

His eyes darkened. "I've already explained this to you. We have to disassociate B & T from you and these allegations of fraud against your great-grandmother."

"My great-grandmother wasn't a fraud!" she hissed, her back straight and her chin high. She'd never thought she would see this day—when a member of the Tate family would have to fight for the company and the integrity of the Tate name.

"Can you prove it?" he said in a lower tone. "Because if you can, great. We could take things public and try to repair the damage done by your cousin. But I doubt that you can, and right now I don't see any other way around this. I'm sorry, Kelsey, but I spoke at length with Rupert Brennan yesterday. He may be a little eccentric, but he's not crazy and he's not giving up the fight. I'd move carefully on this if I were you."

Kelsey wanted to scream. Walter, who should have been her strongest ally, was now her adversary. She wished Great-Grandma Adele were here with her—or her father or someone else she could trust. Someone who would back her up and give her the freedom to do what she needed to do. A week ago she would have turned to Gloria. Tonight, she had been counting on her team. But there was no team, no Gloria, no Nolan, no Adele.

There was just her, and she was alone.

Swallowing the painful lump in her throat, Kelsey told herself to calm down, that she couldn't blame Walter for this. He was only trying to do the best he could to ensure the company would ride out the storm.

"Talk to me, Walter," she said in a more reasonable tone. "We both want this horrible mess to go away. I'm doing what I can from the outside, but there's still a lot I need to know. I deserve some information."

He stood there for a long moment, as if hovering between coming and going. Then he sighed heavily and looked at his watch. "All right. I can give you fifteen minutes."

Together they returned to the restaurant and to her table in the back corner, though when the waitress came to get Walter's drink order, Kelsey apologized, saying that her group wouldn't be coming after all and that they would be happy to move to a smaller one.

"No prob," the woman said. "We don't usually get much of a crowd on Thursday nights anyway."

Once she walked away, Kelsey turned to Walter and asked him to start by explaining to her about the takeover. He gave her a brief summary of events, saying that on Monday afternoon he'd been contacted by Pamela Greeley of Queen's Fleet Management Group, who made him an offer for Brennan & Tate.

"Trust me, that offer was *not* in our best interest. I took it to the board, and of course they rejected it."

Kelsey pondered that. "Were you surprised when the offer came in?"

"Of course. I had no idea it was in the works. And I'm very unhappy about this whole thing, but we're in it now, and I'm doing the best I can—for B & T and for you, Kelsey, whether it feels that way or not."

Deep down, she wanted to take his words at face value, but it was hard. Could she really trust him? How did she know what he was really doing while she was banned from the office and her usual sources of information?

"What did Gloria think about the offer?" she asked. She didn't want to rat out Ephraim and the secret he'd shared with her about the argument he'd overheard on Monday between Gloria and Walter, so instead she left it to Walter himself to tell her. If he answered honestly, it would be a good sign that he was on the up-and-up.

"Gloria was all for it, much to my surprise," he said. "We had words. It didn't go well. The day she died, she was still so angry about it that she wouldn't even speak to me. I figured she would cool down eventually and then we could talk like rational adults. Instead, she killed herself, leaving me to wonder why she'd taken such an absurd stance against the company she loved more than life itself."

The waitress approached the table with the mug of hot tea Walter had ordered and a fresh cup of decaf for Kelsey. Then she asked if she could take their order.

"We're not staying," Walter said to her, and again Kelsey was reminded of how differently this evening was playing out than she had expected. At this point she should have been surrounded by her EA and her top-notch team, fighting over slices of pizza and hashing out the mystery that was quickly consuming her life. Instead, she was here sipping coffee, stomach growling, with the man who had kicked her out of her own family company.

"You say you had words. When was that?"

"Monday afternoon, downstairs in the auditorium."

"And did you call her at home later that night? Around ten thirty?"

Walter looked startled. "No, why would I do that?"

She studied his eyes, trying to decide if he was telling the truth or not. "Vern said someone called her at home Monday night at about ten thirty, and after that she was upset and went back to the office and stayed there till dawn."

A noisy group of diners came in the front door, distracting them both. Once the people were settled at a front table and had quieted down a bit, they resumed their conversation.

"This is the first I've heard of this," Walter said earnestly. "I can't imagine what would have brought Gloria back out at that hour, much less kept her out for that long."

They were both quiet for a moment as Kelsey tried to decide how much to tell him.

"To be honest, Walter," she said finally, "Gloria did several things recently that have me questioning her motives. Things you may not be aware of."

"Oh?"

She nodded. "For starters, did Rupert tell you about the letter he got inviting him to the ceremony?"

"The anonymous one? With the invitation and the cash? Yes, he did. What about it?"

She hesitated, hoping she was right to trust Walter with the secrets she had thus far unearthed. "That letter came from Gloria."

Walter's head jerked back, as if he'd been slapped. "Don't be ridiculous."

Without another word, she reached into her purse and pulled out the printed copy. "I figured out her password and found this yesterday. I brought it up to your office and was about to show it to you when you had me escorted from the building."

He took the letter from her and read it through, several times, his face growing ashen as he did.

"I don't understand," he said finally, handing it back. "Gloria was the one charged with squelching this issue the last time it came up. Why would she turn around now and undo all of her own hard work?"

Kelsey let that question sit there between them as she folded up the letter and tucked it back into her purse. "I don't know, but you might have someone poke around a bit more in her files. Who knows what else you'll find in there? I came across this in less than half an hour, and I had barely scratched the surface."

The poor man actually looked as though he might be sick. "But why?" he whispered, more to himself than to her. "Why would Gloria turn on us this way?"

Kelsey sipped her coffee, studying his face. "I have a theory if you'd like to hear it."

"Please. Something. Anything."

Settling back in her chair, Kelsey told him that she thought it had to do with the situation five years before, when he was first brought in to run the company and Lou and Gloria were both passed over for promotion. She said that Gloria had been extremely hurt by the whole thing and had been harboring resentment ever since.

"Why did my father do that anyway, Walter?" she asked. "No offense, but why did he need you when he already had two outstanding candidates in-house? Both Lou and Gloria were competent enough to step into the positions of CEO and COO. Did my father not trust them in some way?"

Walter shook his head. "No, lack of trust had nothing to do with it. I think in Gloria's case she was *so* competent in the position she already held that Nolan wanted to keep her there forever. His long-range plan for her was to continue to develop her department so that it would eventually become its own division."

"So she never would have risen to COO or CEO?"

Walter shook his head. "Not under Nolan's long-term plan, no. As for Lou, your father had great respect for the man, but at that time he felt he was too immature, too impulsive to become CEO just then. That's one reason I was Nolan's first choice for the job, because I'm not exactly a spring chicken. He told me straight out that he expected me to serve at the helm for ten years and then retire. At that point, his hope was that Lou would have matured enough to step up and take my place."

Walter sipped his tea as Kelsey thought about that. She didn't see Lou as impulsive, just aggressive, which wasn't necessarily a bad quality to have in this business. If she was honest, she had a feeling her father's stance had had more to do with Lou's nouveau riche mentality than his "immaturity." The man wore thousand-dollar shoes and lived in Trump Tower, but every once in a while he'd let slip a "youse guys" and reveal his humble Brooklyn roots. And while her father wasn't exactly a snob, he'd been raised in a far more refined environment. Someone like Lou at the helm of the family company would have been distasteful at best, embarrassing at worst. Nolan had probably hoped that another ten years would serve to file away the rougher edges and make Lou a more suitable representative for the Tate family. She wasn't proud of that thought, but she had a feeling she was right.

"Unfortunately," Walter continued, "while your father's plan was a sound one, he didn't do a good job of communicating it to Lou or to Gloria. In response, Gloria was very upset, from what I understand, but at least she sucked it up and got on with things. Lou, on the other hand, did not. True to his nature, he left B & T in a pique and went to start his own company."

"Which he's been quite successful with, by the way."

"Oh, I know. No one doubted his talents, Kelsey. It was just a question of his readiness for the position at that time."

"But when Lou left B & T, that would have opened up the COO position after all, right?"

"Correct."

"So, once again, Gloria must have expected a promotion into the spot left vacant by Lou's departure."

Walter nodded. "Probably. Instead, your father decided to dissolve the COO position and divide out its duties, most of which came to me."

"Leaving poor Gloria passed over again."

"I'm afraid so. Maybe you're right. Maybe her resentment had festered in the years since. She always worked well with me, but then again she was a professional, never the kind to wear her heart on her sleeve."

Kelsey nodded in agreement. Some of Gloria's biggest lessons to her as mentor involved keeping a level head and making business decisions with facts, not emotions. Acting from hurt feelings wouldn't fit Gloria's character. If she had chafed working under Walter, she had kept her feelings in check and done an excellent job without revealing what was really going on inside.

Which had probably only served to make the situation worse.

"Anyway," Kelsey concluded, "I think Gloria may have taken all of that rejection harder than anyone realized. I think she'd probably been simmering with resentment ever since, just waiting for her chance to get even. That sounds impossible, I know, but it's the best explanation I've been able to come up with."

They were both silent for a moment. Kelsey watched a plate of nachos go by and felt her stomach rumbling. Maybe when they were finished she would order some dinner for herself.

"But why now?" Walter asked. "It's been five years. Why choose this point in time to sabotage the company?"

Kelsey shrugged. "I'm not sure, but I wouldn't be surprised if it had something to do with the big PR campaign we've been conducting to promote the Tate name. How better to bring the company to its knees than by letting that campaign reach a fever pitch—all Tate, all the time—and then slam the Tate name with allegations of fraud? It's brilliant, actually. She sent that letter to Rupert Brennan a few weeks ago and set off a chain of events that just might lead to the end of the company as we know it. Voilà, sweet revenge at last."

Walter sipped at his tea for a moment and then spoke. "Let's say you're right and that's really what she was trying to do. But to what end? What did she hope to accomplish? She's an employee of B & T herself, not to mention a stockholder. By damaging the company, she'd only be hurting herself. As my mother used to say, she'd be cutting off her nose to spite her face."

"Which is why none of this made sense until I heard about the hostile takeover."

He looked at her, squinting, and then understanding slowly flooded his features. "The stock value."

Kelsey nodded. "It's my theory that Gloria wanted to drive down the value of the stock so that the takeover would be more feasible for Queen's Fleet Management Group. I'm sure Pamela promised her a cushy new position after the takeover—maybe even at the top spot. Gloria wasn't just being spiteful for spite's sake, Walter. She was killing two birds with one stone."

"You're talking about corporate sabotage, young lady."

Kelsey raised her hands, palms upward. "Hey, don't shoot the messenger." With that, she sat back and waited for him to process her theory. The poor man looked stunned, a general who'd just learned there was a traitor in the ranks.

CHAPTER
TWENTY-SIX

April 12, 1912

ADELE

The sea was calm again on Friday, and Adele and Jocelyn had spent half the morning on the boat deck, visiting, reading, and warming themselves in the sun. Now that lunch was over, Adele had come back up to the boat deck again, alone this time, to wait for her Uncle Rowan. The air was colder than it had been that morning, but it was still pleasant enough to be outside, thanks to the warm new navy coat Aunt Oona had made for her prior to the voyage. Adele didn't even need her hand muff, though she was glad she'd thought to wear her gloves this time.

At the moment, Jocelyn was three decks down in the enclosed promenade. She had found some storybooks in the library and brought them with her, hoping to help entertain some of the children there. As for Tad, Adele had a feeling he was currently in the smoking room. She wasn't sure what the men did in there all day, but apparently that had quickly become one of his favorite places on the entire ship. At least he seemed to have made some new friends in there. Right now, Adele was grateful for the relative solitude of the boat deck as she waited for her uncle's arrival. They had an exciting appointment coming up in a little while, and she was relieved to have this chance to relax and focus on what lay ahead.

Once Uncle Rowan joined her, the two of them would be going into first class to have tea with Mr. Neville Williams. Only they had been invited, and though Adele wasn't sure why Jocelyn and Tad had been excluded from the event, a part of her was glad. She hoped to discuss matters of business and finance with Mr. Williams, and that would be easier and far more pleasurable without the bored, glazed-over eyes of her cousin or the scornful, dismissive looks of Tad.

At least he had begun to tone down all of that a bit. Last night at dinner, Adele had been trying to calculate how many meals would be needed for the entire voyage. When she expressed her final estimate aloud, rather than ignoring her or making fun, Tad had actually responded with interest. Soon, they were entertaining everyone at the table with various facts they had learned about the galley; for example, that the ship had started out with fifty tons of meat and poultry and five and a half tons of fish, all served on twenty-one thousand plates and washed down with beverages in thirteen thousands cups.

It made for a fascinating discussion, and by the time the meal had drawn to a close and Adele pushed the last of her dessert aside, the two of them had moved on to a spirited debate about how much coal was burned in a single day in order to maintain a speed of twenty-two knots. By the time they finally agreed on six hundred tons a day, the conversation had shifted to whether that speed would allow *Titanic* to break the record for the fastest crossing of the North Atlantic. Tad claimed he had it on good authority that the ship was traveling fast enough to arrive a day early in New York, thus ensuring they would make it into the history books. Adele countered that this was just nonsensical smoking room talk, and it would be far too dangerous to maintain that speed through the ice fields to come.

After dinner, as the men and the women parted ways so that the ladies could visit the library and the gentlemen relax in the smoking room, Tad had actually taken hold of Adele's hand and brought it to his lips in farewell. She wasn't sure how she felt about such an action—or about him, for that matter—but she'd been flattered by his attentions regardless. Perhaps he was the one who had given a bad first impression and was not nearly as obnoxious as she'd thought.

"Adele!"

At the sound of her name, she turned to see her uncle moving toward her across the open deck, a wide smile on his face.

"Oh, good," Rowan said, coming to a stop in front of her. "I had hoped you'd be out here already so that we would have a few moments to chat before going to tea."

Adele noted that her uncle had changed into his finest suit for the occasion. She, too, had taken care with her appearance, styling her hair and donning another of her new dresses, an emerald-green wool crepe with a shadow lace collar and plaited-front skirt.

"You look absolutely lovely, by the way," Rowan said, eyeing her outfit approvingly.

"And you, sir, look as if you must have wandered into second class by accident," she replied with a smile. "Better get back to first class by dinnertime, or they will be missing you at the captain's table."

A trio of female passengers began moving their way, so before the women could attempt to engage the two of them in friendly conversation, Rowan took Adele's arm and steered her in the opposite direction.

"Our mutual good looks aside," he said jovially, "I need to bring you up to date on the situation with Mr. Williams before we see him. I apologize that you and I have not had the opportunity to speak alone prior to this."

Adele told him not to worry, that she had known he would get to it eventually.

"If you recall from our conversation Tuesday night," Rowan continued, "I told you that while I had been quite impressed with Neville's new company, Tad had not shared my high opinion. In the end, he chose not to invest, and so I had followed suit."

"That's what you said on the train. I was disappointed, but I trust your judgment. There will be other opportunities for investment."

"Yes, well, let me continue. You see, at the time I had deferred to Tad's expertise in the matter. He's young, yes, but I assumed Sean would not have sent him as his representative unless he possessed the ability to evaluate an investment properly. After all, Tad came with the authority to commit a much larger sum to Transatlantic Wireless on your father's behalf than the amount I had hoped to commit on yours. If he truly felt the company did not deserve the fifty thousand dollars Sean had allotted for the investment, who was I to think I knew better and hand over the money you had entrusted to me?"

She nodded. "I see what you mean."

"You have strived so diligently over the years to create a large nest egg for yourself, and I have not taken lightly the trust you've given me to make the decision about whether or not to invest it in Transatlantic Wireless."

"I have absolute faith in your judgment, Uncle Rowan," Adele said, glancing at the older man. With a twinkle in her eye, she added, "Though I assume what you are about to tell me now has to do with that last-minute 'change of plans' you had on Wednesday morning, prior to our departure."

He smiled. "You know me well. That's correct. Though I turned Neville down on Tuesday afternoon, I awoke Wednesday morning with a new view of the situation. The man had mentioned he would be attending a breakfast meeting with his partners there in Southampton prior to boarding the ship, and so while you and Jocelyn were dining with Tad at our hotel, I was paying a visit to that meeting to let Neville know that I wanted to invest with him after all."

Adele stopped walking. "And?"

Rowan stopped as well, turning to face her. "And he was delighted to see me. He and I were given access to a private room where we conducted our transaction." Lowering his voice to a whisper, Rowan added, "I am happy to tell you, my dear, that you are now the proud owner of ten one-thousand-dollar bonds from Transatlantic Wireless, Limited. They are in the safe in the purser's office, though I will gladly hand them over once we reach America."

Thrilled, Adele gave her uncle a big hug. This was tremendous news! Not only did this make her a real, legitimate investor at last, it also gave her a wonderfully striking trump card, if needed.

"You must promise me something," Adele whispered eagerly, gripping his hands. "Promise you won't breathe a word of this to my father."

Rowan raised an eyebrow.

"Don't misunderstand. I actually think of this as his money," she continued quickly. "After all, I wouldn't even *have* a nest egg if he hadn't sent funds for my support so regularly all these years."

"Don't be modest, Adele. It was thanks to your tight budgeting and your clever little investments that you were able to grow each month's leftover cash into an amount so great."

Adele shrugged. "Regardless, I would have none of it if not for him. I will be giving the bonds over eventually, but I need to do so in a way that serves as leverage—when I'm finished with college and ready to join Brennan & Company as an employee."

"Leverage? What on earth are you talking about?"

"If my father resists having me in his employ, if he says no, that a woman has no place in business, I will tell him, 'On the contrary, Father,' and then I will pull out the bonds and hand them over with a flourish. They will be proof positive that I *do* know what I'm doing, that by using my money skills I managed to parlay a small portion of the monthly allowance he sent for my support into bigger and bigger investments until I worked it up to ten thousand dollars—which I then invested in bonds. He will have no choice at that point but to welcome me into the ranks."

Adele was grinning at the very thought, but all Rowan could do was groan.

"Fine, I will do as you have requested," he told her, shaking his head piteously, "but I don't think such a presentation will ever be needed. My brother is a fine man and a forward-thinking individual. He also loves you very much and will surely do whatever he can to make you happy, proof or not."

Adele considered his words, hoping he was right but grateful to have the bonds just in case.

"In any event," Rowan said, taking her arm and continuing their walk, "I would imagine that the reason Neville has invited us to tea today is to celebrate your investment and to assure you of its validity and potential."

"You told him it was my money you were spending?"

"Not at the time, no. But after our tour of first class yesterday, he kept saying what an impressive young woman you were, and in the end I was unable to resist. I bragged about how you have strived over the years to amass such a tidy sum. He was deeply honored that I had chosen to entrust that amount to him on your behalf. When his invitation to tea arrived this morning and your name was included, I can't say I was all that surprised."

Rowan took out his pocket watch and flipped it open as they continued to walk. Adele's head was spinning—with excitement, with nervousness, with pride. This was wonderful news, truly wonderful!

"I'm curious, Uncle. What made you change your mind about Tad's judgment on this matter? Is he not as skilled a businessman as you had first thought?"

Rowan looked out at the watery horizon, his face growing unreadable. "I suppose it's just that Tad is…young…and needs to mature. He has much to learn about finance—and about the world in general.

"And about women," she added with a grimace.

"Speaking of women," Rowan said as they rounded the corner and saw the same group of chattering females once again coming in their general direction, "I believe this would be a good time to head to tea. We certainly don't want to keep Neville waiting."

With that they turned and made their way down a flight of stairs to the A deck and the door that divided the first and second classes. After showing their invitation to a steward, they were welcomed into the Verandah Café and Palm Court and escorted to the table of Mr. Williams, who was already there waiting for them.

The room was beautifully appointed, light and airy, with ivy trellises covering the walls and wicker furniture all around. Mr. Williams was at a table near the center and seemed delighted to see them. Soon the three were indulging in a variety of treats, from shortbread cookies to finger sandwiches and more, as they sipped their tea and discussed wireless technology in general and Transatlantic Wireless in particular. Adele didn't know much about wireless, but Mr. Williams was quite knowledgeable about both its current capabilities and its future potential. He said that the equipment aboard *Titanic* was the most powerful on any ship in the world, capable of communicating with stations several hundred miles away during the day and several *thousand* at night. Adele found herself thoroughly encouraged by their conversation and had no doubt that someday her ten bonds would be worth quite a lot more than their original price of a thousand dollars each.

At some point the conversation turned to the world of investment in general. Mr. Williams must have sensed Adele's genuine interest in the topic, because not only did he freely dispense his own advice, but he even began to solicit input from some of his fellow first-class passengers as well. The man was quite popular and seemed to know almost everyone who passed by. More than once, upon making introductions, he would refer to Rowan and Adele as "my newest investors," and then he would lightheartedly ask the people if they had any investment tips to share.

Most responded with an eye to Rowan, but Adele absorbed every word regardless. She was especially impressed with a Canadian named Mr. Charles Fortune, whom Mr. Williams later explained was a self-made real estate mogul who had been born the son of a farmer. In response to Mr. Williams' request, Mr. Fortune seemed to consider the issue for a long moment. Then, looking toward Rowan, he said, "When investing, never forget the value of the people involved. You may sometimes find a better price elsewhere, but never forget to factor in character and integrity—both of which have tremendous worth. In my opinion, the value of a man's good word is much higher than most investors realize." Then, with a smile, he turned to Mr. Williams, adding, "And now I suppose I've given away any negotiating advantage I

might have had between us, eh?" With a laugh and a pat to Mr. Williams'
back, Mr. Fortune excused himself and kept going.

More than once during their time together, Adele thought of Tad and
how much he would have loved meeting the people she was meeting and
having the conversations they were having. Though it would be hard to keep
quiet about it later, she decided not to mention it at all, lest he become so jealous that he revert to his earlier treatment of her.

Still, she couldn't help but wish he'd been there when she was introduced
to the vice president of the Hudson City Hospital in New York. To Adele's
amazement, the person in possession of that title was a woman, a Miss Kor-
nelia Andrews, traveling home aboard *Titanic* with her sister and niece.

As exciting as that was, however, Adele's favorite introduction of all was to
a woman named Margaret Brown. Though the spirited Mrs. Brown seemed
to possess even more American brashness than Tad, she was also quite smart
and witty, and Adele took to her instantly. When Mr. Williams solicited the
same advice from her that he had been asking of the men, she looked straight
at Adele and replied, "If you want to invest, honey, look to the people and
places the big boys are ignoring—women's interests, for example. Show me
a woman with a good idea and a strong work ethic, and I'll show you somebody who can succeed like the dickens if she's given a proper chance."

Adele thought about those words for the rest of their time in the Palm
Court and even once their wonderful visit with Mr. Williams had drawn to
a close and they were back on their own part of the ship. Truly, she felt as if
Mrs. Brown had lit a spark inside her brain.

It is one thing to try and break down those barriers that stand in my way,
Adele thought, *and quite another to help other women get started out as well.
How fulfilling that would be!*

After college, once she joined the staff of Brennan & Tate, she would
try to focus her investments on hardworking women with good ideas who
wanted to go into business. Not only would she be changing lives for the better, but with all that was going on in the world, she had a feeling there had
never been a better time to explore the potential of such an untapped market.

CHAPTER
TWENTY-SEVEN

Walter looked at Kelsey, a frown creasing his brow.

"Wait a minute. You knew Gloria as well as I did. Hidden resentments or not, these are very serious charges. Do you honestly think she was the kind of person who could do something like that?"

"Before this week? No. After all that's happened now? Yes. Needless to say, I've come a long way in a short time."

He put down his mug and leaned forward to speak in a whisper. "As an employee and a significant stockholder, for her to have acted to facilitate the takeover in this way wouldn't just be unethical, it would also probably be illegal. Hidden resentments or not, do you really think Gloria Poole would have gone outside of the law?"

Kelsey felt a surge of guilt as soon as he asked the question. In truth, she could not. But what other explanation was there for what she'd done?

"Maybe that's why she killed herself," Kelsey replied. "Maybe she did it, but then her remorse was so great that she ended up taking her own life because of it. Why else would she send her suicide note to me rather than to her husband? She asked *me* to forgive her for what she'd done. Her crimes were primarily against *me*." Blinking away tears, Kelsey met Walter's eyes, a new thought just coming to her.

"I bet I know what the final nail in this coffin was, so the speak. The thing that tipped her over the edge."

"What's that?" Walter asked.

Kelsey's mind raced. "All the promoting of 'Kelsey Tate'—the Quarter

Club and the *Forbes* honor and all of that. What do you want to bet she saw the writing on the wall and realized that five years from now when you retire, *I* would be the one to hop right over her and land in the spot of CEO myself. Everyone knows my father has always intended for me to run the company eventually. I thought I'd be much older before that happened, but maybe she saw me becoming more successful, more well known, and she panicked, realizing that once again the top spot was going to open up and it would be given to someone else instead of to her."

He nodded, understanding her point. "That makes a lot of sense. I just hope that in five years there will be a company left for you to run."

Kelsey leaned forward, studying Walter's face. "What are we going to do to fight this takeover?"

"There's not a lot we *can* do at this point. We've turned down their offer, so technically it's now in the hands of the stockholders. I've been contacting all of the ones I know personally and presenting our case, but it's difficult."

Kelsey puffed out a breath. "I need to speak to Pamela myself."

"I don't know what good it would do. To be honest, I'm fairly resigned to things at this point. Unless we can come up with some big bucks to save ourselves, I'm afraid the cause is lost."

She thought for a moment. "What about Strahan Realty Trust? Doesn't Lou have a standing offer on the table for a friendly merger?"

Walter nodded.

"Why not go that route instead? Surely a friendly merger with a smaller company is preferable to a hostile takeover by a mammoth one."

He took a deep breath and let it out slowly. "I suppose I could talk to Lou and see if he's still willing to stick to the amount of his previous offer, but I'd rather do neither. With all of Rupert Brennan's talk about Adele's mythical bonds really existing, I just keep thinking, if only those bonds did exist and we had them now..."

He shook his head, his voice trailing off, so she finished his thought for him.

"If only those bonds did exist and we had them now, that would change everything." She sighed. "Those bonds would save this company."

Walter needed to leave the restaurant soon after, but before he left, he reached out to shake her hand, thanking her for having insisted that they talk.

"I'm glad we cleared the air," he told her. "You're a credit to your whole family, Kelsey. I'm just sorry that I have to keep you away from the company for now. I do hope you see that it's nothing personal."

She shrugged, releasing her grip. "Personal or not, Walter, I think it's a dumb move. But I'll live with it for now. I'm willing to do whatever I can to help us through this mess."

"As am I," he said, but neither his tone nor his expression bore any hope of succeeding in that quest.

Once he was gone, Kelsey ordered herself a big, fattening plate of nachos with extra sour cream, but then she thought better of it and asked for soup and salad instead. She ate alone, looking out at the various people in the restaurant, laughing and chatting and having a good time. For some reason, her mind went to Cole and how much fun they had always had together when they went out to eat.

They had been a good couple, well matched in personality and intellect, with similar upbringings and ideals and goals. The closer they came to the possibility of marriage, the more they had talked about those goals. Together, they dreamed of becoming the modern version of Adele and Edwin Tate, with Kelsey out front and Cole behind the scenes, both of them working hard to make Brennan & Tate even more successful than it already was. She'd even teased him one time, saying that Adele changed the name of the company once her husband came on board.

"A tradition you could repeat, eh? Brennan, Tate, & Thornton," he had mused, nodding. "Has a nice ring to it, don't you think?" Pinching his nose, he had droned in a high voice, "'Hello, thank you for calling B & T & T. How may I direct your call?'"

Smiling at the memory now, Kelsey felt a surge of emotion deep in her chest, an aching loneliness, not just for all that she and Cole had shared but for what they would have shared in the future. How could she have destroyed that future simply because of her own ambition? For the past five years she'd been telling herself that Cole was too sensitive, that he should never have allowed their business relationship to affect their personal life. When she was really mad at him, she would even think good riddance, that he was too wimpy for this kind of a job anyway.

The deal he'd offered Lou *had* been pathetically low, considering the man's business plan, his extensive client commitments, and the large amount of his own money that he was willing to put in up front. The offer she had made was far more in line with his prospects than the one Cole had handed him, especially knowing how gifted and driven Lou was. Poor Lou had ended up getting caught in the crossfire and had felt bad about that for months after—especially when Cole had broken away completely and Kelsey had been so devastated. She always assured Lou that it wasn't his fault, that Cole didn't belong in this business without a thicker skin than that anyway. But looking back now, it struck her that it wasn't just her undercutting of a deal that had ended their relationship.

It had been her stubborn pride. Her unwillingness even to consider that she'd been wrong to do what she did. Her refusal to apologize or even feel bad about it. Now, eating her bowl of chicken noodle soup and her house salad with fat-free ranch dressing, Kelsey finally realized something. It was the aftermath of the event, far more than the event itself, that had driven Cole away.

She put down her spoon, suddenly losing her appetite.

In five years she hadn't once apologized to the man or admitted that she had lived to regret her actions. In five years she hadn't given him a call or sent him a note or even dashed off an email saying *I was wrong and I'm sorry*—not in an attempt at reconciliation but as an act of simple human decency. She had been wrong. She was sorry. But she had allowed the blinders of righteous indignation to keep her from seeing that truth until now, much less admitting it to anyone else.

Sadly, even if she did apologize to him now, it would probably be too little, too late. She couldn't give him back what he'd lost. On the phone earlier this morning, he'd said it was all "water under the bridge," but she knew that somewhere inside he must still harbor plenty of resentment toward her. Even so, she had no doubt his current offer to help had been genuine. To his core Cole was a good guy, the kind to set aside personal differences when necessary to deal with the matter at hand.

Poor Cole. At least he'd eventually landed on his feet. She wasn't sure exactly what his new company did, but he'd sounded as though they were making a go of it. For all she knew, he was even married by now. He could have children.

She, on the other hand, had barely dated since Cole left, let alone acquired a spouse and kids. In a flash she saw her own life for what it had become—an empty, work-centric existence that drew all emotion from the job rather than from other people. Now she found herself ostracized and alone, at odds with her firm's management and in danger of losing the family business. In a sense, she realized, Cole had surely come through their breakup in far bet-ter shape than she had.

Now, looking around the restaurant, her nerves jangling with every clink of glass or scrape of silverware, she realized that without her team and with-out insider access, she was never going to preserve her great-grandmother's legacy nor save the company from a hostile takeover. Cole had said to let him know if there was anything he could do to help. How ironic that she now seemed to have no other alternatives. She did need his help, desperately so. She would have to take him up on that offer—it was that or lose everything her family had worked so hard for.

Is this Your idea of a joke, God? she prayed silently as she gestured toward the waitress for her check. *Is going to Cole with my hat in hand my just desserts?*

When she left the restaurant it was dark outside and the temperature had dropped significantly. Shivering in her light jacket, she jogged almost all the way home. Once there, she was so wound up from her run that she changed into sweats and a T-shirt and climbed on the stair stepper. Finally, after a bru-tally long workout, she hit the shower. It wasn't until she was dried off and dressed for bed that she admitted she could stall no longer. She put down the hairbrush and reached for her phone. She pulled up the number she'd used earlier that day and tapped it.

Cole answered on the third ring.

"Kelsey! Glad you called. What's up?"

His cheerfulness and confidence hit her with greater force than she'd expected, and she sat down abruptly on the love seat.

"I...Cole, is the offer still open? I need help."

"Of course. I told you, anytime."

"Well, then, I'd like to take you up on it."

"Sure. Why don't you come to my office first thing in the morning? I'll round up my people and we'll see what we can do."

"That...that would be great. Thank you so much."

"No problem. You okay?"

She closed her eyes even as her ears were straining for background noise, for clues—the voice of a woman, the chatter of a toddler. The proof of a happy life, of having moved on. She heard nothing.

"I'm fine," she replied finally, clearing her throat. "It's just been a rough day."

"I can imagine. Well, not to worry. I'll see you in the morning and we'll try to figure out how we can make tomorrow a lot better."

He gave her the address for his office and then they ended the call.

She went on to bed soon after and dreamed she was floating in a small boat, alone, cut loose from its moorings and drifting slowly out to sea. She woke up after that. Getting out of bed, she went to the window and sat there in the darkness for a long time, looking out at the lights of the city.

She'd always wanted to grow up to be just like Adele. But Adele had found a way to have a successful career and a happy family and a full life. With tears rolling down her cheeks, Kelsey realized things hadn't turned out the way she'd planned at all. These days, she was nothing more than an empty workaholic who channeled all of her emotions and her energies into her career, pursuing success at all costs. Outside of that, she had nothing in her life, nothing else to live for. Swallowing hard, she had to admit the truth.

She hadn't grown up to be just like Adele.

She'd grown up to be just like Gloria.

CHAPTER
TWENTY-EIGHT

The next morning Kelsey approached Cole's office in the Chelsea section of Manhattan with a mix of trepidation and excitement. It would be so great to see him again, but a part of her was afraid it might be too much, that her cool demeanor would slip and she would end up revealing her feelings—about him, about their past, and about how much he still meant to her.

At least she'd made a point of looking her best today, and she thought that added confidence would go a long way toward helping her keep a level head. Cole had always loved her best in blue—the blue of her eyes—and so she had chosen an azure silk shirt dress with a slim silhouette that hung mid-calf with a slit to the knee. She always felt a little uncomfortable at B & T without a suit or at least a jacket, so this dress didn't get much wear. But she loved it, and with the addition of a black belt, her Q pin, and a beaded black necklace, the effect was at once completely businesslike and yet strikingly feminine. Knowing Cole, as long as there was blood still pumping in his veins, his heart would skip a beat or two over this one.

His office was located on a side street off of 9th Avenue. The address certainly wasn't as prestigious as the B & T offices, but not everyone could afford rent in the financial district. Their suite was on the third floor of the building, so she took the stairs, pausing at a mirror on the second floor landing to check her hair and makeup.

Continuing up one more flight of steps, she easily found the door she wanted, the nameplate reading Thornton Resources, Inc. Pausing a moment to collect herself, she steadied her shoulders and then twisted the knob to open the door, entering a pleasant reception area brightly lit by a full wall of deep windows.

"May I help you?"

Kelsey started at the sound, realizing that a woman had come out from the back to stand at the reception desk.

"Uh, hi," she replied, stepping closer. "Kelsey Tate to see Cole Thornton."

"Of course. He's expecting you. Just a moment."

The woman left again, and Kelsey took a deep breath, telling her heart to stop pounding so furiously. After a moment she could hear someone else coming, and then there he was, emerging from around the corner and walking toward her, a smile lighting up his whole face.

"Kelsey, wow, it's great to see you," he said, giving her a quick hug. She hugged him back, hoping he couldn't feel the thudding of her heart as she did.

"Hi, Cole. Thanks so much for this."

"Of course. You look great, by the way."

Kelsey smiled, looking up into his beautiful green eyes. He looked great too. Better than she'd remembered. His new maturity sat well on him. He was wearing a navy blazer with a light blue Oxford cloth shirt and khaki slacks. Apparently Thornton Resources had a business casual dress code. It seemed to fit the office—and its dashing CEO.

"Thanks," she managed to say. "Ditto."

"Why don't you come on back? I have us all set up in the conference room."

He led her from the sunny reception area and down a hall that was much darker by comparison.

"This is a neat space you have here," she said as they went. "Sunbeams shining in a third-floor window. That's awesome."

He flashed his handsome, handsome smile. "Thanks, Kels."

Cole stopped at a conference room doorway and gestured for her to go in. She did, stepping into a large room with a big table at its center surrounded by chairs, everything already set up for their meeting. At the far end of the room was a coffee dispenser, a platter of breakfast pastries, and a pitcher of ice water flanked by drinking glasses.

"I'm impressed," she said, gesturing toward the food service and inhaling the delicious scent of the coffee. "Looks like you went all out."

Cole grinned. "Well, I know you, Kelsey. Can't focus without a cup of joe in your hand."

She smiled in return, thinking, *He does know me. It's been five years, but still he knows me.*

He told her to help herself and have a seat while he left to round up the team. "Just so you know, I'm bringing in my two best guys on this. I'm sure you'll be sharing information with us that's quite confidential, and I just wanted to say that you can trust these two implicitly. They may not be your typical Wall Street suits, but they have been with me since the beginning and have never wavered in their loyalty or dependability. You're safe with us."

She gave him a grateful smile. "Thanks, Cole. That's comforting to know."

After that he was gone, and so she set her things on a chair and went to the far side of the room and made herself a cup a coffee. Grabbing a small paper plate, she chose a blueberry muffin top and carried it and the coffee back to the table. Then she sat, putting her goodies to the side as she placed her briefcase on her knees and popped it open.

Kelsey had managed to eventually get back to sleep last night, but she had gotten up just a few hours later, soon after dawn. She'd spent that first hour of the day at her laptop, organizing her thoughts and preparing her information for the meeting. In a business like theirs, facts needed to be clear and straightforward, preferably laid out chronologically in an easy-to-understand fashion. Though she wasn't coming to Cole for an investment, she was coming to him for help, and considering that he was doing this for free, she wanted to make things as easy as possible.

Thus, she'd assembled her main points into a handout, topped it with a typed-up version of her family tree, and printed out several copies that she'd stapled together. She removed those handouts from her briefcase now, along with a pad of paper and a pen. She hoped she could quickly run through the facts and then get down to the business of figuring out how to find the answers to at least some of her many questions.

She had just placed her briefcase on the floor behind her when she heard voices coming up the hall. Cole reappeared with two other men, a slender young guy with pale skin and brown hair who was in an electric wheelchair, and a tall, lanky African-American man with a shiny bald head and a big gold cross hanging at his neck. She stood as they came into the room, giving them each a smile in turn.

"Wow, boss, you weren't kidding," the one in the chair said, eyes wide and admiring.

She looked to Cole, but he just poked the guy on the arm. "Kelsey Tate, I'd like you to meet two of the most trusted members of my staff." Gesturing toward the tall one, he added, "This is Thriller. He's the best there is for research."

"Hi, Thriller." Kelsey shook his hand, wondering what the story was behind the nickname.

"Pleasure to be working with you, Miss Tate."

"Call me Kelsey."

"Kelsey," he replied, nodding.

"And this is Flash," Cole continued, placing a hand on the shoulder of the younger one in the chair. "He's our techie. Flash can do anything with a computer—and I mean anything."

"Security systems weep when they hear my name," the guy told her with a smug smile. "Nice to meet you."

"You too, Flash," Kelsey said, shaking his hand and wondering if everyone who worked at Thornton Resources had a nickname.

The guys helped themselves to the food and beverages, and then they took their seats at the table. Once everyone seemed ready to begin, Cole turned to her, his posture relaxed as he began to speak.

"Kelsey, why don't you tell us what can we do for you. I've spelled out the situation to the guys, as far as the people and the companies involved, but I didn't have many of the details."

Kelsey nodded, clearing her throat. "Well, basically, there's a big mess at my family firm, Brennan & Tate, and I need help sorting it all out. I have lots of questions I'm not going to be able to answer by myself."

"Then you've come to the right place. Finding solutions is our specialty."

Nodding again, Kelsey told them that the situation was so complicated that she'd decided to lay things out chronologically, from the beginning. She gave each man a handout, and they seemed impressed as they looked over the notes.

"On the first page," she began, referring to her own copy, "you'll see I started with a family tree. This is so you can keep all of the players straight. Things are going to get pretty complicated, so you can use this chart as reference."

The men nodded, studying the diagram.

"Anyway," Kelsey continued, flipping over to page two, "I think it's best if I begin at the beginning and bring it all forward from there."

Glancing down at the first item on her list, she started by saying that her great-great-grandfather Sean Brennan was born and raised in County Antrim, Ireland, and that when he was grown he married a woman named Beatrice and had a daughter named Adele. In 1896 he left his wife and child behind and came to America to build a better life for them all.

She was about to keep going when she realized Flash was giggling.

"Yes?"

He looked up, startled, as if he hadn't realized he was laughing out loud.

"It just struck me as funny that you said you were going to start at the beginning. I was expecting something like last year or last month—not a hundred and sixteen years ago! That's what I call starting at the beginning."

Thriller chuckled as well.

"Sorry," she replied, smiling. "Like I said, it's complicated. We have to go this far back to understand the whole situation." She returned her eyes to the page in front of her but then paused to look back up at Flash. "Sounds like you're a bit of a numbers whiz, by the way. That was some quick math you just did."

Beaming, he replied, "I'm the youngest-ever recipient of the Lobachevsky Award." At her blank stare, he added, "Nikolai Ivanovitch Lobachevsky? Discovered non-Euclidean geometry?"

Suppressing a grin, she glanced at Cole, who gave her a wink in return.

Referring again to the handout, she gave a brief summary of Sean Brennan's life, how his wife died and his daughter was sent to Belfast to be raised by his brother and sister-in-law, Rowan and Oona. She described Sean's professional successes here in New York, and how he worked in a bank and later formed his own investment firm, Brennan & Company, in 1904.

When Kelsey got to 1912 and the part where Adele and her cousin Jocelyn were nineteen and ready to come to America with Jocelyn's father, Rowan, Thriller grunted.

"Don't tell me," he said, interrupting. "They didn't buy passage on *Titanic,* did they?"

Kelsey nodded. "How did you guess?"

He shrugged, looking slightly embarrassed. "Nineteen twelve. Everybody knows that's the year it sank."

Again, Kelsey had to suppress a smile. She was being assisted by one math nerd and one *Titanic* buff. Throw in an ex-boyfriend for whom she still carried a torch, and their group made quite a team.

She continued, telling how the family may have bought some bonds before leaving London—bonds which may or may not have survived the sinking—and then she traced out the rest of the story, including the fact that the uncle and one cousin died but that the other cousin survived and made it to America. She told about what happened a year later, when a young executive who also survived the voyage, Tad Myers, challenged Adele's true identity, claiming she was in fact Jocelyn Brennan just pretending to be Adele. She described the letter Sean sent to Oona in response, and the frustrating lack of the letter she'd written in reply.

"According to my grandfather," Kelsey said, "Adele was keeping a diary back then, but no one knows where that diary ended up. If I could find it, it would probably shed some light on several of these issues."

Moving on, she told them about Adele going to work for her father and marrying Edwin Tate and guiding the company through tough times while also breaking down doors for women in business and becoming a legend on Wall Street. She gave the specifics of the payout from Sean's estate after he passed away and the impact Adele's identity would have on that. All three men nodded, seeming to understand, and the further she went, the more she realized what a great team they were. They seemed to connect the dots almost as quickly as she could lay out the facts.

From there she brought things forward to the early '70s, when Ian Brennan first approached Brennan & Tate about Sean's will and Adele's true identity and ended up with a settlement, and then how his son Rupert picked up that battle once Ian died in 2002 and pursued it some more until he was squelched by Gloria Poole. Kelsey was about to launch into a side explanation of why DNA testing couldn't help settle the question of Adele's identity when Flash cut her off with a brusque, "Of course not," and then, with reference to the family tree on the first page of her packet, he summarized the situation in scientific terms, going on about X and Y chromosomes and the limitations of mitochondrial DNA.

"I think we can take your word for it," Cole said at last, cutting him off. "Anyway, Kelsey, you were saying that Gloria was in charge of keeping Rupert quiet?"

She nodded, glad to be back on track but also sick at heart at the imminent turn in her tale. Her face flushing with heat, she kept her eyes trained on

the page as she got to that time five years ago when Gloria was twice passed over for promotion and ended up feeling so hurt and bitter. As that was also the time Kelsey had undercut Cole in the deal to finance Lou, she was afraid Flash might make some snide comment that would once again refer to their prior relationship. But he either had sense enough at that point to keep it to himself or he hadn't realized their breakup was connected with that specific series of events because he didn't say a word.

Finally, she brought them to one year ago, when her father had a stroke and the company's value began to plummet. She described the path that had eventually led the firm to hire a public relations group to restore consumer confidence by promoting Kelsey as the newest Tate with the golden touch. Moving along in time, she explained how Gloria had most likely been in talks with Pamela Greeley of Queen's Fleet Management Group at some point in the past few weeks, and how she had apparently done an about-face with Rupert Brennan and sent him an anonymous letter encouraging him to come to Tuesday's ceremony—probably to drive down the value of the company and thus make it more viable for a takeover by Pamela.

She had included a copy of the letter Gloria had sent to Rupert, and she paused to let them read it now. When they were done, she went on to reveal how Walter had been contacted by Queen's Fleet on Monday afternoon, at which point they had made an offer to buy B & T. She described how Gloria had been all for it and how she and Walter had fought, and then how Gloria went home early but got a call later that night, one that upset her greatly and brought her back to the office, where she stayed until morning.

Weary from the telling, Kelsey took a deep breath and tried to stretch her neck by tilting her head from side to side. The closer she came to the death, the harder this was for her.

She pressed onward regardless, describing Gloria's odd behavior just prior to the ceremony on Tuesday afternoon. Then she went through the whole Rupert disturbance and the conversation with him afterward. Finally, he voice flat, she explained how at 5:52 p.m. on Tuesday evening, Gloria se Kelsey a suicide note via text and then apparently hung herself from a cc attached to the projection screen in the executive conference room. At t point, the others around the table had grown so silent and still that she c hear the ticking of the clock on the wall.

"There's also a chance her death wasn't..." Kelsey's voice trailed of

cleared her throat and tried again. "The police are still investigating, but they haven't yet said whether it was a suicide or a homicide."

That earned a grunt from Thriller, but he didn't comment.

"Anyway," she said, "I've spent almost all of my time since then gathering the facts I've just gone through with you guys." She went on to describe how Walter kicked her out of the company and his reasoning behind it. Glancing at Cole, she was gratified to see an expression of outrage on her behalf.

She concluded with the last two matters of importance: the status of the hostile takeover, which was in the air pending a meeting and vote by the stockholders, and the conversation with her father about the bonds, when he told her Gloria had been in charge of their safekeeping and that wherever they were, it had something to do with what he'd called "The wonder."

"The wonder?" Flash asked.

"The wonder," Thriller mused, and she could tell that he was thinking the name over closely.

"And so," she said as she turned to the final page of the handout, "this is where we are now. You'll see on the last page that I've written out a long list of questions. And while I certainly don't expect you guys to answer every one of these, I thought the more clearly I spelled out exactly what I need to know, the more easily you can figure out which aspects you'd like to tackle and how you want to approach things."

With that she looked from Thriller to Flash to Cole, focusing in on Cole's gorgeous green eyes. "I'm so grateful for your offer to help, but now that you see what we're up against, I'll understand if you want to take a pass after all."

Cole's eyes widened, and to her surprise he reached out and placed a warm, comforting hand on top of hers.

"If anything, Kels, I'm even more determined to help you now than I was before. You weren't kidding when you said things were a mess. There's no way you should have to figure all of this out by yourself."

As he spoke, he looked to the other two guys, who were both nodding vigorously. Cole removed his hand, but the warmth of it lingered.

"Do you think there are parts of this that you can jump in and tackle?" she asked hopefully. "I know you're used to digging up info on investments, not on things like inside traitors or stolen identities or potential homicides, but I'm hoping maybe there's enough crossover here that you could at least do a little."

"I think we can do a *lot*," Thriller said, standing and going over to the dispenser to freshen his coffee.

Flash nodded. "Several avenues of approach have already occurred to me."

She looked again to Cole, who gave her a reassuring smile.

"Kelsey, our company is what you might call, uh, unique. This team truly is more than capable of meeting your challenge."

"So you really can help me after all?"

"You bet we can," Cole replied. "Looks to me like you need all the help you can get."

CHAPTER
TWENTY-NINE

Within an hour the group had managed to hammer out a full plan of attack. Each member of the team would be focusing on a different aspect of the investigation according to their expertise or access. Kelsey had been charged with two tasks. First, she was to secure some sort of detailed plans or blueprints of the B & T building so that the guys could study them for any logical places where a hidden safe may have been built into the walls. That shouldn't be too hard. From what she could recall, there was a set of plans in her father's home office, acquired a few years ago when they were considering a remodel of the sixth floor at B & T. And though there was no longer any need for that home office to exist, as far as Kelsey knew, it had remained untouched and completely intact.

Her other task was to confront Pamela Greeley, if possible, about her intentions with the takeover and her ties to Gloria. While they were all still there in the conference room making their plans, Kelsey called Pamela's office to ask for an appointment but had to leave a message.

Cole would be focusing on financials—of B & T and Queen's Fleet— while Flash would work on a plan for getting a look at Gloria's recent digitally recorded activities before she died. Finally, Thriller would cover the bonds, from their original acquisition to their current location. More than once she'd heard him mumble "the wonder" as if he had an idea about what that might mean but couldn't quite remember what it was.

The only part of the plan that made Kelsey nervous was the fact that they needed her to get into the Brennan & Tate offices after hours, both to facilitate a digital search and to conduct a physical one. Cole and Thriller both felt strongly that there might be a safe hidden somewhere in the office, and if so that it would probably contain the bonds—if they existed. She wasn't crazy about sneaking in against the wishes of the CEO, but in her heart she knew Walter was wrong to keep her away, dead wrong. If her father were still active and involved, he would have kicked Walter to the curb by now for even suggesting that Kelsey be banned from the family company. She had every right to go back in there and do what she needed to do.

"Can you suggest an optimum time?" Cole asked. "We need to get you in there when the place is empty, but we don't want to look suspicious by doing it in the middle of the night or something."

Kelsey thought for a moment. "Gloria's wake is this evening, and I'm sure most of B & T's management will be there. I thought I'd put in an appearance, but I don't have to stay long. I can be punctual, and most of them will probably come in a little later."

"Good," Cole said. "When does it start?"

"It runs six to nine."

"Perfect. Show up right at six and let them all see you there, but then get back over here as soon as you can, let's say by seven at the latest, and we'll all head down to the financial district together."

"Okay. Sounds good. Should I dress in black? Maybe bring along a ski mask or something?"

Cole smiled. "Slow down, James Bond. You're not breaking in and hopping over laser beams and rappelling down walls. You're an employee and a family stockholder of Brennan & Tate, and you'll be walking in the door like a regular person—well, you'll be walking in the back door. Coming in through the front might be pushing it."

They decided then that they would adjourn until this evening, with everyone working hard between now and then to accomplish their goals. With that, Flash and Thriller grabbed up one more load of pastries and disappeared to their respective offices while Cole offered to give Kelsey a quick tour before she left.

"Yes, please, I'd love that," she said, putting away her papers and then falling into step beside him.

Thornton Resources didn't have a lot of square footage, but they made the most of what they had. Cole explained that they were a small outfit of just twelve employees, but that by keeping the overhead reasonably low and having a talented, tight-knit staff that worked well together meant no duplication and no wasted efforts.

"We're a lean, mean resource machine," he quipped. "And we've accomplished a lot of exciting things in just the few years we've been in business."

"Good for you, Cole," she said, meaning it. "That's awesome."

As the owner of the company, he had the corner office, one with twice the windows and even more sunshine than in reception. Stepping inside, Kelsey felt at once that the pleasing space was both completely foreign and incredibly familiar—on the desk, his old Yankee Stadium pencil holder, on the shelves, his A to Z bookends and his little aquarium. She couldn't help but do a quick scan of the room for pictures or some evidence of his life outside these walls. But the only framed photo in the whole place was one she knew well: sixteen-year-old Cole posing with a gold medalist at the '96 Summer Olympics in Atlanta.

Unable to stop herself, Kelsey picked up the photo and studied it for a long moment. She and Cole had first met just a few weeks after that shot had been taken. How she missed the boy with the easy smile and the beautiful eyes.

"That was the same summer I joined the youth group," Cole said, noting her interest.

"I remember," she replied, placing it back on the desk. "Feels like yesterday sometimes, doesn't it?"

He nodded, eyeing her strangely. "Sometimes. Though usually it's the opposite, as though it were a lifetime ago."

She nodded and glanced away, feeling suddenly shy. To cover her discomfort, she crossed the sunny room to the small tank on the shelf and bent to peer at the goldfish inside.

"That's not still Ginnie Mae, is it?"

"No, she died last year. That's Fannie Mae, and the other one is—"

"Let me guess, Freddie Mac?"

"Nope. Roi."

"Roy?"

He grinned. "With an *i*. R-O-I."

Kelsey chuckled. Only Cole would name a fish after the primary goal of everyone in their line of work, Return On Investment.

"Come on," he said warmly. "I'll walk you out."

She wished she could just ask him if he was married, what his life was like these days, but she couldn't come up with a subtle way to get around to it and finally gave up thinking about it for now.

They headed back through the hallway together, and though she thought he'd only go as far as the front door, he stayed with her all the way down the stairs and even to the outside. He pointed toward the nearest subway entrance and then laughed and said, "Wait. I guess you already knew that. You took it to get here."

Turning to face him, Kelsey wished she could think of some way to prolong their conversation. Somehow, standing in the circle of his gaze was much warmer and more comforting than the cold, empty place her own world had become.

"So tell me, what's up with nicknames like Thriller and Flash? Does everybody at Thornton Resources have one?"

Cole smiled. "Flash is short for Flasininski. His parents were Russian defectors during the Cold War. I've heard rumors they worked for the CIA and that's where he learned all of his skills, but he won't say either way."

"Wow. How about Thriller?"

"Believe it or not, that's his real name. His mother was a big Michael Jackson fan, and the song had just come out when he was born."

Stepping closer to avoid a double-wide stroller barreling toward her on the sidewalk, Kelsey said, "So what nickname do they call you? Coleslaw? Colby Cheese? The Colester?"

Eyes twinkling, he studied her face for a long moment.

"None of the above," he replied, grinning. "In fact, if they know what's good for them, they won't call me anything but 'Boss.'"

They parted after that with another hug, this one lingering slightly longer than the one before.

"Thank you again," she whispered before pulling away.

Cole shrugged modestly, told her he would see her tonight, and turned to go inside.

Kelsey could still feel his strong arms around her as she walked to 8th Avenue and got on the subway. Twenty minutes later, telling herself to take her mind off Cole Thornton and focus on the task at hand, she got off at 5th and 53rd and walked to Park Avenue. There she turned and headed upward toward the offices of Queen's Fleet Management Group several blocks away.

No one had gotten back to her yet from Pamela's office, and she had a feeling no one would, at least not anytime soon. Better to drop in on the woman unannounced, she'd decided, and shame her into giving Kelsey at least a few minutes of her time.

She spotted the building up ahead and slowed down, using the rest of the walk to review in her mind the points she intended to make. Though Pamela Greeley was past the usual retirement age of sixty-five, that didn't mean she was past her prime when it came to business strategy. The woman was as shrewd as they came, and Kelsey knew she was about to face a formidable opponent.

Even so, right now she felt empowered after her morning at Thornton Resources. For the first time she was starting to believe she might have some influence over the situation. She realized that Cole's belief in her had instilled this new confidence. He was so kind, so dependable, so *good*. There weren't many good men left in the world, and she was glad she had one on her side now.

Kelsey reached the entrance to QFMG's corporate headquarters, in which everything shouted success and prosperity. The huge lobby with its luxurious ambiance, Persian carpets, and period furnishings set the tone. Just the open space there spoke volumes about the company's wealth. Square footage was at a premium in Manhattan, particularly on Park Avenue, and a company with this much open space was just plain flaunting its affluence.

Kelsey approached the receptionist, whose vast walnut desk could have accommodated a board meeting all by itself. As expected, when she asked to see Pamela Greeley, the response was, "Do you have an appointment?"

"No, but if you let her know I'm here, I think she'll see me anyway. Tell her it's Kelsey Tate of Brennan & Tate." She held her chin high and met the receptionist's stare, surprised to see that the young woman's eyes were violet. Nobody on the planet had eyes that color. What was the point of tinted contacts if everyone could tell they were fake?

"I'll see if Ms. Greeley has time."

Kelsey nodded and then stepped a few feet away from the desk as the receptionist picked up the phone to call upstairs. At least Pamela was in the building. Now the question was if she'd have the nerve to sit face-to-face with the heir apparent of a company she was trying to steal out from under her.

From what Kelsey could tell, the receptionist had to navigate through several layers of administrative assistants before she got the final word and hung up the phone.

"Twentieth floor, Ms. Tate. Ms. Greeley is expecting you."

Ah, yes, the penthouse suite. Kelsey had been there several years ago with Gloria for a meeting. She entered the elevator now with two perky young women carrying stacks of files and giggling with each other about whether a certain coworker had really left his keys in her office by mistake or whether he'd done it intentionally so he'd have to come back for them later.

Trying to tune them out, Kelsey kept a neutral smile on her face until they exited at the eighth floor. Once she was alone, she tried to calm her nerves by studying the elevator car itself, which was lined with what appeared to be genuine cherry paneling in old growth wide boards. All the fittings were of gleaming brass, with fine art prints recessed into the side walls. They *were* prints, weren't they? Who would put original paintings in an elevator? Kelsey squinted at the nearest one but couldn't tell.

She could, however, continue to hear the screams of the decor: Success! Prosperity!

Good grief.

As the doors opened at the penthouse level, Kelsey was surprised to see that Pamela was standing there waiting for her. The older woman stepped forward and shook her hand, smiling politely. Even in her late sixties or early seventies, she was striking. Her honey-colored hair looked as if it had never heard the word "gray," and her complexion was flawless. Pamela was wearing a navy power suit with a red silk scarf, and for a moment Kelsey felt inadequate in her azure silk dress sans jacket.

"Kelsey, how wonderful to see you. I got your message earlier and was trying to figure out when I could meet with you."

Sure you were, Kelsey thought, but she gave a gracious smile.

"Anyway, here you are regardless."

"Thank you for seeing me, Pamela. I decided to stop by without an appointment in the hopes that we could talk."

"Well, come in, come in. How is your family holding up? I was so sorry to hear the news about Gloria Poole."

They discussed Gloria's death and the funeral arrangements as Pamela led the way through two outer offices that looked more like opulent drawing rooms than places of business. At last they reached the inner sanctum— Pamela's domain, complete with French doors that led out onto a rooftop observatory deck. Two walls held gorgeously carved bookcases, and behind the massive rosewood desk at the center hung several rows of what looked like embossed gold saucers. Peering at them more closely, Kelsey gasped.

"Are these pre-Columbian?" she asked.

Pamela stepped toward her, nodding proudly. "Yes. They are pectoral discs, circa twelfth century AD. They were worn by important chiefs and warriors as symbols of their power."

Pamela's meaning was not lost on Kelsey. The discs themselves were strikingly beautiful, but to mount them on the wall in an imposing arrangement behind the desk of the most powerful chief in the building was downright tacky.

Stepping away to take in the rest of the room, Kelsey decided that Pamela's office had the same effect on her that Pamela herself did. Very classy, very intimidating. At least she didn't have to sit facing her wall of power for their talk. Instead, the woman led her over to a pair of deeply cushioned wing chairs beside the French windows.

"So, Kelsey," Pamela said, smoothing her skirt as she sat, "I'll be frank with you. It looks like Queen's Fleet will soon be taking over Brennan & Tate. I have to assume that you're here to secure a position within the new organization once the takeover is complete?"

Kelsey made herself take a deep breath before answering. She didn't want to blurt out anything stupid.

"Why, no, actually. That's not why I'm here at all."

"No?" Pamela arched a delicate eyebrow at her. "In that case, what can I do for you?"

Kelsey took a deep breath, reminding herself of Cole's words from their phone call the day before. *You may be young, but you're already the lifeblood of that place.* He was right. She might not have the years of experience that a Pamela Greeley had, but she'd accomplished a lot in her time at Brennan & Tate, far more than many others her age, and she was perfectly capable of standing her ground.

"Well," Kelsey said. "First, I wanted…" She faltered for a moment but then cleared her throat and tried again. "I needed to speak with you, face-to-face, to ask how you could possibly be doing this to us. You *knew* my Great-Grandmother Adele, Pamela. You got up at her funeral and told the congregation you wanted to be just like her. Now you're trying to take over the very company her father founded and she helped to build? Trust me, if you see this takeover through, you are nothing like her at all."

And there it was. She'd laid the gauntlet down in front of the head of one of the most powerful conglomerates in Manhattan. Kelsey had no doubt that with the amount of money that flowed through these hallowed halls,

Pamela could buy and sell places like B & T for breakfast and crush a career like Kelsey's for lunch. Yet somewhere inside the woman's polished exterior had to beat a real heart. Surely she could see what a travesty this hostile takeover would be, for the stockholders, for those who worked at B & T, and especially for the legacy of Adele.

"I'm sorry you feel that way," Pamela said. "To my mind this would be a real coup for Brennan & Tate. You need a cash infusion and some new blood. We need a solid name in the investment branch, one that's positioned precisely as you are. Seems to me it's a perfect match."

Kelsey was about to respond, but Pamela continued, cutting her off.

"You do know how you're positioned in this market, don't you?"

Kelsey eyed the woman keenly, not sure if she was trying to lead her into some sort of trap. "Why don't you tell me?"

"Our research shows that B & T projects a dual image—which is not an easy thing to do, believe me. On the one hand, it's thought of as a solid company rooted deeply in the past, but on the other hand, it's one that is known for its innovative, forward-thinking investment choices. Are you aware that the company's early success was due in a large part to the founder's focus on wireless technologies? Here we are a hundred and some years later, and what's one of the biggest slices of the financial pie out there? Wireless technologies! The mechanics are a little different now, of course, than they were back at the turn of the nineteenth century, but I still think it's a delightful example of a business coming full circle. I've already been jotting down ideas for some ad campaigns. For example, I was picturing someone out of history, perhaps Braun or Marconi, sitting at an old wooden desk, tapping out a message in Morse code. Then that message is received as an email by a group of good-looking young executives around a computer at a state-of-the-art company where they make cell phones or GPS units or something. Clever, don't you think?"

Sadly, it *was* clever. But that was beside the point.

"Pamela, B & T didn't earn its reputation overnight. It took years, not to mention the blood and sweat and tears of my forebears. Brennan & Tate is a *family* company—*my* family—not just some clever, well-positioned entity to be absorbed into a faceless conglomerate."

Pamela studied her for a long moment, and Kelsey forced herself not to look away under the scrutiny.

"I'm sorry, dear, but for all intents and purposes Brennan & Tate ceased to be a true *family* company in the thirties, when they had to give out so many stock shares to their creditors that their own holdings dropped below fifty percent."

Wow. The woman had done her homework.

"Need I remind you that was the Depression?" Kelsey replied evenly. "At least they managed to hang on and get through, unlike a lot of other companies. Besides, there has always been either a Brennan or a Tate at the helm from day one."

"Oh, yes," Pamela replied. "How is your father these days?"

Game, set, match. The words hit Kelsey like a fist to the gut, but she managed to keep all expression from her face. This was a formidable opponent, one who knew how to hit below the belt.

Trying to remain calm, Kelsey drew in a deep breath and let it out slowly. Somehow, looking at Pamela Greeley, she could almost picture one of those golden discs from the wall strapped across the woman's chest.

No matter. Kelsey had her own symbol of power, the golden *Q* with the diamond, pinned to her dress. Suddenly, she wished she'd worn Adele's hat pin as well, yet another symbol of all she'd come from and how hard she would fight to preserve it.

She could fight dirty too if need be.

"Actually," Kelsey replied in a calm tone, "he's not doing well at all. And as sad as that is, I'm glad for it right now. At least he'll never have to know that one of his most trusted executives secretly joined forces with the head of a major conglomerate and conspired to drive down the value of the company's stock in anticipation of a hostile takeover."

Take that, Pamela Greeley, Kelsey thought as she sat back in her chair, relishing the shock on her opponent's face. The gloves were off now.

Bring it.

Pamela didn't reply for a long moment. Instead, she worked her fingers at a loose thread on the cuff of her sleeve as she seemed to be forming her thoughts. Finally, with one quick, sharp tug, the thread came loose. Rolling it into a ball between her fingers, she turned her attention back to Kelsey.

"I am going to give you some grace here, *Miss Tate,*" she said slowly, "because I know you've had a difficult week and that you're still reeling from the shocking loss of a woman who was very dear to you. But if you ever make such a slanderous accusation against me again—either in private or in public—I will sue you personally for every penny you have, and then I'll go after your parents as well."

"This idea didn't come from them."

"Where, then?"

"Are you denying that you've been working behind the scenes with Gloria to do certain things to make the company more affordable?"

"I certainly am! How dare you even suggest such a thing?"

"It's not that much of a leap, Pamela. You make an offer, it gets turned down, the next day a man stands up in a public forum and impugns the company's founder. The value plummets, and then immediately you sweep in and announce your intentions for a hostile takeover. How much did that one scene save you in dollars and cents? Whatever you had to promise Gloria to arrange it for you, I'd say you definitely got your money's worth."

Pamela eyes narrowed. She placed her elbows on the armrests and leaned forward.

"Strike two. Say it again, Kelsey, and I'll be on the phone with my lawyer before the elevator doors have closed in your face."

CHAPTER
THIRTY

April 13, 1912

ADELE

Jocelyn *"the Letter-Writer" has struck again,* Adele thought as she sat on the chair in her stateroom and reread for the third time the note that had been left upon her pillow. Jocelyn had the gifts of writing and encouragement, and when the two were combined, they gave a powerful punch.

Today's note admonished as well, and it focused on a common topic between them, namely Adele's tendency to value business and money above all else in life. In an elegant, impassioned plea, Jocelyn's letter was meant to serve as a reminder that life needed a balance between matters of business and those of the heart. Jocelyn urged Adele to open her eyes to what was in front of her and embrace the idea of marriage and children as thoroughly as she had always embraced the hope of a profession.

Adele knew Jocelyn was right. She also knew that she was saying this now because of Tad, for if ever an eligible suitor existed, it was he. Not only was the man smart and friendly and ridiculously handsome, he was also knowledgeable about the topics that interested Adele the most. The two of them had gotten off to a bad start, yes, but perhaps Jocelyn was right. He'd been much nicer lately about her business interests, so maybe she really should give him another chance. It would be quite nice to marry a man who shared her passion for business. That her father had already given his stamp of approval by sending Tad to London on his behalf was an added bonus.

Adele tucked the note away in her new journal for safekeeping and then checked her image in the mirror. She decided she would try to do as her cousin said and open her eyes to what was in front of her. Whether there would end up being a spark between her and Tad or not she wasn't sure, but at least it was worth a try. For all she knew, someday they would be telling their grandchildren about the way he had laughed at her ambitions, only to learn in the end that she was every bit as talented in business as he.

For now, Adele needed to get going. She had promised to meet Jocelyn in the library, so she headed there and found her cousin waiting impatiently near the door.

"There you are! What took you so long?"

"I'm sorry. I know I said I'd just be a minute, but I hadn't expected to find such a long and eloquent note waiting on my pillow."

Jocelyn blushed a pretty pink at those words. Though she frequently dashed off notes to her cousin, they were rarely acknowledged between them with anything more than a whispered thanks or a smile. Leaning close, Adele whispered, "How does one become so wise so young?" With a wink, she added that she appreciated the sentiments and would be happy to keep them in mind.

Jocelyn looked deeply pleased. "Well, then, now that you're here, let's go. I have something to show you." Grabbing her by the hand, she led Adele across the library, saying she had finally found her very favorite place on the ship and wanted to show it to her.

Adele slowed. "Not the enclosed promenade at this hour, please. There must be at least twenty children in second class, and every single one of them will have just got up from their afternoon naps!"

Laughing, Jocelyn gave Adele's hand a tug and said no, this was something quite different. Taking her through the library's aft door and into the C deck entranceway, she brought her up one flight of stairs to B deck. There, at the top of the staircase, was a vestibule comprised of a small sitting area, as elegantly appointed as every other part of the beautiful ship. It had two doors at each side that led to the promenade outside of the smoking room.

"Have a seat," Jocelyn urged, gesturing toward an empty chair along the back wall, beside the main mast.

"Here?" Adele asked. "What is so special about this place?"

"You'll see in a minute," she replied mysteriously.

Adele took a deep breath and let it out slowly, telling herself to indulge this silly whim of her cousin. She had a feeling she knew what the girl was doing. More than likely, Tad would soon be emerging from the nearby smoking room and pass through this stairway vestibule for a "chance" encounter between them. And while Adele found the very thought both manipulative and embarrassing, she would play along. She had decided to give the young man another chance, after all.

She was still trying to relax when suddenly she heard the opening strains of a familiar tune coming from somewhere below. Eyes wide, she looked at her cousin, who clapped her hands gleefully and explained she had discovered this spot just yesterday and realized it was the perfect place to take in the orchestra's afternoon concert.

"Don't you agree? It's comfortable and empty and far preferable to squeezing in with the crowd that will have gathered down there to listen."

Adele smiled, thinking fondly how often her cousin managed to surprise her. Just when she'd learned to expect one thing, Jocelyn would end up coming out with another.

"It's not the full orchestra, of course," her cousin continued. "That's only for first class. But at least we get a few of them, and the combination of instruments is quite pleasing—as is their choice of songs. Yesterday, they even played my favorite."

"Chanson de nuit?"

Jocelyn nodded. "I enjoyed a lovely time of prayer and reflection right here—and admittedly a few tears."

"Why tears?"

"Oh, it's..." She sighed heavily. "I still do not know what my decision will be about staying in America or going home to Ireland. But as I sat here taking in the music and thinking about the rest of my life, I realized how blessed I am regardless. What a problem to have—choosing between two countries that would welcome me, not to mention two families that love me. With that in mind, truly, how can I go wrong with either decision?"

"How right you are." Adele looked into the face of her cousin, thinking that as beautiful as she was on the outside, she was even more so on the inside. "You know, if you go back to Ireland, you and I shall have to split up our hat pin set and decide who gets which pin permanently. Do you have a preference?"

Jocelyn shook her head.

"Good. Then I think you should keep the notes."

"Is that because you prefer the gold one to the silver?"

Taking her cousin's hand and giving it a squeeze, Adele replied, "No, it's because the notes suit who you are. You're like a song, you know, rising up into the air and filling the space with joy."

Tears filled Jocelyn's eyes as she gave her cousin a hug.

"Of course, that makes me the harp," Adele continued lightly. "Big, solid, clunky—"

"Don't! Solid, maybe, but dependable, useful, and elegant."

They were quiet for a moment, just sitting there side by side and enjoying the music.

"You know," Adele said softly, "a harp and its notes belong together. Each is dependent on the other. Without the notes, the harp has no purpose. Without the harp, the notes don't exist."

Jocelyn glanced at her cousin and nodded. She didn't reply, but it was clear she understood exactly what Adele was saying.

CHAPTER
THIRTY-ONE

Such fire filled Pamela Greeley's eyes that Kelsey was inclined to believe her denial—almost, anyway.

"Pamela," Kelsey said in a softer tone, "can you look me in the eye and honestly tell me you had no contact with Gloria before her death regarding the takeover?"

She shook her head. "I didn't say that. As a matter of fact, Gloria and I discussed it a few weeks ago."

Kelsey's pulse surged. "You did?"

"Yes."

"The two of you talked about a takeover of B & T by QFMG?"

"About the *purchase* of B & T by QFMG, yes."

"In what context?"

"She called me up on the phone, out of the blue."

"And said...?"

Pamela looked away, seeming decidedly uncomfortable. "I'm sorry. When she called, she asked that we speak in confidence, and I agreed."

Kelsey raised her hands in a gesture of futility. "Do you think that agreement still holds now that she's gone?"

Slumping in her seat, for a moment Pamela looked every bit her age. "I suppose not, if she acted in a manner that's reflecting poorly on me."

Kelsey nodded, understanding her logic. "Pamela, do you remember the man who stood up in the ceremony the other day and disrupted everything?"

"Yes."

"The reason he was there was because Gloria sent him an invitation, five hundred dollars for traveling expenses, and a letter urging him to come and warning him that if the company were sold, he would lose all rights for any claims against the family fortune."

Pamela's eyes widened. She did look genuinely surprised.

"I'll ask you again. Why did Gloria contact you and what did she say?"

Pamela was quiet for a long moment, and then she spoke. "You have to understand, Kelsey, that I put out feelers all the time, all over the place. In the past twenty years of acquaintance with Gloria, I've probably brought up the topic of purchasing B & T a dozen times. Ask anyone. It's just what I do. I put out feelers."

"I believe you."

"Well, I'm sure that's why Gloria thought to contact me a few weeks ago. She called to ask if we could speak confidentially. Once I assured her we could, she told me she was looking for a buyer for B & T and wondered if I was still interested."

Kelsey blinked. "Gloria was looking for a buyer. For Brennan & Tate."

"Yes."

"She didn't have that kind of authority."

"Oh, I know that. It wasn't an official inquiry. It was more like a testing of the waters, so to speak."

Shifting in her seat, Kelsey leaned forward, placing her elbows on the arms of the chair and clasping her hands together. "What did she say to you? How did she put it, exactly?"

Still reluctant, Pamela took a deep breath before she spoke. "She said that given my interest in acquiring the company in the past, she wanted me to know that if I still wanted Brennan & Tate, now might be a good time to give it a shot. Actually, I believe her words were, 'If you were to make a reasonable offer for the company at this time, I don't think it would be rebuffed.'"

Kelsey's mind raced. What on *earth* had compelled Gloria to say such a thing?

"Did she tell you why she thought the company might be for sale?"

"Not directly, no. But I had the impression that things have been in a bit of a slump since your father's health took a turn for the worse last year. She assured me that the company would rebound eventually, but that for the time being it was in dire need of, as she put it, 'more resources and better management.' She thought the two companies would make a good fit. As it happens, so do I."

Kelsey sat up straight, trying to wrap her head around the idea of Gloria doing such a thing. "Did you promise her anything in return? Compensation for the tip-off? A guaranteed position after the merge?"

Pamela shook her head, bristling. "I did nothing of the kind."

"Fine. So then what?"

"Well, after we had that conversation, I did some research into your company and really liked what I saw. So this past Monday, I contacted Walter Hallerman and said I'd like to speak with him and his management group about buying Brennan & Tate. Needless to say, the man was surprised to hear from me. Very surprised. He told me flat out that B & T was *not* for sale."

"And?"

"We haggled a bit. I made a specific offer, he rejected it outright, I tried again at a higher price, but he said the answer was still no. Then I told him I wouldn't consider that 'no' official until I'd heard it directly from the board. I had no doubt they would see things differently. After all, Gloria had told me this would fly if I came at them with a reasonable amount. Which I had."

"Did you speak with Gloria after that?"

"No. At first I was waiting to hear back from the board. Their answer came the next morning, Tuesday. To my surprise, they also turned me down."

Kelsey nodded, glad for that much at least.

"I tried to reach Gloria after that, to ask her what was going on, but she never returned my calls. To be honest, I had ulterior motives for coming to your ceremony, Kelsey—no offense, of course. I'm a busy woman, and I have to turn down invitations to things like that left and right."

"None taken," Kelsey replied, though she was a little hurt, if only for Adele's sake. When she'd first spotted Pamela from the podium, Kelsey had thought the woman was there in honor of her great-grandmother's memory and legacy.

"Anyway, even though I had no intentions of going to your little event, I changed my mind for two reasons. First, I decided it wouldn't hurt to establish a visible reminder for Walter Hallerman and the board of my intentions to pursue purchase of the company. Second, I was hoping to pull Gloria aside and find out what had gone wrong between the time she contacted me and the time I made my offer. I hadn't treated the matter as a priority, and my fear was that I had taken too long to move on this and that B & T had managed to find some other source of funding in the meantime."

"When was it that she first contacted you about it?"

Pamela thought for moment then rose and went to her desk. "I can tell you exactly. I keep a log of all my calls."

Kelsey expected her to type something into the computer, but instead she opened the top drawer and pulled out what looked like an old-fashioned leather-bound ledger. She flipped through a few pages and then placed a finger on the page and ran it across the line as she read.

"Here we go. Gloria Poole, March ninth, two ten p.m."

Kelsey thought about that for a moment. The letter to Rupert had been mailed eight days later, on March seventeenth. Surely, the call and the letter had been connected somehow. Could she believe this woman's denials of culpability?

Kelsey had trouble understanding why anyone in this business would wait that long to jump on a hot property. When she came across a good prospect for investment, she'd been known to go from square one to a full-on offer within twenty-four hours. At most she'd never gone more than a week. Yet Pamela expected her to believe that she'd received an invitation like that and hadn't moved on it for almost a *month?* Not likely. "So Gloria gave you this tip on March ninth," she said, squinting her eyes, "and you didn't act on it until April first?"

"That's correct," Pamela said, ignoring Kelsey's insinuation as she returned to her chair by the window. "As I said, I didn't see it as a priority. We were embroiled in a deal with a much bigger fish at the time. Between the research and the decision making on that matter, I got to it when I could."

Kelsey felt a surge of anger. If Pamela was telling the truth, then Brennan & Tate—this business that was her family's heart and soul—was nothing but a little fish to these people, a side deal barely worth their time, a mere whim.

Wanting to stay on track, Kelsey took a deep breath and told herself to calm down. "Were you able to speak with Gloria after the event on Tuesday?" she asked evenly.

Pamela shook her head. "I looked for her but never spotted her anywhere, not during the ceremony nor afterward in the lobby. It was such a madhouse that I didn't stay for long. I assumed she would get around to calling me back the next day. Instead, I turned on the news later that night only to learn that she was dead."

Both women were silent for a long moment after that.

"When did the situation turn into a hostile takeover?" Kelsey asked finally.

"Well, once Walter and the board had turned me down, we had to decide whether to proceed regardless. In spite of Tuesday's mess, we still want your company—though, of course, it's worth far less now than it was on Monday. The board should have jumped when they had the chance. Now we're getting an even better price, and there's nothing they can do to stop it."

"So you're definitely proceeding."

Pamela nodded. "I'm sorry it had to come to this, Kelsey, but I'm sure you'll see in the end that this is the best-case scenario for everyone. Your company has the B & T name—which is still an asset, once we're past this current issue—and some talented people. We have the cash to take you to the next level and the personnel to fill the shoes left empty by your father and others."

Pamela leaned forward and fixed her steely gaze on Kelsey. "You can be part of this acquisition too, you know. I feel sure we could find a place for someone of your talents in the new organization."

Kelsey gritted her teeth, eyes narrowing. "Yeah, right. And people call you guys 'Clean Sweep' because you keep your offices so tidy."

Pamela threw her head back and laughed. "You really are a feisty thing, aren't you?" She stood, as if to say their time was up.

"I can be when my back's against a wall," Kelsey replied, also standing.

"Well," Pamela said, leading her out of her office and back through the two outer chambers, "if you change your mind about that position, let me know. I like you, Kelsey. I think you and I could accomplish great things together."

After that they were silent until they reached the elevator and Pamela pushed the button to summon it. Then Kelsey turned and fixed her gaze on the woman, ready to make one last appeal.

"Please, Pamela, won't you reconsider and drop this whole thing?"

"Sorry, but no." She shrugged, holding out both hands, palms upward. "*Les jeux sont faits.*" The die is cast.

Kelsey's eyes narrowed. "Then why on earth would I want to work for someone who would steal my family's company out from under me? You're taking advantage of a difficult situation to give a lowball offer to a bunch of nervous stockholders who don't even understand what a bad move this would be. It's just wrong."

Pamela looked back at her, eyes sparkling, as if she were somehow amused.

"Kelsey, darling," she said, shaking her head from side to side. "Welcome to the real world. This is how business is done. It's nothing personal. It's just how it is."

With that, the elevator arrived and their meeting was over.

Kelsey left the building and began walking off her frustration. She realized she was less than a mile from her parents' house, so she decided to go there by foot rather than grab the subway. The day was getting chillier and she had no jacket, but soon she was moving briskly enough that she managed to warm up anyway.

As she went, Pamela's final words kept ringing in her ears: *"Welcome to the real world. This is how business is done."*

Though she hated to admit it, in a sense Pamela was right. For many, many people, this was exactly how business was done. Never mind if others got hurt. Never mind if lives were destroyed by the decisions made in the upper echelons. Business was business.

But if that was the case, why did it feel so wrong? Why was this whole thing so utterly distasteful? She thought about that, and after a moment she decided it was because it deviated far from the business model established long ago by Adele Brennan Tate.

Adele had been an incredibly keen businesswoman, but she would never have pursued a deal that would bring such grief to so many, much less one that was capitalizing on another's misfortune. She hadn't been about tearing things down. Her focus had been on the building up—of people, of ideas, of businesses.

Kelsey thought again of the "Accomplishment Walks" with her great-grandmother all those years ago. At the time they had made her feel so close to the woman, so connected. But thinking back to the memory of it now, Kelsey wondered if she'd ever really known her at all.

"Were you really who you said you were?" she whispered aloud, wishing that somehow Adele could send her a reply from heaven. Instead, that was the one question in all of this that Kelsey was afraid she might not be able to answer.

By the time she turned onto her parents' street, she was thoroughly depressed, ravenously hungry, and angry with herself for not having thought to bring a pair of flats with her today. She had in fact worn some of her highest high heels as a part of the overall "eat your heart out" package she'd wanted to present to Cole earlier. Now she knew exactly what such vanity had wrought, at least five or six blisters and two terribly sore feet.

When Kelsey reached her parents' brownstone, she was excited to see a familiar blue bicycle chained to the railing out front. Despite the pain in her feet, she mounted the steps quickly and rapped on the door. After a moment it swung open to reveal none other than her brother.

Fifteen minutes later, Kelsey's comfort level had risen considerably. She was in her stocking feet, clad in a cozy fleece sweat suit borrowed from her mother, and sitting at the kitchen table feasting on a giant chef salad topped with Yvette's famous homemade dressing. To her right was Matt, digging into a bowl of ice cream with chocolate sauce, and to her left was their mother, describing the long and futile search Kelsey had assigned to her of digging through all of the various family papers and mementos for Adele's hand-written diary or some sign of the bonds. She had found neither, but she didn't seem all that upset about it, saying at least she had taken the opportunity to get the stuff better organized. Only her mother could find a silver lining in a cloud this dark.

The phone rang and Doreen went to answer it, leaving Kelsey alone in the kitchen with her brother. She was glad. Though she'd kept her mother generally apprised of the overall situation, she hadn't given her the full details or spelled out exactly how bleak the outcome was looking. Matt, on the other hand, wanted to know everything, so while Doreen was gone, Kelsey lowered her voice and told him what she could, omitting only her meeting with Cole and her investigative jaunt planned for later in the evening.

"Did you get your stockholder letter yet?" she asked, wishing Pamela had volunteered the time frame for the takeover.

He shook his head. "I've been watching the mailbox for it, but so far I haven't seen a thing."

"Me neither, though it's only a matter of time."

Matt finished his ice cream and placed his empty bowl and spoon into the sink. "Is there anything I can do to help?"

She thought about that, and for a moment she was tempted to invite him along on her B & T break-in tonight. She resisted the urge, however, knowing that when it came down to it, she had every right to go into the building but he did not. He was family, yes, but he wasn't an employee. If anyone was going to get in trouble for this, it needed to be her alone. At least she had a good defense for her actions.

"Actually, there is one thing you could do for me," she said, thinking of the floor plans Cole had requested. "I need something from Dad's home office, but my feet hurt so badly right now I'm not sure if I could make it up three flights of stairs."

"Sure. What am I looking for?"

"It's a rolled-up tube of paper, and I think it's on the floor of one of the closets, propped against the back corner."

"What is it?"

She shrugged. "Diagrams of the B & T offices. I thought I might look them over and see if they indicate any sort of safe or secret hiding place where Gloria might have stashed the bonds."

"Good idea," he said. "Be right back."

"Thanks, Matt."

"No problem. You're working so hard to save the day, it's the least I can do."

Once he was gone, his words stayed with her.

But what if she didn't save the day?

What if she couldn't find a way to stop the hostile takeover?

What if she did all of this digging around only to lose the family company in the end, or to learn that Adele had actually been Jocelyn?

Kelsey felt so frustrated, so restless. The problem, she decided, was that she was tired of *talk*. All she had done in the past few days was talk—to Pamela, to Walter, to her parents, to Rhonda, to Rupert, even to Gloria. Now, she was ready for some action. She was ready to get into the offices of Brennan & Tate and do some real out-and-out sleuthing—sore feet and all. Thank goodness for Cole and his team! Suddenly, she was counting the minutes until it would finally be time for their mission.

"Ask and ye shall receive," Matt said, coming back into the kitchen. In his hand was a tube of rolled-up paper, which he gave her with a flourish. Eagerly, she took it from him, pulled off the rubber band, and opened it out onto the table just to make sure it was what she needed. They both studied it for a moment, but when nothing jumped out at them, she began rolling it back up.

"I need to run for now," she said, "but I'll take a longer look later when I have the time."

"Sounds good," he replied.

"Thanks again. Sometimes it's actually worth having you around, bro."

Kelsey would have liked to have stayed there with her family all afternoon, but she had other things to do. She needed to get home and get organized for tonight's adventure, including coming up with two different outfits—one for the wake and one for the sleuthing afterward. When she said that she needed to be going, her mother insisted on calling for a cab. Kelsey did not resist, knowing she wasn't up for the walking that the subway would require anyway.

She went in to visit with her father before she left, and though Doreen had said he wasn't having a good day, he didn't seem all that bad to Kelsey. She stayed with him for a good ten minutes, during which she told him that she'd been working hard to straighten things out at Brennan & Tate. She didn't want to give him many details, and the picture she painted was brighter than the reality, but she saw no need to upset the man with the dismal specifics of all the latest developments.

She did, however, confide in him about her sleuthing plans for tonight. She did so because she needed his permission, so to speak, to open up B & T's private computer network to an outside agency.

"They are just going to poke around a bit and see if they can reconstruct Gloria's activities during the last week or so of her life," Kelsey told her father. "They will be looking for 'digital handprints' she may have left behind, not just things like emails but also the times she entered her code to go in and out, any faxes she sent or scans she made or photocopies she ran or whatever. Anything she did that was digital, they can take a look and see if clues or patterns emerge. What do you think?"

He seemed to grasp what she was saying. Fixing his eyes on hers, he said, "You...trust? Trustworthy?"

"Yes," she replied, nodding emphatically. "Dad, it's Cole Thornton. He has his own company now, and he offered to help me out."

At the mention of Cole's name, Nolan's eyes seemed to smile. "Trust Cole," he said, nodding.

"Yes, we can trust Cole. So this is okay with you for me to do this?"

She was surprised when he placed a shaky hand atop hers.

"Fire with fire," he said.

She thought for a moment and said, "Fight fire with fire? Is that what you're telling me?"

"Fire with fire," he repeated, nodding. "Trust Cole."

"Great, Dad, thanks so much. I'll let you know what happens, okay?"

"Okay, but not..." his voice trailed off and she could see he was grasping for the words he needed. "No mushy parts."

She laughed. "Don't worry. There won't be any mushy parts. Cole and I are just friends now."

He merely grunted, but she could tell he didn't believe her.

They were interrupted at that moment by the honk of a horn outside, so she hugged him goodbye and left, meeting up with her mother in the hallway.

Doreen walked Kelsey to the door, asking if they could go to Gloria's visitation together. "You don't have to come all the way back up here. We could meet up outside the funeral home if you want."

Kelsey hesitated, not wanting to tell her mother the truth, that she would be racing in and out of the wake as quickly as possible in order to meet up with a couple of guys to break into her own office. Instead, she just said that she was busy tonight so she was only going to make a brief appearance, right at six o'clock on the dot, and probably wouldn't stay longer than fifteen or twenty minutes.

Doreen's eyebrows lifted a bit, but rather than scolding her daughter for giving short shrift to the woman who had been so important in her life, she said simply that she would have Matt take her instead.

The long cab ride home ended up costing a small fortune, but Kelsey didn't care. It was worth every penny for comfort's sake. The building was quiet when she got there, which wasn't unusual for this time of day. In the lobby, she stopped to grab her mail and then flipped through it as she rode the elevator up to the tenth floor. She spotted the envelope just as the car was slowing to a stop. There, between a bill and a mail-order catalog, was the letter she'd been dreading.

Kelsey waited until she was safely inside her own apartment before she opened it up and took a look. Hands trembling, she unfolded the single page slowly, noting the elegant, gold-embossed header across the top. She skimmed through the words once and then read them again more slowly.

It was official. As a stockholder of the firm Brennan & Tate, she was being given the opportunity to sell her shares of stock to Queen's Fleet Management Group. There would be a meeting of the stockholders on April thirteenth—exactly one week—at which time a vote would be taken and the majority would rule as to whether or not the company would be sold.

Worse than that was the dollar amount being offered per share. Surely, even a character assassination against Adele Tate and the in-office death of one of the company's top executives could not have driven the price this low. How *dare* Pamela and her cronies do this? Kelsey was so furious, she tried to throw the letter across the room. It fell to the floor without drama, so she kicked at the coffee table next, gratified by the crash and clink as it tipped over onto the ground.

Heart pounding, Kelsey stomped down the hall to the bedroom to get ready for tonight. With the amount of adrenaline rushing through her veins at the moment, she felt there was nothing she couldn't do.

If they were able to find a hidden safe, she told herself as she flung open the closet and began choosing her clothes, even if they had no combination for it, she had no doubt she would be able to rip it open with her bare hands.

CHAPTER
THIRTY-TWO

Kelsey arrived at the funeral home at six o'clock on the dot. Fortunately, not many people were there yet, which meant a faster in and out for her. The fewer the people, the fewer the conversations she would be obligated to have.

It wasn't until she walked into the lobby and saw a placard with an arrow and the words "Visitation for Poole" that it struck her what she was really doing there. This was a *wake,* of all things, for one of the most important people in her life. This was goodbye to a woman who had guided her, advised her, and cared about her for years. This was the final send-off for a person Kelsey had thought she'd known intimately, one of her nearest and dearest friends.

Or so she'd thought.

Now she knew differently. Given the many disturbing truths that had come to light in the past few days, what was she to make of this event? How was she to process this tragedy?

Hovering in the entryway, she thought about Wednesday morning, when her mother had talked about the shell of a person she had allowed herself to become. Though Kelsey had been sincere in her desire to change, she decided that tonight that hardness would serve her well. Once she had some answers, once she knew the whole truth, maybe then she would permit herself to mourn. For now, she dared not try to process the fact that Gloria was dead. There was still too much to do, too many facts to unearth, too many questions to answer.

Steeling herself with resolve, Kelsey smoothed her hair away from her face and followed the arrow to the large room on the left. A young woman in a conservative black suit, an employee of the funeral home, was standing near the doorway to receive guests. With a practiced nod, she welcomed Kelsey in a soft voice and gestured toward the guestbook lying open on a nearby podium.

Using the pen provided, she signed her name on the sixth line, taking note of the first five guests who had already arrived. As most of them had the last name of Poole, she realized that family members must have been allowed to come a little early. Setting down the pen, Kelsey turned her attention to the other end of the room, where those five people—plus Vern—were congregating a few feet away from the open casket.

Taking a deep breath and letting it out slowly, she started up the aisle. Let others give Gloria her goodbye. Kelsey refused to do that until she understood exactly who she was saying goodbye to.

As she neared the front of the room, Kelsey got a quick glimpse of Gloria's body, laid out in a mahogany casket with burnished silver-tone accents, surrounded by a riot of colorful floral arrangements. Ignoring all of that, she stepped forward to take Vern's hand.

His eyes swam with tears, and his charcoal gray suit and silver tie made his skin look colorless. At least he was impeccably groomed, as always.

She leaned forward and kissed his cheek. "How are you doing, Vern?"

"Hanging in there. Thanks for coming."

"Of course."

They made small talk for a moment, but half of Kelsey's mind was on her feet. Despite being in high heels, she was grateful she was no longer feeling much pain. Between a foot soak, some numbing cream, and a handful of well-placed Band-Aids, she'd managed to get the problem under control, thank goodness.

Kelsey heard soft voices behind her, and she realized that more people had arrived and were coming up the aisle. As Vern turned his attention toward them, she stepped closer to the casket, trying to look everywhere but at the dead body of her friend.

A spray of pink roses and white lilies spread over the lower half of the casket lid and flower arrangements of all kinds flanked each side. Walking along to take a closer look, Kelsey realized there had to be at least thirty arrangements. She glanced at a couple of the cards. Of course. Business contacts.

Many of the companies Gloria had financed probably sent flowers. They had most likely sent representatives out tonight too.

She found her family's arrangement near the end of the row, a gorgeous pastel-colored display of gladiolas and carnations and at least two dozen roses. Doreen had outdone herself, Kelsey thought proudly. The card read, *Forever in our hearts, Nolan, Doreen, Kelsey, and Matthew Tate.* Very nice.

Even if it turned out not to be true.

Finally, Kelsey forced herself to return to the casket. As she went, she tried to concentrate on the good times she and Gloria had shared, but her mind simply wouldn't go there. It was stuck on all she had learned about this woman in the past few days.

She stood and gazed down at Gloria's lovely face, which was no longer purple and red as it had been the last time Kelsey had seen her, thank goodness. Even at fifty-four, with wrinkles beginning to show, Gloria had been a striking woman, and they had done a pretty good job with her. Her hair was perfectly coifed as always, and they had done a nice job with the application of subtle brown eye shadow and mascara. Something didn't look quite right, however, and after a moment Kelsey realized that there were two problems. The lipstick had obviously been chosen to coordinate with the purples in the scarf at her neck, but that lipstick was definitely not Gloria's shade. More importantly, the woman had never, ever, in Kelsey's memory, worn a scarf.

"She looks so natural, doesn't she?"

Kelsey jumped and turned to see Yanni standing beside her.

"I was just thinking about that scarf," Kelsey replied. "It ought to come off. Gloria was not a scarf person at all."

Even as she said it, Kelsey realized that Yanni *was* a scarf person. She wore them all the time. Maybe she really had chosen the outfit, as Vern had said. Then again, if her visit to his place had been as innocent as that, why had she lied about it?

For a moment, Kelsey considered saying something blunt and provocative, such as, "Amazing how you managed to pick out these clothes while getting your hair done at the same time." But she held her tongue. At least the girl had chosen the rest of the outfit well. Except for the scarf and those too-dark lips, Gloria looked as if she could hop up from the casket and get back to work.

"Actually, I helped choose the clothing. I wanted her to be wearing the diamond necklace she got from her sister, the one who owns the jewelry store," Yanni said softly. "But the funeral home gave it back and requested a scarf instead."

Kelsey looked at Yanni as she processed that thought. She didn't understand until the young woman motioned toward her own neck and whispered, "Some things they couldn't cover with makeup."

A surge of nausea rose up in Kelsey's throat at the memory of Gloria's dead body. Of course. She had died by hanging. Her neck had been a mess.

"Excuse me," Kelsey said, and then she turned and made her way through the crowd, praying she could get to the bathroom before she was sick. She managed to make it, but by the time she got there, the urge had passed. In its stead she just felt shaky and weak, a cold sweat breaking out on her forehead.

How could this have happened? How could Gloria be dead—and in such a violent manner?

Kelsey stayed where she was, leaning her back against the wall of the handicapped stall for a good five minutes, until she felt normal again. Just as she was about to emerge, she heard voices—familiar voices—coming into the room and decided to wait.

"He told me they were kissing in the elevator, no lie," one of them said softly. "He saw it himself on the security camera."

"No way! In the past few days? Or before it happened?"

"Like, a month ago."

"No way! And he never told—" She stopped short, clearing her throat, and then they both fell silent. Kelsey realized they must have come around the corner and spotted feet under the stall.

"Don't stop on my account," she said as she swung open the door to face exactly whom she expected to see: one of her female coworkers and her executive assistant.

"Kelsey!" Sharon cried, throwing her arms open for a hug.

In response, Kelsey took a big step backward, folding her arms across her chest.

"What is it?" Sharon said, looking genuinely hurt. "How are you? We miss you."

Kelsey studied the girl's face, wondering how she could be so obtuse. Just yesterday she had promised to assemble the team and have them meet with Kelsey at their usual restaurant. Instead, Walter had shown up, and Sharon hadn't even had the decency to text her a warning, much less give her a call.

So much for being her eyes and ears.

"You're upset. I'm sorry. We shouldn't be gossiping."

With a soft "Oh, please," the coworker slipped into the nearest stall, but Kelsey and Sharon stayed where they were.

"It's not the gossip, Sharon. What happened last night? You couldn't warn me that Walter had canceled my team meeting? Couldn't even send me a text?"

The girl's face colored. "I'm so sorry about that. But to answer your question, no, I couldn't. Walter specifically said that I was not to communicate with you in any way until further notice or else. What was I supposed to do? Risk my job?"

Kelsey felt a renewed surge of nausea. Why on earth would Walter prohibit communication between them? That was pushing the whole separate-the-company-from-the-Tate-name thing way too far.

Exhaling slowly, she felt the energy draining from her body. Earlier, she had been filled with righteous anger. Now she was just tired of the struggle.

"I understand," she said. "It's not your fault."

"Thanks, Kelsey."

They shared that hug, and as they pulled apart, Sharon began to volunteer the gossip she'd been discussing when she first came in. Unfortunately, just as she said the words, "Guess who's been having an affair?" Yanni strode into the room.

She stopped short, staring at the two women, her face growing ashen.

"K-Kelsey," Yanni uttered in her lilting accent. "I was just coming to check on you. I thought you might need some help."

Cheeks burning, Kelsey stepped to the sink and began washing her hands as Sharon ducked wordlessly into a stall.

"Thanks for your concern, Yanni. I thought I was going to be sick for a minute there, but the feeling passed."

Yanni nodded, and then slowly she turned and walked out. As quickly as possible, Kelsey rinsed and dried her hands and then followed along, terribly embarrassed. Affair or not, unless it was relevant to Gloria's death, whatever was going on between Vern and Yanni was none of her business.

She caught up with the black-haired beauty in the hallway, took her by the elbow, and apologized. In response, a flicker of gratitude flashed in Yanni's eyes, and then they filled with tears.

"For what it's worth, Kelsey, she didn't…" Yanni's voice trailed off as she blinked away her tears.

Kelsey waited, unsure what the girl was trying to say. Yanni cleared her throat and tried again.

"Gloria knew," she whispered. "She knew and she didn't even care."

With that she turned and walked away, leaving Kelsey to stare after her. Behind her, Sharon and the other woman emerged from the restroom and tried to sweep her up with them to head back into the wake. When they reached the lobby, however, Kelsey declined, saying that she had to be going. Sharon gave her another hug and then turned to continue on into the room, which was now full of people. Looking at all of the activity inside, Kelsey noticed that Yanni had taken her place up front beside Vern, shaking hands with well-wishers and acting as if she had every right to be there. Not ten feet behind her lay the dead body of the man's wife.

The queen is dead. Long live the queen.

With a sigh, Kelsey crossed the lobby and moved past a man who was standing off to one side, leaning a shoulder against the wall and chewing on a toothpick.

"Leaving so soon, Miss Tate?"

Kelsey paused to look at him, knowing the face was familiar but not quite able to place him. Then he shifted to stand up straight, and with the glint of a silver badge clipped at his waist she remembered who it was. Detective Hargrove.

"Oh, hi, Detective," she said, stepping closer. "I'm surprised to see you here."

He shrugged. "Never know what you might pick up on at a thing like this."

He was staring off toward the crowd milling about in the large room, and she turned to watch with him.

"Actually, I'm glad I ran into you," she said. "I never did hear the final conclusion about Gloria's death. Has it been ruled a suicide, or...?"

Again, he shrugged. "Still undetermined at this time."

She nodded, thinking about that. "So the investigation is still open."

"Yep."

"Anything I can do to help?"

At that he returned his attention to her. "A question, actually. Gloria Poole received a phone call on her cell Monday night around ten thirty. Did you make that call?"

Kelsey gaped at him. "No, but I've been wondering the same thing since I heard about it from Vern."

"Any idea what it might have been about, or why she went back to the office afterward and worked all night?"

Kelsey shook her head. "I wish I could tell you, but I don't have a clue."

He nodded, popping the toothpick back in his mouth. "All right. Well, thanks anyway."

She started to go but then turned back toward him. "Wait a minute. Don't you have her cell phone, or at least her cell phone records? What number did it say?"

"Call came from a pay phone."

"A pay phone? Do those things even exist anymore?"

He smiled. "Yeah, here and there."

"Where was this one located?"

"Over near Times Square."

Times Square. Kelsey thought for a long moment.

Rupert and Rhonda Brennan.

Their hotel was very near Times Square.

She expressed that thought to the detective, who thanked her, nodding. "Already looked into it. At the time, the two of them were at a Broadway show."

Kelsey shrugged. "It's not hard to slip out, maybe during intermission, make a call, and then come back in."

"Yeah, but intermission for that show ended at nine forty-five, and from what I've been able to ascertain, the two were never seen missing from their seats. They had fifth row center, so it's not like they could have slipped out and slipped back in unnoticed."

"Fifth row center?" She asked incredulously. "Did they get them from a discount booth or something?"

Hargrove shook his head. "Bought separately for full price. Four fifty per."

Their eyes met. Rupert and Rhonda Brennan went to the theater their first night in town and sat in $450 seats? Each?

"Did they pay for that themselves?"

"Nope. They claim the tickets were waiting for them at the front desk when they checked into their hotel, a fun surprise from their anonymous benefactor. Unfortunately, we weren't able to trace the original purchaser. They were bought from a VIP ticket broker two weeks ago, with cash."

"Cash," she echoed. The calling card of the anonymous.

Kelsey was thinking about that when she noticed a taxi pulling up out front and discharging a group of passengers. How much easier and faster it would be at this hour to grab that cab rather than using the subway. Noting her interest, Detective Hargrove shook her hand and said he didn't mean to hold her up. Smiling gratefully, she told him to give her a call if she could help any further.

"Will do," he replied with a nod and a tired smile. "Thanks."

Moments later she was inside the taxi and rumbling across the city toward Cole's office in Chelsea. Though her head was spinning with all she'd learned, she was glad to feel a fresh surge of adrenaline at the thought of what lay ahead. It was time to get into Brennan & Tate and take a look around.

Time to find some answers.

CHAPTER
THIRTY-THREE

Kelsey called ahead, and Cole was waiting for her at the door to the building when she arrived. She paid the cabbie and dashed inside, greeting her handsome ex-boyfriend with a smile.

"Wow, look at you," he said, taking in her styled hair, carefully applied makeup, and black vintage Yves St. Laurent dress. For jewelry, she'd worn just a simple diamond tennis bracelet and her favorite earrings, a pair of diamond studs. Too late, she remembered that the earrings had been a gift from him, a Valentine's Day surprise back when they were dating.

If that registered with him, he didn't show it. Instead, he seemed to be captivated with the overall effect, his eyes dancing with admiration. Kelsey swallowed hard, realizing how much she had missed those adoring gazes of his.

"I brought along a change of clothes," she told him, holding up the black oversized purse she'd been lugging around all night.

"That's good," he replied, motioning toward the stairs. "Somehow, I think our activities tonight will go a lot better in sneakers than stilettos."

They moved up the stairs side by side, and as they went Kelsey stole a few glances at Cole as well. He, too, was all in black: black shoes, jeans, belt, and button-down shirt. Combined with his handsome face and sandy brown hair, the effect was so sexy it was mesmerizing.

"How long will we be here before we head out?" she asked.

"Depends. We have some information to go over, but we'll try to move quickly. How did you do on your tasks?"

In response she reached into her purse and pulled out the Brennan & Tate floor plans, which she'd had to fold instead of roll. "Here you go. I also talked to Pamela, though it didn't go all that well."

Taking the thick, folded pages from her, Cole opened them slightly and peeked inside. "Nice. I forgot what a whiz you are at getting things done."

She smiled. "How about everyone here? Any success?"

Cole grinned as they reached the door for Thornton Resources and he swung it open for her. "Oh, we have a few surprises in store. Why don't you go change in the bathroom and then meet up with us in the conference room?"

"Yes, sir," she said, pulse surging. Cole wouldn't be smiling like that unless he'd found something good.

She dressed quickly, donning her own all-black outfit, nearly identical to Cole's, except that he wore black loafers while she was in black sneakers. When she reached the conference room, she saw that both Thriller and Flash were in dark clothes as well.

"Look at us," she quipped as she came into the room and set her purse aside. "Throw in a couple of wigs, and we could be an eighties hair band."

They laughed.

"Personally, I'd rather be the Man in Black," Thriller said.

"You mean like Will Smith?" Flash asked. "Tommy Lee Jones?"

"No. Johnny Cash," Thriller replied, shaking his head.

"You need a better belt buckle if you want to be Johnny Cash," Cole said, carrying a cup of coffee over to the table. Seeing that, Kelsey headed for the pot at the end of the room and poured one for herself as well.

"Oh, I got the belt buckles for it, don't you worry," Thriller replied. "I just can't wear 'em on surveillance. They might draw too much attention, not to mention blind somebody with their silver brilliance."

Cole and Flash both laughed heartily, and Kelsey smiled as she carried her coffee to the table and took the same chair she'd used earlier.

"All right, gang, let's get down to work," Cole said, placing both hands on the table and looking at the others assembled there. As he did, Kelsey couldn't help but notice the solid biceps under the taut, dark fabric of his sleeves. Obviously, he'd kept up with his workouts since their breakup. Good for him.

Turning to her, Cole explained the order of events for the evening. First, they would go around the table and quickly share the information they had each managed to gather since their meeting that morning. Then they would wire her up, give her instructions, and head out. Once the mission was complete, their evening would be over and they could even drop her at her place if she wanted, since it wasn't too far from where they would be.

"Wire me up?"

"You'll see," he replied. "Okay, since my info is the most depressing part of the agenda, I'll go first to get it out of the way." In front of him was a neatly typed page of columns and numbers, a copy of which he slid over to Kelsey.

She picked it up and studied it, noting that the page was in three sections divided by horizontal lines.

"My job was to check out all of the financials. At the top is a profile of Queen's Fleet Management Group. As you can see, they're quite liquid and fully capable of affording this acquisition."

Kelsey nodded, scanning the numbers. She was stunned by the size of their retained earnings. She'd known it was a big company, but this was impressive.

"Below that," he continued, "in the middle section, is a breakdown of B & T. As you know, it's a lot harder to come up with a specific value for a privately owned company, even one with shares and stockholders. But your father has always obtained an annual estimate, and fortunately Walter has continued the practice in his stead. You're right that the company's value peaked shortly before Nolan's stroke and then dipped the following year."

Kelsey scanned the numbers, seeing that in December 2010—just two months before her dad's stroke—B & T had been valued at $70 million. By December 2011, that figure had dropped to $36 million. She'd already known this, of course, but it still hurt to see it spelled out in black and white.

"There have been no official numbers compiled since December," Cole continued, "but I did find a report done just last Friday that estimated a nice rebound back up to around fifty-eight million. In other words, Kelsey, your PR campaign was working."

She nodded, waiting to hear his opinion as to the impact the past week might have had on that number.

"Of course, it's hard to say what *today's* exact value would be, given what has happened, but we can look at the offer given by Queen's Fleet to get an idea of what their estimate is." Looking directly at Kelsey, he said, "If you've received your stockholder's letter and done the math, you already know what Queen's Fleet thinks you're worth."

Nodding somberly, she replied, "Yeah. About twenty-two million. That's why my coffee table is upside down and coasters and magazines are all over my floor."

Cole gave her a sympathetic smile as Thriller let out a low whistle.

"Are you saying that in less than a year and a half, the value of the company went from seventy million down to twenty-two million?"

Kelsey looked to Cole, who shook his head. "No. It didn't really—at least, not yet. That may be what Queen's Fleet wants to think, but it won't be true unless the stockholders vote to sell at that price. In my opinion, I believe a more accurate figure would be right around the previous low of thirty-six. That's not great, but it's a lot better than twenty-two. Which brings us to the bottom section of my report."

Kelsey returned her attention to the page in front of her and felt a tiny surge of hope at the heading he'd put there, *Recommended Recourse.*

"As you can see," he said, "I came up with three scenarios that your board could try in order to circumvent this hostile takeover. Scenario one would be to do nothing. Reject the offer and ride out the current troubles until things are back on track."

"Nice dream," Kelsey replied, "but the board has no control over that. It's up to the stockholders now."

"Which is why I included more than one option. Scenario two would be a friendly merger with another company. By combining forces with someone of equivalent or slightly lesser value, you might not see an immediate return, but at least you could stave off the hostile takeover—and if you play your cards right, retain all current positions and complete control of operations. Choose well, and their good will could also help B & T overcome the current publicity issues."

Kelsey nodded. "This is exactly what I told Walter last night, that a friendly merger with a smaller company had to be preferable to a hostile takeover by a mammoth one." Kelsey leaned forward, looking at Cole. "Lou Strahan has been wanting to merge with us for a long time. I don't know the specifics of his current offer, but I have to believe he could beat Clean Sweep's paltry twenty-two million."

Cole's eyes narrowed, and after a moment Kelsey remembered what a touchy topic this was for them both. "Lou's only been at it for five years, Kels. Is he really all that big yet? Big enough for something like this, I mean?"

"Absolutely. As predicted, he's been extremely successful. He also knows that the realty trust area is a good fit and something we currently lack at

B & T. From what he's told me, his long-range goal has always been to grow big enough to buy back in. In the beginning, even I thought that was a tad optimistic, but given how low our value has fallen, at this point it actually seems plausible."

Cole nodded, avoiding her eyes. Once again, they were in tricky emotional territory. "And what was Walter's response to that suggestion?"

"He told me he would look into it, but I don't know how aggressively he's going to move on it."

Leaning back in his chair, Cole finally focused his gaze on Kelsey. "You know what, Kels? Depending on how things work out tonight, you might consider going over Walter's head and convening an emergency meeting with the board of directors yourself." Glancing toward Flash, he added, "In our research, we turned up a rather...uh...troubling fact."

"What's that?"

Cole hesitated, so Flash jumped in and spoke.

"Fifteen years ago, Walter Hallerman was working as a consultant, and his biggest client was none other than Queen's Fleet Management Group."

Kelsey's eyes widened. "Wait a minute. You're telling me the man at the helm of Brennan & Tate used to be aligned with Queen's Fleet?"

"That's what we found out," Cole replied. "He may be completely on the up-and-up. But for all we know, he could have been working this from the inside all along, trying to bring everything at B & T to this point."

Kelsey shook her head, refusing to believe it. She had never been crazy about the man, and she'd been especially frustrated by the choices he'd made in the last week, but she also knew that her father was a tremendously gifted judge of character. Nolan Tate had believed in Walter one hundred percent. Thus, she had always believed in him as well. She said as much now.

"We have no proof of any wrongdoing," Flash said. "We just thought we would bring the matter to your attention."

They were all quiet for a long moment, and then Cole returned to the financial report.

"Anyway," he said, "the third scenario I'm recommending is to secure a significant cash infusion and buy out any stockholders who would otherwise force the sale of the company. Buy enough shares, and the Tate family could even regain control of B & T for the first time in decades."

Kelsey liked the sound of that. "Have you done the math? Exactly how much money would it take?"

"It's hard to come up with an exact figure, but if I had to guess I'd say somewhere between seven and ten million dollars—seven to stave off the takeover and ten to get your family at fifty-one percent. Then you reject Pamela's offer and do your best to ride out the storm until the publicity crisis is past and the value recovers."

"Obviously, this would be my choice," Kelsey said. "But a cash infusion from where? Are you recommending that we acquire some sort of debt? Or maybe a liquidation of some kind?"

Looking to the two men at the table, Cole shook his head. "No, I was thinking more along the lines of cashing in some bonds."

It took a moment for Kelsey to understand. She was about to give a sarcastic reply, like, "Bonds? Sure. No problem. Let me get my purse," when she realized that all three men were smiling at her.

"What?" she asked warily, not daring to hope.

"Got something to show you," Thriller said, turning to pick up a large, heavy book from the chair beside him. Standing, he opened it and began flipping through the pages. She tilted her head, trying to read the spine. She couldn't quite make it out, but from the cover photo it looked to her like some sort of antiquing catalog.

Thriller found the page he wanted, flipped the book around, and slapped it down on the table in front of Kelsey. Leaning forward, he pointed toward an old black-and-white photograph.

She sat up straight and took a look. Sure enough, it was a catalog of antiquities with photos and descriptions of various items. The photograph to which Thriller was pointing was of an old black safe. There didn't seem to be anything special about it that she could see. Its door was outlined with a decorative square of shiny metal, and inside that square was some writing, a combination lock, and a wide handle.

Peering more closely, she read the decorative script on the door, which said, *Cramer Bros. Safe Co.*, and under that, *Kansas City, MO*. Still not sure what she was looking for, her eyes went to the only other writing on the safe. Those letters had faded, but she squinted at them until she could make out what they said. Then she gasped.

In big block letters across the top, over the door, were two words, the best two words she'd seen in a long time.

THE WONDER.

CHAPTER
THIRTY-FOUR

April 13, 1912

JOCELYN

Jocelyn was feeling quite melancholy as the final song of the concert came to a close. How would she ever make her decision? Why was God being so silent in this matter?

As sounds of applause drifted up from the audience below, the doors to the outside burst open and several men entered, laughing and talking loudly.

"Ladies!" one of them cried, and Jocelyn realized it was the voice of Tad.

The three men stumbled toward the couch, arms around each other, and for a moment she feared they were drunk. Then she realized that while the one in the middle was indeed inebriated, the other two were sober and simply holding him up so he wouldn't fall.

"Hey, Clancy," Tad said, turning to the fellow on the other end, "this is the girl I was talking about. Why don't you stay here and chat with her for a few minutes while I get our friend here tucked into bed and then come back and join you?" Turning to Adele, he said, "You don't mind, do you?"

Adele seemed to recoil. "I don't—"

"Oh, wait," Tad said with a laugh, "I guess I should tell you what I'm talking about. My friend Clancy here needs some business advice, and I thought you might be the one to help him."

"Advice?"

"He'll explain. His company has run into some troubles. See what you can do. I'll be back in just a bit."

With that Tad was heading off down the stairs, one arm supporting his friend and the other firmly gripping the rail. Clancy was left standing there, looking embarrassed and nervous, clutching the brim of his hat and focusing his eyes on the floor in front of him.

"I'm sorry about that, ladies," he said. "You're both otherwise engaged. I don't mean to interrupt."

He turned to go, but Jocelyn spoke. "No, please. Obviously, Tad wants you to stay. Have a seat. I'm Jocelyn Brennan, by the way, and this is my cousin Adele."

"How do you do?" the man replied with a polite nod. "Clancy O'Connell. I only met Mr. Myers yesterday, but I could tell straight off he was a man of ideas. Unfortunately, none of those ideas will fix my problems."

He sat down on a chair to the right of the couch, hat still in his hands, and his eyes returned to the floor. "My music store is going under, you see, and I don't know how to stop it. I thought perhaps a loan or an investment might help, but Tad took a look at my financials and said I'm in such bad shape that I couldn't get money from St. Nicholas himself on Christmas Day."

"I'm sorry to hear that, Mr. O'Connell," Adele told him kindly. "I'm not sure why Tad thought I might be able to help. I've not worked in business and have no formal education on the topic."

Clancy shrugged. "He said you had a natural gift."

"Well, then, why don't you give me some background and I'll see if any suggestions come to mind?" Adele said. Her cheeks were flushed, but Jocelyn could tell she was deeply pleased.

Nodding, the fellow began his tale. From what Jocelyn could tell, it sounded as though the company had suffered several big blows in a row, including a dishonest cashier who had been dipping into the till and a piano factory that had gone bankrupt with numerous orders still pending. Adele asked the man some questions, and they were still exploring various options when Tad returned and took the space on the sofa next to her.

Eventually Mr. O'Connell said he had to leave to meet up with his wife, but he thanked them for their help and asked if they might talk again later. Once he was gone, Adele turned to Tad and said she appreciated the fact that he respected her abilities enough to suggest such an encounter.

He smiled shyly. "It's not exactly a secret. You just have a way about you. I thought he might find your assistance encouraging—and that you might even come up with a solution to his problems."

Tad held Adele's gaze for a long moment, and suddenly Jocelyn felt very much like a third wheel. She wanted to slip away and give them some time alone together, but she needed to do so without being rude.

Then it came to her. Stifling a smile, she announced it was time for her to head to the enclosed promenade and help entertain the children. "Would you two like to come with me?"

"No," they replied in unison, and then they all laughed.

Soon Jocelyn was on her way. She had accomplished her goal of moving them toward a relationship, which was a good thing.

So why did that thought make her feel so sad?

CHAPTER
THIRTY-FIVE

Thriller looked as excited as Kelsey felt.

"See, as soon as you said that stuff this morning about 'The Wonder,'" he explained, "my brain started working on it. I knew I had seen or heard that phrase somewhere before. Then this afternoon it hit me. It took a while to find a picture of it, but there you go. The Wonder safe, made by Cramer Brothers Company in Kansas City, Missouri, in the year nineteen fifteen."

"Do we know where it is?" Kelsey whispered.

"Not yet," he replied. "But hopefully we will by the end of the night."

Kelsey continued to stare in shock at the photo of the old safe. Even if they couldn't find it, even if nothing came of this at all, just seeing that photo reaffirmed something far more important, that her father was still *there*, that he wasn't just a mindless shell who sat babbling nonsense. "The Wonder!" he had cried in response to her questions about the bonds. Looking at the photo, she felt a flutter of release, of hope, deep in her heart. Maybe he would never return to the man he'd once been, but at least a part of him remained. For her, that was enough.

Drawing in a quick breath to ward off happy tears, she asked Thriller if he had seen one of these before in person.

"One or two."

"Where?"

"Let's just say I have some *familiarity* with safes."

Kelsey looked at him, slightly startled, wondering if he'd been a thief or a safecracker in the past. Cole had always been the type of person to give a fellow a second chance. For all she knew, he hired ex-cons.

"I used to work for a locksmith," Thriller said with a faint smile.

"Ah," she said, embarrassed for her assumption. "So what's our next move?"

"We'll get to that," Cole said. "But let's finish up our review first. Thriller, why don't you tell us what you learned about the bonds themselves?"

Thriller retook his seat. "Flash, you helped me out on this. Why don't you explain?"

"Gladly." The young man sat up a little straighter in his wheelchair and looked at Kelsey. "Good news. With some digging we were able to confirm that on April tenth, nineteen twelve, a Mr. Rowan Brennan purchased ten bonds for a thousand dollars each from a company called Transatlantic Wireless Limited, in England."

Kelsey gasped. "Are you sure?"

Flash nodded, looking vaguely insulted at the question.

"Transatlantic Wireless?" she asked. "What is that?"

"Primarily, they sold telegram and telegraph equipment to companies like those owned by Marconi. In fact, *Titanic* was using some of their equipment on board, so we assume Brennan was able to see it in action during the trip."

"Wow." Kelsey sat back in her seat, astounded at what she was learning. "But how do we know if the bonds made it off the ship or not?"

Flash grinned. "Oh, they did. I tracked the serial numbers and found that two of them were cashed in nineteen twenty-nine, another in nineteen thirty-five, and yet another in nineteen seventy-three."

"That means they were still worth something as late as the seventies," Kelsey said softly.

"Yep," Flash replied. "Three hundred and forty two thousand dollars each, to be exact. They would be worth more than that now, maybe even twice as much."

"How about the other six bonds? Any idea what happened to them?"

Flash shook his head. "My search was pretty exhaustive. I found no other evidence of the remaining serial numbers. There's a chance that only four of the bonds made it off *Titanic*, of course, but it seems unlikely they would have become separated. Our conclusion is that your father was correct. Some of the bonds still exist, unredeemed, and they are being stored somewhere in a Cramer Brothers safe."

Closing her eyes, Kelsey verbalized the one question she was afraid to ask.

"Is Transatlantic Wireless still around? I can't imagine that bonds from a tele-graph company would be worth anything in this day and age." She opened her eyes, and once again she realized that the three men were all smiling at her.

"The good news," Cole said, picking things up from there, "is that TW is now part of a larger conglomerate. They're owned by BAE Systems, which is one of the UK's largest corporations."

"So it's a viable company?" she said.

"Quite."

"And they would honor these bonds?"

"We believe so." His smile faded. "There's just one big problem."

"What's that?"

Cole glanced at Flash and Thriller and then back at Kelsey. "The bonds purchased by Rowan Tate were hundred-year bonds. If we can't find them and cash them in by April ninth, two thousand twelve, they'll expire."

Kelsey swallowed hard. "Expire? Then what?"

He shrugged. "Essentially, they'll become worthless."

"You could probably sell them on eBay, as collectibles," Flash interjected. "But you wouldn't get that much for 'em. Maybe forty, fifty bucks a piece."

Kelsey's mind was whirling. April ninth? That was... "Cole, today is Fri-day the sixth, right?"

"Yes."

"That means we have to find them and cash them in by Monday or we lose everything."

He nodded grimly. "Guess you could say we have our work cut out for us. It's time to take a good look at these floor plans to see if we can figure out the most logical places where that safe might be hidden."

Cole then unfolded the plans Kelsey had brought and spread them open on the table. As he and Thriller studied them closely, Flash suggested it might be a good time to wire her up. Soon she had a transmitter/battery pack tucked in a pocket, a tiny mic fastened inside her collar, and a small, flesh-colored triangle wedged in her ear.

Using a headset and his laptop, Flash had her walk through the Thorn-ton offices as he tested out the sound. And though the vibrations of the ear-piece tickled a bit when he spoke, otherwise she was amazed at the quality of the reception.

"What exactly do I do once I'm in there?" she asked Flash when she rejoined the others in the conference room.

Handing her an iPad, he said, "The first thing is to use this to log onto the network and go into your email. You'll accept an email from me, and that will serve to open a channel. After that, I'll take over and get the electronic info we need remotely."

"Remotely?"

"From the van. We'll be parked right outside."

She was suddenly nervous. "Will I be able to talk to you while I'm in there?"

"Absolutely, like you did just now."

"Okay."

"After that I may need you to take other actions, depending on the data that comes back to me. Otherwise, Thriller will be guiding you to look for the safe."

She nodded, the butterflies in her stomach suddenly going wild.

"I was able to get information about the security system the B & T building uses," Flash continued. "Fortunately, you can still get in the doors with your regular code, and there's only one security camera on the fifth floor. It shows the elevator landing, the restroom doors, and the reception area. Avoid those, and you won't be spotted."

Kelsey nodded, remembering that from a conversation with Ephraim.

Glancing at his watch, he added, "The security team doesn't start making rounds till midnight, and the cleaners come on Sundays rather than Fridays, so you should be clear of all interruptions. Unless some employee decides to come back to the office, you'll have the place to yourself."

Kelsey sank into a chair. "You guys certainly seem to have thought of everything," she said gamely, wishing she felt more confident.

Flash nodded. "That's our job. And we're as thorough as they come."

They both fell silent, and Kelsey turned her attention to Cole and Thriller. The two men were leaning intently over the plans, deep in discussion, pausing occasionally to make notes on a pad.

"How are you guys coming over there?" Flash asked, glancing at his watch. "We ought to roll soon."

"Just about finished," Cole replied. Then, after another minute, both men sat up straight and Cole gave Kelsey a nod. "Just one more thing, and then we can go."

Nodding, she moved back to her place at the table.

"No offense, Kels, but I need you to sign this." Cole pulled a piece of paper from a manila folder and slid it in front of her. "It's a waiver, and it says you have the authority to grant us remote access to your computer network. What we're doing is legal as long as it's done with the permission of someone who already has access to the data."

"We won't be hacking any firewalls," Flash added. "That's why you have to be inside, online, to grant us the permission electronically."

Kelsey nodded, skimming the wording on the form. It all looked reasonable to her, and she had no hesitation in signing. Not only did she feel that she had every right to do this, but she had also obtained permission from her father, who was still the president of Brennan & Tate, technically speaking.

Cole handed her a pen. After she had signed the document and handed it back to him, he thanked her, adding, "I won't work outside of the law, and I can't have my employees doing so either. I'm glad you understand that."

She nodded, their eyes holding for a long moment. "Knowing you, Cole, that doesn't surprise me in the least."

Smiling, he tucked away the waiver and then stood.

"Guess that's it, folks," he told them, eyeing his troops one by one. "Let's roll."

Soon the four of them were in a dark blue, handicap-accessible van, Thriller at the wheel, driving down Broadway toward the financial district. The back of the vehicle was filled with all sorts of electronic equipment, and the more Kelsey took it all in, the more confident she began to feel about the whole thing. These guys really did seem to know what they were doing. Glancing at Cole, she felt her heart surge with gratitude.

"Thank you," she whispered when he returned her gaze. "I know you guys offered to do all of this for free, but I say if we find those bonds, you've earned yourselves a finder's fee."

"*That's* what I'm talking about!" Thrilled cried, slapping a hand on his thigh.

"Thanks, Kelsey," Flash said from where his wheelchair had been strapped in behind her.

Cole gave her a wink and said, "I'll pass, but that's kind of you to do that for the guys."

"Aw, shut up, boss," Thriller said. "If you don't want it, Flash and I will split your share."

They all laughed.

As they continued onward, Cole asked Kelsey about her other assignment, the confrontation with Pamela. She sighed and then related their entire encounter, and by the time she was finished, they had nearly reached their destination.

When they were just a half a block from the office building, Thriller said, "Looks like we got lucky, boss," as he pulled into an open parking place. Kelsey stifled a smile, not bothering to explain that in this business-centric area, empty spots could almost always be found at night.

As Thriller cut off the engine, Cole handed Kelsey a piece of paper, explaining that he'd jotted down a simplified version of the office layout and put an *X* everywhere that there was enough excess wall space that a recessed safe could possibly fit. Next, he gave her a small flashlight, saying she should turn on lights only where they wouldn't shine through to the areas seen by the security camera. She nodded, remembering at that moment that she was going to have to access the fifth floor via the same conference room where she'd found Gloria's dead body. Swallowing hard, she tucked the flashlight into her pocket.

"And I guess that's it," Cole said, giving her a reassuring smile.

She nodded again, her heart racing.

"Quick sound check," Flash said from behind her, and she turned to see that he was now unhooked from the safety straps and facing the equipment as though it were a desk. He handed two headsets to Cole, who kept one and passed the other up to Thriller. Then each of them put them on and spoke to her in turn.

"Why can't we just use cell phones?" Kelsey asked once they were finished.

"Not secure," Flash replied. "Trust me. I know what I'm doing."

"Oh, I believe you," she said, gripping the door handle. "Do you think I'd do something like this if I didn't?"

Cole placed a warm hand on her arm. "You'll be fine, Kels."

Looking into his eyes, she very much wanted to believe that. With a final nod, she slid open the door, got out, and started walking.

CHAPTER
THIRTY-SIX

A s Kelsey went toward the building, clutching Flash's iPad to her chest, she wanted to look over her shoulder toward the van, but she resisted the urge. When she arrived at the door, she tried to act nonchalant as she punched in her code and waited for the click.

Oddly, nothing happened.

She must have keyed it in wrong. She tried again and waited. Nothing. She tugged on the door handle, but it was locked up tight. Unbelievable.

"I think Walter invalidated my security code," she hissed, heart pounding. "What now?"

"Hold on," Flash's voice said in her ear. "Let me see if there's anything I can do."

She waited, trying not to look guilty or feel paranoid, grateful at least that the street was deserted for the moment. Inside, her blood was pumping, not just with fear but with rage. Walter had canceled her code! If her father knew about this, he would—

Kelsey gasped, the idea coming to her in a flash. Quickly, she keyed in her father's code. Almost instantly she heard a soft click in response. Swinging the door open, she whispered, "Crisis averted. I'm in. Walter may have canceled me, but he forgot about my dad!"

In her ear she could hear the guys softly cheering. When the cheer faded, she gave them the code that had gotten her inside, just in case they might need to come in after her.

She sprinted silently up the stairs, but after two flights she began to feel a sharp pain in her left heel. Oh, great. One of the Band-Aids must have slipped out of place. Slowing slightly, she continued onward, wondering why she hadn't thought to shove a few extras into her pocket.

When she reached the fifth floor, she again used her father's code. *Please, please, please, let it work.*

Click.

"I'm in."

"Fantastic!" Flash replied.

Not until she pushed the door open did she realize what room she was entering—that it was the place where Gloria had died. Hand to the wall, she fumbled around for a light switch and then flipped it on, exhaling in relief to see that there was nothing amiss now. No dead bodies. No hanging cords. Instead, in the wall where the screen had previously been mounted was just a row of empty holes.

Kelsey pulled the door shut behind her, stepped to the nearest chair, and sat.

"Okay, signing into the network now," she whispered as she pushed the button and the iPad sprung to life. She went into the settings, waited until B & T's wireless network popped up in the list, clicked on it, and then entered her password. Holding her breath, she feared that Walter might have canceled this as well, but after a moment it was accepted and she was in.

"Done," she whispered.

"Good," Flash replied. "Now log into your inbox and look for something from Superstudonwheels."

Smiling, she did as he said, and once she'd clicked on his email, she watched as he took control of the screen from a block and a half away.

"Cool," she whispered.

"Okay, Kels," Cole said. "You can leave the iPad where it is for now. We need you to keep moving."

"All right."

She placed it on the seat of the chair next to her and then slid that chair under the table so that it was out of sight. After that, she forced herself to walk across the room, but when she reached the other door, she realized that this next part of her task would have to be done in the dark.

Pulling the flashlight from her pocket, she turned off the light switch in the conference room, plunging herself into blackness, and then she quietly opened the door and peeked out into the hallway. At least it wasn't totally black out there. Safety lights glowed softly from several places along the wall, and at the far end of the hall she could see light flowing in through the windows in the front offices facing the street.

She took two steps and stopped, listening. At that moment she felt more like an intruder than the rightful heir. The honk of a horn reached her from far away, but inside all she could hear was the pounding of her own heart. Her knees felt weak, and her breath came in short gulps. Was she in danger?

She stood for a long time, blinking as her eyes adjusted to the darkness.

"Kelsey?" She jumped. It was Flash who spoke softly into her ear.

She hauled in a deeper breath and whispered, "If I say the word 'help,' you guys will come running, right?"

After a couple of seconds, Cole's voice came over the earpiece. "It's me, Kelsey. Trust me, I won't let anyone or anything harm you. Do you want me to come up there now?"

"No, I'm okay."

"Does something seem wrong or unsafe?"

"No, not really. I'll be fine. It's just…creepy. Keep listening though, okay?"

"I'm not going anywhere," Cole said, the tone of his voice helping to calm her beating heart.

Slowly, she tiptoed down the long, dark hallway toward the executive suite up front. She kept the flashlight off but clutched it like a weapon just the same.

"You okay?" Cole asked in her ear.

"Halfway there," she whispered in reply.

It wasn't until she had to walk past the open doorway that led to reception that she saw something in her peripheral vision. She swung her head to the right and gasped, freezing in her tracks.

"What is it?" Cole asked.

She didn't answer immediately but peered toward a human form standing in the corner, past the reception desk.

"Kelsey, are you okay?" Cole asked more insistently.

Then she realized what she was seeing. Blowing out a long, slow breath, she continued down the hall.

"Yes, but for a moment I thought I was done for," she said, chuckling softly.

"What happened?"

"I saw the glass display case with the *Titanic* memorabilia. Do you remember the mannequin wearing Adele's outfit? I thought it was a person standing there."

He chuckled as well. "I guess that could be pretty startling."

"Yeah, well, it's not the first time that's happened," she admitted.

She reached the executive hallway, turned right, and walked all the way down it, past Gloria's office and the executive washrooms, to the last door on the left. The placard read "Nolan Tate," but long before this had been her father's office, it had been used by Adele herself. The guys all thought this room was their first, best chance for finding the safe. Placing a hand on the knob and giving it a twist, she whispered, "Made it to the office. I'm going in."

"Roger that."

She opened the door and stepped inside, breathing in the stale, unused smell that hung in the air. Closing the door behind her, she was glad she didn't need the overhead lights or her flashlight. The wide front windows let in so much brightness from outside that she could see just fine.

Kelsey pulled the paper Cole had given her from her pocket. She unfolded it and studied the diagram, searching for Xs. Instead, this entire room had been circled.

"Cole, I thought you said this was the best place to start," she whispered. "You don't have any places marked in here at all."

"That's because three of the four walls are deep enough to handle a recessed safe. If you can't find anything in there, the Xs will guide you to other places in the building where you could also look."

"Okay."

Shoving the diagram back into her pocket, Kelsey slowly circled the room, lifting framed art out from the walls and checking behind each one. She peered around all of the furniture.

Nothing.

Next, she opened the door to the closet and was hit with an even staler whiff of air. She clicked on her flashlight and shone it on the shelves that lined the closet walls from ceiling to floor. They were packed with office supplies, manuals, and old boxes.

Nothing.

She stepped out of the closet, her flashlight beam sweeping across the floor as she did, and she noticed something gray on the carpet. Kneeling, she studied it more closely. Dust. Lots of dust. Like a squared off ridge of dust.

"Kels?"

"Just a sec. I have an idea."

Shining her flashlight on the lower shelves, she saw that they were packed tightly with old records and file folders, all coated in a deep layer of dust. She tried to see if any of them looked as though they had recently been disturbed, but she couldn't tell. Still, she had a feeling that the dust mark on the closet floor had come from a stack of these old papers that someone had placed there. Given that the things in here were ancient, and the fact that this office wasn't currently being used anyway, she felt that the dust marks had to be significant.

With a heavy sigh, she began removing items from the shelves so she could peek at the walls behind them. She started at the bottom right, pulling boxes out, looking, and putting them back. Pulling out, looking, putting back. It wasn't until she got to the second shelf, left side, that she pulled a stack of file folders out, looked, and gasped.

Black. She could see black. The black of metal.

The black of an old safe.

"I think I found it!" Heart pounding, she pulled out more and more things from the shelves until she had exposed the recessed wall safe in its entirety. It was about two feet high and a foot and a half wide, and it was in better shape than the one in the photo. The letters on this one had barely worn off at all. The "Cramer Bros." was clearly visible on the door. And above the door, across the top, were the words, "THE WONDER."

"Do you have something?" Cole asked urgently.

"Do I ever!" Kelsey replied, grinning. "We found it, boys. We found The Wonder."

Another cheer rang out from the van, this one louder than before.

She reached out and touched the cool, black metal. Could it possibly hold the bonds? Or had whoever made that dust mark on the floor already gone inside and taken them?

Gloria's words rang in her memory, *"Have you ever done something bad out of good intentions?"*

Please, let the bonds still be there. Please.

"Guys? What do I do now?"

"Okay, Kelsey, it's Thriller here. We have two choices. One, you close things back up the way they were and we come back tomorrow with a locksmith."

She sighed. She was unwilling to wait that long—not to mention that she couldn't exactly sneak one in through the back door. "You said you used to work for a locksmith, Thriller. Can't you crack this safe yourself?"

He chuckled. "Locksmiths don't 'crack' safes, Kelsey. They bring in tools and equipment and open them up other ways."

She sat back on her heels. "What's the other option? Got any explosives out there in the van?"

"Hey," Flash snapped. "Don't kid around like that. We're on wireless here."

"Sorry." She took a deep breath and blew it out. Apparently they were getting a little tense.

"According to the book," Thriller said, "The Wonder's combination was configurable by the customer. If your great-grandmother was the one who had it installed, chances are it still has the combination she gave it originally."

"You want me to guess the combination?"

"Well, it takes three numbers. A lot of people use dates."

"You mean like birthdays and things?"

"Yeah. Any idea of a date she might have used?"

"I don't know. I could try her birthday and her son's birthday, but those are about the only dates I have. I don't know her father's birthday, or her anniversary, or her husband's birthday, or anything else like that."

"Okay, well, at least give those two a shot. Just remember to spin it three revolutions, clockwise, each time before you start."

"Got it."

Tentatively, Kelsey reached up and placed her hand on the dial. After doing as Thriller instructed, she tried right 7, left 21, right 93. Adele's birthday.

Nothing.

After spinning it clockwise several times again, she tried once more, right 11, left 14, right 23. Grandpa Jonah's birthday.

Nothing.

She shifted to a more comfortable position and tried to think how they could figure this out. If only her father could tell her.

She sat up straight. Maybe her father *could* tell her.

"Guys, I have an idea. I'm going to call my dad and ask him. I'll have to take out the earpiece for a minute."

"Okay," Cole replied, "but don't talk any louder than you've been talking to us."

"I won't."

She dialed her parents' house. Then she pulled the triangle from her ear and held her cell phone to it instead. Her mother answered, and Kelsey asked to speak directly to her father.

"What did you say, dear? Speak up."

Kelsey shifted further into the closet and pulled the door shut, nearly choking from the dust. "I need to talk to Dad for a minute. Can you put him on the phone? It's urgent."

"Is it something I could help you with?"

"I don't think so, Mom. I need the combination to an old safe at the office."

"Oh, well, then you do need him. Hold on."

After a good minute, Nolan finally came on the line. He didn't speak, but she could tell from the sound of his breathing that he was there.

"Dad? Can you hear me?" she asked.

He grunted in return.

"Good. Listen, I'm at B & T, in the closet in your office, looking at The Wonder."

"The Wonder! G-great."

"It is great, Dad, but I need the combination. Do you remember what it is?"

The line was silent for a long moment, and then he said, "Birthday."

"Adele's birthday? I tried that and it didn't work."

"No. Hoppelin."

"Hoppelin?"

"Joplin."

She closed her eyes, desperate to understand.

"Jock. Jock." He couldn't seem to get it out. Then, "Josh."

Her eyes flew open. "Jocelyn? Are you trying to say Jocelyn?"

"Yes. Joshen."

"Jocelyn's birthday. That's the combination?"

"Y-yes."

"Okay, Dad, put Mom back on the phone."

Once her mother came on, she explained that she needed to know Jocelyn's birth date. "Try looking in Adele's book. I think it's in there."

"Hold on, I'll check."

While she was gone, Kelsey thought about running out to the glass case in reception and grabbing the copy that was kept there. If not for the security camera, she would have done so already.

"Okay, here it is," her mother said, finally, coming back on the phone. And then she gave the date of October 23, 1893.

Quickly, Kelsey thanked her mother and then hung up. Replacing the earpiece and tucking away her phone, she opened the closet door for air and light, and then she knelt down again in front of the safe. Hands shaking, she gave the dial several revolutions, and then she tried right 10, left 23, right 93.

Nothing.

Her heart sank. That *had* to be it. It just had to. She tried again, to no avail.

Finally, she stood, brushed off her pants, and exited the closet as she explained to the team in the van what had just happened.

"I don't think he was wrong," she whispered. "I think someone went in there and changed it. I guess that means we'll need a locksmith after all."

Everyone was silent for a long moment, their disappointment palpable.

"Well, all is not lost," Flash said. "There's something else I need you to do."

"What's that?" Kelsey asked, looking down at the stacks of folders on the floor of the closet and trying to summon the energy to put them all back on the shelves.

"I've been sitting here going through Gloria's digital activity the night before she died. Looks like she made photocopies on a copy machine. If you can go there now, I'll talk you through reprinting whatever it was."

"Okay."

Kelsey turned off her flashlight, crossed to the door of her father's office, and pulled it open as quietly as possible. Listening intently, she peered down the darkened hallway. She still seemed to be alone.

Summoning her nerve, she emerged and padded softly down the hall, limping a little from her sore heel, and went past Gloria's office to the alcove next door, where Yanni and the other executive secretaries had their desks. Though there were other copy machines in the building, the one that sat there against the back wall under the window was the one Gloria used most often.

Once Kelsey was there, Flash told her how to use the digital panel to scroll through the machine's history until she found a printing job that had been done Tuesday morning at 12:25 a.m.

"Got it," she said, and then she pressed Print.

With a flash of light and a noisy whirr, the machine sprung to life. Quickly, she ducked down behind a desk to hide, just in case, and then she finally allowed herself to peek around the side toward the hallway. No one appeared. She was still alone, and now copies were coming out onto the tray. Rising,

Kelsey told herself to get a grip. She grabbed the first sheet and held it up to the light coming in through the window to see some sort of fancy scrollwork covering the page. Needing a better look, she turned on her flashlight and directed the beam of light at the piece of paper in her hand.

"Oh, wow."

"What is it?" Cole asked.

"Bonds," she whispered. She grabbed another from the tray. "Each one is a copy of a very old bond."

"How many?"

"Uh…hold on."

She waited until the machine went silent. "Six." She picked up the rest of the copies. "Gloria came here that night and made copies of the six bonds."

"Check the date on 'em," Thriller said. "Does it say they were issued April ninth, nineteen twelve?"

She scanned the various markings on the page until she found the numbers 09-04-12 with the word "Date" underneath.

"I don't understand. Does this mean the bonds were purchased in September?" she asked. "I thought you said Rowan Tate got these in April, the day before boarding *Titanic*."

"He did."

They were all quiet for a moment.

"Wait," Cole said suddenly. "You're talking about England here. What we write as four-nine-twelve, they would have written as nine-four-twelve. Kelsey, do you know what this means?"

"I'm on it!"

With the copies gripped tightly in her hand, she dashed back down the hall to her father's office, ran inside, and fell to her knees in front of the safe. There, hands trembling, she tried Jocelyn's birth date again, only this time, she flipped the month and day: right 23, left 10, right 93.

She could hear the tumblers click in response.

"I think that did it," she whispered.

Gripping the handle, she twisted and pulled. The door opened with a loud, rusty squawk. Her heart pounded as she swung it wide. She shone the beam of her flashlight inside. The safe was empty except for a small leather-bound book. With trembling hands, Kelsey pulled it out, realizing almost immediately what it was.

"No bonds," she whispered.

"I'm sorry," Cole replied.

"Is there anything in there at all?" Flash asked.

"Yes," she said, cradling the book in her hands and gently turning a few of the pages. She blinked, sending tears of gratitude down her cheeks. "It's Adele's original diary," she told them. "Written in her own hand."

CHAPTER
THIRTY-SEVEN

April 13, 1912

ADELE

Adele could not make up her mind about Tad. At times she felt quite fond of him, yet at other times she bristled at his behavior. He was handsome and charming and attentive, yes, but he was also brash and impulsive and immature. And though they had shared a fun afternoon together and were now eating side by side in the beautiful second-class dining saloon, a part of her felt exhausted, almost as if it were an effort to keep up the attraction between them.

Shouldn't romance be easier than this? Shouldn't it feel more natural?

Adele wasn't well versed in male–female relationships, but she had to believe that most happy couples craved each other's company rather than grew weary of it—especially in the beginning.

But weary was the word she was looking for. A part of her just felt weary.

At least their dinner companions tonight were interesting. Clancy O'Connell and his wife had taken two of the spots at their table, and because Uncle Rowan was dining with new friends at another table, there were three remaining places to give over to the Brown family from South Africa, including Thomas, his wife, Elizabeth, and their teenaged daughter, Edith. Tad had orchestrated the gathering, and soon Adele understood why. The Browns were quite knowledgeable about business, and they, too, were eager to pitch in on finding solutions for Mr. O'Connell's failing music store.

Adele knew that their behavior—hers included—bordered on rude, that business and finance were not suitable dinner conversations. Yet the subject was so fascinating that she couldn't bring herself to change it. The Browns discussed everything from hiring competent staff to negotiating a lease to launching a publicity campaign. Both of them were highly knowledgeable and seemed eager to share what they could. At least poor Edith had ended up next to Jocelyn, so the two tablemates who couldn't care less about any of it were able to entertain each other with more appropriate dinnertime talk of fashion and celebrities and the day's activities.

After a while Adele found herself so comfortable with the Browns that she decided to share her decision to invest in female-owned businesses. They strongly endorsed her idea, but Mr. Brown also suggested she include another demographic as well—that of the immigrant.

"For example, take an acquaintance of mine on this ship," he said. "He's a third-class passenger named Austin van Billiard. The van Billiards have been diamond mining in Central Africa for the past six years, and now Austin and his two eldest sons are on their way to America, where he hopes to become a diamond merchant."

"That sounds exciting," Adele said.

Mr. Brown shook his head. "He has a long road ahead of him. He has family in Pennsylvania, but how much can they do, really? He needs a big, solid loan to get started in his own business, but who will give it to him? He's good for it. I've never known such a family of hard workers. Given a chance, I have no doubt the man could succeed brilliantly, yet I fear he'll not find the capital he needs to get things off the ground."

Adele understood what he was saying, and she agreed that her business model could certainly be improved by offering funding to both women *and* immigrants.

By the end of the meal, though her head was spinning with all of her new knowledge, a consensus had still not been reached as to how the poor O'Connells were to go about saving their music store. Pushing away his empty ice cream dish, Tad leaned toward Clancy when the others weren't listening and said quietly, "I told you this morning, buddy. There's only one way out of this thing, and you know what it is."

In response Clancy's eyes grew guarded, his mouth tight. Soon he and his wife excused themselves, leaving Adele to ask Tad what that had been about.

"Let me walk you to your room and I'll tell you on the way."

Adele readily agreed. Jocelyn came along with them but was soon sidetracked when a little girl of about six came running up to her the moment they exited the dining saloon. Jocelyn introduced the child to Tad and Adele as Daisy.

"Daisy and I have become great friends, haven't we?" she asked the little girl.

"We played shifflebird!" she replied, excitedly.

"You mean shuffleboard," Jocelyn corrected with a smile.

"Mommy said we can play one more time before bed. Can you come too?"

The girl's mother gave a wave from across the lobby.

Turning to Tad and Adele, Jocelyn asked if they would mind, and when they told her to go ahead, she took the delighted child's hand and they headed off.

"Children certainly take to your cousin," Tad said, holding out his arm for Adele.

"And she to them," she replied, slipping her hand into the crook of his elbow.

They walked to the staircase and began to descend slowly, side by side, talking as they went. Tad seemed to have something on his mind, and soon he brought up Brennan & Company.

"Your father is an outstanding leader," he told her, "but he needs to plan for the company's future and his eventual succession. I have always hoped to fill that role, but since I met you, my dream has been altered somewhat."

"Oh?"

Pausing at the C deck landing, he turned to face her and took her by both hands.

"We could do it *together*, Adele," he whispered eagerly. "Can't you just picture us, you and me, at the helm of the company? I know we have only just met this week, but I feel a deep connection to you. I think we are each what the other needs. Smart, business minded, hardworking. I know your father well, and he would be pleased with such a union."

Adele was dumbfounded. She was flattered, of course, but he had to know it was far too soon for such talk. Gracefully removing her hands from his, she said, "Is this a business proposal or a declaration of your romantic intentions?"

He grinned. "Both, I suppose."

Her mind was racing. While she needed to set the man straight, she also didn't want to humiliate him.

"I'm afraid it's a bit too soon for either," she said after a moment. "Surely you must see the…inappropriateness…of your words at this time."

His grin began to fade. They were blocking the stairwell, so she took him by the arm and directed him toward the promenade. It was crowded, however, so he didn't respond until they had reached the other end and stepped into the vestibule above the aft staircase.

"This is how I work," he told her. "I'm decisive. I get things done. And if I see something I want, I go for it, plain and simple."

"What you call decisive, some might call impulsive," she replied as they started down the aft stairs. "I'm afraid you're moving much faster than I am comfortable with, Tad. That doesn't mean I don't like you. Just that you need to slow down a bit."

He nodded, but she could tell by the set of his jaw that he wasn't happy about it. They were both quiet for a long moment. Adele tried to think how she might change the subject to lighten the mood.

"Those were lovely dinner companions you arranged for us tonight," she said, again slipping her hand into the crook of his elbow. "The O'Connells were sweet, and I thoroughly enjoyed meeting the Browns."

"I'm glad you were pleased."

"So tell me what you were talking about with Mr. McConnell," she continued lightly, ignoring his petulance. "His 'only way out,' you called it. What was that about?"

With a deep sigh, Tad seemed to shake off his bad mood. Glancing around, he leaned closer and lowered his voice. "Let's just say that between a spill of kerosene from a wobbly lamp and a carelessly dropped cigar, that place could go *poof* real fast. Pianos and violins would make excellent kindling. As long as he has good fire insurance, that's probably his only option left."

Adele was dumbfounded. She pulled her arm loose and faced him.

"Option? That's not an *option*, that's a *crime*. No wonder the poor man looked so upset when you suggested it!"

Tad rolled his eyes. "Come on, Adele, don't hide your head in the sand. This is the real business world now. It's not all nicey-nicey and helping the immigrants. Sometimes you have to make choices that save what otherwise would be lost. Mr. O'Connell has a disaster on his hands that could ruin him. I was merely suggesting a last-ditch way to keep that from happening. Don't you know how huge the insurance companies are? They could easily handle such a small payout. If you think about it, it's his own money anyway, with all the premiums he's paid to them over the years."

Adele couldn't believe her ears.

"I don't want to have any part of this," she said, shaking her head. "And I am sure my father wouldn't be pleased to know this is the kind of advice his company is dispensing." With that she turned and continued down the stairs alone, much more quickly now.

After a beat she could hear Tad protesting as he followed behind.

"It is not what you think, Adele. That wasn't official advice from Brennan & Company. I was just speaking one buddy to another. There's a difference."

Adele reached F Deck and moved quickly down the corridor toward her room. Halfway there, Tad caught up with her and grabbed her by the arm, stopping her progress.

"Please listen to me," he implored, "I would never sanction such an action. I just think that if you are going to be in the business world, you had better understand the full realm of what goes on out there. There is no need to talk to your father about this."

Adele took a deep breath, trying hard to control her anger.

"Let me go," she said softly, refusing even to look at him. "I would like to retire for the evening."

"Fine. Sorry."

Tad released her arm, but instead of going away, he fell into step beside her and walked with her the rest of the way down the corridor to her stateroom. As she paused at the door and pulled out her room key, she said a curt goodnight and turned to slip the key into the lock.

The lock was temperamental, however, and before she could get it to work, she was shocked to feel Tad's body suddenly pressing against hers, forcing her against the solid door, his hands encircling her waist from behind.

"I'm crazy about you," he whispered, burying his face into the side of her neck and kissing her furiously. "Why don't we forget about this whole mess and instead spend time getting to know each other better."

She tried to pull away but he was stronger than she. Only by stamping her heel down onto the top of his foot was she finally able to wrench herself loose from his grasp and step away. Why was the hallway empty now, of all times? Where was her steward? Where were the other passengers?

"How *dare* you! How could you possibly—"

"Grow up, Adele," he said, moving toward her menacingly. "I'm not leaving until things are settled between us. I need to know you're not mad at me, that at least we can still be friends."

She looked up at him, eyes wide. "Friends? Since when does a friend force himself upon another friend?"

"You brought that on yourself. I felt sure you had feelings for me. If those feelings weren't genuine, then I'm afraid you've been leading me on."

Adele's heart was thumping furiously. "Listen, I don't know who you think you are," she hissed, "but I find you rude, inappropriate, and extremely unethical. I don't want to associate with you in *any* manner ever again! Does that make it clear enough for you?"

She heard a noise from down the hall and turned to see a steward walking in their direction. Unfortunately, he paused halfway up to knock on someone else's cabin door and then, when it was opened, stepped inside.

Tad seized the moment to move even closer, again pressing himself against Adele. He placed his hands against the wall on each side of her and then leaned forward until his lips were at her ear.

"If you say a word about this to anyone," he whispered, "I will say that you were the one who threw yourself at *me*. Even Jocelyn will believe it. She's seen you flirting with me all day. And don't imagine for one second that your father wouldn't believe me, either. He completely trusts me—and he hardly knows you at all. You make trouble for me, and I'll make sure he sends you back to Belfast so fast you won't know what hit you. You can live out your days walking the streets of that city for all I care."

His threat finished, Tad stepped back and dropped his arms just as the steward emerged from the cabin and continued in their direction.

"Is everything okay, miss?" the man asked, looking doubtfully from Adele to Tad and back.

"Yes, thank you," Adele replied. "But I believe this man has lost his way. Could you please escort him to his own stateroom?"

"Certainly. Come with me, sir. What's your stateroom number?"

As the two men headed off down the hall, Adele finished unlocking the door with trembling hands, slipped inside, and closed it tight. Turning to lean back against the solid surface, she could feel her entire body shaking. Carefully, she moved to the wash basin, filled it with water, and splashed it onto her face. That didn't help. Shivering, she quickly changed into her nightgown, climbed up to her berth, and slid under the covers.

Pulling them tightly to her chin, she lay there staring at the ceiling, overcome with exhaustion and wondering if this trip would end up being the biggest mistake of her life.

CHAPTER
THIRTY-EIGHT

Kelsey could hear the disappointment in the men's voices, but for some reason she wasn't nearly as let down as she should have been. She didn't have the bonds, that was true, but she did have Adele's whole story, in her own words. With this diary they might be able to prove the facts about the woman's identity. More importantly, Kelsey thought as she knelt there on the closet floor and quickly but carefully flipped through the pages, she could finally learn the truth about the woman she'd kept on a pedestal her whole life. Did Adele really belong up there? Or had she been a fraud all along?

"Uh-oh," Flash said.

Kelsey's head jerked up. "Uh-oh what?"

"Kelsey, I think you need to get out of there."

"Why? What's wrong?"

"Hyper surveillance."

"In English, please?"

"Somebody's watching what we're doing. Electronically. The trackers are being tracked."

She pressed herself farther into the closet. "Is someone coming up here after me?" she hissed.

"There's been no activity that I can see, but I don't like this. I don't like it at all. Somebody knows we're poking around—and from what I can tell, they are letting us get away with it."

"Kelsey, come on out," Cole added. "Right now."

"On my way," she replied.

Quickly, she closed the safe door and gave the dial a twirl. Setting the diary and the copies of the bonds aside, she hastily shoved the records back onto the shelves. Once she was done, she looked around to be sure she hadn't left anything and closed the door to the closet.

Nervous about her possessions and wanting her hands free in case she had to defend herself, Kelsey slid the photocopies and the diary down the front of her blouse until they came to rest where it was tucked in at her waistline. Then, clutching the flashlight in one hand, she left her father's office, moving as fast as she could along the eerie hallways and through the conference room, grabbing the iPad as she went past and then racing down five flights of stairs.

By the time she stepped out the back door of the building and pulled it shut behind her, the van was idling just half a block away, waiting for her. She quickly walked straight to it, climbed in, and they drove off.

"Are you okay?" Cole asked.

"I think so." Kelsey's heart thumped furiously in her chest. "Give me a minute."

"You did a great job," Flash told her as she handed him the iPad.

"You sure did." Cole reached out and gave her shoulder a gentle squeeze.

"Thanks." Kelsey took a few more calming breaths and turned slightly away to pull the photocopies and the diary from her shirt. "These are the copies of the bonds," she said, handing them over.

"Terrific." Cole turned on a penlight and hunched over the papers, silent as he studied the top sheet and then examined each one in turn.

"Kelsey, what's the best way to get to your place from here?" Thriller asked, and she named off the three turns that would get her home.

"Well, this is definitely proof that the bonds exist," Cole said once she was done.

"And proof that they were in Gloria's possession late Monday night," Flash added.

"But if we can't find the actual bonds..." Her voice trailed off.

Everyone was quiet for a long moment as they rode along Battery Place.

"Here's what I suggest," Cole said, turning to face her. "I know a scripo-philist in Chinatown—"

"A what?"

"A scripophilist." Cole smiled. "That's someone who collects antique stocks and bonds."

"Oh."

"Anyway, why don't we take these copies and show them to him first thing in the morning? At least he should be able to tell us more about them."

"Good idea."

He handed the pages back to her, and she put them with the diary, which she'd been holding tightly to her chest. Cole eyed her curiously, but he didn't ask for it. Kelsey was glad, because she wasn't eager to let it out of her possession, not even for an instant.

She twisted around in her seat. "Flash, did you figure out who was watching us?"

"No. I'll keep working on that. In the meantime, even though we had to cut things short in there, I got a lot of good data."

"Like what?"

He gestured toward the computer screen. "Gloria Poole's electronic trail for the past two weeks—phones calls to and from her extension, the times she coded in to work, the times she logged onto the computer, what equipment she used and when, things like that."

"Wow."

"This data will take some analysis, but you'd be surprised at what can be gleaned from this sort of thing."

"Other than making copies of the bonds, can you tell about any of her other activities that Monday night?"

He typed on the keyboard and then scanned the screen. "Let's see…for one thing, I see that she googled 'Transatlantic Wireless LTD' and eventually clicked her way to 'BAE Systems.' So we know she was researching the bonds."

"Probably trying to figure out if they still had any value," Cole said.

"And if so, how much," Kelsey added.

Thriller turned onto her street and then pulled to a stop in front of the building. Before she got out, Cole suggested they meet up at Columbus Park at nine in the morning. The man he wanted to visit was just a block away, in Chinatown.

"Sounds good," she replied. "I'll bring the copies of the bonds."

She climbed out of the van and then turned to look back at the three men inside. "Listen, 'thank you' doesn't begin to express—"

"No thanks necessary," Cole cut her off. "We're happy to help. And we're not done yet."

"Okay, then," she said, smiling at each one of them in turn. "Thanks for everything so far, at least. You fellows have no idea how alone I felt until you came along."

At the word "alone" she let her eyes meet Cole's. He held her gaze, and she wondered if he knew what an understatement that was.

Minutes later, upstairs in her apartment, Kelsey heated a quick frozen dinner and ate it standing at the kitchen bar. Though her mind kept going to Cole, she forced herself to focus on tonight's incredible find, the handwritten diary of her great-grandmother Adele. Soon she was ready for bed and under the covers, propped up with pillows, the diary on her lap. She opened it up to the first page and read the inscription that had been written there:

> *Dear Adele,*
>
> *As you begin this next part of your life, may you use this diary to reflect and record the many blessings the good Lord brings your way. You will be sorely missed, but we will keep you in prayer always.*
>
> > *With love forever,*
> > *Uncle Rowan and Aunt Oona*

Oh, boy, Kelsey thought, reaching for the box of tissues on the bedside table. She was on page one, and already she was crying! Smiling at herself, she wiped her eyes, took a deep breath, and then turned the page.

The diary's first entry was dated April 8, 1912. It read:

> *I will give this a try, but only because Aunt Oona says it is important to record my thoughts and experiences as I embark on this next part of my life. She seems to have forgotten that Jocelyn is the writer in this family, not I. Already I am feeling quite silly, writing down things I could more easily say.*
>
> *As for the day, we have arrived in London and are now tired and quite overwhelmed. The architecture here is lovelier than in Belfast, and our hotel is especially grand. But the people look at us as if we are culchies, and I can tell that our frocks— perfectly suitable for home—do not begin to suffice here. Jocelyn cannot wait to go shopping, but I am far more excited about*

meeting Mr. Williams of Transatlantic Wireless and discussing
our investment.

Off to sleep for now.

Kelsey read the page several times through, pausing to look up the word "culchie" with her phone. She learned that it meant country folk, though it was most often used derogatorily, something akin to a "hick" or a "bumpkin." Poor Adele! Here she'd come to London for the first time in her life and felt completely out of place from day one.

Unfortunately, as fascinating as this was, Adele's handwriting was difficult to read. She wrote in a tight but messy script, and to make matters worse, the ink had faded over the years. Continuing on to the next entry and then the next, Kelsey saw that the handwriting only grew worse. It was such slow going that after a while she almost felt as though she were translating from another language.

Still, it was worth the trouble. Kelsey had only known Adele as an older woman. What an amazing treat to meet her on these pages at nineteen. She sounded wise for her years and yet in many ways naive. Several times she referred to America as "the land of opportunity," but from her entries it was clear she expected that to include opportunities for women in business. What an awakening she must have had once she arrived and learned that many of the limits imposed on women in the United Kingdom prevailed on this side of the ocean as well. At least she would no longer be bound by the class system that had further served to dampen her prospects back in Ireland. In the States she would probably find that a man could become whoever he wanted to be if he was willing to work hard enough for it. She would struggle to make that true for women too, but at least she would eventually prevail, as everyone who was familiar with the legend of Adele well knew.

Kelsey persisted in reading the difficult script. Soon her head was hurting from the strain, but her heart was full with the joy of experiencing Adele's journey in her own words. The entries grew quite expansive, and her first day on board *Titanic* merited the longest entry of all. Near the end of that one, Kelsey turned the page and was surprised to see a folded piece of onionskin paper tucked into the margin. Carefully, she pulled it loose and unfolded it to take a look. She realized it was a note from someone else, written on *Titanic* stationery. At the top left was the logo of the White Star Line, a red flag with a white star at the center. Across from that, on the right, were the words *On board*

R.M.S. Titanic. Below that was a line where someone had filled in the date, April 10, 1912. The note itself was brief and had been written in a different hand, a lovely, flowing script that was far easier to read than Adele's. All it said was:

> *Dear Adele,*
>
> *Pay no attention to the opinions of others.*
> *Everything will turn out fine.*
>
> > *Love,*
> > *Your cousin Jocelyn*

Smiling, Kelsey returned her attention to the diary entry, eager to see what this was about. She finally came to it near the bottom of the next page, where Adele had written:

> *This afternoon as we were crossing to France, Tad asked us about our plans upon reaching America. I told him I hoped to attend college in New York, followed by a career in finance. To my surprise, he laughed as if I had made a joke! I am used to the odd looks and discouraging comments whenever I speak of my intentions, but this was the first time I faced such a blatantly cruel reaction. It made me very uncomfortable.*
>
> *Ever sensitive to the needs of others, not half an hour later I felt Jocelyn press a note into my hand. How does she always know the right words at the right time? It is a skill I lack entirely but one which I find utterly enchanting in her. I thank the Lord for her sweet spirit each and every day. How I will miss her if she ends up choosing not to stay with me in America!*

Adele's diary went on to a new topic from there, so Kelsey paused to reread Jocelyn's note. *Pay no attention to the opinions of others. Everything will turn out fine.* With just those two sentences, she had provided comfort and encouragement to her cousin in the wake of someone else's cruelty. Adele was right. Jocelyn did seem to be a natural encourager.

On a hunch, Kelsey decided to flip ahead and see if there were any other notes hidden within the pages of this book. To her delight, she spotted quite a few, though of course there were none beyond the date of April 14—the day *Titanic* struck the iceberg.

With a mixture of excitement and dread, she forced herself to wait and read each note in context. She picked up the story where she'd left off and continued reading. Again, it was slow going, but a few pages later, she ran across the next note and soon found its related passage:

> *This morning while I was out, Jocelyn left a letter on my pillow. As usual, she knew exactly what I needed to hear. Her words were regarding priorities, and I shall take her message to heart. I am so blessed to have someone in my life who is willing to speak the truth in love.*

This note looked thicker, and as Kelsey unfolded it, she saw that it covered two pages of the White Star stationery, front and back. She was eager to read it, but she paused first to go to the kitchen for a glass with water and some ibuprofen for the headache that persisted. Glancing at the clock on the microwave, she was surprised to see that it was after midnight. As much as she wanted to keep reading, she told herself that she should probably stop after this letter and pick things up again in the morning. She didn't have to meet up with Cole until nine, so she would set her alarm for six, knowing perusing the diary might go faster after she'd had some rest, not to mention once her headache was gone.

Yawning, Kelsey returned to the bedroom, settled down against the pillows, and began to read. Jocelyn's letter was quite heartfelt, filled with lots of underlined words and exclamation points. Already, Kelsey was getting a sense of who young Adele and young Jocelyn were, but this letter opened up another level of understanding for them both. It read:

> *Dearest Adele,*
>
> *Today we watched the last of Ireland disappear on the horizon behind us. Now we are only ship and water and sky. What freedom! What excitement! What fear!*
>
> *And yet I know whatever fate befalls us, perfect love casts out that fear. God holds us in His mighty hands, and with Him we can bear all things, believe all things, hope all things, and endure all things. I* know *this to be true!*
>
> *My sweet cousin, as gifted and ambitious as you are, you must promise never to neglect two matters.*

One is <u>love</u>. I know you love your numbers and your ledgers, but God's plan for your life includes far more than just those things. He wants you to live <u>completely</u>, Adele, in a way that has room both for your ambitions and a family. You deserve the love of a husband and of children! Please always remember this! There is room in life for many kinds of blessings. Seek them all, every single day that you live.

Two is <u>God.</u> Mother says that at the center of each human heart lies a hole, one that man forever attempts to fill with all the wrong things. She says that this hole has a unique and specific shape, the shape of God Himself. Please always remember that this place in your heart can never be filled with work <u>or</u> with love but with Christ alone. Allow Him to continue to fill that empty space and be the Lord of your life!

I am reminded of Ecclesiastes 1:7, especially now in this land of ship and water and sky. With this verse in mind, we would both do well to remember what is truly important and what is meaningless under the sun. Whether we live to be 100 or we die within the year, I know that the time we have left is in God's hands. Let us go forward to this new world embracing that truth, clinging to Him and to each other, and determined to pursue balance in work <u>and</u> love. This is God's plan for us, my cousin, and despite our occasional differences, I am so thankful that you and I are embarking on this journey <u>together</u>.

With love,
Jocelyn

What special women they both were. Deeply touched, Kelsey got out of bed, walked over to her desk, and turned on her printer, which also worked as a copier. She knew she would be reading this letter again and again, but she didn't want to damage the paper. Better she make a copy for reference and return the original to the diary for safekeeping.

That done, she put the diary safely away in the bedside drawer and then got back under the covers with a copy of the letter. Reading through it again, more slowly this time, it struck her not just how relevant Jocelyn's words were but also how much Kelsey really was like her great-grandmother. People had always said so, and even as a girl she'd known it to be true, but only now did she realize their similarities went much further than mere common interests. From Jocelyn's letter—and from the diary entries that preceded it—it was clear that Adele had had the same tendency as Kelsey did to place work above everything else in her life. Even at nineteen, she was blessed to have someone in her life to point that out to her, just as Kelsey's mother had confronted her the other day.

Yet there was something about this letter that took the issue so much further than Doreen had. It went beyond a mere matter of priorities and into the realm of faith—real, gut-level faith. And even though these words had been written one hundred years ago, they were every bit as relevant now. More than that, they were relevant to Kelsey specifically—to *her* situation, *her* life. Jocelyn Brennan had been dead since 1912, and yet she might as well have been sitting here tonight and telling her these things face-to-face.

Kelsey realized that God really did want her to live completely, in a way that had room both for her ambitions and for love. More importantly, however, was this truth about the God-shaped hole in everyone's heart. *Please always remember that this place in your heart can never be filled with work or with love but with Christ alone.*

Her eyes slowly filling with tears, Kelsey read and reread that sentence, its truths washing over her like a balm. How much she'd needed to hear that. How simple it sounded now.

In the last paragraph, Jocelyn referred to a verse in the Bible. Kelsey had no idea where her Bible was or even if she still even owned one, but she wanted to look up that verse, so she grabbed her iPhone instead and checked to see if there was an app for that. Sure enough, there were dozens of Bible programs, many of them free. She picked one to download and a minute later was looking at Ecclesiastes 1:7, which said, *All streams flow to the sea, yet the sea is never full. To the place the streams come from, there they return again.*

That didn't make much sense to her out of context, so she ended up reading the whole chapter—and then she went on to read the entire book of Ecclesiastes. Back in her youth group days, this was a part of the Bible that hadn't made much sense to her. But now, with added years of maturity, she was able to understand what the writer was saying. Everything in this world was an endless cycle. Life was a drudgery. There was nothing new under the sun.

All that really mattered was God.

With that thought filling her mind and her heart, Kelsey found herself moving from the bed to the floor and kneeling there, almost as if her body were acting independently of herself. Placing her elbows on the mattress, she clasped her hands together, closed her eyes, and bowed her head. There she remained for a long time, simply praying at first but soon listening and thinking and worshipping and confessing as well. Then and there, deep in the night, she could literally feel herself being heard and forgiven and, most of all, healed.

When she was finished, she offered one last prayer of gratitude and a heartfelt "Amen," and then she slipped back into the bed and nestled under the covers. Soon she was drifting away, sleeping the sleep of the forgiven, dreaming the dreams of the redeemed.

CHAPTER
THIRTY-NINE

April 14, 1912

JOCELYN

In spite of the wonderful food and spectacular service, Sunday lunch was not pleasant as far as Jocelyn was concerned. The O'Connells were avoiding Tad, Tad was avoiding Adele, and Adele was so withdrawn she'd hardly spoken to anyone all day. Jocelyn had no idea what was going on and could not imagine what had changed so rapidly from the lovely time they had all shared the evening before.

As it was, Adele had slept so late that morning that she nearly missed the worship service entirely, slipping in at the last moment and sitting in the back by herself despite the empty seat next to Tad. After the church service, Jocelyn had pulled Adele aside and tried talking with her to see what was wrong, but she merely shook her head and said she was having a bad day.

"You're not getting sick, are you?" Jocelyn had asked, placing the back of her hand on her cousin's forehead. It felt cool.

"No, just tired," Adele replied, adding that she thought she might take an afternoon nap.

"There's not some problem between you and Tad, is there?"

Adele looked away. "I'm not interested in him, if that's what you mean."

"You're kidding! But everything looked so promising yesterday—"

Adele turned to face her, a new sadness in her eyes. "Some things become clearer in the light of day. He's..." She hesitated. "He's not who you think he is, Jocelyn. I don't want to say more than that."

After that Adele simply turned and walked away. Disappointed and more curious than ever, Jocelyn headed up to the promenade deck to think things over and review the situation in her mind. What on earth could have happened to destroy such a promising relationship? She knew Tad could be a bit forward, but from what she'd seen, many Americans were that way. Rough edges could be smoothed with time, which Adele surely knew. It had to be more than that.

At the top of the stairs, she was pleased to see young Edith Brown from dinner last night, who immediately waved her over.

"Look, Jocelyn!" she whispered, gesturing toward a cluster of first-class passengers standing at the rail one floor above them. "It's the film star! Miss Gibson!"

Sure enough, the woman stood at the rail, gazing out at the sea, looking every bit as beautiful in person as she had in her photographs. Then, after a long moment, she turned and went inside.

Once she was gone, Edna sighed loudly and said, "I do so wish we were traveling first class."

Ten minutes later, as Jocelyn was again alone and walking along the deck, it came to her. Tad had said almost the same thing their first day on board. Suddenly, Jocelyn realized what must have gone wrong between Tad and Adele: the tea with Mr. Williams in first class! Adele had said she wasn't going to tell Tad about it at all, but he must have found out somehow and become as upset as she had feared he would.

Shame on Tad for being so shallow, Jocelyn thought as she made her way to the stairs. Her dear cousin didn't deserve this kind of treatment, and someone needed to tell him that!

She found Tad exactly where she'd expected, in the second-class smoking room. As women were not to go inside, she had to stand at the door and wait until she caught his eye. Fortunately, he was facing in her direction at a table not far away. From what she could see, he was engaged in a game of cards with several other young men.

When he finally spotted her, she gave a subtle flick of her hand and he came out of the room. Soon the two of them were together in the vestibule of the aft staircase, near the back side of the smoking room, where they could speak privately.

He sat on a sofa and she followed suit, apologizing for the interruption but saying they really needed to talk.

"It's not a problem. What's wrong? You look upset."

"I have to ask you something, Tad, and I want you to be honest with me. It's obvious you and Adele have had a parting of the ways. Forgive my bluntness, but I'd like to know if this has anything to do with her visit to first class on Friday."

He studied her face for a moment. "Her visit to first class?"

Jocelyn nodded. "The reason she didn't tell you about it was because of exactly this. She knew you'd feel hurt at having been excluded, so she thought it best not to bring it up at all."

Tad thought for a long moment. "It is hurtful that she didn't tell me about it. In fact, I still don't know many details. Do you?"

"Oh, yes. I was quite excited for her and my father after I heard all about it. Mr. Williams is such a nice man, and Adele said the Palm Court was fantastic."

"So you weren't invited either?"

"No, for the same reason you weren't."

"Which was…"

She exhaled. "Because of the bonds, Tad. What did you think? Mr. Williams invited Adele because of the bonds my father bought on her behalf, and he invited my father because he'd been the one to do the purchasing. The three of them had a lovely time together, talked some business, and then came back. That's all it was. I certainly don't think that's worth ruining a relationship over."

Tad shook his head. "I'm still a bit unclear, though. I know for a fact that Rowan did not buy any bonds from Mr. Williams on Tuesday."

"That's correct. On Tuesday, he did not. But by Wednesday morning he'd had a change of heart. They conducted the transaction then, before breakfast."

He seemed to think that over. "Where are those bonds now?" he asked. "Surely they didn't bring something so valuable onboard the ship, did they?"

Jocelyn shrugged. "I think he said they are in the ship's safe, but that doesn't matter. What matters is that you forgive Adele for not telling you, and then you accept the fact that you were excluded. These things happen. She had no control over Mr. Williams' guest list, you know. You can't expect her to have turned it down just because you weren't invited as well."

Tad stood and walked to the nearest porthole, where he lingered for a while. Jocelyn was afraid she had also made him angry, but if she had, well, that was too bad. These things needed to be said regardless.

After a long minute or two, Tad returned to the sofa and sat, an odd expression on his face.

"May we speak confidentially?" he asked, sitting at an angle to face her.

"Yes, of course."

"There's a bigger problem than that between me and her."

"Oh?"

He nodded. "Last night, when I walked Adele to her room, she…" His voice trailed off as he ran a hand across his face. "She said nothing of the interaction between us to you?"

"No, not a word."

"Well, to be honest, she professed her love for me."

Jocelyn's mouth fell open in surprise. "You're kidding! That's great news, isn't it?"

The man shook his head miserably.

"She practically threw herself at me. I like her well enough, and I tried to make a go of things yesterday, but the honest truth is that I cannot love Adele because I am already in love with someone else."

Jocelyn's heart sank, realizing he must have someone back home, perhaps even a fiancée. Before she could decide how to respond, he leaned closer and locked his gaze on hers.

"To be honest, Jocelyn," he said softly, taking her hand, "I'm madly in love with *you*."

CHAPTER
FORTY

Kelsey awoke slowly, but as she came to consciousness, she realized some thing was wrong. Her alarm hadn't gone off, which meant it wasn't even six a.m., yet the room was bright with sunshine. Twisting around to see the clock, she saw that it was eight twenty-five. Immediately, she knew what had happened. She'd never actually set the alarm but only thought about it—and now she'd overslept!

Jumping out of bed, she got ready as quickly as possible, brushing out her hair and dabbing on some makeup and dressing in jeans and a light blue sweater. As she did, she sent Cole a text to let him know she was running late. He responded with an easy, *No prob. Will use the time to grab a bagel. Something for you?*

Smiling, she texted back, *One guess.*

Without missing a beat, he replied, *One sugar, two creams?*

You know me well. See you soon.

Tucking her phone into her purse, Kelsey retrieved the diary from the bedside table. She didn't want to let it out of her sight, so she carefully wrapped it in a soft scarf for protection and put it in her purse, along with the copies of the bonds. Finally, she grabbed a prewrapped cheese square and a bottle of water from the kitchen, took her favorite casual jacket from the coat rack by the door, and headed out.

The morning was sunny but chilly, so she pulled on her jacket as soon as she stepped outside. She half walked, half jogged to Rector Station and got on the train, which was nearly empty. She sat across from the door, her purse in her lap, and glanced around at her fellow passengers. This was definitely a Saturday bunch—everyone looking relaxed, with no suits or ties in sight. At the far end of the car sat a trio of teenagers, each of them sporting an instrument case. One lifted his case onto his lap and pulled out a violin, and for a moment Kelsey hoped he might play something. Instead, he simply began changing a string.

Settling back in her seat, she pulled out her cheese and nibbled at it as she thought about last night. Not only had she gotten a glimpse into the life and times of her forebears, but she had somehow managed to find her way back to God again as well. Closing her eyes, she inhaled deeply, wondering how she could have wandered so far away from Him. How could she have endured that feeling of emptiness for so long? How could she have forgotten what it felt like to be washed in God's grace, to be filled with His love?

Though she knew that today's spiritual high was probably just a temporary emotional thing, she didn't even care. Euphoria or not, from here on out she was in it for the long haul. Now that she had once again given her life over to God, she knew without a doubt that He was present, that He loved her, and that He was in control. And though she was still determined to save her company and her great-grandmother's legacy, she had a new peace about all of it, regardless of the outcome. Now, more than anything, she just wanted to live in a way that was pleasing to Him. She would trust Him to work out the details of the situation according to His plan for her life and the lives of all involved.

Three stops later, Kelsey got off at Canal and began the short walk to Columbus Park. She spotted Cole from half a block away, and just the sight of him sitting there on a park bench waiting for her took her breath away. Just as she'd been wearing blue because she knew he loved it on her, she noticed he had on her favorite dark brown jacket, a rich chocolate leather that they had chosen together back when they were dating. It still looked amazing on him, especially when he spotted her in return, stood, and gave her a broad smile.

When she reached him, Cole gave her the coffee and a warm hug.

"Even when she oversleeps and has to get ready at super speed, she still looks amazing," he said as they pulled back apart.

"Not looking half bad yourself, Thornton," she replied. "You know I always loved that jacket on you." She took a sip of the coffee, which wasn't exactly piping hot but would do. "Thanks for this. What do I owe you?"

"Oh, please," he said, eyes twinkling. "My treat."

He held her gaze for a long moment, and though she tried to think of some joke about how indebted she was to him already, she found herself so distracted by his beautiful eyes that she couldn't speak at all.

"I'm not kidding though. You really do look…" his voice trailed off. "Different somehow. I'm guessing you read the diary last night? Is that where this is coming from?"

She smiled, wondering how to respond. "I did read some of it, yes," she replied. "But if I seem different this morning, that's not exactly why. It's kind of hard to explain."

"Well, then, let's walk and you can tell me as we go."

He gestured to the right and they set off, walking briskly through the cool morning air toward Chinatown. As they went, she meant to give him the facts in a nutshell but soon found herself revealing more than she'd intended. She told him about the letter Jocelyn had written to Adele and how her words had spoken to Kelsey as well. When she got to the part where she'd fallen to her knees and recommitted her life to Christ, he responded by putting an arm around her shoulders and giving her a tight squeeze.

"That's wonderful, Kelsey," he said as his arm again dropped to his side. "I've been wondering how you were doing, spiritually speaking. This is great news."

"Thanks, Cole. I just can't understand why it took me so long to get back to this place."

He nodded thoughtfully. "Don't feel bad. I have to admit, I wandered away there for a while myself. I'd say it was probably a year, year and a half, before I got back on track."

"That's better than five."

He shrugged. "Yeah, but we're talking about God. To Him, five years is like five seconds, as long as you ended up in the right place."

"Guess so," she replied, grateful for his perspective.

They turned right on Mott Street, walked past several restaurants, and were engulfed by the delicious, pungent smells of real Chinese food—the kind the Chinese themselves ate—with ingredients like *daikon* and *jie lan* instead of plain ol' American carrots and broccoli. Kelsey inhaled deeply, surprised that the scents appealed to her so early in the morning. It wasn't yet ten o'clock, and already she felt herself craving a plate of Dongpo pork.

Cole stopped halfway down the street and swung open the door to a small shop that was tucked between a restaurant and a florist. The writing on the door was in Chinese, so Kelsey wasn't sure what kind of establishment it was until they stepped inside and she saw the walls and counters lined with all sorts of paper-based collectibles, from rare autographs to old manuscripts to foreign currency. Walking up to the main counter, Cole greeted the young woman by name and asked if he could speak with her father.

Nodding with a shy smile, she slipped through a curtain into the back, and after a moment a man emerged in her place. Short and slender with stooped shoulders and graying hair, Mr. Hu looked quite old until he smiled, and then his deep brown eyes were young and lively.

"Mr. Cole!" the man cried happily, shaking his hand. "What a pleasure to see you." He spoke with an accent, but his words weren't at all difficult to understand. Turning to Kelsey, he shook her hand as well, greeting her warmly as Cole introduced them.

Soon, Mr. Hu had been brought up to speed on the situation. They gave him the copies of the bonds, and he spread them out on the countertop in front of him, studying them closely with a magnifying glass.

As he was silently perusing the documents, his daughter emerged through the curtain with a tray of beverages.

"Melon tea?" she asked, and all three accepted a glass.

The beverage was chilled, not hot, and to Kelsey's surprise it wasn't tea at all but instead a sweet, syrupy liquid that tasted like an odd mix of Hi-C, grass, and honeydew melon. After a few tentative sips, the strange drink began to grow on her, and she'd nearly finished it off by the time Mr. Hu looked up at her and spoke.

"You have some very old bonds here, Miss Tate. Quite interesting. Excuse me for a few minutes while I am on the computer."

With that, he picked up the papers and disappeared into the back with his daughter.

"You really trust this guy?" Kelsey whispered to Cole, nervous about being parted from the pages for a moment, even if they were just copies.

"A hundred percent."

As they waited, she used the time to look around. Though the room was quite small, it held numerous items of interest. Not surprisingly, some were very old, some very rare—and all seemed very expensive.

"How much is this appraisal going to cost?" she whispered, hoping the man would take credit cards.

"Nothing," Cole replied. "Though it would be polite to buy something as a thank-you."

Her eyes widened as she gestured toward a $695 price tag. Cole smiled, pointing to a shelf lined with books, near the floor. Nodding with relief, she knelt down and flipped through them, surprised to see that more than half were in English and none was more than $20. She finally picked a photographic history of Wall Street, which looked fascinating and was on sale for $16.99.

Her decision made, Kelsey waited at the counter, anxiety building in her chest. What if Mr. Hu came out and told them that the bonds were worthless? Could they save the company without them? If the bonds *were* valuable, on the other hand, where could they possibly be?

How were they ever going to find them?

"Okay," Mr. Hu said, coming back in through the curtain and setting the papers down on the counter in front of them. "What would you like to know first?"

"Present-day value," Cole said without hesitation.

"Well, the good news is that they are still valid. This is only an approximation, you understand, but my guess is that these would be worth just under two million dollars—each. Probably about one point seven million to be exact, so all six combined would come to around ten point two million dollars."

Kelsey exhaled slowly. That would be enough to stave off the takeover. *Please, Lord, if it's Your will, help me find the bonds!*

"There are two issues here, however," he continued. "First, as I am sure you are aware, these are hundred-year bonds, purchased on April ninth, nineteen twelve. That means they will expire on April ninth, twenty twelve—which is Monday."

Cole and Kelsey looked at each other and then back at him, both nodding somberly. "We know," Cole said.

"Second," Mr. Hu continued, "as you probably also realize, these are bearer bonds."

Cole gasped, flipping the pages around so that he could take a closer look. "Oh, man. I can't believe I didn't catch that before."

"What?" Kelsey asked, looking from one man to the other. "What does that mean?"

"It means anyone can cash them in," Mr. Hu told her. "Bearer bonds are always paid out to whoever is bearing them."

"Oh, no," she whispered, the blood draining from her face.

"Oh, yes. They are like a winning lottery ticket without a name written on the back. Whoever turns it in gets the cash."

"Is there any way that we can find out if someone else has already cashed them in?" Kelsey asked.

"I tried, but that information is not available on a Saturday. I put a request in to one of my contacts in London and he will reach out to BEA Systems on Monday."

Kelsey thanked him and asked, "If we can find the bonds, can we still cash them in then?"

"Yes, should you be fortunate enough to locate them, I can facilitate their surrender to the company on Monday," Mr. Hu replied. "But we will need to contact them at the beginning of their workday, even if that means you have to get up at four in the morning."

"That's good advice. Thank you."

Mr. Hu nodded, and then he looked from Kelsey to Cole. "That is about all I can tell you. I hope it is helpful."

"More than you can imagine," Cole replied, shaking his head. "You always come through for me, Mr. Hu."

"It is an honor to do business with the man to whom I owe so much."

Looking embarrassed, Cole glanced toward Kelsey and gestured at the book in her hands. "I believe Miss Tate would like to make a purchase before we go."

"Yes, thank you," she said, handing the book over.

Mr. Hu rang up the transaction, and soon they were ready to leave.

"Thank you again," Kelsey said to the older man with a slight bow of her head as she accepted her bagged purchase.

"You are most welcome," he replied, bowing to each of them in return.

As they went outside into the chilly morning air, Kelsey tried to remind herself that all was not lost. They still had the rest of today and all of tomorrow to find the bonds.

If someone else hadn't already stolen them and cashed them in, that is.

CHAPTER
FORTY-ONE

April 14, 1912

Adele

After watching the sunset, Adele returned to her stateroom. Though she would rather have spent the evening in her room, Uncle Rowan convinced her to go to Reverend Carter's hymn sing in the dining saloon. Fortunately, Tad did not attend, so it wasn't as uncomfortable as Adele had expected. In fact, she ended up enjoying herself. The reverend introduced each song by describing the history of how it had come to be written, and as a special treat they enjoyed several solos by Miss Marion Wright, a beautiful soprano who was bound for marriage in Oregon.

When the final hymn was sung, "O God Our Help in Ages Past," Adele lingered for a while in conversation with some of the other passengers, including the Browns. She wasn't sure where Jocelyn had gone, but she had a feeling her cousin was wherever the families with children were. That poor girl needed a husband and kids of her own soon so she would have a place to pour out all of that love.

The crowd eventually began to disperse. Uncle Rowan was headed to the smoking room, so Adele bid him good night and went back down to her cabin. After last night she would have been frightened to be by herself in the corridors, but at least a hundred people had attended tonight's hymn sing, and they were still getting settled, so the hallways were populated the entire way.

When Adele reached her stateroom and stepped inside, she was surprised to see Jocelyn already there. She was still fully dressed, sitting in front of the mirror and fooling with her hair. Adele knew she needed to apologize to her cousin for having been in such a foul mood all day. Though she wouldn't share the particulars about last night's incident with Tad, she didn't have to take out her frustrations on her cousin.

Tonight Adele had worn the most modest dress she owned—a pale blue silk messaline with a high collar, long sleeves, and a loose-fitting overlay down the front—which was also her most comfortable garment. Without changing, she went to the sofa, kicked off her shoes, and pulled her feet up under her as she attempted to chat with her cousin.

She began with simple small talk, but when the conversation allowed, Adele made a point of saying how sorry she was for having been such a dour traveling companion today. Jocelyn simply waved off her words, saying not to give it another thought.

While sitting on the sofa, Adele noticed a folded piece of paper on the lower bunk across from her and feared she might have dropped one of Jocelyn's notes out of her diary earlier. She reached for it without thinking and unfolded it to read, only then realizing it hadn't been written by Jocelyn at all. The note said, *Meet me at the sitting area behind the smoking room, 11 p.m.* She would have thought the note was from Uncle Rowan except that it wasn't in his handwriting.

"What is this?"

Turning, Jocelyn snatched the note from Adele's hand and tucked it into her pocket. "That's mine!"

"I'm sorry. I wasn't trying to be nosy, but it was on the same Titanic stationery you've been using, and I thought it was one of your notes to me."

Their eyes met in the mirror, and Adele realized that Jocelyn's cheeks were flushed a bright pink. A moment later, it also struck her that Jocelyn had been putting her hair *up*—not taking it down.

Jocelyn sighed and then said, "I've been invited out by a young man."

"Who?"

"I…I'd rather not say."

"Is it the Frenchman with the two young boys? I've yet to see a wife. Is he a widower?"

"Adele, I don't want to talk about it."

"Fine." Adele plopped back onto the sofa. "So what are you going to do on this date of yours?"

"It's not a date. We're just going to take a stroll on the promenade."

"Do you think that's appropriate?"

"Why not?"

Adele shrugged, watching as her cousin placed a velvet hat onto her head and slid in the silver musical notes hat pin to hold it there. "It's late. There won't be many people about…"

"It's a beautiful night. I'm sure there will be more than you think. And remember, my father's right inside the smoking room if I need him."

"True."

Adele knew she should offer to chaperone, but the thought was too exhausting to consider. She rose and went to the wardrobe to gather her nightclothes, telling herself that Jocelyn was a grown woman who could take care of herself. But then she thought about her own evening with Tad and how easily he had overpowered her. She couldn't bear to imagine what might have happened if the steward hadn't shown up when he did.

"Just remember, cousin," she said, wishing she *didn't* remember, "not all men can be trusted. Sometimes, they can be downright evil."

CHAPTER
FORTY-TWO

O ut on the street, Cole suggested they find somewhere they could sit and think. "Why don't we grab a bite to eat? That bagel didn't do much for me, and knowing you, you had no breakfast at all."

"I most certainly did. I ate some cheese on the subway ride over."

"Uh-huh. Like about this much?" He held up his thumb and forefinger an inch apart.

"No, more," she replied with a chuckle as she reached up to separate his thumb and finger by several inches.

Laughing, he evaded her grip and then held his hand up higher, this time showing just half an inch. "This much?"

Jumping, she tried again to grab his hand.

"This much?" he teased, thumb and finger almost touching now.

Finally, she managed to jump high enough to take his hand. To her surprise, as she jokingly struggled to pull his thumb and forefinger apart, he suddenly relaxed his fingers and intertwined them with hers. In that moment their eyes met. Time froze.

On a busy Chinatown sidewalk, with people milling all around them, Kelsey and Cole simply looked into each other's eyes, hands clasped, hearts pounding. After a long moment, as if he only just realized what he was doing, Cole gently extracted his hand from hers and took a step back.

"Sorry about that," he mumbled. "Let's go."

Turning, he began to walk up the street in the same direction they had come, hands shoved firmly in his pockets. Stunned and hurt and excited all at the same time, once Kelsey recovered from her surprise she followed along behind him. She caught up to him near the end of the block, and they both walked briskly side by side, Cole leading the way and neither of them saying a word.

She didn't even know where they were going, but she could tell he had some destination in mind. Silently, she kept up the pace next to him, wishing yet again that she'd thought to grab a few Band-Aids for her blisters. He finally slowed once they reached Tribeca, and eventually he came to a stop in front of a little diner on Church Street.

"This okay with you?" he asked brusquely, gesturing toward the door.

"This is fine," she replied softly, trying not to feel hurt by his complete change in demeanor. Why was he acting this way?

They went inside, where Cole greeted the hostess by name and asked for a booth at the window. The restaurant was buzzing with chatter and the clink of silverware on china. Smells of bacon, coffee, and toasting bread hovered in the air, stirring up Kelsey's appetite as they were led to their table.

"This was a good idea," she said, sliding onto a bench and focusing on the menu handed to her. "I didn't realize how hungry I was."

Cole sat down opposite her and became equally absorbed in his own menu. It wasn't until the waitress had come to get their food order and taken the menus away that he finally looked her in the eye.

"Listen, I'm sorry about that..."

"About what? About holding my hand? Or about acting like I had cooties afterward?"

He smiled in spite of himself. "Cooties? What are we, in kindergarten?"

She shrugged, feeling a little belligerent. "I don't know, Cole. It feels more like high school drama to me."

Looking weary, he ran a hand over his face as he slowly exhaled. "I know. It's just that I promised myself I wouldn't..."

Again he met her eyes, and she could tell he felt genuinely pained. Now she was the one to be sorry. Dropping the attitude, she leaned forward and spoke. "You wouldn't what?"

He shrugged. "Rekindle. With you. So to speak."

She sat back, suppressing a smile. Leave it to him to find just the right word. Rekindle. That was it exactly.

She was about to say something flirty, such as, "And what would be so wrong with that?" when she was struck by a disturbing thought. Her smile faded.

"Are you…You're not married, are you?" she asked softly. "If you are, then I'm sorry too. I would never—"

"No, Kelsey. I'm not married."

"Engaged?"

He shook his head. "I was, almost. Engaged, I mean. But it didn't work out."

"I'm sorry."

"This has nothing to do with anyone else. It's about us, about our history. I just…it took me a long time to get over all of that."

She swallowed hard. "I can imagine."

"Then, when I heard about what was happening to you this week, I wanted to contact you, just to check on you and offer my support. I never stopped caring, you know. But I was afraid that if I talked to you again, much less spent time with you in person, I would…" He shook his head, cheeks flushing "I don't know. I sat and thought for a long time before I picked up that phone on Wednesday. This…thing…between us, Kelsey, it's always been there, always will be. But that doesn't mean we have to succumb to it. I offered you my help as a friend, and that's how I'll get through all of this and wrap it up once we're done. As a friend."

Kelsey sat there trying to process his words, but he wasn't making any sense. If there wasn't someone else in the way, and he was enjoying being with her as much as she was with him, then why not go with it and see what happened? They weren't a couple of kids in youth group anymore, nor were they naive twentysomethings fresh out of grad school and just starting out in their first real jobs. They were in their thirties now, for goodness' sake. Clocks were ticking. Life was progressing. They were maturing. Now that they had managed to find each other again, what was to stop them from giving it another try? Surely he could feel the connection they still shared as strongly as she did.

She was trying to think of a way to put all of these thoughts into words when she realized what might really be going on. As the thought came to her, she could feel her own face flushing with heat. Unable to meet his eyes, she looked down at the table and spoke.

"For the past few days, there's something I've been wanting to say to you, but the right moment hasn't presented itself before now. It's just that…you don't know how ashamed I am about what I did to you five years ago, how sorry I am for everything. I'm not just talking about undercutting your deal with Lou Strahan. I'm talking about how I acted afterward. Unrepentant. Indignant. Condescending, even. Looking back, I can't believe how badly I acted toward you. I *loved* you, Cole. I truly did. I wanted to spend the rest of my life with you, but I was too proud to see my own actions for what they were."

Her eyes filling with tears, she forced herself to look him in the face as she continued. "I have *always* loved you," she said miserably. "But I have not always acted with love. I don't blame you for walking away after it happened. I deserved that. But if it makes any difference, at least I have finally seen my actions in all of their ugly reality. And I am ashamed. Ashamed and so, so sorry. I understand why you don't want to see me that way anymore. I can do the friend thing if I have to, but someday, Cole, I hope at least you'll be able to forgive me."

On the verge of breaking into sobs, Kelsey placed her napkin on the table, grabbed her purse, and slid from the booth.

"Excuse me," she whispered. "I need some air. I'll be back."

With that she stood and made her way from the restaurant, blindly pushing her way through the door. Out on the sidewalk, she turned to the right and walked away, not stopping until she came to a wide, square column that she thought might give her a modicum of privacy. With her back to the street and her shoulder to the column, she allowed her sobs to bubble to the surface. Clutching her stomach, all she could do was weep—for them, for him, for herself. At least now she understood the truth. Cole Thornton would never allow himself to date her again because he knew the kind of person she really was. Considering how badly she'd hurt him, she couldn't blame him for that, not one bit. Not at all.

A few minutes later she was rooting through her purse for a tissue when Cole suddenly appeared there in front of her, bearing a tissue of his own.

"This what you're looking for?" he asked gently.

Mortified, she took it from him and wiped her face and blew her nose. Once she did, he moved closer, taking her into his arms.

That act of kindness brought on a fresh round of tears, but this time as she sobbed, she did so against his broad chest, wrapped in the warmth of him. She cried for a long time, allowing all of the hurt and pain and loneliness of the past five years to come out. She had loved him *so much*. She had loved him and she had hurt him and he had gone away, and she would never forgive herself for any of that. She still loved him, but it was too late.

"Shhh," he cooed finally, offering up more tissues and patting her on the back in a brotherly sort of way. He continued to hold her until she was all cried out. Finally, she just leaned into him silently and held on tight, knowing this was probably the last time she would ever be in Cole Thornton's arms.

"You okay?" he whispered.

She nodded.

"Good. Why don't we get you cleaned up? Come on."

With one strong arm still around her, Cole led Kelsey back toward the restaurant. When they got there, he asked her to wait outside, and then he went in through the door, leaving her alone. A moment later he reappeared, carrying a plastic bag that held two Styrofoam boxes.

"I had told her we'd take it to go," Cole explained as he once again slipped his free arm around Kelsey's shoulders and pulled her close. "Come on."

She didn't know where they were going and she didn't care. She just let him lead her down the street as she focused on the solidity of his hold, the warmth of his body, the comfort of his presence.

They had already been through so much together. At least there was no need for embarrassment or pretense anymore. Now that he'd been honest with her and she with him, there was nothing left to do but be themselves. And if they each had wanted something different to come from this brief period of time they had been spending together, that was okay. She would respect his wishes, he would show her some tenderness despite his resentment, and somehow they would each pick up the pieces and go on.

If only it didn't hurt so badly.

Finally, Cole came to an old, industrial-looking building and stopped, pulling out a key card and sliding it through a scanner at the door. With a buzz it popped open and then they were inside, moving across a bare lobby toward a freight elevator on the far wall.

Kelsey was quiet as they rode it upward, counting five floors before it came to a stop. Cole slid the cage door open and they stepped into a long, dingy hallway.

"Where are we?" she asked.

Again, he scanned his key at a door, and then he swung it open as he replied, "Home sweet home."

Kelsey sucked in a deep breath. This was where Cole lived now? Stepping into the broad, open space, she could barely believe her eyes. It was huge and beautiful, the wood floors gleaming, the furniture spare and modern, the whole space warm and welcoming. He closed the door behind them and then led the way to the kitchen area, where he put the bag down on the table and then went about retrieving plates and silverware and napkins.

"I can't believe you live in a Tribeca loft, Cole. This is amazing." She had no idea his business was doing so well. The only people their age who owned a loft in Tribeca were movie stars or sports figures.

He shrugged, grabbing two glasses from the cabinet and filling them with water from a recessed spout in the door of his stainless steel fridge.

"Technically, you're off a little. We crossed Chambers a few blocks ago. This is the upper limit of the Financial District. Trust me. I couldn't afford a place this big in Tribeca. No way."

She smiled at his typical modesty. "So what happened to the old apartment on Twenty-Ninth?"

He shrugged. "I got tired of having roommates. I cashed in every single investment I had, bought some tools, and used the rest as a down payment on the cheapest loft I could find in a decent neighborhood. Most people seem to think the Financial District is too boring to live in, but I really like the quiet. And with this much space, if I ever get married, at least my kids will have plenty of room to toddle around in."

She swallowed hard, the pain of his casual remark like a knife to her heart.

"You renovated yourself?" she asked once she found her voice.

"It's a work in progress," he replied modestly. "I still have a long way to go. But, yeah, I did the renovating with a lot of help from my friends. And don't forget that my dad owns a home supply store in the 'burbs. I get most of my materials at cost."

"Well, it's really awesome."

"Thanks, Kels. The bathroom is around there, if you want to get yourself cleaned up before we eat."

Thanking him, she went where he indicated, once again impressed by the space. The half bath was all beige-and-brown tile, with modern fixtures and bright, recessed lighting. Gazing at herself in the mirror, she was shocked to see how truly awful she looked. Between the raccoonlike mascara smudges and the splotchy cheeks, she had her work cut out for her. Unfortunately, though she usually carried a small makeup repair kit in her purse, all she could find in there now was some lip gloss and an old tube of mascara. At least it would feel good to wash her face.

A few minutes later, she returned to the kitchen looking a bit better, though her eyes were still swollen and she was in a subdued mood. She was surprised to see that Cole was already at the table eating his meal, a laptop open in front of him. He glanced up as she came in the room and said, "Make yourself at home. I already said a blessing."

"Okay. Thanks." Kelsey took a seat at the table across from him.

"Sorry if I'm being rude. It's just that I'm super hungry, but I had a thought and I wanted to look into it right away."

Glad for the apology, she said a quick, silent prayer of her own and then nibbled on a piece of bacon as he explained what he was doing.

"Remember the report I gave you last night and the three scenarios I out-lined for you at the bottom? Plan one was to do nothing and hope the stock-holders vote in your favor, two was to orchestrate a friendly merger, and three was to buy up enough shares to regain control of the company and stop the hostile takeover."

"Right."

"Well, considering that option one isn't likely to happen, we need to focus on options two and three right now—and three will only work if we can find those bonds. In either two or three, we need to take a look at your stockhold-ers. We have to figure out who might be willing to side with you in scenario two or sell to you in scenario three."

"Okay, go for it," she said, still feeling somewhat shell-shocked but know-ing there was no more time for matters of the heart. They were in the midst of a crisis, and they needed to return their focus back where it belonged.

"Two questions first," he said. "I assume you have voting power for the four percent owned by current employees?"

"Yes. All employee stock options include terms that grant voting rights to the company for as long as they are employed."

"And how about the five percent Gloria owned before she died? Until her estate is settled, do you control those shares as well?"

She nodded, taking a bite of her bagel and trying not to think how good it felt to have someone else take charge of the situation for a while.

"Well, then, if you combine that with the shares owned by you, your father, your grandfather, and your brother, it comes to thirty-nine percent. Add Walter's four percent, and you're up to forty-three."

She sat back, wiping her mouth with a napkin. "Which means I need just eight percent more to gain control and prevent the takeover."

"Exactly. So whether you go with scenario two or three, I think our next move should be to look at this list of the remaining stockholders and try to figure out where that eight percent might come from."

Cole moved around to her side of the table and sat next to her, laptop in front of them, so they could view the screen together. For the next half hour, they hashed out various possibilities for who might be swayed to vote her way. In the end, they decided to let Walter work on the six percent owned by retired employees of the company and to ask Jonah to do the same with the four percent owned by more distant relatives of the Tate family. That left two categories of ownership for Kelsey to work on herself: banks and trusts, which held twenty-seven percent, and private investors, with the last twenty percent. The biggest opposition in this situation were the banks and trusts, who weren't likely to be swayed. Thus, they agreed she would focus on the private investors. God willing, between long-standing relationships she and her father had established in the industry and general goodwill toward B & T, she might be able to convince enough of them to vote her way so that when added to the votes secured by Walter and Jonah, they could gain control in the end.

Before she started making the many phone calls this was going to take, she decided to contact Lou, just to let him know about scenario two—a friendly merger—and get the specifics of his offer. He sounded thrilled to hear from her.

"From what I understand," Lou said, "Queen's Fleet offered twenty-two million, right? So how about we say twenty-five?"

She hated to haggle with a man who had been so good to her, but twenty-five was ridiculous. She closed her eyes and pinched the bridge of her nose. Lou was a good guy, but he was also a savvy negotiator—and not someone she'd ever want to go up against in a financial fight. Though it was a risky move, she decided to tell him to take it or leave it. They both knew Pamela's offer had been absurdly low.

"Sorry, Lou. It's thirty-one or not at all. I'm going to have to go to the mat for this with the stockholders, so it needs to be an attractive offer."

"What do you mean? Even if I came in at twenty-three, my offer still beats theirs."

"You know as well as I do that any stockholder selling less than their full amount of shares will go with the lower offer if it means Queen's Fleet will be at the helm from here on out. I'm sorry, Lou, but I think they will see that as a much safer long-term investment."

"Okay, okay. I understand where you're coming from."

"Are we agreed on thirty-one? Like I told you, I'm working on several different scenarios, so if you can't make this work, no problem. I'll just move on to the next approach."

He was silent for a moment, and then she heard him let out a soft chuckle. "Half of me wants to yell at you right now, and the other half couldn't be more proud."

She grinned. "Are we in business or what?"

"I'll go thirty," he replied, "but not thirty-one, and here's why. Unlike Queen's Fleet, I will not be cleaning house. In fact, a large part of what I'm buying are the very people they would be letting go. When I made that original offer, it included getting Gloria Poole as a part of the package. Now that she's gone, I'm sorry, Kelsey, but the value drops for me, regardless of any of these other current factors that are also dragging things down."

Kelsey thought his words made sense, but she asked him to hold so as not to lose the upper hand. Pressing the mute button on the phone, she bounced Lou's offer off of Cole, and he agreed that $30 million seemed fair, given Lou's logic.

Back on the line with him again, she agreed to his price. They arranged to get together later in the day to go over specifics and present their plan to the board, if she was able to convene a meeting that quickly. At the very least, they should be able to sit down with Walter this afternoon over at B & T and crunch some numbers together.

Before they hung up, Kelsey reminded Lou she was pursuing one other option, and there was a slight chance it might pan out.

"If it does, that's the option I'll be going with," she said. "No offense, but it's the more favorable outcome for me and my family." She didn't elaborate beyond that and he didn't ask, but he probably knew it had to do with the securing of enough funding to buy out a majority herself. What he didn't know was that the only way she could acquire that much cash that fast was to find the missing bonds.

CHAPTER
FORTY-THREE

April 14, 1912

JOCELYN

Jocelyn walked out into the corridor, closing the door behind her with a mixture of guilt and relief. Guilt that she hadn't shared the whole truth. Relief that Adele hadn't figured it out anyway.

Jocelyn knew she was going about this wrong, that her first outing with Tad should be a far more public affair. But before she decided whether or not to let the world know about their feelings for each other—and possibly alienate her dear cousin in the process—she wanted to share one stolen hour together tonight, just the two of them. There would be time tomorrow to make the bigger decision of when and how to break this news with others.

She made her way to the aft stairwell and began climbing the steps. When she reached the B deck, where they were to meet, she saw Tad already waiting for her. Unable to hold in her smile, she was beaming as she went up to him and he took her hand in his.

"Tad," she said softly.

"You came," he replied, also smiling, his eyes holding hers. Then slowly he lifted her hand to his lips.

Pleased but surprised, she could feel heat rise to her face. She looked around, realizing that this part of the ship was completely devoid of others at the moment.

"I didn't realize we would be quite so alone here," she said. "I think it would be more proper for us to be among passengers on the promenade deck."

"I agree," Tad replied, "but only after you allow me to kiss you."

Eyes wide, she nodded, tilting her face upward. He leaned toward her and lightly touched his lips to hers in a chaste kiss, her first. Afterward, she gazed into his eyes, unable to understand how Adele could be so immune to his charms.

"That's better," he said with a grin. "Shall we take our walk?"

Holding hands, they stepped into the chill air outside on the promenade deck. It was much colder now than it had been on any other night of the trip, but at least she had someone to keep her warm.

As they gazed up at the stars on this perfectly clear night, Tad put an arm around her shoulders and sighed contentedly.

"This is the happiest night of my life," he said. "There's only one thing that keeps my joy from being complete."

Jocelyn nodded sadly. "The fact that we can't yet reveal our relationship openly?"

"No, that will happen in time. I'm bothered by the fact that your father left me out of the bond deal he made on Wednesday morning. That really hurt. I thought he respected my opinion, but his actions show me that he doesn't." He hung his head and looked away.

"Oh, Tad, I am sure it wasn't like that. He had a change of heart, is all. It had nothing to do with you personally."

"You're probably right. I'll try not to worry about it." He pulled her closer. "It has made me rethink my position, however. Your father is a wise man, and I am starting to believe that he may have been right and I was wrong. Do you know where the bonds are so that I could inspect them? I'm thinking perhaps I should reconsider my investment."

"I believe they are in the purser's office."

Turning toward her, Tad took both of her hands in his and looked deeply into her eyes. "Perhaps you could request them from the purser for a while, just so I could get a closer look. But don't tell your father. It's too embarrassing to have him know how stupid I'm feeling."

Jocelyn was about to reply when she realized that he was leaning toward her for another kiss. Not ten feet away was another couple, so before his mouth met hers she placed a gloved finger against his lips.

"Not here," she whispered.

"Where, then?" he replied in a husky voice, eyes filled with passion.

Standing there in his embrace, her back against the rail, Jocelyn suddenly felt a tremor running through her body, one so strong she actually lost her balance. Tad's strong arms kept her from falling, but then he released her and took a step back, a puzzled expression on his face.

"What was that?" he asked. "The whole deck shook."

CHAPTER
FORTY-FOUR

Two hours later, Kelsey and Cole were still at it. Comfortably ensconced on the couch, she was surrounded by a mess of crumpled-up papers, and the pad in her hand was covered with copious notes. Cole and his laptop were equally buried over at the kitchen table. Between the two of them, they had managed to convince several of the private investors to let Kelsey serve as their proxy, voting in whatever way she thought best. Grandpa Jonah was also busy on the phone, trying to convince the various Tate relatives to do the same.

Walter, too, was handling his part with the retired employees of B & T, though Kelsey had yet to speak with him directly. She was still so upset about the fact that he'd invalidated her security code that for the time being Cole was handling communications with him on her behalf. She wasn't sure if she could trust Walter or not, especially given the information Cole's team had turned up about the man's previous ties to Pamela Greeley. Better she bide her time and see how he handled this current assignment. If he really could sway some votes in her direction, maybe that would be proof enough that he was on the up and up after all.

He didn't know about the copies of the bonds, of course, so he hadn't been told about scenario number three. But at least he was on board with scenario number two, the friendly merger with Strahan Realty Trust for $30 million. Walter, Kelsey, and Cole would be meeting with Lou at the B & T offices at four p.m. to hash out the details, and then the board members would be joining them there two hours later, when Walter would present the full plan and they could make the decision as to whether or not that was how they wanted to proceed.

And even though Kelsey needed to be on hand for both meetings, her continuous presence would not be required at either. Her plan was to slip out whenever possible and do some digging around in Gloria's office in the vague hope that the woman might have hidden the bonds there somewhere before she died. Kelsey knew that Gloria's files had been removed by the police, but she had a feeling that if the bonds were in the office, they would be in some place the police would not have thought to look, such as taped to the underside of a drawer or slipped into the back of a picture frame. It was definitely worth a shot. With Monday's deadline looming, she didn't know what else to do but keep looking—and keep praying.

If the bonds didn't turn up during this afternoon's surreptitious search, then the only choice left was to take steps for a more open and direct exploration tomorrow, perhaps by closing tonight's board meeting with the big news that not only were the bonds real but that Gloria had them in her possession on Monday night—and they were now nowhere to be found.

By one thirty Kelsey's efforts came to a standstill as she reached the end of her calling list. She was still waiting for a number of people to get back to her, but for the moment she had done all she could do. Cole was still working away at the table on his laptop, so she decided to change course, dig out Adele's diary, and keep reading between callbacks. There was still the question of the woman's true identity, and Kelsey's hope was that the diary contained some sort of irrefutable evidence that she really had been who she'd said she was.

At one point, Kelsey was deeply engrossed in Adele's description of the ship's library when she had the feeling that she was being observed. Glancing up, she caught Cole looking at her from across the room, his expression unreadable. He glanced away, and when she asked if something was wrong, he simply said he was getting hungry and wondered if she was ready for lunch yet.

She wasn't exactly starving, but her eyes and brain needed a break, so she put the diary aside and offered to pull something together. She dug through the fridge and came out with some sliced deli meat and other sandwich fixings, glad to have a physical task after a morning filled with so much mental effort. Cole put his laptop aside and joined her as they made themselves ham-and-cheese sandwiches, and after a while she realized he was joking and she was laughing and it felt perfectly natural and easy. Maybe they could be friends after all.

Then again, did friends ache to be held by their friends? Did they yearn to be pulled into their arms and kissed and told that they were loved? She needed to face the fact that once they had navigated through these current troubles, they would pretty much have to wrap things up for good. At least this time around they had found some closure, and she'd even been able to apologize for her past actions. And as hard as it was going to be to see Cole walk out of her life yet again, in the long run it would be the easier choice—like ripping off a Band-Aid all at once instead of enduring a long, slow, excruciating pull.

Once their sandwiches were ready, they took a break and ate together at the table.

"Can I ask you a question?" Kelsey asked, placing a napkin on her lap. "What did Mr. Hu mean this morning when he said he owed you so much?"

"A few years ago I helped find funding for a nonprofit organization the Hu family created, one that helps immigrants get settled in America."

"Interesting."

"Yeah, they had a great business model but couldn't procure any start-up funds. I found some grants for them and helped them get rolling. Nowadays the organization is doing quite well. They have even taken over their own fund-raising."

Kelsey took a bite of her sandwich, considering his answer. She didn't know much about the nonprofit world and asked if he dealt with that type of thing very often.

"Yes, actually," he replied. "Thornton Resources has a specialized team that works exclusively with nonprofits, linking them with grants, donors, government programs, and other sources of funding. In the past five years, we've helped more than thirty-seven organizations get their start."

"Is there money in that?"

Cole chuckled. "Not much. I mean, we do all right, but it pays off in so many other ways. I really enjoy working with the nonprofit sector. They are just as driven as the for-profit world, but their overriding goal is to help, not to make money."

Kelsey put down her sandwich and looked at Cole. "That's really quite amazing. I should hire you to work with the foundation that B & T has started in memory of my great-grandmother. I could use some advice."

"I'd love to hear more about it."

Kelsey was eager to discuss it, but just then his phone rang, and then her phone rang, and soon they were back at their separate stations, finishing up their lunches as they continued to work.

At one point she could tell Cole was disturbed by something, so when she wrapped up her next call, she asked him what was wrong.

"Two things, actually," he said, glancing her way and then returning his eyes to the computer screen. "One to do with Lou and one with your brother Matt."

"Oh?"

"Yeah, let's talk about Lou first. I've been running through his financials, like I did with B & T and Queen's Fleet, just to head off any potential problems with the deal, but I'm seeing some figures I don't understand. Can you give him a call and see if he can bring along a copy of his most recent certified audit when he comes to meet with us today at B & T?"

"Sure."

"Also, I'd like to get contact info for some of his investors. There seem to be some discrepancies, but if I could just verify a few things, I think I could clear this up."

Standing, Kelsey crossed the room to stand behind Cole and look at his screen. All she saw were rows and columns of numbers, perfectly understandable to him and utterly Greek to her.

"Should I be concerned?" she asked, resisting the urge to place her hands on his broad shoulders and give him one of the quick massages he used to love so much. "We are about to put all of our eggs in his basket."

"Yeah, I know. That's why I'm going through this now. I hope it's just a case of insufficient info. If I can get some more facts, I should be able to figure it all out."

"Good. I'll give him a call now. Before I do, though, tell me about Matt."

With a few clicks, Cole changed the screen, pulling up what looked like a telephone list. There were two columns. The one on the left showed a bunch of names, both businesses and people, and the one on the right was a column of 10-digit numbers separated by dashes.

"Flash sent this over a little while ago," Cole explained. "This is a record of all phone calls made to and from Gloria Poole's office extension in the fourteen days prior to her death."

"Impressive. But what does this have to do with Matt?"

Without speaking, Cole pointed to the screen, left column, which showed the name *Matthew Tate* about halfway down. "Any reason Matt would have been calling Gloria?"

Kelsey shrugged. "Not necessarily, but they certainly knew each other. It doesn't seem all that weird. Maybe he was trying to find me and I didn't answer, so he called her office instead to see if I was up there."

Cole glanced her way, eyes narrowing. Then, with a few more clicks of the mouse, he sorted the name list in alphabetical order. On the screen *Matthew Tate* appeared five times in a row.

Five calls in two weeks?

Cole scrolled to the right, revealing the next few columns, which showed the dates and times and origins of those calls. They seemed to alternate—him calling her, her calling him—and were evenly spaced, every other day or so around two or three in the afternoon.

"Doesn't that seem just a little bit odd to you?"

Again, Kelsey shrugged. "Sort of, I guess, but I feel sure there's a logical explanation for it. Maybe she was handling an investment for him. Maybe she needed some information, the kind only a professor can give. I've called him a few times myself over the years whenever some new economic development cropped up I didn't understand. Matt's a great teacher. When it comes to financial theory, he can explain things better than anyone I know."

"Kelsey—"

She cut him off, growing irritated. Exactly what was he trying to imply? That her brother had been involved in some sort of sneaky dealings with Gloria before her death? She took a step back, shaking her head.

"Give him the benefit of the doubt, would you? I don't know why he was calling her, Cole. Maybe they were in the same book club and wanted to chat about the latest selection."

"Oh, come on—"

"I'm just saying that it could be almost anything. Gloria wasn't just an employee of my father's; she was also a friend of our family. She's known Matt since he was a little boy. If they were having a flurry of communications near the end of her life, I'm sure it was perfectly innocent and completely explainable."

"I hope you're right, but do me a favor. Once you're finished talking with Lou, why don't you give Matt a call and ask."

"Don't worry, I will."

Kelsey returned to the couch and fiercely pressed the buttons that would bring up Lou's number. As she listened to the ring, she told herself to calm down. Why was she being so defensive? Was this just her inner big sister coming out in defense of her little brother?

Or was she thoroughly rattled by the possibility of having been betrayed, yet again, by someone she loved?

Lou answered on the second ring, his voice sounding so light and happy that she instantly felt bad for having to dampen his mood. Putting the Matt question out of her mind for the moment, she relayed Cole's request, making sure to phrase it in such a way that it came across as standard operating procedure and not as a response to some red flags. Even so, he sounded somewhat offended. For a moment she felt guilty about that, but then she realized she shouldn't. Lou might be like family, but they were about to enter into a major business transaction together. He had to know that any good businessperson would be doing their homework right about now.

In the end he agreed to bring along the items she had requested. Once they wrapped up their call and she hit the speed dial for Matt, she decided to relocate to a different room, preferring that their conversation be private. Unfortunately, this being a loft, there weren't exactly separate rooms, just "areas" that had been demarcated by various architectural elements, such as half walls and big plants and glass block towers. She thought of Cole's vision of filling this place with a wife and kids. Without a doubt, if that ever did happen, she felt sure some walls would go up real fast.

She ended up making her way to the half bath, her best choice for privacy, just as her brother answered the phone.

"Kels? Hey. What's up?"

"Quick question. Do you have a sec?"

"Sure, but not much more than that. Tiff and I are about to play racquetball, and we only have the court from two thirty to three thirty."

Kelsey glanced at the clock on the wall, not surprised to see that it was two thirty-five. Matt was running late, as usual, a bad habit that had only grown worse since he'd started dating Tiffany—who was even more punctuality-challenged than he was.

"This'll be fast. As you know, I've been looking into things with B & T and with Gloria's death. Something a little odd has come up, and I wanted to ask you what it was about."

"Okay."

Kelsey took a deep breath, sick to her stomach that she even had to ask such a question. "I managed to get a copy of Gloria's telephone log, and I see that the two of you had a flurry of phone calls back and forth in the two weeks prior to her death."

"Yeah, so?"

"So I was just wondering what that was about. I've been trying to understand her mind-set and her various activities there at the end and all." She closed her eyes, telling herself it was only half a lie. She *did* want to understand about Gloria, but she also needed to know what Matt's connection was.

Unfortunately, he didn't give her an answer she wanted. Rather than freely coming out with an explanation, his voice sounded tight as he said, "Yeah, well, I can tell you all about that later."

"It would be a lot easier if you could just tell me now," she replied, trying to keep her own voice even and light.

In the background, she could hear a woman speaking, and then Matt said, "Look, Kels, I gotta go. I'll call you back when I get home in a couple hours."

In a couple of hours she would be deeply embroiled in business matters at B & T. "Matt, really, this is more important than you think. Can't you just give me the quick version now and go into more detail later?"

"All right, then. Thanks for calling. Got to run for now. Bye."

With that, he hung up. What on earth? She held out her phone to look at its face, to verify that their call had actually been disconnected. Sure enough, her little brother had hung up on her. And as hard as that was to comprehend, it was harder still having to go back out there and tell Cole what had just happened.

With a deep breath, she tucked the phone away in her pocket and returned to the main living area.

"Well?" Cole asked. "Were you able to reach him?"

Turning away so he couldn't see her face, she headed over to the couch and began cleaning up the mess she'd made. "Yeah, but he was just heading into a racquetball game and couldn't talk. He's going to call me back later, once he's done."

If Cole realized she wasn't giving him the full story, he didn't show it. Instead, he asked her to come take a look at his computer. When she did, he gestured toward an email that was up on his screen. "This just came from Flash."

Kelsey quickly scanned the note, which read:

> You're right, boss, things totally don't add up here. I'm even
> picking up a whiff of Ponzi. You?

"I don't understand," Kelsey said, returning to the task of straightening. "What's he talking about?"

Cole hesitated momentarily before speaking. "I sent him the numbers from Strahan Realty Trust and asked him to look them over. He came to the same conclusion I did."

"Which is?"

He took in a deep breath and blew it out slowly. "That Lou's company looks like it could be a bunch of smoke and mirrors. Frankly, we're both concerned he has a kind of a Ponzi scheme going on over there."

Kelsey spun around, angry with Cole for impugning the integrity of yet another of her loved ones.

"A Ponzi scheme? The man is offering thirty million dollars for my company. Where do you think that money's coming from? Is he going to pull it from a hat?"

Cole's eyes narrowed. "I'm just saying that his financials are looking very fishy."

"And yet I've been getting regular dividends—healthy dividends—from him for several years. How do you explain that?"

"You know how a Ponzi scheme works, Kelsey. Of *course* he's paying out dividends. That's how he keeps up the facade. But his corporate structure is all wrong. I'm afraid the money you're seeing may not be an actual return on investment at all. I think he may just have been bringing in new investors and using their money to make payouts to old investors. Classic Ponzi—and then it all comes crashing down."

Kelsey shook her head. "Look, Cole, I know Lou is a little slick, but that's just his way. When you get down to it, he's a sharp guy and a born salesman. If things over there look a little investment-heavy, I'm sure that's just because he's so good at sharing his vision and bringing other people in on it."

"The numbers don't lie, Kelsey. I know a pyramid when I see one."

"Oh? Like you know a good investment when you see one?"

As soon as the words were out of her mouth, she regretted them with all her heart—but it was too late to take them back. From the look on his face, he knew exactly what she was saying: Cole Thornton didn't always know a good thing when he saw it. Worse, if that particular offer was indicative of his skills, he didn't have the instincts their line of work required.

"Wow," he said, rising and moving into the kitchen area. "And here I thought that apology of yours today was sincere."

Cole filled his glass with water from the fridge, his jaw tight, veins bulging in his neck. Kelsey knew his expression well, and she could feel the situation spinning out of control. Forcing herself to sound calm, she stepped forward and spoke.

"Cole, look, I'm sorry it came out that way just now. I really am. But if we could talk about this rationally—"

"Rationally? I think I left rational behind on Wednesday when I decided to give you a call."

"Stop. Please. Don't say something you'll regret."

He dumped his water back into the sink, the liquid splashing over the sides. "Regret being the operative word here. Do we really want to talk about regrets? Because right now I'm starting to regret an awful lot."

She blinked, willing herself not to cry. "Please don't do this," she whispered.

Ignoring the spilled water, palms flat against the counter, Cole met her eyes and said grimly, "Do you have any idea what all of that did to me back then?"

"Yes, I—"

"Do you have a clue how long it took me to get over you and go on with my life?"

"Please, Cole, let me talk. *Yes*, I know I hurt you. *Yes*, I deeply regret all of it. But if you put everything else aside and just look at the facts of the situation, you have to agree that your offer to Lou back then was not a good one. The man was a known entity with a proven track record—a friend and former coworker, no less. He had a top-notch business plan. He had, what, something like five hundred thousand dollars' worth of client commitments? The man was even putting up almost a million dollars of his own money. And yet you came at him with an offer so low it was an insult. Give me a break, Cole. He was opening up a realty trust, not a Popsicle cart! B & T's reputation has always been about building people up and helping them succeed, not insulting them and taking advantage of them. Lou was deeply offended by your offer. We would have lost his business entirely if I hadn't stepped in when I did."

Cole ground his teeth. "You're confused about the actual numbers, Kelsey, but whatever. I stand by my offer. It was right in line with my analysis. Yours is the offer that was ridiculous—not to mention out of line with the rest of B & T's reputation for being wise and conservative investors. There was nothing remotely conservative about what you gave him. Your risk factor was way too high. Frankly, I think you let your friendship with Lou cloud your judgment. Just because someone's a trusted coworker and friend doesn't mean you should invest with blinders on."

Kelsey gasped. "Blinders? That's not how I do business *ever*—friend or not. The cold, hard truth here is that your research was insufficient. You didn't do a proper analysis of the potential. *Five hundred thousand* in client commitments, Cole. *A million dollars* of his own money. I knew exactly what I was doing."

He shook his head. "First of all, review your facts and stop exaggerating. It was more like a hundred thousand in client agreements, and his personal investment was nowhere near half a million. His was a high-risk case, and if you didn't recognize that, then your research was insufficient."

Her head began to throb. "Fine, whatever. I don't remember the exact specifics right now, but the truth is that when all was said and done, in light of those facts my offer made a lot more sense than yours did. I know I went about things totally the wrong way, and I take full responsibility for that, but you have to admit that you weren't completely without blame. If you can't do a proper investment analysis, Cole, you shouldn't even be in the business."

With that the room fell silent. Kelsey hated the turn their discussion had taken, but at least she'd finally said what she'd been wanting to say for five years. If only she could have done so in a less emotionally charged moment. Now it was almost time to head over to B & T to meet with Lou, and she'd never felt so unready for anything in her life.

"Where do we go from here?" she asked softly. "Are you done with me now, or are you still in my court?"

He didn't answer right away, and that was all she needed to hear.

"Never mind," she said. "I've obviously taken up enough of your time. Thank you for your help. I'll be sure and let you know how things turn out."

Walking stiffly to the couch, Kelsey gathered up her papers and shoved them in her purse. "I'll see myself out," she told him, hoping he would try and stop her, but he didn't move, didn't reply.

So that's exactly what she did.

CHAPTER
FORTY-FIVE

April 14, 1912

ADELE

Adele felt an odd shudder, the water in the basin sloshing from side to side. The sensation didn't last long, so after a moment she went back to washing her face, wondering if something had gone wrong with the ship's engine or perhaps its propeller. Either way, everything seemed fine now. She patted her face with a towel, straightened the basin area, and climbed into bed.

Even though her body was tired, her mind was wide awake, so she pulled out the book she had been reading and turned to the page where she'd left off. After a while, however, she was distracted from that pursuit when she realized that something was wrong. Looking around the room, she tried to decide what it was.

Nothingness.

It was nothingness. Used to the constant hum of the ship's engine and the vibrations and propulsions of a vessel cutting through an open sea, she suddenly felt as if all was quiet and still. Someone had turned the ship off.

More curious than alarmed, she went back to her reading but soon heard a commotion outside her stateroom. She got up, donned her robe, and opened the door to peer out into the corridor to see what was happening. Other passengers, some in their nightclothes, were emerging from their rooms, and a small group nearby was speaking with a cabin steward. From what she could gather, it sounded as if the ship had either lost a screw from the propeller or had somehow collided with some other vessel.

Adele wanted to know more. She closed her door and hastily changed from her nightclothes back into the dress she'd worn earlier in the evening. She wished Jocelyn were here. This was not a good time to be separated.

There was a knock at the door, and she opened it to see Uncle Rowan standing in the hallway speaking to the cabin steward.

"I'll see to it that they respond," Rowan told him, gesturing toward Adele.

"Thank you, sir," the man replied, moving along.

Leaning forward to watch, Adele saw that he was going room to room, knocking on doors and asking that passengers don their life vests and head to the boat deck, "Just as a precaution."

Eyes wide, Adele looked to Rowan for an explanation.

"Where is Jocelyn?" he said, moving into the room and looking around.

"She...she went up to her favorite sitting area at the top of the aft stairwell. She'll be back shortly." Adele could hear the commotion out in the hallways begin to increase. She looked at her uncle with some concern. "What is going on?"

"It appears that the ship has grazed an iceberg," Rowan replied, his expression grave. "They stopped the vessel so the engineers could assess the damage. Our purser has asked that we put on our life vests and go to the boat deck. Once we are given the all clear, we will be allowed to return to our rooms."

"So should we go now or wait until Jocelyn returns?"

He thought for a moment. "I need to go to the purser's office first and retrieve our valuables. Hopefully, she will have returned by the time I get back."

Adele nodded, praying it would be so. "I'll prepare the life vests for wear," she told him.

"Dress warmly first, and then put on the life vest over your coat. Bring your hat and hand muff too. It's bitterly cold outside tonight. I'll be back soon."

He opened the door and walked out, and as he did Adele could hear the increased noise level of the corridor.

Where was Jocelyn? Was she on her way back?

Feeling deeply unsettled, Adele decided to go and retrieve her. She rushed from the cabin but was stopped by a steward, who told her to don her life vest first.

"But I'm just going—"

"All passengers in life vests," he repeated sternly, so she returned to the room and quickly threw it on, still fastening it as she made her way through the crowds clogging the halls and the stairs, trying to get up to the place where she knew Jocelyn would be. The vest was bulky and cumbersome and felt quite uncomfortable, but Adele realized that nearly every person she passed was wearing theirs as well.

Despite the urgency, her trip was slow going. There were just so many people in the way. As she moved up the steps, she could tell that most of them had no idea what was going on. At every level, people were just standing around, wondering what they were supposed to do or where they were supposed to go. Others were grumbling and complaining about the lateness of the hour or the coldness of the night. Most were calm, but some seemed frantic. There seemed to be no order or reason, but at least there was no general panic. She pushed her way past as many people as she could until she reached the sitting area at the top landing.

Jocelyn wasn't there.

Opening the door to the outside deck, Adele pushed her way into the cold night. Her heart filled with joy as she finally spotted her cousin, off on the far side of the promenade beside a young man. They were both facing away from her, leaning over the rail, looking toward the bow of the ship. As she got closer, she saw the young man slip an arm around Jocelyn's waist, and in response Jocelyn looked up at him and smiled.

Things with this fellow were further along than Adele had realized!

Just as she was about to call out to her, the young man turned and Adele saw his face. The sight hit her like a punch to the stomach.

Tad.

The young man Jocelyn had met up with tonight was Tad.

CHAPTER
FORTY-SIX

Kelsey walked away from Cole's building in a daze, her feet pounding rhythmically against the pavement. Despite what had happened, she felt oddly calm and subdued, and she supposed that the full impact of the scene she'd just been through would hit her later. For now, she was simply numb—numb and empty and sad. Poor Cole. Poor her. As much as it felt as though the two of them were soul mates, it was clear they were not meant to be. Perhaps at some point they could revisit the situation one last time, just to make some final peace about it, but any hopes she'd had of Cole coming back into her life in a significant way were now gone. Maybe it was good that this had happened how it did and when it did. That ripping Band-Aid was a killer, but it was still preferable to the torturous alternative of a longer, more excruciating split.

Cole's new place was only about half a mile from Kelsey's own apartment, and once she was out on the street, heading down West Broadway toward Vesey, she considered running home to fix herself up and change into something nicer before going over to the office. After all, she would be addressing B & T's board of directors later this evening.

Then again, she thought as she checked her phone, it was nearly three o'clock, and the meeting with Lou and Walter would be starting at four. If she wanted to be ready in time, she needed to get on over there now. In the long run, if she couldn't save her company, what difference did it make whether she was in jeans or a suit tonight anyway? Decision made, when she reached Vesey Street, she turned left, went one block and turned right on Church to angle her way down to Brennan & Tate.

As she went, she tried to regroup now that she would be heading into this situation alone, with no Cole-the-money-guy at her side, running the numbers and serving as her wingman. While she might not have his mathematical skills, she knew she'd be okay. She was far more savvy about investments, after all, and probably contracts too. The hardest part wasn't going into this alone. It was grasping the fact that for the first time in her experience, B & T was going to be sitting on the other side of a deal—the "for sale" side. That thought simply broke her heart.

If only she could locate the bonds!

At least she had a little time left. Whatever details were hammered out this afternoon, and regardless of any decisions made tonight, the sale itself would not go through until next week at the earliest. In the meantime, she would take an extremely close look at Strahan Realty Trust. Though she doubted it with every fiber of her being, Kelsey had to acknowledge there was at least a slight chance Cole and Flash were right about Lou's company being set up like some sort of Ponzi scheme.

Even if it turned out that they *were* right, this meeting she was about to head into was not a waste of time—at least not for her—because while Lou and Walter sat and hashed out specifics, she had plans to go and search for the bonds in Gloria's office. Ditto tonight with the board meeting. Kelsey would do whatever it would take to dig up those bonds—which had to be cashed in on Monday, the day after tomorrow, or they would expire and become worthless.

She made it to the office by three fifteen, and she went straight to the front door, not the back. Sneaking in at night with her father's code was one thing, but trying to pull the same stunt in the light of day—especially when she knew Walter would be coming in soon as well—would have been, at the very least, unwise. If the front desk was manned, she wouldn't need a code at all.

When she reached the front door, just as she'd hoped, she spotted someone there despite the fact that it was a Saturday. Even better, the person currently on duty was Ephraim, who buzzed her in the moment he spotted her through the glass entrance.

"Hey, Eph," she said as she stepped inside. "I'm surprised to see you here on a Saturday. Are you guys still on a ramped-up security schedule because of last week?"

Ephraim stared at her strangely before answering. "Nope. We're on a ramped-up security schedule because of last night."

"Oh?" She kept her expression blank as she continued across the wide lobby toward his desk.

"Yeah, it's the strangest thing. From what I hear, your pop is pretty incapacitated these days. And yet somehow he managed to get into the building anyway—and up five flights of stairs, no less. Amazing, isn't it?"

Kelsey hesitated before answering. "Wow. That is amazing. Have you told anyone else about this incredible development?"

He held her gaze for a long moment. "No. I reviewed the security footage from the fifth floor elevator bay and reception area and didn't see anything or anybody. Then I took a look around up there myself, in person. Considering that I couldn't find any signs of, uh, maliciousness or vandalism or anything like that, I figured it could wait until my Monday morning report for Mr. Hallerman. Doesn't seem to be any need to rush and let him know 'bout it today."

She wanted to hug him, but instead she just gave a quick nod. "My father has always appreciated your loyalty to this firm and to our family."

"Well, I hope your father—or somebody else in your family who happens to work here—will be able to straighten out this mess real soon and it won't matter anyway." His expression was stern but loving.

"That's the plan," she replied, forcing a smile. "Or, I guess I should say, that's the prayer, anyway."

"Amen to that."

With a grateful smile, she continued on to the elevator, took it to the fourth floor, and headed down the hallway toward her office. Despite being fully in the right, it felt odd to be here now, almost as if she were an intruder. Nevertheless, Walter knew she was coming in today, so at least she wasn't breaking his ridiculous rules at the moment.

Flipping on the lights, she stepped into the room and looked around, glad that nothing seemed amiss. Her favorite sweater still hung from the peg on the wall. The files she'd been working on Tuesday morning still sat neatly at the corner of her desk. It was almost as if she'd been gone ten minutes, not three days.

She couldn't believe so much had happened in such a short time.

Kelsey would have liked to process things a bit, mentally speaking, but she knew she couldn't dawdle. With less than forty-five minutes until she was to meet up with Lou and Walter in Walter's office, she needed to get busy. Even without taking Cole's Ponzi theory into consideration, there was still more homework to do on the merger she would be proposing later tonight.

Her laptop was at home, so she flipped on her desktop computer instead. As it powered up she went to the file drawers on the far wall, her own personal archives. Digging through them, she pulled out all the paperwork she had ever acquired regarding Strahan Realty Trust. Besides the large original investment she had orchestrated five years ago, there had also been several small loans in the years since. Back at her desk, she signed into her computer and then pulled up the record of all payments—both loan repayments and dividend earnings—that B & T had ever received from Lou's company. She printed out that information and then returned her attention to the files she had taken from the drawer. Reaching for the earliest one, she flipped it open and began skimming through it, just to refresh her memory of the terms of their original agreement.

As she worked, it wasn't long before she came across the old investment analysis sheet Gloria had first given her to start the ball rolling. Unable to resist, Kelsey looked for the figures Cole had accused her of remembering incorrectly. She felt a surge of righteous indignation when she spotted them, two items in a list of specifics about the deal. First was the line that read, *Client commitments totaling $485,000*, followed by the one that said, *Personal investment totaling $950,000*.

She was right! Cole was the one with the faulty memory.

A part of her—the childish, vindictive part—wanted to scan a copy of that page and email it directly to him with the words "I told you so!" written in big block letters across the top. She didn't, of course, but just in case she ever had the opportunity to share that information with him in a less vindictive manner, she scanned it in anyway, feeling smug and guilty at the same time.

Returning to her work, she continued to review the files. Once she was finished, she went into her email and was relieved to see that Cole had sent over his reports, just as she'd hoped. They were attached to a brief note, one that said, simply:

Kelsey, thought you might find these helpful. Best wishes on your merger and your life.

Cole

Ouch. In just two short lines, he had managed to convey every ounce of his anger—and twist the knife a little further into her heart. Deeply saddened, she printed out the information he'd sent and was about to click out of her email when another message from Cole popped up. Opening it, she expected to see another attachment or two, but instead it was just a note, which read:

Sorry about that last email. I should have cooled down before I hit send. Just because it's clear that you and I are better off apart doesn't mean I have the right to be hurtful to you. I do wish you the best with whatever solution you end up using to solve your company's current problems. I'm sorry my team and I couldn't be more help. Please feel free to contact Flash or Thriller directly if you have any further questions.

I also really do wish you the best in life. You are a special person and will always have a place in my heart.

Cole

Kelsey stared at the screen for a long time. In a way, this second letter pained her even more than the first. Words of farewell said in anger seemed far less permanent somehow than those said with kindness.

Their relationship really was over.

With a heavy heart, she rose from her desk. It was almost time to go upstairs to meet with Lou and Walter, almost time to get the ball rolling. The success of scenario number two contained a lot of contingencies—it could work, *if* Lou wasn't running some elaborate scheme, *if* he and Walter could hammer out the specifics, *if* the board approved the deal, *if* Kelsey didn't find the bonds in the meantime—but at least laying the groundwork for a deal was better than doing nothing.

She headed to the printer, pulled off the pages Cole had sent to her, and took a moment to look through them. When she came to the last one, she did a double take. Like her, he had managed to dig out his old investment analysis sheet for Lou Strahan's business venture. His sheet also had a list of specifics about the deal, including client commitments and personal investment. Except his said, *Client commitments totaling $125,000,* and *Personal investment totaling $400,000.*

Overcome with a wave a dizziness, she reached out and placed a hand on the wall to steady herself. She reread the document two more times, just to be sure she was seeing what she thought she was seeing. The forms were identical—same date, same executive summary, same exact info—except for those two amounts, which had been altered.

It was clear as day. They had each been working from different figures.

One of them had been given fabricated data.

She pulled out her phone and dialed Cole's number, praying he would take her call. He answered on the fifth ring, his voice flat and distant.

"Yes?"

"I'm sending you an email right now. Can you take a look while we're on the line?"

"I guess. Hold on."

Dashing over to her desk, with trembling hands she sent off her version of the form she held in her hand, the one she had scanned earlier. "There," she said softly. "It should show up any second."

She held her breath as she waited. Finally, she heard him gasp.

"Do you see what I see?" she whispered.

"Kelsey, where did you get this?"

"I did the same thing you did. I looked up the old numbers. *My* old numbers. I wasn't going to send them to you. I just needed to reassure myself that I was right. But then I got your version, and I realized—"

"We were set up. We were working from different figures."

They were both silent for a long moment.

"Do you understand what this means?" he said. "For one thing, it means Lou was lying."

"Or Gloria. She's the one who gave me this information."

"It means you made an investment based on vastly inflated numbers," Cole said.

"It means you may be right about Lou's pyramid business structure," Kelsey replied.

"It means…" His voice trailed off.

"It means you and I were both right, because we didn't have the same information. I would never have made such a high offer based on your figures."

"I would never have made such a low offer based on yours."

After a beat, he ended with the obvious. "It means our breakup was predicated on someone else's lie."

Kelsey closed her eyes. "Oh, Cole," she whispered. "If only we could turn back the clock…"

"I know, but don't say that, Kels. There's nothing we can do about it now. And we both had a lot of growing up to do. I truly think God used that time apart to make us stronger, to lead us to new places, new challenges."

"Judging by today's fight, I don't know that we got all that far."

He groaned. "Look, I overreacted and I'm sorry. I didn't realize how much of that stuff I was still holding on to until it came up this afternoon. Obviously, forgiving you all those years ago wasn't enough. I needed to release it completely and let it go. I thought I had, but… Well, let's just say I should never have let you walk out of here earlier like that, much less sent you such a cutting email once you were gone."

"At least you followed that up with another, kinder version."

"Yeah, also intended to cut, just couched in a little more civility."

She couldn't help but laugh. "What a mess we are. Will we ever get this right?"

"At the moment, Kels, I think our relationship is not our most urgent problem. It's almost four o'clock. What are you going to do?"

She hesitated, relishing the way he'd referred to their "relationship." Did that mean they still *had* a relationship, one that might possibly be saved after all?

Your will, Lord, not ours.

Trying to focus, she looked at the clock. It was three fifty-two.

"First things first," she said. "Can you hold on a sec?"

"Of course."

Setting her cell on the desk, Kelsey reached for her office phone and called down to security. When Ephraim answered, she asked if Walter had come in yet.

"I haven't seen him, but he usually goes up the back stairs anyway, so that doesn't necessarily mean anything. Want me to check the security code log-in?"

"Um…no. I'm sure he's here by now. How about Lou Strahan? Has he come in yet?"

"I haven't seen him either. Is he supposed to?"

"Yeah. Walter and I have a meeting with him."

"Okay. Well, he hasn't shown up so far."

She exhaled with relief. "Good. When he does, could you detain him for a few minutes? Walter and I need to speak privately first, and we don't want to be interrupted."

"Sure. Just call back when you're ready for him. What time is he supposed to come?"

"Any minute now. Our meeting's at four."

"Okay. You got it, Kelsey."

She hung up and returned to her call with Cole. "All right, at least I've headed Lou off at the pass. What's my next move, other than alerting Walter to all of this?"

"I was just trying to figure that out. Do you think I should come over there? I could gather more information for you. There's a chance Lou is innocent in this, you know. Maybe it was all Gloria's doing."

"Maybe."

"Then again, maybe they did it together. There's a chance something was going on between the two of them we didn't know about."

"You mean like they were in cahoots?"

Cole cleared his throat. "Yeah, well, or maybe they were even in a, uh, relationship."

A relationship? Lou and Gloria? With a start, Kelsey remembered her conversation with Yanni at the funeral home, about her and Vern's affair. *"Gloria knew,"* Yanni had said. *"She knew and she didn't even care."*

Was it possible the reason Gloria didn't care was because she was involved in an affair of her own?

Her mind racing, Kelsey thought back to the time when Lou worked at B & T. He and Gloria had been close friends and colleagues, but to her recollection there had never been even a hint of impropriety between them. Gloria was an attractive woman, but she was older than Lou by a good ten years— and in many ways she acted even older than that. If anything, her demeanor toward him back then had been that of elder stateswoman, so to speak, the same as she'd been with almost everyone in the company—superiors, peers, and underlings alike.

"This may be tacky, but I think I need to call Vern," Kelsey said to Cole. "He'd tell me the truth."

"If he knew about it."

"Who else could we ask?"

They both thought for a moment.

"Didn't you say your EA keeps an ear to the ground?" Cole asked.

"Yeah, but if Sharon knew Gloria was having an affair, she would have told me already. Besides, she's only been working here for two years, so if it's something from before, back when Lou was still on staff, she wouldn't have any reason to know about it."

"True...wait. Remember Brooke, who used to work in human resources?" Cole asked.

"You mean 'Babbling Brooke'? The office gossip?"

"That's the one. She might know something. Back when I was at B & T, she knew everything about everyone."

"Maybe, but do you have some way to reach her?"

"As long as she hasn't changed her number since she retired. How about this, you call Vern and I'll try Brooke. Between the two of us, we might find some answers."

Kelsey glanced at the clock. Three fifty-four.

"Okay. Let's text each other when we're done, and then we can talk."

"Sounds good."

Once they had disconnected their call, Kelsey pressed the speed dial marked *Gloria—Home*. With a surge of sadness, she realized she'd have to change that now, removing it from speed dial and changing the listing to read *Vern Poole* instead.

Fortunately, Vern answered her call right away. She felt terrible having to ask such a question the very day of his late wife's funeral, but in light of all Gloria had done lately, she really had no choice in the matter.

"Vern, it's Kelsey. I am so sorry to bother you, especially today, but I need to ask you an important question—and it's really urgent. Are you where you can speak privately?"

"I can be. Hold on a sec."

Listening, she could hear the murmur of voices in the background and then the sound of a closing door.

"Sorry about that," he said, coming back on the line. "I have family staying here, and we were just going through some old photos."

"No, *I'm* sorry. This shouldn't take long."

She looked at the clock. Three fifty-six. Time to head upstairs to talk to Walter. She could finish her call on the way.

"I don't know how to say this other than to just come out with it. Vern, do you know if Gloria was involved with Lou Strahan?"

"Involved?"

"Were…were they having an affair? Either recently or at some point in the past?"

Vern was silent for a long moment. "Funny you should ask that. I was wondering that very thing myself, a few weeks ago."

Kelsey's eyes widened. "You were?"

"Yeah. It's a long story."

"I'm listening," she told him as she gathered up her papers, turned off the lights, and headed down the hall.

"Well, it started one night when we were getting ready to go to the ballet. She was in the shower and I was in the bedroom, getting dressed. I accidentally dropped a cuff link into one of her open drawers. While I was digging around in there trying to find it, I ran across an envelope hidden under some clothes. It was one of those brightly printed folder envelopes, the kind you get when you buy tickets to a show. Anyway, I was nosy enough to take a peek. Like I expected, there were tickets inside, real expensive ones, for VIP seats to a big Broadway musical. I thought they were for the two of us and she was going to surprise me with them."

"Let me guess," Kelsey replied, remembering her conversation with Detective Hargrove about Rupert and Rhonda and how they had spent their first evening in town. "Were the tickets for a Monday night show? This past Monday night?"

"Yes, actually. How did you know that? There aren't that many Broadway shows that even run on Monday nights."

"Just a guess. Keep going." Kelsey reached the elevator and pressed the "up" button.

"Well, like I said, I thought she was going to surprise me with them, but as it got closer and closer to the date, she never said anything at all. To make matters worse, she'd been acting pretty strange for the past month, kind of secretive and evasive. Finally, on Sunday night, I asked her about the tickets. She got real weird and flustered, and she said they weren't for us at all but instead a professional gift for a colleague. I took her at her word. What other choice did I have?"

Kelsey didn't reply. She just thought how much better Vern and Gloria's relationship could have been if only they had *talked* to each other more. Then again, who was she to judge? Her and Cole's original breakup could have been avoided entirely if only one of them had thought to bring up the exact figures of the deal involved.

"Anyway," Vern continued, "that next afternoon was the day she came home from the office a little earlier than usual. Around six o'clock I was in the kitchen, cooking supper. I thought she was in the living room, just resting her eyes for a bit, when I heard the front door open and close. Curious, I went to the door myself and looked out in the hallway—and that's when I saw her getting on the elevator, tickets in hand."

Kelsey thought about that as her own elevator arrived and she stepped on board and pressed the button for the fifth floor. Monday afternoon was when Gloria had fought with Walter and gone home soon after.

"I'm not ashamed to say I followed her down. By the time I got off the elevator, she was out in front of the building, handing off the envelope to somebody in a taxi. I tried to get a better look through the front window and realized it was Lou Strahan, of all people."

Kelsey closed her eyes, swallowing hard. Lou and Gloria. Together.

"I wanted to bust out the front door and punch him in the face," Vern said, "but standing there at the window, watching them, I realized they really were acting like colleagues, not lovers. When Gloria came back inside, I confronted her, and she just said that she and Lou had been working on some big business deal recently and that's all it was. I believed her, Kelsey. I can't explain it—and goodness knows I had no room to judge—but I really think their relationship was platonic."

The elevator came to a stop at the fifth floor and opened up. Kelsey stepped off but hovered there for a moment, wanting to finish her call before she continued on to Walter's office. "Lou hasn't worked at B & T for five years. Why would he and Gloria have been involved in a business deal together?"

"I don't know, but she said it had something to do with both companies, like B & T and Strahan Realty Trust were going to be aligning somehow. Merging, maybe? Are the two companies planning to merge?"

"Over my dead body," she replied. Then she thanked him for his help and said she had to go but would be in touch later.

After she hung up, she took a moment to shoot a quick text off to Cole:

Talked to Vern, learned a lot. Call me when you're finished. I'll be in with Walter.

She was halfway across the reception area when he responded, so she paused again to read his text.

Am on my landline with Brooke now. I forgot what a
talker she is!

Smiling, Kelsey responded, No problem. I'll text you once
Walter and I have finished.

Cole replied, Sounds good. Let me know if/when you
want me to come over there.

Kelsey typed, Will do, and then she slid the phone into her pocket. Going
to Walter's door, she gave it a light rap before pushing it open.

As expected, he was already there, sitting behind his desk, though the
room around him was a disaster, with papers strewn everywhere and the furniture turned on its sides.

Something was horribly wrong. Looking again at Walter, she saw that he
wasn't just sitting there; he was *taped* there. Numerous bands of duct tape
were encircling his chest and upper arms, affixing him firmly to the chair.
Each wrist was taped to an arm rest, and his feet were bound together at the
ankles and to the metal base of the chair.

Worse, he looked as though he'd been in a boxing match. His eyes were
dark and swollen and his nose looked broken, with blood trickling from his
nostrils and down across the strip of duct tape that covered his mouth.

Their eyes met. Kelsey froze, unable to move or speak or even breathe.

Who did this to you? She could hear the words screaming silently in her
mind.

But she already knew. Lou had done this to him.

It had been Lou all along.

Before she could speak, something caught Walter's attention behind her.
His eyes widened in terror. Sucking in a deep breath, Kelsey forced herself to turn around. Lou was standing there, just a few feet away, holding a
black metal rod with one hand and smacking it lightly against the palm of
the other. Staring at the rod, Kelsey saw that it was a tire iron. A big, black,
heavy tire iron.

"How could you?" she managed to utter, her mind racing to think of
some escape.

"It's not like I enjoyed it," he replied defensively. "Well, okay, maybe a little, but only because it's Walter. I sure don't want to have to do that to you.

Believe it or not, I really am fond of you, Kels. You've always been like the daughter I never had."

Kelsey shook her head side to side. "You're an animal."

"Not really," he replied, taking a step forward, his voice oddly calm. "I just felt sure Walter knew where those bonds were. Turns out I was wrong. That leaves you. Give them to me and I'll go away quietly. Nobody else needs to get hurt."

"And if I can't?"

Lou shook his head sadly. "Hold out on me, kiddo, and I'm afraid I'll have to do to you what I did to him. Those bonds are all I have left. And as much as it pains me to hurt you, trust me when I say I'll do whatever it takes to get them in my hands."

CHAPTER
FORTY-SEVEN

April 14, 1912

JOCELYN

Jocelyn smiled warmly at Tad, grateful he had been willing to miss out on the fun for her sake. Apparently, *Titanic* had struck an iceberg. Soon after it happened, another passenger told them that some of the young men were having a great time playing with the ice that had fallen onto the ship's open deck. Tad had wanted to go up and join them, but Jocelyn asked him to stay with her. He'd agreed, remaining at her side and keeping her warm as they watched all the goings-on together.

It was just like him to value her wishes over his own personal desires.

Suddenly, Jocelyn felt someone grab her arm and give it a jerk. She turned, stunned to see Adele standing there in her coat and a life vest, her face screwed up in a dark scowl. Adele's grip tightened, and she pulled again, this time wrenching Jocelyn from Tad's side.

"You're coming with me," she snarled. "Back to the stateroom. Your father wants us to meet him there *now*." Not letting go, she pulled her cousin toward the door.

Stunned, Jocelyn turned to Tad for help, but he was holding himself back, still standing at the rail and glaring angrily at Adele. Then his features softened as he shifted his gaze to Jocelyn.

"It's okay," he called out to her. "You go ahead. I'll wait for you right here. Just come back as soon as you can."

"I will!"

"And don't forget to bring me what we talked about when you come back."

She gave him a nod even as her mind was racing. *That thing we talked about? Oh, he must mean the bonds.*

Jocelyn asked Adele to let go of her arm, promising she wouldn't try to break away. Reluctantly, Adele released her, and the two of them wove together among the other passengers as they made their way to the stairs and began to descend.

"Please don't be angry with me," Jocelyn pleaded as they reached the next deck and continued on. "I know I should have told you I was meeting with Tad, but I didn't want to upset you when you already seemed to be having such a bad day."

Adele did not reply, so Jocelyn continued.

"Remember, just this morning I asked you what was going on with the two of you, and you said you weren't interested in him that way."

Still she did not respond, though at least they were making progress against the crowds. Perhaps Adele was waiting until they were in the cabin before she spoke her mind.

"Otherwise, I never would have agreed to see him," Jocelyn tried one more time. "We were going to tell you eventually."

Adele remained silent all the way back to the stateroom. When they finally got there and stepped inside, Adele spoke, just as Jocelyn had expected.

"You cannot possibly be interested in Tad," Adele said fiercely. "He's not good enough for you!"

Jocelyn blinked, trying to understand what was really going on.

"I'm sorry if the sight of us together made you feel jealous, Adele, but—"

"Jealous? I'm not jealous!"

Before she could speak further, there was a knock at the door. Jocelyn opened it to see her father standing there, his face pale and lined.

"What's wrong, Da?" she asked, fearing that he, too, had learned of her relationship with Tad and had come to try and talk her out of it.

"Sit down, both of you," he said in a low voice, moving inside and lowering himself to the chair. "Quickly now."

Adele responded by sitting on the sofa, but Jocelyn moved to the lower bunk and sat there instead, not even taking the time to remove her coat.

"This situation is bad," he told them solemnly, "much worse than many of the other passengers realize."

Jocelyn swallowed hard. What was he talking about?

"Listen to me very carefully," he said, looking from one to the other. "This ship is sinking, and it's sinking fast. It'll be under the waves in less than two hours. We must get the two of you to a lifeboat. The crew has already started uncovering them and readying them for launch."

A lifeboat? Sinking?

Jocelyn's heart began pounding furiously in her chest. How stupid could she have been, how blinded by love that she hadn't grasped the seriousness of the situation? The amount of people surging up on deck after the impact had seemed odd, especially as most of them had been wearing life vests, but she'd merely attributed all of that to curiosity and not any real danger.

Swallowing hard, she realized she had to get back to Tad as quickly as possible, to warn him and make sure he got into a lifeboat as well.

"Before we go, I need to give you the bonds to hold onto, Adele." Rowan pulled an envelope from his inside jacket pocket and handed it over to her. "Is there somewhere safe you can hide them on your person?"

"I can keep them in my bag," she replied, suddenly looking as frightened as Jocelyn felt.

"We need to do better than that. These are *bearer* bonds, which means that anyone who gets hold of them can cash them in."

"Oh!" She clutched the bonds tightly in her hand.

As she tried to think of a safe place to hide them, Rowan grabbed the cabin's other life vest, told Jocelyn to stand, and helped her put it on over her coat. He placed the belt around her and pulled it tight, and suddenly she felt like a small child again, being dressed and cared for by her loving father.

"There is something else I need to tell you both," he said, his eyes growing watery. "The purser shared this with me, and it is a serious problem."

Jocelyn had rarely seen her father cry. With her heart feeling as though it would break, she reached out and placed a comforting hand on his arm.

"There aren't nearly enough lifeboats necessary to save everyone on board," he continued. "Not all of us will make it off the ship. Right now, they are calling for women and children only to board the lifeboats."

Jocelyn gasped. "What about you, Da?"

"I will do my best," he replied, but before she could protest he continued. "You must understand that we don't have much time and have to think clearly. It's pandemonium up there, and I'm sure it's grown worse while we have been down here. We may get separated. If that happens, promise me you'll continue on toward the boat deck and get yourselves on a lifeboat. Promise me."

"We promise," they said in unison.

"Stay together, and no matter what happens, get on a lifeboat."

Adele nodded. "But what about you, Uncle Rowan?"

"I will do everything within my power to get off this ship alive. But whether I manage to do that or not, I need to know the two of you are safe. Do you understand?"

Both girls threw themselves in his arms, crying as well.

"No matter what, always remember that I love you," he said, hugging them in return and giving them each a kiss. "Now grab your coats, hats, hand muffs, and whatever else you have to keep you warm up there. We have to go *now*."

They did as he said and were still wiping away their tears as the three of them moved into the hall. As they quickly walked toward the stairwell, Jocelyn was shocked by how much emptier their deck was now than it had been before. Were they already too late?

As her father had said, the higher they went on the ship, the greater the pandemonium they encountered. The upper corridors were full of people pushing and shoving, all trying to get to the same place, the deck where the lifeboats awaited.

Jocelyn could hardly breathe from the crush of the people. It felt like an eternity to her, climbing the steps, trying to hold tightly to Adele's hand, trying not to get knocked down and trampled by the crowd. The process was made harder by the listing of the ship. Halfway there, she realized that they were no longer upright but tilted somehow.

Titanic really was sinking.

When they finally reached the open air of the boat deck, it was hard to know what to do. Her father moved them into what seemed to be a queue of women and children moving toward the boats. He told them to stay there and get into the first boat they could reach.

"I'm going to look further ahead and see if I can get some more information," he said. "I'll be back."

Once he had given them each another hug and disappeared into the crowd, Jocelyn felt a greater panic begin to overwhelm her. Turning to Adele, she grabbed her hands tightly and spoke.

"I know I promised Father I'd get on a lifeboat," she said, "and I will. But I have to go get Tad first. He's waiting for me on the promenade deck, but he needs to be up here, where there's still a chance of rescue."

She moved out of line, but Adele tightened the grip of her hands and held her firm.

"No! Jocelyn, I won't let you risk your life for his!"

She tried to pull free but Adele was stronger—and even more intense. Eyes blazing, Adele suddenly began to make all sorts of absurd claims against Tad. He was a liar. He was only using her to advance himself in her father's company. He made lewd suggestions. He pressed his body to hers and touched and kissed her against her objections.

It was insane. Absurd.

"Stop!" Jocelyn shouted. "You're lying. Tad already told me what happened last night."

"He did?"

"Yes. You professed your love to him and he spurned it."

"I *what*?"

"I'm sorry, cousin. I know you want him for yourself, but he loves *me*. And I love him."

Adele began to shake her head furiously from side to side. "No, Jocelyn, that wasn't it at all. Listen to me. You can't trust him. He doesn't care about you. That's not what happened—"

"Don't do this," Jocelyn pleaded, her eyes filling with tears as she looked at the grip Adele had on her hands. "Please let me go."

"I can't. I won't."

Pulling back, Jocelyn looked into her cousin's face, knowing she had to do something extreme. "Don't you understand?" she whispered. "If I have to choose between him and you, I choose *him*."

Chaos reigned on every side, but in that moment there was only the two of them. Cousins, raised as sisters, the best of friends. Jocelyn could clearly see in Adele's beautiful blue eyes the hurt her words had caused. She felt bad about that, but surely someday her cousin would understand and forgive her. Jocelyn had dreamed of a husband and children of her own her whole life. Now that the chance was within her grasp, she refused to leave it behind.

As expected, Adele released her grip, dropping her arms to her sides. "You fool," she said, her voice quivering. "I hope you do find Tad. The two of you deserve each other."

Her heart heavy, her mind swirling with guilt and regret and fear, Jocelyn slowly stepped away. Then, picking up speed, she headed for the stairwell, desperate to find the man she loved before it was too late.

CHAPTER
FORTY-EIGHT

I know the bonds used to be kept in a safe." Lou gestured toward the far wall in Walter's office.

Kelsey turned to look, surprised to see a safe there, albeit one that looked far newer and more modern than Adele's. Mounted in the wall at shoulder height, it was hanging open, the picture frame that had apparently kept it hidden lying broken on the floor underneath.

"The bonds may have been in there before," Lou continued, "but they are not there now. I think Gloria took them out on Monday night and hid them somewhere else in the building so I wouldn't be able to find them."

Kelsey swallowed hard, her brain still trying to grasp the situation she found herself in.

"Where are they?" Lou persisted, glaring at her. "Where are the bonds? Where did she put them?"

Kelsey shook her head from side to side. "I promise you, Lou, I don't know. I really don't."

"Okay, we can start there, no harm done yet." He moved a step closer, still slapping the tire iron rhythmically against his palm. Behind her, Walter began rocking fiercely in his chair, trying to get loose, but it was no use. He was taped up tight with no hope of escape.

"Look, that's why I came here today," Kelsey said, taking a step backward, "to search for the bonds myself. I was hoping they might be hidden somewhere in Gloria's office. While you and Walter were in here having your meeting, I was going to go in there and root around till I found them."

"Uh-huh. Well, been there, done that. Got any other theories?"

"No, but I've been racking my brain trying to figure it out."

He glared at her, eyes narrowing. "You sure you didn't already find them when you were here last night?"

Kelsey resisted the urge to look over at Walter, who could hear their exchange.

"How did you know about that?" she asked. "Were you the one tracking us?"

Lou shrugged. "Jumping in on your transmission was the only way I could follow your activities, seeing as how you didn't think to wear your pin."

Kelsey gasped, one hand flitting to her collar, though of course the pin wasn't there. She hadn't worn it since yesterday afternoon. "My Quarter Club pin? What did you do, Lou? Put a bug in it or something?"

He shrugged. "Not exactly. A tracking device. It was the best way I could think of to keep an eye on you and those bonds."

Kelsey was dumbfounded. How had she ever trusted him, much less defended him to others?

"Speaking of transmissions," he said, holding out a hand. "Give me your cell phone."

Only then did she realize that she'd missed an opportunity, that she could have dialed with one hand in her pocket and somehow summoned help. Now it was too late for that. Reluctantly, she handed it over to him and watched as he slipped it into his jacket pocket.

"Back to the matter at hand," he snapped, "are you sure you didn't already find them when you were here last night? Walter says the bonds were never in the safe at all, but I know he's lying. Now I'm thinking maybe *you* did something with them."

"He's not lying. The bonds were kept in *Adele's* old safe, not this one."

Lou eyed her suspiciously. "Adele's old safe? There's another safe somewhere else?"

Kelsey nodded. "I found it last night and even managed to get it open. But it was empty except for my great-grandmother's diary. The bonds weren't in there."

"Where is it?"

"The safe? It's in my father's office—which used to be Adele's office, as you probably recall."

"I want to see it. Let's go."

"I'll show you, but it won't do any good. I'm telling you that it's empty."

Lou snarled, quickly losing his patience. He gestured toward the other end of the hall. With a last, desperate glance at Walter, Kelsey began walking, with Lou following closely behind. Passing the main hallway, she desperately wanted to dash out toward the reception area. Even if she couldn't get away from Lou completely, at least her actions might be noticeable on the security camera and would alert Ephraim that something bad was going on up here. But then she felt a sharp jab to her shoulder and realized it was the tip of the tire iron. Swallowing hard, she continued forward. As they passed Gloria's office, Kelsey paused, stunned at the mess she spotted inside.

"You did this?" she gasped, looking at Lou.

"I was trying to find the bonds, but no dice. Wherever she hid them, it wasn't in there. Now keep moving."

Kelsey kept going until she got to her father's office at the end of the hall and opened the door. The smell inside was the same as it had been last night—dusty and unused—but as she flipped on the light, she realized that it looked completely different now. This office had been tossed as well, with papers strewn everywhere, cabinet doors open, drawers upended onto the floor.

"When did you have time to do all of this?" she couldn't help but ask as she gazed at the mess in dismay. "How did you even get in without security seeing you?"

"It wasn't difficult. You had set up our little meeting for four o'clock, so I called Walter directly and suggested he and I get together an hour early. I told him we needed to speak privately before you joined us. When he showed up at the back door at two forty-five, I was already there waiting for him, so he let me come on in and we walked up the back stairs together. What an idiot."

Eyes scanning the disaster he'd made of the room, Kelsey tried to understand what he was telling her. "I'm confused, Lou. What about the merger? Was that just some sort of ruse to get into the building?"

"Not at all. I really wanted that to happen, more than you can imagine."

She turned to look at him, wishing she could find inside the man she'd always thought she knew.

"Then why do all of this? You had to know that once you roughed up Walter and trashed everything the deal would be off."

Lou shook his head sadly. "Kiddo, I knew the deal was off the minute you called and asked me to bring along an audit and the contact info for my investors. You were on to me. You'd figured things out. At that point the only option left was to get the bonds and get out of town. It wasn't my first choice, but ten million dollars, give or take, can go a long way in helping a guy get established somewhere else with a new identity. A new life."

She looked at him, sickened by the normalcy of his tone, his face. They might as well have been discussing dinner plans, not theft and lies and brutality.

"Enough talk. Keep moving." With the tire iron, he poked her again on her shoulder blade, harder this time, so she continued on to the closet and opened the door. Though he had clearly rifled through the shelves during his search earlier, it seemed that he hadn't thought to clear them off completely so he could see what was behind them.

Pushing aside some papers that had fallen to the floor, she knelt down in front of the left wall and pulled off the stacks of old files. Lou came and stood behind her, and as soon as the black metal door became visible, he let out a low whistle.

"Good girl. I knew this was going to work out well, having you here. Open it up."

Kelsey turned to look at him over her shoulder, realizing for the first time what a strong, imposing figure he was. For years, she'd thought of this man as all bark and no bite.

Now she realized nothing could be further from the truth.

"I'll open it, Lou, but there's nothing in there."

He didn't reply, so she reached up and began twisting the dial, her hands trembling fiercely. In fact, they were shaking so much that she messed up twice and had to start over.

"Come on, come on!" he snapped.

"I'm trying! You're scaring me."

He grunted as he took a step back. "I don't want to hurt anybody. I just want what's coming to me."

"What's *coming* to you? Those bonds belong to my family and to this company, not to you. How could you possibly think you have the right to take them for yourself?" She glanced back to see him shaking his head.

"This is a last resort, kiddo. It wasn't the original plan, not by any means."

Jaw clenched, she told herself to calm down as she turned to the numbers in the combination. "And what was the original plan?"

He didn't respond, so she added, "I'm assuming Gloria was in on it with you?"

Again, he was quiet for a long moment. "Yeah. We've been working toward this for five years, ever since the day your father passed us over for promotion and brought in someone else from the outside."

Kelsey swallowed hard, her fingers still slowly turning the dial. "What were you guys hoping to accomplish?"

"Can't you guess? We wanted to set things right, to establish the leadership structure your father should have put in place when he first retired—me as the CEO, Gloria as the COO, and Walter nowhere to be found."

"And how were you going to do that?"

"It was all a matter of mathematics. We knew that with Nolan no longer at the helm and stupid Hallerman in his place, this company would eventually devalue enough that I could afford to merge back in. That's all we wanted, to be in the top two spots at B & T. Nothing else would have changed. You would still have been our rising star. All we were doing was fixing what your father broke when he made the wrong decisions five years ago."

"And that's why you gave me faked data in your financing request?"

"Oh, you figured that out too? Gloria worried that you and Cole would talk, but when Cole quit in a huff over your beating him out on the deal, we knew we were set. He played right into our hands."

Kelsey's mind worked hard to grasp what he was telling her. She couldn't fathom how they allowed her to suffer such collateral damage.

"And where did the bonds figure into that plan?" she asked tightly.

"Don't be naive, Kelsey. The bonds were the key to everything. It was to be a simple acquisition asset sell-off."

Stunned, Kelsey spun around to face him. "Do you mean to tell me you were going to use this company's own assets to finance your purchase?"

He grinned proudly. "That's the way it's done, kiddo. With the bonds as collateral, I could easily get a short-term loan to buy controlling interest of B & T, and then once I had control, I could authorize the sale of the bonds to pay back the loan. It's brilliant, don't you think?"

She merely glared at him.

"Oh, don't look so shocked," he sneered. "You were trying to do the same thing—find the bonds, cash them in, and use the money to buy controlling interest and stop the Queen's Fleet takeover."

"That's not the same thing at all! B & T has a right to those bonds. You don't."

"A mere technicality. The end result would have been the same, except with my plan, the leadership would have been far more effective. Walter Hallerman is a fool—and so was your father for putting him at the helm. This company needed the vision and the experience that Gloria and I would have brought to the table instead."

"That's debatable, Lou. I think we were starting to do pretty well without you."

"Are you kidding me? Five years ago this company was worth upwards of seventy million dollars! By December it was down to less than half that much."

"Well, sure, but an initial dip was to be expected, especially after my dad's stroke. We've been rebounding lately."

"Yeah, I know you have. That's what finally forced our hand. We knew if we didn't move soon, the value would rise so high that I'd lose any chance of buying back in forever. That's where your cousin Rupert came in."

Kelsey's eyes widened. She wanted to stall so he would keep talking, but he was watching her too closely. When he slapped the tire iron in his hand again, she had no choice but to end the turn of the dial at the final number in the combination.

With a click of the tumblers, the safe was unlocked. Kelsey gripped the handle, twisted, and pulled the door open to reveal the small, empty chamber inside. She was tempted to say, "I told you so," but she didn't want to antagonize Lou. Instead, she just sat back on her heels so that he could peer inside. "See? Like I said, they're not here."

Bending, he craned his neck to take a look, his face hardening into stone. Terrified that his next move might be to rough her up as he'd done to Walter, she tried desperately to think of some way to change his focus and calm him down.

"Listen, Lou, we're not going to get anywhere if you keep insisting I have the bonds. I don't. But if we put our heads together, maybe we can still figure out where they are."

He didn't reply, but neither did he strike out against her.

"Obviously, Gloria took them out of the safe and put them somewhere else," she continued. "It would help if I understood why she did that. Can you explain it to me? What were you two planning, and how did Rupert Brennan fit into that plan?"

Lou stood up straight and walked to the doorway of the office. Then he gestured for her to get up and move to the nearest chair. Was it now her turn to be bound and gagged and beaten? Her eyes scanned the room for any potential weapons she could grab, but nothing was within reach that could begin to compete with his tire iron—especially given the muscle he could put behind it. She sat and waited for him to continue.

"Rupert, right," he said, going on with his story. "Like I said, B & T was starting to rebound. We had to do something to reverse that upward trend, so I came up with the Rupert idea. Gloria had dealt with the man in the past and had his address and stuff, so I made her type up a letter that would convince him to come to the meeting. She gave it to me, along with an invitation to the event, and I was supposed to add in some cash and send it on. But then, when it was almost time to put the letter in the box, she chickened out. Told me to wait, that there was something else she wanted to try first, something that would be far less damaging to the company in the long run."

"What was that?"

"What do you think? The threat of a hostile takeover. She figured if Pamela Greeley started breathing down everyone's necks, B & T's board might just get nervous enough to accept my offer for a friendly merger instead. It wouldn't be ideal, as far as they were concerned, but it was still better than getting Clean Sweeped, if you know what I mean."

Kelsey felt nauseated. She had played right into Lou and Gloria's hands, encouraging Walter to reconsider Lou's standing offer. She'd even said something like, *"A friendly merger has to be better than a hostile takeover."* How could she have been so blind?

"But you got your hostile takeover attempt," she said, shaking her head. "Why did you end up playing the Rupert card too?"

Lou switched hands with the tire iron and began slapping it against his other palm. "Because Pamela took too long. Gloria gave her the tip about making an offer almost a month ago, but the woman didn't act on it until Monday. By then it was too late. We had already given up on that and gone back to plan A."

"But actually you got both—a takeover attempt *and* Rupert's outburst."

Lou nodded gleefully. "I know! We didn't plan it that way, but it ended up being a real one-two punch. It worked like a dream. Between those two events, the value of B & T fell to an all-time low."

Kelsey closed her eyes, terrified to ask the obvious question. "So if everything was going so right with your plan, what went wrong? How did Gloria end up dead?"

Lou began to pace, holding the metal rod in front of him as if he might strike out with it at any moment.

"Gloria killed herself out of remorse, I'm sure. She started going weak on me in the eleventh hour, losing her nerve."

Kelsey held her tongue, waiting for him to continue. When he spoke, it was in a high-pitched imitation of Gloria.

"'We can't destroy the Tate name just for our own selfish gains,' she told me. The closer it got, the more she kept talking about Adele and the legend and the legacy and all that. Give me a break."

As he spoke, an idea came to Kelsey, a way that she could get in front of a security camera after all.

"The display case!" she cried suddenly. "What if Gloria hid the bonds in the display case?"

Lou hesitated, his eyes narrowing. "Out there in the lobby?"

Kelsey nodded. "Yeah! I saw the key to that cabinet just the other day in Gloria's desk. What do you want to bet that the reason she had it out was because she went in there the other night and hid the bonds inside?"

He studied her suspiciously, but after a few moments he nodded, gesturing toward the hall. "Worth a try," he said. "Let's take a look."

Kelsey stood and began moving up the hall, praying that Ephraim was still downstairs and that he was watching the security screen. Stopping by Gloria's office to get the key, she had to dig through the rubble but finally found it. Holding it aloft like a prize, she looked to Lou, who nodded approvingly. They continued onward. As they went past Walter's open door, she tried to look inside but felt the sharp jab of the tire iron. Even the brief glimpse she'd gotten told her that nothing had changed. The man was still bound and gagged in his chair.

Out in the reception area, Kelsey walked straight to the display case and unlocked it with trembling hands. She wasn't sure of her plan, but somehow she needed Ephraim to notice what they were doing. How could she send him a signal of some kind? As she swung open the mahogany-framed side door of the case, it came to her: The slower she worked, the more frustrated Lou would become. Eventually, he might even start waving around the tire iron or even push her aside and start trashing the case's contents himself, the same way he'd torn up the offices. Ephraim would never miss that.

Kelsey dragged things out as long as she could. Slowly, she began by removing Adele's old Bible with care, and then she flipped through the pages one by one, searching for the bonds inside.

"Hurry up," Lou barked, crossing to a nearby chair and having a seat. Though he rested the tire iron on his lap, on the camera it probably just looked like some innocent cane or a pole.

Kelsey set down the Bible and moved on to the next most logical hiding places for the bonds—the memoir, the menu, and the stationery. As she carefully flipped through each, she glanced at Lou, looking for signs of frustration to appear. Nothing else yet.

The clothing would have to be next, she realized, so she started with the hat, and even as she reached for it, she wondered if perhaps she might actually be onto something. This case would have made an interesting hiding place for the bonds—at least on a temporary basis. With trembling hands, she lifted the hat from the display but was disappointed to see that it was empty.

She reached for the hand muff and then the gloves, also to no avail. Finally, she was just peering down inside the second glove when she heard the "ding" of the elevator. The doors whisked open and off stepped Ephraim. Immediately, he came through to reception.

"Kelsey, what are you doing with those things? I'm not comfortable with this, not comfortable at all."

At that moment he glanced over toward Lou and something seemed to register in his face. Was it the tire iron? The aggressive posture? Whatever it was, Ephraim reached for something at his waistband just as Lou's hand slid into his jacket. In a flash, Lou drew his hand back out, bearing a gun.

Then he shot.

Ephraim crumbled to the ground.

Not caring if her actions ended up getting her shot as well, Kelsey dropped the glove and ran to her friend, trying to cradle his massive frame in her arms. As she did, her fingers grazed something hard and square at his back. Heart racing, she discreetly pulled it loose from where it was clipped to his belt, praying it was a Taser. As she bent over Ephraim, she slipped the device into her pocket.

He was either unconscious or dead, but before she could figure out which it was, Kelsey felt the cold steel of the gun against her temple.

"Enough talk," Lou said softly. "I love you, kiddo, but I promise I'll pull this trigger if you make me. I'm asking you one last time. Where...are... the...bonds?"

She closed her eyes, praying God would protect her.

Then she heard the click of the safety being released.

CHAPTER
FORTY-NINE

April 15, 1912

ADELE

A dele hovered there, stunned and furious as she continued moving with the mass of people toward the waiting lifeboats.

She could hear the crew yelling for women and children. She could see the men and older boys being pulled from the line. She could feel the push of the hands behind her, everyone impatient to get off the sharply tilting ship before it went down. She looked back and could no longer see Jocelyn. She looked forward but saw no sign of Rowan.

Then she looked to her right and met the eyes of the crewman who was assisting people into the lifeboat. He nodded at her and she knew her time for a decision had come.

He reached for her, and after a moment's hesitation, she took his hand. He guided her into the boat, and she dropped onto a seat. Another young woman was pushed in next to her, and Adele turned to look at the terrified stranger.

A shiver ran through Adele's body. The person sitting next to her should be *Jocelyn*. Instantly coming to her senses, she jumped up and grabbed onto the crewman's arm. She knew what she had to do. She had to get out of this lifeboat and go back and get her cousin.

She wouldn't leave without her, even if it meant not leaving at all.

CHAPTER
FIFTY

"O kay, okay!" Kelsey cried, wincing at the feel of the metal against her skin. "You win. Cole has them. Cole Thornton. We found them last night and decided he would hold on to them for safekeeping."

With that, she felt the gun being removed from her temple.

"Thank you," he said softly. "That's what I needed to know."

Eyes still closed, she buried her head against Ephraim's broad shoulder, praying she hadn't just taken them from the frying pan into the fire. And while she would never, ever want to put Cole in danger, at this point he seemed to be their only hope.

"Call him."

Opening her eyes, she looked up to see Lou with the gun still in one hand and her cell phone in the other.

"What?"

"Call Cole. Tell him you need him to bring you the bonds right away. Have him go to the back door and tell him you'll meet him there."

Her hands trembling so violently she could barely function, Kelsey reached up for the phone.

Trying not to fall apart completely, she dialed Cole's number. As she did, she discreetly turned down the volume with her thumb in the hopes that she could pull this off without Lou being able to hear what she was doing.

"Put it on speaker," he commanded, dashing her hopes.

She did as he directed, her pulse surging at the sound of Cole's voice.

"Kelsey? Hey. That took longer than I expected. You okay?"

"Hi, Cole. I'm here at the meeting and need you to do me a favor. Lou and Walter need to see the bonds. Can you bring them over to B & T?"

"Bring you the bonds? What are you talking about?"

Kelsey took a deep breath and let it out slowly. *Please, Lord, help him understand what I'm doing.*

"It's okay, Cole," she said. "I've already told them. In fact, they're here on the speakerphone with me now. You don't have to pretend. I just need you to bring us the bonds right away, okay?"

Please let him get the message loud and clear.

After a beat he said, "Sure, but it might take a while. I moved them to the safe down at the office."

Kelsey looked up at Lou apologetically. Then she said, "I thought we agreed you'd keep them at your place, Cole."

"We did, but I got nervous. Sorry for being extra cautious. I was trying to protect them."

"Well, whatever. Go get them and bring them here as quickly as you can. Come to the back door. Text me once you've arrived, and I'll come down and meet you there."

"Will do."

"Thanks, Cole," she said softly, and then she disconnected the call.

Placing the phone back in Lou's waiting hand, she looked up at him, hoping he'd bought their performance.

"All right, get up," he told her, gesturing with the gun. "Time to take a walk."

Grabbing her firmly by the wrist, he pulled her away from Ephraim and to her feet. Overpowered by his brute strength, she was unable to resist as he began dragging her down the hall. Soon they were in the executive conference room and then in the stairwell.

"Where are we going?" she demanded, wishing she could take just five seconds to examine whatever it was she had taken from Ephraim. If it was a Taser, she just might be able to stop things from going any further.

If it wasn't, she might end up getting herself shot.

"Let's just say I need a little insurance policy," Lou told her as they went down the stairs.

She thought they would go down to the first floor and then wait at the bottom, but instead, when they got there, he surprised her by pressing the gun to the small of her back and pushing open the door.

"Here's what we're going to do," Lou whispered in her ear as they both stepped outside. "We're going to cross the street and wait over there in the alley. Then we're going to watch. If Cole shows up alone, no problem. But if he shows up with some friends, specifically friends in blue uniforms, then you and I are out of here. It's that simple."

With that, he gripped her elbow and began to propel her forward. With his gun still pressed discreetly at her back, Lou forced her to walk to their vantage point about a hundred feet away. Once there, they stood in the shadows of the alley where they could see the back side of the Brennan & Tate building without being seen. Unfortunately for Kelsey, as was typical for a Saturday, this part of the financial district was practically deserted.

Perhaps that was for the best, she decided. At least this way, if there were gunplay, fewer people were around to get hurt.

Hoping to distract Lou from his vigil, Kelsey tried to pull him back into their earlier conversation, but he wasn't having any of it. The third time he told her to be quiet, he emphasized the point by jabbing the gun's barrel into her spine. Wincing from the pain, she kept her mouth shut after that.

Finally, after the longest ten minutes of her life, some sort of movement caught their eye. With a gasp she realized what they were seeing: Three police cars were coming up the road behind the building and pulling to a stop about a block away.

"Looks like my insurance policy paid off. Make one sound, Kelsey, and you're dead."

With a jerk Lou turned her around and forced her to walk up the alleyway in the opposite direction. As they went, she said a silent prayer for protection, followed by thanks that at least Walter and Ephraim would now be discovered and get the medical attention they so desperately needed.

At the other end of the alley, they emerged at a cross street and kept going, angling down the sidewalk to a parking garage halfway up the block. It, too, seemed deserted, and soon Kelsey was being shoved into a vehicle—not onto a seat but into its trunk!

She tried to struggle against Lou as he forced her inside, but it was no use. Between his strength and his gun, she was outmatched. With panic rising in her throat, she watched as he closed the lid down on her, and then she was lying alone in the dark.

Bracing herself, she listened as Lou got into the driver's seat and closed the door. She waited for the car to start, but instead all she heard was Lou's voice, and it sounded as though he was having a telephone conversation.

"Nice try. Did you think I was stupid enough to wait there for you? Tough luck. We're long gone."

Cole. He must be talking to Cole.

"Here's what you're going to do now," Lou continued. "Without telling the police or anyone else this time, you're going to bring those bonds somewhere else."

Another long silence.

"Thatta boy. Go to Bowling Green Park and have a seat on a bench to await further instructions."

And that was it. He must have hung up, because the car roared to life and then they were off.

Kelsey tried not to panic. She told herself not to cry. Instead, as she was bounced and jostled in the tight space, she willed her eyes to get used to the darkness, pulling out the item she'd taken from Ephraim.

She needed to see what it was, but it was just too dark in there. At least she could feel the size and shape. It was smooth, about the size and weight of a man's electric razor and had an ergonomic shape to it, her hand fitting naturally around one end. At the other end was some sort of symbol, and as her eyes adjusted she thought she could make out a lightning bolt.

It had to be a Taser.

Feeling more empowered now that she had a weapon, Kelsey studied it to make sure she understood how it worked. On one side, near the front, was a round button with an arrow pointing forward. She assumed this was a safety of some kind and would have to be pushed in the direction the arrow was showing before the weapon could work.

Finally, she eased the Taser back into her pocket and began to look around for some sort of latch or hook that she might pull to release the trunk lid. Before she could find anything, however, she realized that the car was slowing to a stop, and then it turned off. The drive had been so short, she knew they couldn't have gone more than half a mile.

Kelsey braced herself for the trunk lid to fly open, but instead she heard the sound of Lou making another call from inside the car. He spoke more softly this time, which made her wonder if they were in a more populated area. She couldn't make out all of his words, though she felt sure he was talking to Cole again and that he was giving instructions for where he was to go next with the bonds—bonds Cole didn't even have. Thank goodness for the Taser.

The call finished, Lou was making a new kind of noise, some of it directly behind her, when suddenly light came spilling in over her shoulders.

"Come out this way," she heard him say. "It's less noticeable."

Twisting around in the tight space, Kelsey realized he had pulled down the seat back, which gave access to the trunk from the backseat. Unbelievable.

She managed to work her way out through the opening, and soon she was climbing from the car onto pavement, blinking at the vivid sunset on the distant horizon. They were at the river, the Statue of Liberty standing in proud silhouette against a yellow-and-orange sky.

The heliport. They were at the Downtown Manhattan Heliport.

Lou would be making his getaway by helicopter.

He gestured for her to walk, and so she did, the now-familiar gun pressing into her back as they crossed the paved surface that jutted out into the East River like a big cement peninsula. They reached the edge, where concrete met water. Turning around so they were facing the parking lot, their backs to Lady Liberty, they leaned back against the low railing. The gun remained where it was, but now that she knew she had a Taser, Kelsey wasn't nearly as frightened as before. Mostly, she just needed the right opportunity to use it.

"What are we doing now?"

"Waiting on Cole," Lou replied. "He has ten minutes to get here from Bowling Green Park. If he has the bonds, everything will be fine."

Kelsey wanted to turn and look at Lou, to ask him how he could have done any of this. But instead she continued to face forward and asked him to finish his story from earlier.

"You were telling me how Gloria began to lose her nerve," she prodded, hoping to distract him with his own words while she got a good grip on the Taser in her pocket. To her relief, he picked things up right where he'd left off.

"Yeah, it all started falling apart on Monday. I called and set up a meeting with a creditor for later in the week so I could line up financing and be ready to roll with a merger if everything went as planned. The problem was, they wanted collateral. The bonds *were* my collateral, so I called Gloria Monday night and told her I needed to borrow them for a few days. She agreed to meet up with me Tuesday morning and hand them over, but then she never showed."

"Wait a minute," Kelsey said. "You called Gloria Monday night? About what time?"

He shrugged. "I don't know. Ten? Ten thirty?"

"From a pay phone near Times Square?"

"Yeah," he said, sounding surprised. "How'd you know that?"

"The cops are stumped and asking around. What were you doing over there?"

"I was sticking with the plan. See, Gloria and I knew that Rupert had gotten to town, and we were afraid he might try to speak with you that night, privately, instead of waiting to confront you the next day at the ceremony. So we left show tickets for him and his sister at the hotel's front desk just to be safe. My job was to keep an eye on the two of them from a distance to make sure they didn't take any detours or anything. While they were in the theater, I was checking my voice mail when I heard that message from my lender about needing collateral. So I called Gloria to tell her I had to borrow the bonds."

"Why use a pay phone?"

He chuckled softly. "Gloria said Vern had been acting real suspicious of her lately, hinting that he thought she might be involved in an affair. What a joke, a player like that being suspicious of his own wife. I didn't want my name popping up on her cell phone and making him think she was involved with me, so I used a pay phone instead."

Kelsey let that sink in, thinking how every piece seemed to be falling into place like a puzzle—yet there was still so much she didn't know.

"Okay, keep going," she said. "Gloria was supposed to bring you the bonds Tuesday morning, but she stood you up. What happened next?"

"Not much. I kept calling her all day but she wouldn't answer and she didn't return any of my calls. Finally, after the big blowup at the ceremony, I sent you on your way and then I called her and told her I wanted to come upstairs so we could have this out then and there. I knew she was losing her nerve, but I had worked too hard for too long to let it all go now."

Kelsey blinked, trying to remember the sequence of events from that insane afternoon. The last she'd seen of Lou that day, she'd been riding away in a taxi and he was trying to hail a cab of his own to head to a meeting uptown. Her face flushing with heat, she realized now that there had been no meeting. He'd been lying to cover his tracks.

"How did you get back into the building?"

"Gloria gave me her security code. By that point she was as ready to be done with things as I was."

Kelsey tried not to shudder as she thought about where the story was leading. "So you used her code to get back in and headed up to her office—"

"Not to her office, too risky. She was waiting for me in the conference room off the stairwell. We talked there."

Kelsey closed her eyes. There. Where Gloria died.

"She was a mess," Lou continued, "all in a tizzy about 'we shouldn't have done this' and 'we shouldn't have done that.' I thought it was a little late to put a stop to things by that point. Rupert had already spoken out at the meeting. Pamela had already initiated the takeover. Everything was falling perfectly into place—and all of a sudden Gloria wanted to pull the plug? That was crazy."

Kelsey's eyes opened, for the first time feeling some hint of gratitude for the person Gloria had been. If she'd had remorse, that had to mean she hadn't been completely bad to the core.

"Any idea why she changed her mind?" Kelsey asked softly, watching the Brooklyn skyline as the last reflections of the sunset faded from view.

Lou stiffened as a family emerged from the nearby heliport building and noisily began making their way across the parking lot. Once they were in their car and on their way, he relaxed and answered her question.

"At first I thought this was all about the bonds. She told me that when she got them out of the safe on Monday night, she saw they were bearer bonds and realized she couldn't let me borrow them after all. She had made photocopies for me to take to the creditor instead."

The photocopies of the bonds. Kelsey nodded.

"The problem was that along with bonds, she found Adele's old diary. Said she stayed up all night to read the stupid thing. By morning she'd done a full one eighty. Said she just couldn't go through with it, couldn't do this to the Tates or to the memory of Adele. 'Adele Tate went through so much,' she told me. 'Now that I've read the diary, I believe she really was who she said she was. How can we challenge that for our own selfish gain?' It was ridiculous."

Kelsey realized Gloria must have known Lou would try to take the bonds from the safe himself, so she'd hidden them somewhere else, somewhere he wouldn't think to look for them.

"So she really did commit suicide out of remorse," Kelsey said sadly.

"Yeah, something like that," Lou replied.

Then they grew silent, his words hanging in the air between them. There was something about his tone, his attitude. Stunned, Kelsey turned to face him despite the gun in his hand.

"You killed her, didn't you?" she whispered, all of the pieces finally falling into place.

"Look, Gloria was my friend. I just wanted her to stick with the plan."

"What did you do, Lou?"

At least he had the nerve to look ashamed, his cheeks flushed and his eyes darting away nervously. "It was an accident. We were arguing. I had backed her up against the wall. The cord was hanging there, so I used it. By then I was just trying to scare her into giving up the bonds. If she wasn't going to follow through with the merger, those bonds were all I had left for my trouble. I *earned* them, but she didn't see it that way."

"No…" Kelsey whispered.

"I gave her a couple chances," Lou continued, "but she just wouldn't tell me. I guess maybe I choked her too hard, or one time too many. I didn't mean to kill her. I only wanted her to cooperate. She did it to herself, really. If only she had talked."

Kelsey had been right earlier. This man *was* an animal.

"Anyway, once I realized what had happened, it wasn't hard to set things up to look like a suicide. I knew if it was going to be convincing there had to be a note, so I grabbed her phone and sent you that text."

Kelsey remembered every word:

> Goodbye, Tater Tot. I'm so sorry for what I've done. Please forgive me for taking what wasn't mine and for ending my own life. With love and regret, Gloria

"It was pretty convincing," she said evenly. "You even thought to call me Tater Tot."

Looking less ashamed, he met her eyes and smiled. "Nice touch, huh? I had to find some way to make you believe it really had come from her. Then I remembered her pet name for you and that was that."

Kelsey took a step back and placed her hands on her hips, in preparation for pulling the Taser from her pocket. "You even managed to write the note in such a way that it led all of us to put the full blame on her for everything."

Lou straightened his shoulders, almost proudly. "Once I got over the shock of what happened, I realized my original plan could still work, even without having her help from the inside. I just needed someone else who would go to bat for me instead."

Kelsey studied his face, trying to understand what he was saying. Then it hit her.

"That's where I came in," she said slowly. "You used me. Planted suggestions in my head. Tracked my every move."

"Hey, it wasn't hard to manipulate you five years ago. I figured it was worth a shot again now. I knew if I played my cards right, you could be my biggest advocate."

Kelsey felt like such a fool. With anger rising up inside her, she slid her hand into her pocket and gripped the barrel of the Taser. Just as she was about to pull it out, Lou glanced over her shoulder and said, "Well, here's lover boy. It's about time." Then he reached out, grabbed her arm, and jerked her back around against him and pressed the gun's barrel into her back.

Heart pounding, she had no choice but to watch as Cole came walking toward them, an envelope in his hand.

"That's close enough," Lou said. "You have the bonds?"

Cole nodded as he came to a stop.

"Take 'em out so I can see."

"Why don't you do it yourself?" Cole challenged.

"Because my hands are full," Lou replied simply. "Or at least one of them is."

"He has a gun," Kelsey added.

Watching Cole, she could see how hard he was working to restrain himself. He looked ready to pounce, but not at the risk of her life.

"Take out the bonds and hold them up," Lou repeated evenly.

Kelsey knew it was the moment of truth. There were no bonds. No doubt, inside that envelope were just blank pieces of paper. Again, she slid her hand into her pocket and wrapped it around the barrel of the Taser.

Cole turned his attention to the envelope, pulling open the flap and then removing the folded-up contents from inside. Hands surprisingly steady, he unfolded the pages and then turned them around for Lou to see. Kelsey was shocked to realize that these weren't blank pages at all but were instead what looked very much like the actual bonds themselves. Was it possible he'd found them in such a short time?

"All right, good enough," Lou said. "Put 'em back."

Cole did as Lou instructed and then handed over the envelope. Lou used his free hand to slip it into his inside jacket pocket.

"Nice doing business with you kids," he said with a grin. Then he pulled out his car keys and tossed them to the ground several feet beyond where Cole was standing. "Here's the plan. Cole, I need you to get in my car, the silver Lexus in the first row there, and wait. Don't call anyone, don't signal anyone, don't tell anyone. Just sit and wait. I'm taking Kelsey on a little helicopter ride. Once I'm certain that my escape arrangements haven't been compromised, I'll drop her off and text you with instructions on where you can find her."

"Don't you dare hurt her," Cole hissed between clenched teeth.

"I won't unless you talk. Keep your mouth shut, and she'll be fine. Otherwise, the deal's off. Just ask Kelsey. She can tell you exactly what I'm willing to do to get away with these bonds."

"Do as he says," she pleaded.

Cole gave her a long look, picked up the keys, and began walking toward Lou's car.

It was now or never. Summoning her nerve, Kelsey eased the Taser from her pocket and pushed the safety button forward to arm the device. Suddenly, it seemed to spring to life in her hand, a tiny green light glowing in the darkness.

Lou didn't seem to notice. His hand tightened on her elbow, and just as he turned them to go, she suddenly twisted her body in the opposite direction and managed to break free. She raised her weapon and pulled the trigger before he even had time to react.

It worked!

Almost instantly, the gun fell from Lou's hand and he fell backward against the low railing. As his back hit the rail, the momentum forced his body over the side of the pier and into the water. Except there was no splash.

Kelsey yelled for Cole as she ran to the rail and looked down to see Lou. He was flat on his back on some sort of dark gray metal support structure that surrounded the pier. The wires from the Taser were still hooked to his chest, and when he tried to sit up, she pressed the trigger again. In an instant, he was down. Cole appeared at her side, taking in what had just happened and giving her a quick hug.

"Better lie still, Lou," he called out gleefully. "Something tells me Kelsey's worked up enough to keep pressing that button for a good long while."

CHAPTER
FIFTY-ONE

April 15, 1912

JOCELYN

With everyone moving upward, it was nearly impossible for Jocelyn to get down the stairs, but somehow she managed to push her way through and finally reached her destination. Breaking free from the crowd, she ran to the place where Tad had said he was would wait for her.

He wasn't there.

In a panic she moved across the deck and into the smoking room, ignoring the rule against women. There were people in there, but no one seemed to notice or care. Her heart felt as if it would split in two, but then she spotted Tad across the room. Exhilarated, she ran to him and tumbled into his arms. He gripped her tightly in return. The ship was listing even further now, and he let go of her to steady himself against a table.

"Do you have the bonds?" he asked.

She looked at him, blinking. "The bonds?"

He nodded. "I saw your father in line at the purser's desk. I know he must have retrieved them. Given that they are not letting men onto the lifeboats, I feel sure he handed them over to one of you."

"He gave them to Adele."

Tad looked at her in disbelief, disappointment shining in his eyes.

"They're her bonds, not mine," she hurriedly explained, though she didn't know why it mattered. They needed to get outside. They needed to get in a lifeboat.

Fearing she might fall from the steep tilt of the room, she gripped his muscular arms and looked into his eyes. "Tad, we're together now, and that's all that matters."

"That's all that matters," he echoed. "It would be good to find Adele too. Do you think I can locate her on the boat deck?"

"Yes. We should go now. There aren't many lifeboats left."

To Jocelyn's surprise, Tad said no. He pointed toward a group of men sitting together across the room and explained. "They say a rescue ship is on the horizon. We should just wait for it here."

"But I promised my father I would get on a lifeboat—"

Gently, Tad cupped his hands on each side of her face and gazed into her eyes. "Are you a child or are you a woman? Because a woman makes her own decisions."

Her eyes filling with tears, she knew he was right. She'd already rejected Adele in Tad's favor. Now she would reject her own father as well.

"I love you," she whispered.

Stepping back and taking her hands in his, he helped her into a nearby chair and then knelt beside it.

"Tell you what," he said, reaching up to brush an errant lock of hair from her cheek. "You wait right here. I'll go find out for sure about that rescue ship and then I'll come back."

"Tad, no—"

"Shhh," he said, putting a finger to her lips. "Don't panic, don't fear. Don't move. I promise you that we will make it off this ship one way or the other. Do you trust me?"

Eyes swimming with tears, she nodded and whispered, "I do."

"Then do as I say and stay here. I'll be right back," he said, and then he walked away.

She did as he told her, still feeling frightened but somehow safe in the protection of his love. Time moved slowly as she waited, the many minutes that passed clearly marked by the continued tilting of the room. She watched as items started to fall off the shelves. She watched as the men who had been waiting for the rescue ship left, one by one. She watched as no one came back for her.

She was still sitting there when a man approached, asking if she knew where he could find pen and paper.

"I need to write a note to my family in America," he explained hurriedly. "If I can do that, perhaps someone can carry it onto a lifeboat for me."

She directed him to the second-class library, and then she sat there and watched him go.

Looking around, she saw that the room was nearly empty. She saw the angle of the ship. Stunned, the reality of the situation finally closed in on her.

Tad had abandoned her. He wasn't coming back. He lied.

Adele had been right about him after all.

CHAPTER
FIFTY-TWO

An hour later, Lou had been driven away in handcuffs, his car impounded, and Kelsey and Cole had been delivered back to the much warmer and brighter Brennan & Tate offices. They were sitting in a fifth floor meeting room and telling their story to Detective Hargrove while other police personnel once again processed the scene around them. At least there had been no deaths this time.

Kelsey had been concerned about the health of Ephraim and Walter, but according to the detective, both men had already been taken to the hospital, treated, and released.

"Released? But Ephraim was shot!"

"Fortunately, he was wearing a vest. From what I understand, he has a nasty bruise on his chest, but otherwise his biggest problem is the blow he took to the head when the impact knocked him onto the ground. He has a mild concussion."

Kelsey nodded, just then realizing that would explain the lack of blood from a gunshot wound.

"Security guards in bulletproof vests?" Cole asked skeptically.

The detective shrugged. "What can I say? This is Lower Manhattan in a post nine eleven world. These days, that's SOP."

"Thank goodness," Kelsey added.

To her surprise, the detective admitted they had known all along Gloria had been murdered but had kept the possibility of suicide out there, hoping that would allow the killer to let down his guard.

"The ligature on the neck for a self-inflicted hanging is completely different than that for a strangling done by someone else," he explained. "So we knew right away what had happened. We just needed to find out who did it. Now we have our answers, thanks in a large part to you, Kelsey."

Though the police would be keeping the Taser and eventually returning it to Ephraim, they let her have her cell phone back. She also learned the truth about the bonds Cole had given to Lou. Thinking fast after her strange phone call earlier requesting the bonds, Cole had scanned the photocopies, pulled them into a photo editing program, and quickly played with the images. Then he'd printed them out in color and shoved them into an envelope. Voilà. At a quick glance in dim light, they had looked like the real thing, which was all he'd needed to accomplish.

"I guess we may never know where Gloria hid the real bonds," Kelsey said sadly.

"Don't be so sure about that," Cole replied. Eyes twinkling, he added, "I have an idea, anyway."

Rising, he led Kelsey and the detective back out into the reception area. Things were a mess there, the items she had pulled from the case at gunpoint exactly where she'd left them. Only now they were marked with little plastic numbers, which the detective explained had been added by the crime scene photographers.

"May I?" Cole asked, looking to the detective as he gestured toward one of the items on the floor.

"Go ahead."

Carefully, Cole picked up the white fur hand muff that had once belonged to Adele. Kelsey's heart sank.

"The bonds aren't in there," she said. "I already looked."

"Maybe so," Cole replied, "or maybe I know something you don't."

"Oh?"

"When you walked out of my place earlier, you accidentally left the diary behind," he explained. "I saw it on the couch once you were gone and took a quick look inside. Mostly, I was just interested in reading the part about the sinking of *Titanic* before I returned it to you."

"I hadn't reached that part yet," Kelsey admitted. "What did it say?"

"It told how, once the ship hit the iceberg and Adele's uncle realized it would sink—and that only women and children were being allowed onto the lifeboats—he gave the bonds to Adele and told her to hide them in a safe place. I didn't think much more about it until just a little while ago, when you were explaining to the detective about Gloria's change of heart after reading the diary. I realized that maybe, just maybe, when Gloria started looking for a hiding place for the bonds, she took a cue from Adele."

With that, Cole turned the hand muff on its side and felt around on the inner silk lining until his thumb slid under an open seam. Pulling that seam wider revealed the perfect hiding place for a woman's valuables. There, tucked inside the muff under the fabric of the liner, were six of the most beautiful papers Kelsey had ever seen.

The bonds.

Another half hour passed before they were finally finished and free to go, the bonds securely given over to Mr. Hu, who had come the moment they had called, accompanied by Thriller and Flash. First thing Monday morning, London time, Mr. Hu would initiate the necessary steps to cash in the bonds on B & T's behalf.

While they were there, Kelsey thanked all of them for their efforts. "I haven't forgotten about that finder's fee I promised."

"Neither have we," Thriller replied with a wink and a smile. "We can discuss the terms next week."

Once they were gone, the detective offered Kelsey and Cole a ride to wherever they wanted. They thankfully declined, knowing they had some business of their own to settle and preferred to walk.

When they stepped outside, they realized it was even colder than before. Cole insisted on placing his jacket around Kelsey's shoulders. They were trying to make their way through the gauntlet of reporters clustered near the entrance when a taxi pulled to a halt at the curb and out jumped Matt and his girlfriend, Tiffany.

Matt explained that as soon as they had heard on the radio what happened, they had grabbed a cab to head straight over. The four of them talked for a few minutes, and then Matt offered to go from there to their parents' house to give them the full story so they wouldn't worry when they saw it on the news. Kelsey thanked him gratefully.

"But before you go," she added, pulling him over to the side and lowering her voice so the reporters couldn't hear, "you have to explain your part in all this. Why were you and Gloria talking so much on the phone lately?"

"Aw, man, I knew you were going to bring that up," he replied, his face turning beet red. "Mostly, we were playing phone tag. Why do you always have to be so pushy anyway?"

"Answer the question, little brother. Why were you trying to reach Gloria?"

Swallowing hard, he leaned close and whispered, "Because I needed her advice."

"Advice?"

Without another word, Matt reached into his jacket pocket and discreetly pulled out a small velvet box, which he popped open with his thumb to show to Kelsey. Inside was a beautiful diamond ring, the telltale logo of Gloria's sister's jewelry store embossed in the satin lid.

"What is that?" Tiffany asked, stepping toward them.

With a heavy sigh, Matt turned toward his girlfriend and slowly lowered himself to one knee right there on the sidewalk. Holding up the box, he said, "This isn't exactly how I planned for this to go, but, Tiffany, will you marry me?"

Instantly, the throng of reporters and photographers raced their way, snapping pictures and milking the moment for all it was worth. Kelsey was thrilled, especially when Tiffany responded with an enthusiastic "Yes!" After a few minutes, Cole suggested to Kelsey that this might be a good chance for them to slip off. With a final hug for her brother and her future sister-in-law, Kelsey moved in step with Cole and they continued on their way alone, side by side, leaving the happy couple and the reporters behind.

They both seemed to have the same destination in mind, Battery Park, just a few blocks ahead. They were quiet as they walked, and as they reached the Promenade, Kelsey could feel her phone vibrating in her pocket. She glanced at the screen, surprised to see Walter's name there.

"Sorry, I need to take this," she said to Cole, and then she answered.

She and Walter talked for several minutes. The man sounded weary but assured her he was doing well. He thanked her numerous times for what she'd done to save the company and his life. She thanked him in return for his own efforts on B & T's behalf, not adding that she hoped the days of banning her from that company were a thing of the past.

"We can discuss the details later," he told her as they were wrapping up the call, "but before we hang up, I thought you'd like to hear some good news. Between the efforts of you, your grandfather, and myself, we were able to secure enough votes to gain control of the company and avoid Pamela's takeover attempt. As soon as Lou showed up today, I was going to tell him that we would be turning down his offer. My mistake was in letting him come upstairs with me before I did so. So much for trying to be polite."

"I'm so sorry for what you went through," Kelsey whispered, tears filling her eyes.

"What's done is done," he replied. "We'll pick up and move on from here. At least I didn't suffer the same fate as poor Gloria. I just wish we could have stopped this in time to save her as well. And remember Kelsey, she hid those bonds, so ultimately, at least, she tried to do the right thing. She knew those bonds would give you the funds to buy back control of the company and stop both Pamela's takeover and Lou's merger."

Once they ended their call and Kelsey hung up the phone, she dried her eyes and then looked around to see that Cole was waiting for her nearby, standing at the railing overlooking the water. Behind him was the bay and a thousand sparkling lights beyond.

Moving toward him, Kelsey could feel her heart swell with love and regret and hope all at the same time. She stopped just short, but then he opened his arms to her and she moved into his embrace. They were such a perfect fit together, like two pieces of a tightly molded puzzle. Looking into his eyes, she could see so much there. Peace. Passion.

Love.

"Remember when I told you I was almost engaged a while back but it didn't work out?" Cole whispered softly, gazing down at her as he gently brushed a lock of hair from her cheek.

She nodded, not trusting herself to speak.

"Would you like to know *why* it didn't work out?"

Again, she nodded.

"Because the night I proposed, she told me, 'You're still in love with Kelsey Tate.' She turned me down. She said she wouldn't go through life with a man whose heart wasn't a hundred percent hers."

Kelsey swallowed hard. "That must have been devastating for you," she managed to whisper.

Placing his hands on each side of her face, Cole looked intently into her eyes.

"Not at all," he replied. "Because the moment she said it, I knew it was true. I've been trying to get over you for five years, but I should have known I never could. I *love* you, Kelsey. I have never stopped loving you."

"I love *you*, Cole. I always have. I always will."

The words had been said. There was no turning back now.

Slowly, ever so slowly, he leaned his face down toward hers, both of them closing their eyes as their lips met. Their kiss was tentative at first, as if testing new territory, but then memories began to return, that delicious, familiar feeling of his mouth on hers, the kiss growing longer and deeper and more fulfilling than any they had ever shared. When it was over, he pulled her even closer and they simply clung to each other, two lost souls who had finally made their way back together, two broken hearts that had found healing in the arms where it had all begun.

"So what now?" she asked, praying this wasn't some momentary passion that he would later regret.

"I say we pick up where we left off."

"Sounds like a plan," she said, realizing how perilously close they had come to missing this second chance.

"This time around," he added, "we're a little older, hopefully somewhat wiser, and, when those inevitable conflicts arise, more willing to find a meeting point rather than walk away. I know it's been a long time, and that people can change a lot in five years, but somehow I just feel it won't be all that difficult to catch up. Who knows? Maybe someday soon we can come back here and I can take a cue from your brother's playbook."

She chuckled softly, daring to dream. "Sounds good to me."

Pulling her even closer, Cole pressed his lips to her forehead and gently kissed her there.

"Poor Gloria. She paid a heavy price for trusting Lou," she said. "But I take comfort in the fact that at least she had an eleventh hour change of heart. Lou said it was Adele's diary that did it. I just wish we could have found a way to prove Adele's identity once and for all. The diary will help, but it may not be enough to counteract the damage done by Rupert's claims."

"I guess we may never know for sure," Cole said, holding her tight.

"I guess you're right," she replied, resting her face against his chest.

At least now they knew how Gloria died, and why, and who had killed her. They had answered a myriad of questions, found the bonds, and managed to save the company.

Most importantly, along the way, Kelsey had come back to God.

Tonight Cole had come back to her.

As she looked out at the water and the sparkling lights of the shores beyond, she remembered the Bible verse Jocelyn had referred to in her letter to Adele.

All streams flow to the sea, yet the sea is never full. To the place the streams come from, there they return again.

Life was coming full circle.

Cole Thornton still loved her.

She had found strength and peace in relying on God.

Despite all they had been through, she had managed to rediscover her faith, her need for balance, *and* her true love along the way. For her, that was more than she deserved, and far more than she'd ever had the right to expect.

CHAPTER
FIFTY-THREE

April 15, 1912

ADELE

Adele knew she had to find Jocelyn. As she scrambled up to climb out of the lifeboat, an officer pushed her back onto her seat.

"Sit down and don't move!" he shouted at her. "You're unsettling the boat!"

Crewmen were in her way, pulling on the lines, as she tried again.

"But I have to get out!" she cried. "Please let me through!"

"You can't do that now!" another one yelled. "Sit down and be still, or you'll kill us all!"

Stunned, Adele did as he said, gripping tightly to the side as she felt the jerky back-and-forth motion of the lifeboat being lowered to the sea. Down and down it went toward the black water below. She looked to the ship, the commotion and noise nearly unbearable. She heard the piercing screams and cries. She saw the debris that rained down around them. She felt the shame of what she had done, and it gripped her heart like a vise.

In a moment of anger, she had abandoned the person she loved most.

When they finally landed on the water and were free of the doomed liner, she could see swimmers in the swells, trying to move toward them. But the cold water made them lethargic, and few got very far. None reached them before the crew started yelling for someone to grab an oar and pull.

She and the girl beside her both sprang into action, quickly grabbing the closest oar and pulling on it together. At first it seemed as if they were getting nowhere, but they pressed onward and gradually made progress. They rowed and rowed until a crewman said they had gone far enough. Then they released the oar and sat back in their seats. Adele looked at *Titanic*, its lights blazing, its orchestra still playing, its passengers leaping and falling into the water.

She couldn't watch any longer. She turned her attention to a sobbing old woman near her, trying to give her some comfort. A cold chill settled upon them as they floated aimlessly in the vast ocean. She thought of the bonds, safely hidden away in her hand muff, and wondered if the technology those bonds backed would end up saving her or not.

Had other ships heard the distress calls from *Titanic*'s wireless system? If so, were any of those ships on their way? Adele wondered if they would ever be found or if they would simply float here until they had all frozen to death.

Then she heard a sound like a distant explosion, and she jerked her head up. The crash and crunch of metal rang across the water as if the great ship were splitting in two. No one said a word or made a sound.

All they could do was watch in horror. Suddenly, the lights blinked and went out. The stern began to rise in the air, higher and higher until it was nearly vertical. They all looked on in shock and awe. Then it began its final descent.

Adele could barely make out the silhouette of the sinking ship in the distance. As it slowly lowered straight down into the sea, she thought absurdly what a contradiction it made—the movement of the ship itself so smooth and graceful, but the sounds so horrifying and wrong. The screech of metal. The cries of the doomed.

She closed her eyes, listening for the voice of Rowan, the voice of Jocelyn, in the crowds, but it was a cacophony of screams. Soon the sounds lessened. Eventually, they ceased.

"God help us," the woman next to her whispered, but Adele didn't know if she was asking God to get them to safety or if she was begging His forgiveness for having left others behind.

God help us, Adele echoed in her mind, her own meaning clear. She hoped desperately that Jocelyn had made it, but somehow in her heart she knew she had not. Holding in her sobs, Adele looked up at the starry sky, at the endless black horizon. For the rest of her life, she would have to live with the truth of this night.

Jocelyn was dead because she let her walk away.

CHAPTER
FIFTY-FOUR

Chelsea Piers, New York
April 15, 2012

Nine days later, Kelsey sat on a folding chair on the very pier where *Titanic* should have docked so long ago. Sadly, the great ship had never made it to these shores. On its way here, out in the frigid north Atlantic Ocean, *Titanic* struck an iceberg and sank less than three hours later. This ceremony was but one of the many events being held around the country—and indeed the world—to commemorate the anniversary of the historic event that had happened one hundred years ago on this day, when the unsinkable ship had sunk. Though they had had other options, this was the event Kelsey's family had chosen to attend, mostly because of the ease of logistics for wheelchair-bound Nolan.

A chilly wind blew off the Hudson River, undermining the sun's efforts to warm the participants who had gathered at Chelsea Piers for the occasion. Several hundred people had turned out for it, and as each speaker took his turn at the dais, loved ones huddled together to ward off the chill. To Kelsey's left was Cole, looking incredibly handsome as usual in a black double-breasted coat over a dark gray suit and maroon tie. To her right was Grandpa Jonah; her parents, Nolan and Doreen; and finally Matt and his new fiancée, Tiffany.

As chilly as it was, something about the cold seemed right to Kelsey. A number of descendants of *Titanic* passengers had turned out for the event, and together they were all feeling just a fraction of the cold that had been experienced by their forebears that fateful night so long ago.

The ceremony itself was lovely, with uniformed officers of the coast guard in attendance and several prominent speakers, including a *Titanic* historian; a representative of Harland & Wolff, the company that built *Titanic*; and even the mayor of New York City. Near the end, a commemorative marker was unveiled by two members of the coast guard as a bugler gave a painfully perfect rendition of "Taps." Watching the tribute and hearing the mournful music played, Kelsey found herself rifling her pockets yet again for tissues.

Finally, a Navy chaplain took the podium and offered a prayer to close the somber ceremony. Cole took Kelsey's gloved hand in his as they bowed their heads. After a beat, she reached out and took her grandfather's hand as well. He gave hers a tight squeeze in return, the three of them linked not just by love but by their faith.

When the prayer was over and the crowd began to disperse, Cole put his arm around Kelsey's shoulders and drew her a little closer.

"You okay?" he asked quietly, offering up a clean tissue of his own.

She accepted it gratefully and dabbed at her eyes, assuring him she was fine.

"Such a needless tragedy," she said, gazing out at the horizon and thinking of all the lives that had been lost that night for want of enough lifeboats. "I can't imagine what those people endured."

Finally, they stood and began to mingle with the others, all of them agreeing that it had been a beautiful ceremony. Gazing around at her loved ones, Kelsey couldn't help but think how grateful she was for each of them. How blessed she'd been—both with the family members who were here and those who had passed on before. Now that she had studied Adele's diary at length, Kelsey felt a kinship not just with her own great-grandmother, but also with Adele's father, Sean, and with her cousin Jocelyn and Jocelyn's parents, Rowan and Oona.

A hundred years ago, the two young women, cousins as close as sisters, had left their home in Ireland and all they had ever known and set off for America and the dream of a better life. Only Adele had made it here, but through the life she'd lived and the things she'd accomplished, she'd managed to leave a legacy for them all.

Kelsey had given her Quarter Club pin to the police last week and was back to wearing Adele's golden harp hat pin instead. Today, she had affixed it to the lapel of her navy blue wool coat. She touched the cold metal of the harp with her fingers now, still wishing they had been able to find concrete proof about Adele's identity.

A strong gust of wind sent many of the attendees toward the building at the head of the massive pier. There was to be a brief reception inside, and then the event would be complete. Kelsey's group began moving as well, Matt taking the handles of their father's chair to lead the way.

As they neared the building, two women seemed to be waiting for them. Attendees of the event, one was about forty years old, wearing a black winter jacket. The other was a white-haired lady in an old gray tweed coat, balancing with the aid of a cane.

"Excuse me," the younger woman said as they drew closer. "Are you the Tate family?"

Kelsey and the others stopped walking, several of them nodding.

"Yes?" Grandpa Jonah said, moving forward to take charge of the situation.

The younger woman smiled, introducing herself and the older woman next to her, who was her grandmother, saying that they had come from their home in western Pennsylvania specifically hoping to speak with the Tates.

"My nana has something she'd like to give to all of you," she added.

Kelsey glanced at Cole, wondering what this could be about.

"What sort of something?" Jonah asked genially. "Are you two descendants of *Titanic* passengers as well?"

"Yes, we are," the older woman said. "My grandmother's name was Annie Devlin, and she and her husband and daughter were traveling in *Titanic's* second-class section."

"Did they all survive the sinking?" Jonah asked kindly.

"Annie and her daughter made it, yes. Annie's husband did not."

Everyone nodded somberly, all too familiar with the thought.

"Annie's daughter, Daisy, was just six years old the night the ship went down. She and her mother were on one of the last lifeboats to leave the ship. The story of how they ended up on that lifeboat has been passed down through our family. Daisy grew up to become my mother, and she told the story to me. I have since shared it with my own descendants. Now I want to share it with you."

Interested to hear what she had to say but concerned about her father being out in the cold for too long, Kelsey suggested they proceed to the reception inside. They all moved together as a group into the building and followed the signs to the large room where the reception was being held. It was nothing fancy, just a few tables with finger foods and punch and a chance for attendees to mingle and to observe the various nautical mementoes on display. Kelsey, Cole, Matt, and Tiffany rounded up enough chairs so that they could sit together in a circle with the two women. After supplying the older folks and themselves with some food, they all sat, and then everyone was ready to hear the rest of what she had come here to tell them.

"The night the ship sank," the older woman said, looking from one to the other, clearly in her element as a storyteller, "Annie clung to her husband and her little girl, watching as one lifeboat after another was lowered over the side of the ship. She couldn't bear to leave her husband a moment sooner than she absolutely had to, but by the time he finally forced her to go, they realized it might be too late. With only a few lifeboats left, and hundreds of passengers crowding toward them, they feared that Annie and Daisy might not make it on one after all."

Kelsey listened, rapt. This woman's words were far more real now that she had devoured Adele's diary and experienced the sinking through her eyes.

"Somehow, with Daisy in her arms, Annie managed to push her way through the crowds. As she got closer to a lifeboat, and it looked as if they might make it on after all, people began thrusting hastily scribbled notes toward her, people who knew they were going to die and wanted to send some final word to their loved ones. Annie did what she could and ended up putting six different envelopes in her bag. Soon she and Daisy found themselves at the edge of a lifeboat behind someone they had made friends with during the voyage, a young woman named Jocelyn."

More than one gasp could be heard around the circle.

"Everything was so chaotic that night," she continued. "The next thing my grandmother knew, someone had scooped up little Daisy and plopped her into the overcrowded lifeboat. Jocelyn climbed in next, but when Annie also tried to step aboard after her, an officer pushed her away, saying that the boat was overfull and in danger of sinking if even one more passenger forced their way aboard."

Kelsey glanced at her own mother, her pulse surging at the thought.

"Annie accepted her fate, but as she was climbing down from the rail, Jocelyn must have realized that mother and daughter had been separated. Looking from one to the other, she called out to Annie and offered up her place on the lifeboat."

Tears sprang unbidden from Kelsey's eyes, and she noticed Doreen tearing up as well.

"As the women traded places, Jocelyn gave Annie a small, fat envelope with a name on front. Much like the others, she asked her to deliver it on her behalf. Of course Annie agreed. She owed her life to the girl."

Kelsey and her family members glanced at each other, and she knew they were all marveling at the incredible sacrifice of the young woman. Kelsey liked to think she would have done the same, but who could know until they were actually in such a position?

"Sadly," the old woman continued, "over the next few hours, as they floated in the ocean and waited to be rescued, that lifeboat took on some water. Annie's bag was on the floor, and the water soaked through. Several of the letters she'd promised to deliver were ruined, the ink completely washed away."

At that, she placed her purse in her lap and unzipped it with help from her granddaughter. "Jocelyn's letter wasn't ruined, but her envelope was. The salutation inside was to someone named Adele, but with no last names and no address, Annie could not figure out who that was or where it was supposed to go. Months after the sinking—years, even—she pored over every published *Titanic* passenger list she could find but never ran across anyone by the name of Jocelyn or Adele."

"I know why that is," Jonah interrupted. "Both girls had been named for their mothers. Their full names were Oona Jocelyn Brennan and Beatrice Adele Brennan. The ship's roster had them as Oona and Beatrice, not Jocelyn and Adele."

"Oh, my. Well, that makes perfect sense, then," the older woman said as she dug through her bag. "In the end, the best Annie could do was to preserve the letter and pass down the story in the hopes that someday it might make its way to the rightful owner."

She then produced a small but thick yellowed envelope that had been placed inside a baggie. She handed it over to Jonah, and though he accepted it reverentially he made no move to open it just yet.

"I doubt the connection would ever have been made if not for a recent spate of headlines and news stories," the old woman continued. Looking directly at Kelsey, she said, "You're practically a celebrity, my dear, even out in our neck of the woods. I'd read all the stories about the…situation…with you and your company, but it wasn't until I saw an interview the other day where you discussed your great-grandmother Adele, *Titanic* survivor, that my memory was stirred. There was one photo of you in particular, where you were wearing that same pin you have on today. Once I saw that, there was no doubt. This letter was meant for your great-grandmother, Adele Brennan Tate. It may have taken a while, but I'm thrilled to have delivered it to this family at last."

The woman sat back proudly and looked to Jonah, who took that as his cue. Carefully, he pulled the envelope from the baggie, opened it up, and removed the contents. As he gently unfolded the letter, Kelsey gasped, for tucked inside it was a small silver hat pin with a curve of tiny musical notes at one end.

"The pin!" Doreen cried, looking to Kelsey. Soon everyone was talking at once, especially when Kelsey removed her own, accepted the other one from her grandfather, and slid the two together. A perfect match. The pin had found its other half at last.

Next came the letter. With a strong voice and eyes soon swimming with tears, Jonah read Jocelyn's brief note to those gathered there:

> *Dear Adele,*
>
> *It appears Tad has left me on board to die. You were right; I shouldn't have trusted his word over yours. I'm sorry. I love you. Please wear the pin in my memory. May I always be the notes of your harp.*
>
> *Goodbye my cousin, my sister, my heart.*
> *Jocelyn*

By the end they were all crying. They passed the letter around, and Kelsey's fingers shook when it came to her. These were Jocelyn's final words, her last note, written in her own hand. Oh, how Kelsey wished Adele had been given this in her lifetime!

Kelsey's father was the first to say "Thank you" to the two women. Those were followed by many more expressions of appreciation. Knowing Doreen, Kelsey thought, these two ladies were probably going to be thanked in some especially generous manner in the long run.

She continued to hold the pins in her hand, marveling at how the notes nestled into the niche on the instrument and rose upward from it like a song. *May I always be the notes of your harp*, Jocelyn had said. What a lovely sentiment. What an amazing young woman.

An hour later, the family reconvened at their final stop for the day, the family memorial stone in Battery Park. Though the gathering at the pier had been a public commemoration, this was a far more private affair. They hadn't planned any sort of service, just the placing of a wreath, a prayer from Jonah, and a bit of quiet reflection. For some reason, Cole had told Kelsey it would be best if she rode from the pier to the park with her parents instead of with him. He said he had an errand to run on the way, and it would be faster if he could do it alone. She wasn't sure what that was about, but she had complied.

Once they were at Battery Park, Kelsey placed a special wreath beside the Irish blue limestone memorial. Across the front of the wreath was a ribbon bearing the word "Adele" in an artful script.

While they waited for Cole to arrive, Kelsey stepped away from the group to make an important call. She dialed Walter's home number and explained to him about Jocelyn's letter and all they had just learned from the Devlin descendants.

"The diary was already quite convincing," she said, "but the letter they gave us today is proof positive that Jocelyn was the one who died on *Titanic* and Adele is the one who survived."

Just saying the words gave her such closure, yet a part of her felt sorry for Rupert, whose long and futile crusade would finally have to draw to a close. She said as much to Walter, who surprised her by replying that Rupert had read the copy of the diary she had sent him and had already decided to let it go.

"It was never about the money," Walter added. "He just wanted the truth. Now that you have this final proof, I think in a way he'll almost be glad. At least now he can know for sure and put the matter to rest."

They concluded their call and then she returned to the fold. It had gotten colder, and she was worried about her dad, so she suggested they get started and Cole could join in once he arrived.

They were about to do just that when Kelsey spotted Cole coming toward them, carrying what looked like another wreath. With a sharp intake of breath, she realized what he had done, that somewhere between the two locations he had managed to acquire a second wreath. When he arrived at the stone, he turned his wreath around to reveal that it, too, had a ribbon across the front, this one adorned with the word "Jocelyn." He placed it beside the other, the two wreaths touching in the middle.

A murmur of appreciation went through the small group. As Cole stepped into place beside Kelsey, she gave him a loving hug. Somehow he had known exactly what this day required: an honoring not just of Adele but of her beloved cousin as well. When they were finished with their little service, she decided she would snap some photos and send them to Rupert and Rhonda along with a note, an olive branch for these distant members of their family tree.

"Thank you for that, Cole," Jonah said as he stepped forward to give his prayer. "We would do well to always bear in mind the sacrifice made by Jocelyn that night. The Bible says that greater love has no man than this, that he lay down his life for his friends. I think we all learned today how that verse was lived out in our family. I, for one, am humbled and grateful to have descended from people of such fine character. Let us pray, and then we'll share a moment of silence together."

They bowed their heads as Jonah spoke from the heart, praising God and thanking Him for the gift of life and family and faith. In the silence that followed, Kelsey grew vividly aware of her surroundings: the laughter of children in the distance, the smell of the salty sea air, the warmth of Cole beside her. Slipping one hand into his, with the other she reached up and touched the dual hatpins now on her lapel, the golden Irish harp with the silver musical notes rising up from it like a song.

Kelsey thought of these two great women who had come before, and she knew one thing for sure. With God's help, the legacy of Jocelyn and Adele would continue to live on.

EPILOGUE

Lower Manhattan, New York
April 15, 1913

Adele joined the small group of mourners gathered at the memorial stone her father had placed in Battery Park. She made a point of standing as far from the man in the black coat as possible, but once the service was complete and the attendees began breaking off into small clusters to chat, he approached her directly. She would have simply turned and walked away if not for the fact that he was holding her hat in his hands.

"I saw this blowing across the grass," Tad told her, handing it over, "so I thought I would fetch it for you."

She took it from him with a curt "Thank you" and turned away as she tucked her windswept hair under the hat and affixed her pin to it. As she took a step, he reached out and gripped her arm to stop her. Then he spoke in a low, menacing voice.

"Time's up, Adele. It's been a year since the ship sank. I've already told you what I wanted—and what I would do if I didn't get it."

Summoning her nerve, Adele faced him, her chin jutting out defiantly.

"And I told you that there *are* no bonds. They went down with the ship."

He studied her face, his beady eyes narrowing in the shadow of his hat's brim. "You're lying," he said. "You've been lying since the beginning."

Adele felt her stomach clench. He was right. She *was* lying. She had carried the bonds off the ship hidden in the lining of her hand muff, and that was where they were going to stay until the day came when she could safely hand them over to her father. But she had no intention of doing so as long as Tad was still in the employ of Brennan & Company. Though her father was still fooled, she knew all too well the kind of man Tad Myers really was. Somehow, if he learned for sure the bonds still existed, he would find a way to steal them.

"You'll give me those bonds, Adele," Tad pressed now, squeezing her arm even harder, "or I'll make it very clear to everyone that *you* are the reason Jocelyn didn't make it. It's *your* fault she didn't get onto a lifeboat in time. *Your* fault she died. Do you really want people to know that?"

Again, Tad was right. Ultimately, it *was* her fault that Jocelyn hadn't survived. Thanks to their argument, Adele had turned her back on Jocelyn and gotten into a lifeboat without her. By the time she calmed down and realized what she'd done, it was too late. The boat was already being lowered down to the water. Though she prayed desperately for the next two hours that somehow her cousin would find her way to another lifeboat, deep in her heart she knew she would not.

Adele hadn't known Jocelyn's fate for sure until the next morning when she was rescued and onboard the *Carpathia*. Clinging to the rail of the ship, she had watched as lifeboat after lifeboat was unloaded, to no avail. Jocelyn was not among the survivors.

Adele knew then that if not for her anger that night, if not for her abandonment of her cousin because of that anger, Jocelyn would still be alive.

But for Tad to use her sorrow and regret against her now was needless and cruel. She knew a secret about him as well, one that was equally damaging. She knew how he'd made it onto a lifeboat despite the fact that he was a man. Dressed in clothing snatched from an employee's locker, he had pretended to be a crewman and volunteered to row.

"You tell people that Jocelyn's death was my fault," Adele whispered now, "and I'll tell them about your costumed escape with the women and children from a sinking ship."

Stepping closer, he squeezed her arm so hard that it brought tears to her eyes.

"You do that," he snarled in reply, "and I'll tell them that you're not even Adele. Remember, when I first met you, you said your name was Jocelyn. For all I know, that was the truth. I'll say you're Jocelyn posing as Adele to take advantage of Sean Brennan's money."

Adele stared into the man's wild eyes. What an absurd claim! Surely he knew that such a lie would be found out. She'd been buried in her grief for so long that she and her father were still just getting to know each other, but surely he was smart enough to realize that she was his direct flesh and blood.

"Go ahead," Adele said bravely. "I'd rather live with the shame of Jocelyn's death than break a promise to the man who raised me, or to give away an investment that belongs to my family."

"Fine." Tad released his hold and took a step back. "We'll just see who wins in the end."

With that, he turned to go, the tails of his dark coat flapping in the spring wind. Whatever he did now, Adele realized, didn't really matter. She'd already lost the dearest friend she'd ever had, the cousin who was like a sister.

"Adele?"

She turned to see her father calling to her from across the grass. "Yes, Da?" "Are you ready to go?"

Looking at his kind blue eyes, she felt safe and protected somehow. Though she had lived virtually all of her life without him, she was with him now, and she knew he loved her and that he put a great value on family ties. No matter what Tad might do, she knew her father would see that she was vindicated in the end.

"Just another minute," she responded. "I'll meet you at the carriage."

With a nod he turned to go. She turned in the opposite direction and moved back toward the water for one last glimpse of the dark and choppy horizon.

Today was a day for goodbyes, not just to her cousin Jocelyn and her Uncle Rowan, but to all who died that fateful night. Adele thought of the people whose paths had crossed with hers while aboard that ship who had not survived the sinking:

> *Mr. Neville Williams, their gracious host in first class.*
>
> *Mr. Hoffman, the enigmatic father of the two little French-speaking boys.*
>
> *Mr. O'Connell, the one with the failing music store, and his wife and daughter.*
>
> *Mr. Thomas Brown, their dinner companion from South Africa.*
>
> *Mr. Austin van Billiard, the aspiring diamond merchant, along with both of his sons.*
>
> *So many more.*

Closing her eyes, Adele bid them all farewell.

Now she had one last goodbye to give. Opening her eyes, she stood at the bulkhead, facing out toward the ocean and her homeland beyond, and said goodbye to the life she'd thought she would have here, to the dreams of two idealistic young women who thought that whatever they hoped for, they would achieve.

As it turned out, the world was a much harsher place than either of them had ever imagined. Life was more tenuous and fleeting than they had known. The Bible said that tribulations taught patience, which led to experience, which led to hope. Someday, she prayed, her heart would find that hope. Until then, she would focus on patience and experience and live her life in a way that honored those she had lost.

Looking up to the heavens now, she held out her arms from her sides and gave a final farewell.

"I love you, my sweet uncle, my precious cousin," she said aloud. "May you both rest in peace until we meet again."

DISCUSSION QUESTIONS

1. As the story begins, we see that Kelsey is a singularly focused workaholic who is both talented and successful. Which elements of this story lead her to question this behavior? By the end of the book, who do you think has had the biggest impact on helping her change her ways: her mother, Cole, or someone else? How does Gloria's death play into this transition? How does Kelsey's relationship with God affect it as well?

2. Rupert Brennan claimed he just wanted to know the truth and he was not interested in money. Do you think that is true? Why do you think Brennan & Tate settled with his father years before? Was that a good idea? Was there any other way the company could have handled this situation?

3. As the CEO of Brennan & Tate, Walter is responsible for putting the company's interests first. In that regard, is he justified in his treatment of Kelsey? How could he have handled things differently? Do you think he came to realize her value to the company in the end?

4. Kelsey and her father have always been close. In the wake of his stroke, does this element of their relationship still shine through? How did you feel about their interactions? Do you think he will ever recover enough to become a viable part of Brennan & Tate again?

5. Cole contacts Kelsey when he discovers that she is in trouble. Do you think he did this purely out of an altruistic desire to help her, or do you think he knew it might lead to a rekindling of their relationship? In what ways do Cole and Kelsey make a good match?

6. Gloria paid a heavy price for her actions. What set her down this path? What could she have done to avoid her fate? In your opinion, is she redeemed for having changed her mind near the end?

7. As the ship is sinking, Jocelyn makes a surprising choice to ally herself with one person rather than another. Why do you think she made such a choice? What was it about her character that influenced that decision?

8. Cole thought he had forgiven Kelsey and moved on, but during a conversation one insensitive comment from her was like gasoline on flame, causing his anger to explode anew, surprising him. Have you ever thought you had forgiven someone, only to find out you were still dealing with the issues that upset you? Do you find that forgiveness is an ongoing process or a one-time event, or different for each situation you face?

9. Both Adele's son, Jonah, and her grandson, Nolan, indicated they weren't completely certain Adele was who she said she was, and yet it did not seem to matter to either of them. How hard would it be to live with that question hanging over your life? As a parent, like Adele's father, Sean, how much investigation would you do? As a son, how much trust would you have? And as a grandson, especially one who worked so closely with her, how much skepticism would you have?

10. More than 1500 people on *Titanic* never reached America. Can we ever assess the impact of such a huge loss? Why do you think people are still fascinated by what happened with *Titanic* 100 years later?

Whispers of the Bayou
by Mindy Starns Clark

What mysteries lie hidden beside the dark water of the bayou?

Swept away from Louisiana bayou country as a child, Miranda Miller is a woman without a past. She has a husband and child of her own and a fulfilling job in a Manhattan museum, but she also has questions—about the tragedy that cut her off from family and caused her to be sent her away, and about those first five years that were erased from her memory entirely.

Summoned to the bedside of Willy Pedreaux, the old caretaker of her grandparents' antebellum estate, Miranda goes back for the first time, hoping to learn the truths of her past and receive her rightful inheritance. But Willy's premature death plunges Miranda into a nightmare of buried secrets, priceless treasure, and unknown enemies.

Follow one woman's search through the hidden rooms of a bayou mansion, the enigmatic snares of an ancient myth, and the all-consuming quest for a heart open enough for love—and for God.

Shadows of Lancaster County
by Mindy Starns Clark

What Shadows Darken the Quiet Valleys of Amish Country?

Anna Bailey thought she left the tragedies of the past behind when she took on a new identity and moved from Pennsylvania to California. But now that her brother has vanished and his wife is crying out for help, Anna knows she has no choice but to come out of hiding, go home, and find him. Back in Lancaster County, Anna follows the high-tech trail her brother left behind, a trail that leads from the simple world of Amish farming to the cutting edge of DNA research and gene therapy.

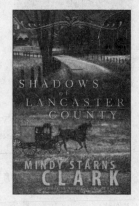

During the course of her pursuit, Anna soon realizes that she has something others want, something worth killing for. In a world where nothing is as it seems, Anna seeks to protect herself, find her brother, and keep a rein on her heart despite the sudden reappearance of Reed Thornton, the only man she has ever loved.

Under the Cajun Moon

by Mindy Starns Clark

What Secrets Can Be Found by the Light of the Cajun Moon?

New Orleans may be the "Big Easy," but nothing about it was ever easy for international business etiquette expert Chloe Ledet. She moved away years ago, leaving her parents and their famous French Quarter restaurant behind. But when she hears that her father has been shot, she races home to be by his side and to handle his affairs—only to learn a long-hidden secret that changes everything she knew to be true about herself and her family.

Framed for murder, Chloe and a handsome Cajun stranger must search for a priceless treasure, one whose roots weave through the very history of Louisiana itself. But can Chloe depend on the mysterious man leading her on this cat-and-mouse chase into the heart of Cajun country? Or by trusting him, has she gone from the frying pan into the fire?

SECRETS OF HARMONY GROVE

by Mindy Starns Clark

What Secrets Lurk Deep Inside Harmony Grove?

Philadelphia advertising executive Sienna Collins learns she is under investigation by the federal government for crimes she knows nothing about. Suspecting the matter has something to do with one of her investments, the Harmony Grove Bed & Breakfast in Lancaster County, she heads there only to find her ex-boyfriend dead and the manager of the B and B unconscious. As Sienna's life and livelihood spin wildly out of control, she begins to doubt everyone around her, even the handsome detective assigned to the case.

As Sienna searches for the truth and tries to clear her name, she is forced to depend on the faith of her childhood, the wisdom of the Amish, and the insight of the man she has recently begun dating. She'll need all the help she can get, because the secrets she uncovers in Harmony Grove are threatening not just her bed-and-breakfast, but also her credibility, her beliefs, and ultimately her life.

The Amish Midwife

by Mindy Starns Clark

*A deathbed confession...a dusty carved box containing two locks of hair...
a century-old letter about property in Switzerland...*

Nurse-midwife Lexie Jaeger's encounter with all three rekindles a burning desire to meet her biological family. Propelled on a personal journey of discovery, Lexie's search for the truth takes her from her home in Oregon to the heart of Pennsylvania's Amish country.

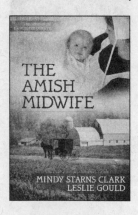

There she finds Marta Bayer, a mysterious lay-midwife who may hold the key to Lexie's past. But Marta isn't talking, especially now that she has troubles of her own following the death of an Amish patient during childbirth. As Lexie steps in to assume Marta's patient load and continues the search for her birth family, a handsome local doctor proves to be a welcome distraction. But will he also distract her from James, the man back home who lovingly awaits her return?

From her Amish patients, Lexie learns the true meaning of the Pennsylvania Dutch word *demut*, which means "to let be." Will this woman who wants to control everything ever learn to let be herself and depend totally on God? Or will her stubborn determination to unearth the secrets of the past at all costs only serve to tear her newfound family apart?

The Amish Nanny

by Mindy Starns Clark

A cave behind a waterfall...a dying confession...
a secret agreement hidden for a century...

Amish-raised Ada Rupp knows nothing of these elements of her family's past. Instead, her eyes are fixed firmly on the future—for the first time in her life. Now that a serious medical issue is behind her, Ada is eager to pursue her God given gifts of teaching at the local Amish school and her dream of marrying Will Gundy, a handsome widower she's loved since she was a child. But when both desires meet with unexpected obstacles, Ada's fragile heart grows heavy with sorrow.

Then she meets Daniel, an attractive Mennonite scholar with a surprising request. He needs her help—along with the help of Will's family—to save an important historic site from being destroyed. Now Ada, a family friend, and a young child must head to Switzerland to mend an old family rift and help preserve her religious heritage.

In order to succeed in saving the site, Ada and Daniel must unlock secrets from the past. But do they also have a future together—or will Ada's heart forever belong to Will, the only man she's ever really wanted?

To learn more about Harvest House books and
to read sample chapters, log on to our website:

www.harvesthousepublishers.com

HARVEST HOUSE PUBLISHERS

EUGENE, OREGON